Allbrite
by
Anne Attias
ISBN: 978-1-9164271-9-8

PUBLISHING

i2i Publishing, Manchester.
www.i2ipublishing.co.uk

Dedication

In memory of Mrs Gertrude Morgan.

Books by Anne Attias include:

The Paradise Scheme my original novel was meant to illustrate a healthy lifestyle, environmental issues, ideal climate, scenic surroundings, flexible working, equality, would that be enough to satisfy people?

Lifetimes tried to reflect the enormous changes that took place from the 1950s-2000s, through the eyes of a modern independent contemporary female.

Allbrite a family saga coping with modern life. Each generation faces new challenges. What happens when Mama disappears? Will Eric ever settle down? Does success bring happiness?

Consequences is the follow up to **Allbrite**. One innocent act has consequences leading to Allbrite, the O'Brien family and the future. The family are growing up and have big issues to face in a changing world.

Double Mystery covers identity theft, cybercrime, fame, brands, underworld, adoption. How do you get your life back when everything is stolen?

Timespan (in progress) is a ghost story relating to two time spans

THE O'BRIEN FAMILY BACKGROUND

Originally Irish immigrants

Grandpa Christian O'Brien migrated to America with his parents to seek a better life as a youth. His father moved from Chicago in search of open space. He rented a plot of land which he farmed in Montana, where Christian went to high school and met a Puerto Rican girl called Anita. They got married and farmed the land in Montana. Christian's children moved away when they grew up. His son Shaun returned to Chicago where he became a fireman and married Bernadette, Poppa's parents.

Poppa **Michael O'Brien** was born in Chicago in 1924. When he was 10 years old his father died and he was sent to live with his grandpa Christian in 1934. His grandpa taught him carpentry skills. When he was 15, Poppa accompanied his school friend to Idaho for a weekend event where he met Mama at a dance.

Mama, **Rachel Clifton** was born in 1925, middle daughter of Mildred and Samuel Clifton from Idaho.

They married in 1945 and had six children

Ryan born in 1947

Marshall born in 1949

Matilde born in 1951

Eric born in 1953

Dan born in 1955

Candice born in 1959

Ryan received call up papers for the Vietnam war in 1965

Marshall was called up in 1967

Gradually the children grew up, married having children of their own

O'Brien family	Married	Son	Daughter	
Ryan (builder)	Marie		Sophie	
			Chloe	
Marshall (accountant)	Linda	Hal		
		Jake		
Matilde (Chef/caterer)	Phil Taylor	Eithan	Scarlett	
Eric (photographer)	Betsy	Ben		
Dan (carpenter)	Claire	Leo		
		Ollie		
Candice (Designer)	Dr Martin Wood		Zoe	

Introduction

Growing up we were a close family, looking out for each other. Poppa worked hard and did his best for us. Mama cooked, sewed and worked hard doing laundry. She was a thrifty woman, aged before her time, but always supportive and kind-hearted. A small woman, she made sure her boys toed the line in the home and taught her daughters all that she knew. We were all encouraged to become independent, we all had to learn to cook, sew and make-do.

We were diverse in looks as well as in temperament. Ryan and Marshall favoured our father in looks, Matilda also took after him in a feminine fashion. Dan and Candice took after our mother in colouring. I didn't look like any of them. The boys shared a room, the girls were squashed into the attic. We lived in a log cabin that our father helped to build, near a creek in Montana. Being isolated meant a long trek to school and favoured forward planning. Being disorganised meant missing out on stuff.

When we were young, we didn't have much in the way of toys so we improvised and played outside, running wild when the weather was favourable. Ryan and Marshall attended school when I was born. As we grew older we were given chores. The boys helped papa with the community farming work. Matilda helped our mother preparing food to take to market to sell, she made excellent cookies. I had to help look after Candice, the baby of the family, although she often bossed me about.

Poppa worked with his hands as a craftsman, he could make furniture, fixtures and fittings, even do stone work. Due to his high-end finishes, he was in demand but was limited in the quantity he could supply, though he always managed to pay his way and put food on the table. He used to go out hunting and sometimes took the boys with him to learn, but I was never interested. Poppa also taught Ryan and Marshall to box, he was big on self-defence and said a man needed to look after himself. He hated bullies and tricksters who preyed on weakness.

Our parents met at a community dance to celebrate Easter. It was our mother's first grown-up outing with her sister. Our father had been passing through Idaho visiting with a friend from school. They were introduced and over time a courtship followed. Poppa was the only boyfriend Mama had. As they had no inheritance or wealth, they moved out to Montana to Poppa's grandfather's place where Poppa extended the cabin as the family grew. Poppa wanted to purchase the land, but the owner refused to sell.

Our parents managed to buy a small parcel of land to farm but it was not enough to cover all their needs. It gave them healthy food and an understanding of hard graft. From being youngsters, we all had to pitch in especially at harvest time. The nearest neighbours were a few miles away. The small town of Allbrite, seven miles away, was where we went to school, worked on the market and did our shopping. Poppa had an old truck to get us to places and transport his goods.

We did not hear much about Poppa's early days, he was too busy or tired to reminisce much. Nobody thought to ask him. We knew he was one of six children, he was number four, his siblings emigrated to Australia, South Africa and Canada. Poppa worked from his teens and did not have the chance to complete his education. Everything we had was thanks to his endeavours. His grandfather had taught him skills in woodwork, craft and general maintenance, so with his trade he had always been employed. With experience Poppa had honed his skills to a very high standard. He wanted his children to have a good education and do better than himself. School was important to Poppa. To miss attending school we had to be unable to stand. Homework was essential, we could not play out or go anywhere until it was completed. Only sports events were permissible postponements for completed homework.

My name is Eric and I fit in after Matilda and before Dan, I don't resemble any of my family much although when we are lined up on photographs, you can tell I belong. We fought and squabbled at times over sibling rivalry or suspected favouritism, but usually looked out for each other. At home, when time permitted, we had wide open spaces to run around in. We made our own friends at school although we could not visit much because of the distances. Once we grew up, we all seemed to settle into city suburbia, or perhaps there were fewer open spaces.

Life continued pleasantly for many years. Sometimes it was a struggle when the weather was unpredictable and crops were threatened. Mama canned, pickled and bottled everything she could find to see us through the cold winters when we were often snowed in. Mama came from Idaho so we did not get to visit her family. We did not question her about her family. She revealed that her parents did not approve of Poppa, they had planned an arranged marriage for her, so cut her off. Mama did not regret her choice but was sorry she hadn't managed to do more to ease our lifestyle.

Our nearest neighbours were the Miller family about three miles away. We met up on the road, in Allbrite, at markets, in school and sometimes walked along routes together. In the opposite direction were the Taylors who were a family of farmers. Everybody knew each other and most of the Allbrite town folk. In times of need, community labour and assistance would be provided by all. Without being intrusive, people were friendly but private. The distances made it impossible to be spontaneous and drop by for a coffee and gossip.

We liked going to Allbrite to see the shops, the ambience of the coffee shops, parks and bustle. As kids we did not see any major cities so Allbrite was town to us. It was interesting to watch town folks go about their business. We enjoyed market days when we could get treats and if time permitted, go exploring. It made an interesting contrast to the quiet of the countryside where we lived. We had birds and wildlife for company. There was always something that needed attention in the country. In Allbrite people seemed to have time to saunter and enjoy casual activities. We usually went to the library there to stock up on reading material and browse magazines and catalogues.

Life seemed to be predictable with a regular annual routine until mid 1964 when disaster stuck. The land owner informed us he was selling his land, he gave us a couple of months grace to move out. This was a shock as the land we farmed and owned was too small to house us. Our home was built on the land we rented. My father was horrified. He also received papers stating that the land he owned would be taken over by compulsory purchase to make way for new development. He was offered a paltry sum of compensation. Poppa sought legal advice but there was nothing he could do. It seemed we would have to move to Allbrite.

Poppa found a house on the outskirts of town with a large shed attached where he developed his furniture business. As soon as we moved into the new place, Poppa got the boys and some buddies together and dismantled our old home. He sold some of the wood or took it in the van to use. Every scrap of our habitation was removed whether wanted or not. Poppa would not give the landlord a single screw. He also uprooted all the crops and vegetation leaving the land upturned. In Allbrite, Poppa bought some small plots and used allotment space to grow vegetables and planted fruit trees. It was limited space but productive soil.

Mama baked and sold produce on the market, as well as taking in laundry. That left Dan, Candice and myself at school. Ryan received call up papers to join the army to go to Vietnam.

Marshall would get his papers the following year. Although Ryan knew how to handle a gun, he often accompanied Poppa hunting, the idea of killing people made him uncomfortable. A big farewell party was held to wish Ryan and some of his buddies a good send-off.

Without saying a word to anyone, Ryan left his party and disappeared. He crossed the border into Canada and did not come back again. We did not find out until the army came around to seek Ryan's whereabouts. Poppa was shocked and mortified. We did not know where Ryan was or how he fared for years. Mama worried constantly about Ryan's welfare, so we learned not to mention his name. The girlfriend Ryan left behind married somebody else. It made it difficult when Marshall's turn came. There was no big send-off and we all waved goodbye feeling subdued.

Marshall barely lasted 18 months when he returned wounded with half his right leg missing. He did not talk about his experiences, from a bright cheerful boy, he became a quiet, haunted man. It took him a long time to adapt to town life and his artificial leg. He found clerical work and studied accountancy at night school. A librarian called Linda became Marshall's sweetheart and managed to lighten his disposition. At their wedding he walked down the aisle proudly. Candice was bridesmaid.

Poppa always told us that we had to earn a living. "Nobody gives you anything for nothing, there's always a catch," he would say. He told us that whatever we did, we should do the best we could. Second best was not good enough. If a job was worth doing, it should be done well. Health was important, so he drummed into us the dangers of polluting our bodies with booze and drugs. Mama cooked fresh meals, often growing the ingredients in her kitchen garden. We had limited amounts of candy, homemade ice cream and chocolate, so our teeth remained strong.

In Allbrite there were temptations in all the store fronts, but we knew not to ask. If we wanted something, we had to save our meagre allowance until we arrived at the required sum. Often the thought of parting with our hard-earned savings was enough to change our minds. Kids at school seemed to get everything given to them. We were good at improvising from anything lying around. We also used our childhood imaginations to create epic adventures where we were always the heroes.

Our childhoods were spent handing down outgrown clothes and belongings. Ryan's bike passed to Dan, Marshall's bike passed to Matilda then me. Mama would repair and make clothing which she kept crisp and clean. Some of the boys ruined their jeans and trousers so she bought a bale of material and sewed new ones. Knitted sweaters were warm in the winter, coats and jackets passed along the line and we didn't know any different. Fashion was just something we saw in movies and magazines.

Poppa's Story

Grandpa Christian O'Brien migrated to America with his parents to seek a better life as a youth. His father moved from Chicago in search of open space. He rented a plot of land which he farmed in Montana, where Christian went to high school and met a Puerto Rican girl called Anita. They got married and farmed the land in Montana. Christian's children moved away when they grew up. His son Shaun returned to Chicago where he became a fireman and married Bernadette.

Michael Richard O'Brien was the fourth child born in 1924 to Shaun and Bernadette who were living in Chicago in a poor tenement building. Shaun worked as a fireman, Bernadette looked after the children and earned some money as a seamstress. Michael had a big brother Anthony and two older sisters, Katherine and Maggie. They all attended St Patrick's school and church. Money was tight, but they were a close-knit family and all their neighbours were in a similar position.

Shaun was a sociable man, fond of playing the accordion when he had company. He enjoyed a glass of beer when he could afford it and was popular in the neighbourhood as he was always willing to lend a hand. Bernadette did her best to run the home, keeping the children clean and fed. She was always busy and tired. After Michael was born, Bernadette produced another son Brendan and a daughter called Maureen. Life centred around the church, school and the community. Their home was basic but welcoming.

An unfortunate accident at work led to the death of Shaun in 1934, due to smoke inhalation. He had been the wage earner for the family. This meant that Anthony and Katherine had to find work, Bernadette took in more sewing jobs and Maggie helped part time at the grocers. Poppa was too young to work so was given household tasks and duties. He grew up very quickly. Instead of playing outside, Poppa was busy doing errands and chores to help the family. When Shaun died, Bernadette was devastated. She could not imagine how she could support her family on Shaun's pension and her meagre earnings.

As a result, Poppa aged 10, was sent to live with his paternal grandpa Christian in Montana. Grandpa Christian had emigrated to America earlier in his teens with his parents who taught him carpentry. Christian's father wanted space so had moved from Chicago to Montana where they rented land and farmed. At high school Christian met a Puerto Rican girl Anita who he married. They now farmed the land.

Due to the distance, the children had not met their grandparents before. At Christmas time and for birthdays, the family exchanged cards with both sets of grandparents but there was no time nor money for visits. Poppa had a change of clothes and a second-hand coat. He hugged his mother goodbye and felt sad to leave all his siblings behind. He did not know that he would not see his mother again. At the same time, Poppa felt a sense of adventure to be setting off to a new world.

Grandpa Christian turned out to be an older version of Poppa with a small white beard. Poppa was obviously a chip off the old block. Grandma Anita was from a Puerto Rican family, with dark hair and pretty features. Initially there had been opposition to their union from both families, but as they had all known each other for many years there was a sense of inevitability. Christian and Anita had walked to school together, he carried her books. They were not interested in anyone else. Both families agreed to make the best of the situation and gave them a good wedding celebration.

Poppa continued with his education in Montana whilst learning his woodwork skills from his Grandpa. He had to travel a long distance to get to school, a bus picked him up and dropped him off halfway. Grandpa made Poppa his apprentice and he learned many skills and techniques from him. Grandma tried to build Poppa up by making savoury meals and delicious baking. Poppa had a skinny, wiry build all his life. Initially, Poppa found the wide-open spaces daunting, it was strange to look around and not see another soul. Later he thrived on the majesty of the place.

At school, Poppa made friends but lived too far away to engage in much social activity. To go to parties or community events, Poppa had to stay over. His best friend Stephen invited Poppa to accompany him to Idaho to a family wedding for the weekend. Whilst there, Stephen and Poppa went to a community dance where he met Mama. She was at her first dance accompanied by her sister and girlfriends from school. Poppa thought she looked like a film star and was smitten by her big brown eyes. When she agreed to dance, he felt thrilled.

Poppa had not taken much interest in girls before he met Mama. He had noticed the pretty ones and avoided the pushy girls. When people tried to introduce him to their daughters, he moved away swiftly. Aged 15, Poppa did not feel ready for commitment. When he met Mama, he felt inside that he had found the woman he wanted to grow old with. Mama was shy and Poppa had to meet her parents to ask permission to write to her until he could prove he would be able to support her. All this would take time. Due to the distance between them, they had to write to each other. Occasionally, Poppa would manage to hitch a ride.

At age 21, Poppa was considered ready to run the business. Grandpa relied on Poppa's assistance more and felt ready to retire. Grandpa played a more supervisory role and began to suffer from dementia. Grandma Anita was aging too but helped Poppa with advice and contacts. In time, customers went straight to Poppa who gained a reputation for fine craftsmanship. Poppa wanted to marry Mama whilst his grandparents were able to travel to Idaho for the wedding. A summer wedding was planned and although invitations were sent to Chicago, nobody was able to attend.

After Poppa left home it seemed Anthony had joined the army, Katherine had married and moved away, Maggie was apprenticed to a professional dressmaker. Poppa's mother was bringing up Brendan and Maureen who were at school. She lived in one room and did laundry and sewing to earn a living. When she died of tuberculosis, the younger children were sent to live with relatives. Poppa did not see any of them again. He missed his mother's funeral because the post arrived too late. When the other children were old enough, they emigrated to Australia, Canada and South Africa. Poppa lost contact with them.

Grandma Anita had moved Grandpa and herself into a little annexe attached to the back of the home, leaving the main living quarters for Poppa and his new wife. Grandpa was ailing and becoming frail. Poppa adored Grandpa and did whatever he could to ease his condition. When he passed away, Poppa was heartbroken. Grandma gave up without her husband and gently faded away within the year. Before she died, she enjoyed meeting her first grandson Ryan with Marshall on the way.

The newlyweds had the cabin to themselves plus a patch of land Grandpa had bought to grow crops. The land the cabin was built on had been rented cheaply. Grandpa had not thought to purchase it because living there was so cheap, he felt it was not worthwhile, or had not got around to sorting out the paperwork. It was the only mistake Poppa felt Grandpa had made. Grandpa had been clean living, even tempered and hardworking, a fine example to follow.

Mama came from a middle-class family living in Idaho. Her papa was a school teacher, her mama worked with a local charity affiliated with the church. They made sure she and her sisters had a good education. They had expected her to marry well and were disappointed when she chose Poppa. Until Poppa proved to be a good provider, they were distant with him. Mama was adamant she wanted Poppa, so the family said that after the wedding she would have to make her own life as they were too far away to help. Mama accepted this and did not return until their funerals.

Poppa enjoyed married life, he learned to be patient and uncritical. It took a period of adjustment on both sides to get the hang of partnership. Mama had not had to cook or do laundry. With Grandma Anita teaching her home skills, Mama proved to be an able enthusiastic beginner. Mama wanted the best for her family. She ensured a hot meal was ready for Poppa every night. The hardest part was the forward planning, she had to store, pickle, bottle ingredients, plan the growth of the crops, make a list for town store shopping in advance and have enough for unexpected situations or for when they were snowed in.

As the family grew, Poppa tried to interest the boys in his skills. Ryan showed promise but lacked aptitude, he preferred to be outside. Marshall was not really interested so he lacked enthusiasm. Matilda was good with her hands but tended to bake and cook for sale to the markets. I was keen to learn, but I lacked commitment. Poppa started to teach Dan and Candice from a younger age, so they were talented. Everybody admired Poppa's work, but choices were open regarding future careers, so it seemed wrong to tie ourselves down.

As a father Poppa was strict but fair. Proud of our achievements, Poppa was sparse with words of praise, but when it came to education, he gave every encouragement. It seems he would have liked to have become an architect. When he was a young boy he was always sketching and studied buildings from any books he could find in the library. There was neither the money nor the opportunity to develop any career, architecture was one of the longest and most expensive courses. Poppa hoped his children would be able to achieve their ambitions.

On special occasions and festivals Poppa arranged events full of fun for the family. He would arrange treasure hunts at Easter with clues hidden along a trail. The family had a big old patched tent, so we occasionally went on camping trips. For birthdays or when suitable, we took long walks with picnics. Poppa also joined in ball games and the whole family were fond of riddles and jokes. It was simple clean fun; no vulgarity or bad mouthing was allowed. When we were naughty Poppa was a frightening adversary, so we toed the line.

Through church and his work Poppa met many of the town's men. He would meet a group to socialise and put the world to rights over a beer. Poppa was not interested in card games or strong spirits, but enjoyed dominoes, darts and music. The new town life was easier for Poppa as he grew older. Having grown up in Chicago, Poppa was used to the amenities and comforts of town life. Allbrite was small in comparison, but very convenient. Poppa missed the open countryside but not the challenging work. He was able to focus on his work and was close enough to get supplies if he ran out.

Poppa missed Ryan and wanted to know what happened to him. He employed a private detective to search. None of Ryan's friends claimed to have heard from him. One of them, Tom Stringer, thought Ryan had gone to Canada because originally, he wanted to accompany Ryan. Tom had been stricken with flu at the time, so he missed the rendezvous. The detective discovered Ryan was living in Montreal and was working in construction. Poppa told the detective to return without making contact. Mama was relieved Ryan was alive and well but felt hurt because he did not get in touch.

Of all the family, Dan was most interested in Poppa's work, so he became his apprentice. I was studying engineering but was really interested in photography which was my favourite hobby. I won a few competitions and was invited to pursue a new vocation. Poppa was sceptical, he felt taking photos was something people could do themselves, whereas a good engineer was worth his weight in gold. I was not interested in photographing weddings and celebrations, but I managed to get a wildlife assignment for a major media company, so I packed in the engineering course and left home to go travelling with the best camera equipment I could afford.

Candice, as the blue-eyed blonde baby of the family was the apple of Poppa's eye. She could get away with so much more than the rest of us. Although she looked like an angel, her core was made of steel. Long before equality for women, Candice knew what she wanted and how to succeed. When it suited her, Candice used her feminine charm but if told something was not suitable for her because she was a girl, sparks would fly. From a young age Candice decided she would take a business course and planned to start her own chain of fashionable clothing. In Allbrite she had little competition.

As Poppa gained a good reputation in Allbrite, he was nominated to stand for Mayor in the Republican Party. This was an unexpected honour for the family, who had always kept abreast of the news but not been politically motivated. Poppa honed up on politics and took his nomination seriously. Accompanied and briefed by experienced officials, Poppa began to make public speeches defending the rights of the community to earn a decent living, emphasising family values. Poppa could be seen to be a regular family man, clean living, sincere compared to the sleek, smooth talking Democrat opposition nominee.

With assistance from Candice, Mama obtained a new wardrobe of suitable outfits for social occasions when she was obliged to accompany Poppa on his campaign. She made regular hair appointments and started to wear foundation and lipstick in public. This opened new avenues of socialising for Mama, she entered a world of ladies of leisure, media scrutiny and invitations. At first daunted, Mama pretended to be a famous actress playing a part on stage which gave her the confidence and skills to succeed.

Mama was witty and attentive, studying her colleagues' behaviour and attitudes whilst remaining private herself. Mama became a good listener and helped Poppa to understand society views and expectations. It was a door to a new world, unexpected but interesting. After leading a quiet rural life for most of their marriage, my parents understood the community they came from whilst embracing the town folk who were trying to better their lives.

Whilst the campaign ran, the family was expected to be more independent. Instructions were left on the table regarding meals and activities. Mama had a housekeeper because she was too busy to remain at home. Dan and Candice still lived at home and often featured in family photos when they were scrubbed up. Candice looked a wholesome pretty star and described herself as a fashionista, promoting her outfits shamelessly. Dan looked like the wholesome boy next door. I was pursuing my career as a media photographer and gaining credentials, constantly moving around.

Poppa was in the lead and to stop him, the Democrats dug out the fact that Ryan was a draft dodger. The Democrats played dirty, this was their main card. It fell to Poppa to explain that he knew nothing of Ryan's whereabouts, there was no contact between them. He told the nation how Ryan disappeared after his farewell party and the family knew nothing until the officer arrived at the house. He mentioned proudly how his second son Marshall served courageously for his country and lost half a leg. Ratings flickered but Poppa's integrity came over well.

Poppa was a faithful husband, neither an alcoholic nor gambler, a regular church goer and his business was straight, so no more dirt could be found against him. None of the family took drugs or engaged in violence. Candice, still a teenager, was targeted whilst out on several occasions with offers of drink or attempted seduction. Poppa had taught her judo and had advised her to remain in control in public, so despite her angelic appearance, her attackers were slayed. In public Candice chose soft drinks, she remained razor sharp and was always seeking new opportunities to promote herself.

On one occasion Candice had been out with her girlfriends celebrating a birthday. Somebody slipped something into her drink and she passed out. Poppa was called, he had the drink analysed and went on television advising the public of the danger of unguarded drinks. When pictures of Candice were shown, the public rallied round indignantly and slated the Democrats who were assumed to be behind the incident. It increased support for Poppa. Many families had a black sheep. Ryan was assumed to be ours.

Poppa's main competition in the Republican party had to withdraw due to ill health, so he became the front runner. Although Poppa had managed to buy our home and a small amount of land, he was not a wealthy man. Poppa's campaign was funded by financial backers who were influential in the Republican Party. They believed Poppa would be a successful candidate amongst the voters. Advisors were on hand to brief my parents on their daily lives. Dan had to hire an assistant to run the business and relied on his own judgement instead of asking Poppa.

When it looked like Poppa might win the election against his sleazy opponent, he was invited to attend a meeting with party officials including his backers. They told Poppa they would continue to advise him every step of the way. The implication appeared to be that Poppa would be represented as an upright clean-living man, but power lay behind the scenes. He would be expected to toe the party line which included looking the other way occasionally. Poppa felt humiliated and foolish, he could not be a puppet mayor. His integrity would not allow him to act the part. Poppa knew there would be compromises but had expected to hold some influence. He withdrew despite all protests.

Life continued except Poppa followed politics more closely and thrashed matters out with his cronies. He was disillusioned and when moved to protest, he led campaign groups. It gave Poppa an interest and a zest for life. As he grew older, he left the business to Dan, rarely taking part. Poppa had time to socialise and even enrolled on a few courses that took his fancy. Occasionally he went to lectures and musical events with Mama. It seemed Poppa had mellowed as he aged, his maturity suited him, he had a full head of grey hair, clear sparkling eyes and a pleasant expression. The only disappointment in his life was the lack of communication with Ryan.

Mama's Story

Rachel May was the second daughter born to Mildred and Samuel Clifton in Idaho. Her father was a high school teacher and her mother worked for a local charity. She had an older sister Stella and a younger sister Theresa. They had a comfortable middle-class lifestyle and enjoyed a good education plus extras including piano playing and horse riding. Each year the family had vacations travelling around the States. There were many social events from the church and community, so the family enjoyed a large circle of friends. Their neighbours were considered extended family. The community shared its highs and lows.

Of the three girls Rachel had mousy hair with luminous large brown eyes and an elfin chin. Stella was blonde with blue eyes, Theresa dramatically dark haired with hazel eyes. All three sisters had different temperaments with Rachel usually acting as peacekeeper. Rachel shared a room with Theresa, so they were closer, Stella had her own room and was the most aspirational. Rachel joined the girl guides and dutifully participated in activities deemed suitable by her mother. She was an obedient, quiet child. In their teens the girls listened to Frank Sinatra big band music.

The first time Mama was allowed to go out with her girlfriends to a community dance unsupervised was the night she met Poppa. She had worn a new cream dress dappled with rosebuds, her underskirts pushed out, her new shoes had small heels. Mama felt happy, she had entered the room and was standing with her friends whilst one of them went to purchase soft drinks. Poppa came from behind and asked her to dance. Mama's heart fluttered when she looked him in the eyes and nervously she accepted. When Poppa turned on the charm Mama could not look at him again, she felt flustered. Poppa was enchanted by her. Before the evening ended as Mama had an early curfew, Poppa took down her name and address and said he would be in touch.

Mama knew that Poppa lived in Montana so she did not hold out much hope. When his first letter arrived, Mama blushed and was delighted. She read it alone in her room. Her parents would not approve of a relationship as they thought she was too young. Stella had only just started courting an approved local banker. Poppa only wrote a short message saying how he had enjoyed meeting Rachel, he hoped they would be able to meet again. He explained he lived and worked in Montana so he would have to wait until he had leave to be able to visit again. This enabled Rachel to write back and enquire what work he did and what Montana was like where he lived.

Gradually, through correspondence the couple got to know each other's likes and dislikes, ambitions, dreams, thoughts and expectations. Rachel's parents thought she had found a penfriend through school so did not interfere. One Easter Poppa wrote to Rachel asking if he could visit. He needed a place to stay overnight. Rachel spoke to her parents who were not enthusiastic, so she arranged for Poppa to stay at her friend's place. Poppa came wearing his Sunday best, he brought flowers for Rachel's mother and a bottle of wine for her father who interviewed him in his study.

Poppa asked permission to court Rachel. Her father said Poppa was too young, he needed proof that Poppa would be able to provide for Rachel and a family. The furniture business was thriving, Poppa had more orders than he could handle. He had grandpa's home and had a new extension built on. There was scope to extend when he needed to. Poppa said he would cherish Rachel and always do the best he could. Rachel's father said they were both too young, Poppa could write to Rachel and see next year how they were both situated. Poppa told

Rachel's father he would wait for eternity to have Rachel for his bride.

Mama knew that her parents wanted her to marry a professional man like Stella. She also knew that she felt an overwhelming desire to be with Poppa. He made her feel precious and feminine. Mama was not interested in the local boys or high society. With Poppa she knew she could develop as a person without pressure or having to keep up with society. The fact that Poppa lived in Montana pleased her enormously. They would be free to raise a family and grow food. It all seemed very romantic. A year seemed a long time, but she knew it would pass quickly. Let Stella and Theresa marry professionals - Rachel knew she would have the best furniture. Frances was Rachel's best friend, she confided in her and the two girls often discussed their futures. Although Frances was dating Leslie, she wanted to study nursing before settling down. Rachel wanted to be the best wife and mother she could. She asked her mother to teach her to cook and bake, although her mother never excelled at either, spending too much time watching her weight to remain fashionably slim. Rachel worked in the sheriff's office as a clerk/typist to fill in time until Poppa could rescue her. Rachel's parents would not allow her to visit Poppa, especially as his mother was in Chicago, so she had to wait impatiently.

When the year was completed, Poppa closed his business and set off to Idaho where he stayed at Maureen's house. Rachel's father's permission to marry was sought. On this visit Poppa had a new suit and was groomed to perfection. Rachel's father reluctantly agreed. Rachel glowed with happiness as they chose her ring in the local jewellers. The whole brief visit filled Rachel with joy. They talked endlessly and found they had much in common and shared similar views. Rachel did not want a big wedding and pleaded with her parents for a small, low key event as soon as possible. Her mother frowned and said people would think the worst if they rushed it. A compromise was reached, however, and they would have a small wedding. The couple were determined not to wait.

Rachel built up a bottom drawer with linens and housewares. She imagined the cabin to be furnished but felt she could choose some accessories to make it homely. She wrote almost daily to Poppa and although the time dragged, the big day finally came around. Rachel's wedding dress was made by her mother's dressmaker, a long simple affair, very modest and plain. Theresa and Stella were bridesmaids in pale apricot. Poppa invited all his family but only his grandparents came. A room was booked in the local hotel for Poppa and his grandparents. The wedding meal was held in the same hotel, all courtesy of Rachel's parents.

After the wedding and speeches, Mama and Poppa disappeared. Poppa had booked a honeymoon suite in the best hotel in the area where they spent their wedding night accompanied by champagne. The next day the newlyweds bid goodbye to Rachel's family and accompanied by Poppa's grandparents, caught the train back home. Rachel adored Poppa's grandparents instantly, they had such kind welcoming faces. Her own family remained detached but civil throughout. When they left Idaho, Rachel had no regrets nor plans to return. Apart from birthdays and Christmas, Rachel's family did not maintain contact and did not see their grandchildren.

When Mama arrived in Montana she was in awe of the landscapes and wondered where all the residents lived. She had no idea how to manage the household. Poppa's grandmother took Rachel in hand, taught her everything she needed to know and treated her like a daughter. Mama loved her as much as Poppa and they enjoyed each other's company. As Grandpa grew increasingly frail, both women took turns to nurse him. When he passed away, they were heartbroken. Grandma Anita lost her will to live without Grandpa. She was around for the birth of Ryan and just after Marshall was born, she faded away. Mama felt her loss eternally. In the brief time they had been together, Grandma had been more of a mother to her than her own.

Mama was busy looking after two little boys and running the home. She was always making and baking, ensuring Poppa had a hot meal when he finished work. For Mama the family came first, she came last. A few ladies had made friends with Mama from church and school, she also got on well with the neighbours when they met. If she missed town life and friends on her doorstep, she never complained.

Occasionally Mama would write to Frances but nobody else. As more children arrived, Mama just sent Christmas cards. Idaho was another world. Stella had married her banker, Theresa married a socialite who moved in high circles. Rachel did not go to her wedding as she was pregnant and was disinclined.

Through the church circles, Mama took part in activities when she was able. Sometimes she would accompany Poppa when he was delivering his furniture and spend a few hours in town. Her baking was successful, so along with some fruit and vegetables, she began to sell some on the market. Matilda had a light touch and made the best cookies. As soon as she was old enough, Matilda accompanied her mother and they would go for coffee and ice cream afterwards in town. From an early age Candice would study the fashions and shop windows. Mama drilled good manners into all her boys and taught them to be respectful and decent men.

Life continued smoothly with established routines and demanding work until the landlord gave them notice. Poppa had not realised that his grandfather still rented the land. This was a traumatic shock to Mama. When the plot of land where they grew crops was sold by compulsory purchase, Mama felt devastated. When Poppa found a place to live in Allbrite with the shed to work in, Mama and the girls moved in with their belongings whilst Poppa and the boys demolished every trace of their cabin and previous existence.

It felt strange but convenient to Mama to live in a town again. She appreciated the proximity to meeting all the family needs but missed the wide-open vistas. It made her realise that she could take nothing for granted.

When Ryan was called up to the Vietnam war in March 1965, Mama's hair began to turn grey. She was so worried about him. After his party when Ryan disappeared, Mama thought he had left without saying goodbye because it would be too upsetting. Ryan always hated fuss. Secretly, Mama was pleased Ryan had not gone to Vietnam. She worried about Ryan's situation but felt he was alive and well.

By the time Marshall left to fight the war there had been no news of Ryan. Marshall did his best but was injured in an explosion and lost part of his leg. Mama was relieved to have Marshall back home with an artificial leg. He would not have to fight again. Despite his difficulties, Marshall managed to study and make a decent life for himself and his family. Mama liked her daughter-in-law Linda and was pleased her son had a good wife to look after him.

In January 1977 when Jimmy Carter became president of the United States, he pardoned draft dodgers who had fled the States to avoid serving in the Vietnam War. The pardon was unconditional and was part of his campaign promise. This gave Mama hope of Ryan's return. She waited for him to make contact. One day whilst she was alone in the house she had a phone call from Ryan. He told her he lived in Canada, was married to a French-Canadian girl called Marie and had two daughters, Sophie and Chloe. He invited Mama to visit him. It seemed Ryan had learnt the building trade and started up his own business. Mama was overjoyed and said she would think about it.

Mama asked Matilda to help her get a passport and think about visiting Ryan in Canada. Matilda helped Mama with the passport but her husband, Phil, had served in Vietnam and had a low opinion of draft dodgers, so Matilda did not want to upset him. As Canada was cold in winter, Mama decided to wait until the summer to think about the visit. Ryan did not want to return to the States even for a visit, said he needed to maintain his business. If Mama wanted to see her firstborn, she would have to travel to see him. The younger family members could barely remember him.

Poppa felt Ryan should return home to pay his respects and apologise for all the distress he had caused. There was no inclination on Poppa's part to visit Ryan although internally, he longed to be reunited with his son. Mama knew she would have to go with one of the family if she was to go abroad for the first time. Candice agreed to accompany Mama when the time came because she wanted to see the Canadian fashion trends. Candice wanted to see if she could expand her connections.

Mama joined a choir and a women's activity group so she had a busy social life. She did keep fit and volunteered helping to deliver meals for the elderly and infirm. Sometimes Mama went on outings, concerts and did sewing classes. Life was busy and entertaining, Mama made good loyal friends and enjoyed life virtually commitment free. All her married life Mama had served and maintained the family first. At this stage, Mama felt she had done her duty and began to choose her lifestyle for the first time. It was fun and filled her with confidence.

Dan worked alongside the house but also had a factory on the outskirts of town for established lines of furniture sold in shops throughout the area. The original shed next to the house was used for fine craftsmanship. One day Mama came home to find she'd been burgled. Poppa was out with his cronies, Dan had gone to the factory and nobody had been at home. Drawers were tipped out, cupboards awry and Mama's jewellery and family heirlooms had been taken. Mama was upset at the intrusion of her sanctuary and the loss of a few sentimental items that could not be replaced.

Poppa installed an up to date security system for home and the factory, but Mama still did not feel safe and wanted to move. The house was too big now that all the family were grown and independent. Mama suggested Dan and his family inherit the house whilst Poppa and she downsize in a central location, keeping a spare bedroom or two for visitors and grandkids. Poppa needed time to reflect before agreeing reluctantly to Mama's wishes. Dan was not sure about the inheritance but his wife, Claire, felt it would be good for their boys, Leo and Ollie, to have the freedom to run around and grow in the spacious environment.

Living in town suited Mama, she filled her days with activities she had previously not had time for. She also embarked on a course about environmental issues and saving the planet. Mama realised she had the freedom to learn and grow in any direction of her choice. Although Mama was one of the older students, she mixed well with all ages and was really motivated. In her younger days she had gone from home to marriage with no interval in between to discover any personal interests. Her life had been devoted to raising the children and keeping the house running. She began to discover her true interests and potential.

Ryan's Story

As the first-born son, I was given responsibilities from an early age and expected to be a good example to the other children that followed. I looked like Poppa, but I did not inherit his temperament. I liked to be outdoors playing and investigating, loved sport and was too impatient to follow in Poppa's footsteps. I learnt how to make and mend furniture and stuff but knew it was not for me. In school I was among the top few pupils but I was not academic, so I did not want a professional career.

Once I completed my chores I would escape and run wild. We lived in the middle of nowhere so as soon as I could I rode my bicycle for miles. My friends did not live locally but we managed. Occasionally, I was allowed to stay over in someone's house. Often, I would have to take Marshall along with me. He was almost two years younger and a completely contrasting character. As brothers, we tolerated each other but we had no common interests. Marshall was a swot and serious minded, whereas I have the quota for adventurous spirit.

Poppa taught the boys to hunt and also taught us self-defence. We would accompany him on trips and assist with gutting and preparing the meat. I took up boxing and self-defence with Poppa giving me a challenging time. Marshall learned beside me but lacked the conviction. I found release by honing my body and finding confidence in the knowledge that I could defend myself. It also helped being fit as I managed to attract some female interest in school and around town. As a teenager I had a girlfriend called Angie, but we rarely managed to get together due to the distance.

As a family we bonded well of necessity, we worked the land, did our chores jointly and had good ball games and picnics. Our parents encouraged us to be independent, to be curious and to develop our potential. We all went to the library on each visit to town. There was a set of encyclopaedias at home to help with our studies. Mama also taught us all to be basic cooks and to sew enough to make repairs. I also learnt to knit (although I kept that secret) because once when I was recovering from flu at home and was bored, Mama taught me in front of the fire.

In our teens some of the boys talked about an illegal still producing hooch. When I managed to stay over, we would consume some until my head was spinning. I learnt how to get drunk but never dared to go home smelling of booze, Poppa would have lynched me. We were taught to retain self-control, to respect women and to help out when required. If something seemed wrong, we should analyse the situation and act if appropriate. If it was not appropriate, we should mind our own business. There was no answering back in our house, even when riled we submitted.

I went camping with my school, taking part in ghost stories, archery and adventures and met a diverse bunch of kids from other States at the site. It was an eye-opener to me to learn how other kids lived. I never got homesick and started to get restless as my hormones developed in my teens. By then our family was complete and I was the big brother who acted as intermediary to the folk. Candice always followed me around from when she learnt to walk. She was the cutest little doll but sharp as a razor. I cared for them in a protective big brother way but was only close to Eric because he was the least judgemental.

At school we began to receive career advice. I did not know what I wanted to do but I felt the need to travel, to explore my country before settling down. Commitment was an alien word to me. I was young, strong, capable of many skills and felt the world was my oyster. To my dismay, I received my draft papers for the Vietnam war. All my friends got theirs at a similar time. Although I had hunted and killed animals for the table, the idea of killing a human being did not appeal to me. I read the politics, followed the news, but the concept of killing some unknown Vietnamese who was probably called up as well to defend his country, miles away from us, became abhorrent. I did not want to be part of it.

I passed the medical and had a date set for departure. Apart from a few close friends who also had reservations, there was nobody to discuss it with. Everybody assumed I would go. Poppa felt it was my duty to defend our great nation. There were a few options to avoid the draft, but I did not fit into any of the categories. I was not a homosexual, not a student, not sick, I objected but could not be classed as a conscientious objector due to beliefs, I could not buy my way out, so there was nothing I could do. If I raised the issue, I would be considered a coward. I felt it took courage to avoid my fate.

Through the grapevine I discovered an escape route to Canada, I knew a couple of guys who were going. It would mean leaving at night, telling nobody and taking the minimum luggage with me. I had to keep it secret and leave as if I was just out walking. Using all my savings, I had enough money to pay my way but not much more. With the confidence of youth, I felt certain I could earn a living on arrival. My folks threw a leaving party for me with some other families in Allbrite which helped. I packed my rucksack with a change of clothing, shaving, toothbrush and soap, spare underwear and my favourite book.

Sneaking away late into the party I felt ashamed, mean and scared. Everybody was enjoying themselves. I slipped out the back of the hall, collected my rucksack hidden behind some bushes and got picked up along the dirt road leading out of town. No questions were asked, money exchanged hands and I sat in the back of a truck with some other silent boys. The remainder of the journey was equally silent. I crossed the border half asleep huddled between a truck driver and his mate, I had a false passport and did not say a word all the way. The story was I was the truck driver's son being trained up.

In Canada I was dropped off at a centre for draft dodgers. I was given food, drink and a place to sleep. I was too exhausted to do more than eat and sleep. It felt cold and I was glad I had brought my winter coat. The next stages of my escape were assisted by Canadian volunteers who provided me with appropriate papers, transferred me to Toronto and got me work on a building site as a general labourer. They also equipped me with some warm clothing, work boots, plus some extra 'Welcome to Canada' snacks.

I was given a copy of *The Manual for Draft-Age Immigrants* to Canada which was a best seller when it first appeared. It explained how to negotiate with the government, how much rent to pay and other issues like how much to spend on food in the supermarkets. It offered facts to immigrants learning about life in Canada and rules to follow. It also brought immigrants up to date on crucial national events.

In 1965 Canada became a welcoming place for American draft dodgers and deserters. There were no official records of how many were admitted to Canada during the Vietnam War because we were admitted as immigrants not refugees. Registration to enrol for the war stated: "Knowing and wilful refusal to present oneself for and submit to registration as ordered was punishable by a maximum penalty of up to five years in Federal prison and/or a fine of US$250,000."

Since January 1986 there were no prosecutions of draft resisters. Between 1965 and 1975 more than 40,000 draft dodgers fled to Canada. Like me, many stayed in Canada when the war ended even when President Carter pardoned us. American dodgers and their Canadian supporters felt the war was immoral. The Canadians welcomed the resisters. CBC and newspapers made draft dodgers a favourite subject. Canadians held the moral upper hand over Americans. A few Canadians disliked the draft dodgers in private, but nobody expressed that view in public.

Our dodgers formed one of the most interesting groups in Toronto, centred around Baldwin Street, slowly assimilating into town. Along with many of my counterparts who stayed in Canada, I became a citizen. The Ottawa's Citizenship and Immigration website later declared us to be: "the largest, best-educated group this country ever received."

Poppa had taught me well, I worked long hours and did all the hard jobs. I wanted to learn and studied the techniques of all the trades. This was noticed and encouraged. Builders had specialist skills and were proud to show a young boy how the professionals did the job. I absorbed knowledge like a sponge. After work we would go for a few beers and I was happy to listen to the stories and banter. I began to progress up the ladder. Heights and balance served me well and I wanted to learn everything.

For almost three years I did a full apprenticeship. I suffered the cold in the winter but adjusted. I tried not to think of home or family because I could not make contact with them, so I put the memories aside to be able to cope. I fervently hoped they were all well. I realised that in their eyes I had set a bad example to the others, but I knew Marshall would go to do his duty on behalf of the family.

Toronto was busy, bustling and thriving. It was a far cry from Allbrite but not hard for me to adjust. Everything could be easily located, and convenience was abounding. I ate out or bought in ready prepared meals from the local bakery. I lived in a small studio apartment which was sparsely furnished but adequate for my needs. I made friends on the job, sometimes got invited to family meals. It was at one of these I met my wife Marie who was visiting for the week. For me it was love at first sight, she was introduced to me and my knees wobbled. I felt conscious of my calloused hands and beating heart.

Marie said afterwards I made her nervous by my unwavering stare. It was hard for me to eat or talk, I just couldn't take my eyes off her. She was not beautiful in the conventional sense like Candice for example. Marie was slim, dark haired with luminous brown eyes and an elfin face, smart in a classical way and well-spoken. I felt inadequate and did not know what to say to impress her. I made us both nervous and conversation was stilted but somehow, I obtained her telephone number and arranged to take her out on a tour of Toronto. I barely slept or ate until I was able to see her again.

I knew that Marie was the girl for me, I spent most of the date telling her why we would make a wonderful couple. I even looked in jewellers' windows asking her to pick an engagement ring. I was lucky Marie did not flee in fright but somehow despite her protestations, she began to fall for me. I described our future life together, my ambitions to run my own business and the family we would create. Marie tried to slow me down, explaining that she lived in Montreal. Her father was an important businessman and both her parents would have to meet me. They would not be impressed with my job, although she could see I had ambitions.

As an only child Marie had been well brought up and indulged. She had exacting standards and was expected to marry into society. The family spoke French at home. Marie had been visiting her friend Janice from university for the week, they had shared an apartment whilst studying. Marie was due to return to Montreal. I obtained her address and asked her to invite me to meet her parents when she returned. I decided to buy a new suit and a couple of smart shirts and ties, visit the barber and invest in new shoes. I even bought hand cream and face cream to try to smooth my appearance.

I knew my future lay with Marie, so I quit my job with good references, packed my bags and set off for Montreal. Upon arrival I went to the Tourist Information who found me a bedsit in Westmount. They gave me directions from Atwater metro telling me to take the exit through Westmount Square Plaza, to Greene Avenue, then along Sherbrooke Street West until Victoria Avenue where there were lots of shops, cafés, some Victorian houses and the Westmount Park which was all very Anglo, even shopkeepers greeted customers in English in that section of central Montreal. I paid my deposit and got directions to the newspaper office.

At the Montreal Gazette the clerk helped me put in an ad with a telephone number advertising my building and maintenance services. I had brought my tools with me and realised I needed a street map, a second-hand vehicle and a decent phone. I paid for a telephone answer service which I called at regular intervals. The answer service was instructed to be very polite, take down full addresses and postal codes plus contact telephone numbers. I made friends with the operator Celia and we have kept in touch. Celia helped me find the addresses and was a font of information.

Marie's parents lived in Rosemont–La Petite-Patrie, a borough in the city of Montreal, Quebec, located in the centre-east of the city. Celia told me it was upmarket and for the well-heeled. I realised I would have to try to learn French to impress her parents. I did not realise that they were religious Catholics and their daughter had to marry in church. I also felt I needed to get established in my new business before I could visit to ask for Marie's hand. My rock at this time was Celia who found out how much to charge for my services, she found my jobs, spread the word amongst her friends and neighbours and helped me get established.

In the beginning I turned nothing down however small. I had an old van with second-hand tools and I worked all hours as I had no home to go to. I listened to French language tapes in the car and on headphones at work. People seemed to be bilingual and friendly. When I tried to practice my French with my customers, they were amused by my American accent. When they realised it was for love, they gave me every assistance. I focused on the French and began to pick it up. One elderly man recommended a good shop selling used tools. He had been in the trade and offered me the use of his tools for my endeavours. I arranged a service contract to maintain his home in exchange.

I was a good listener, so I heard all kind of stories. I also tried to save for the future. Work rolled in with harsh winters and old properties, there was plenty to keep me busy. I always remembered Poppa's advice that if a job was worth doing, it meant doing it well. Whatever needed doing, I stayed until I was satisfied. If I needed to get a part or order something, I left some tools behind to prove I would return. I tried never to let anybody down. If a job ran over and I couldn't make it, Celia would call to advise them. My reputation grew until I felt confident to arrange a visit with Marie's parents.

Marie and I had corresponded spasmodically. She did not know I was in Montreal, our paths never crossed. I told her I was establishing my business and would put funds away for our future. I don't know what she told her parents but eventually it was time to meet. I groomed myself at the barber's as if for my wedding. I bought a big bouquet of flowers for Marie's mother, a bottle of whisky for her father and Marie had a bottle of perfume that Celia told me was suitable. I had my dilapidated van valeted, wore my best suit and set off with trepidation. Whilst I sought favour to win Marie, I would not be defeated.

They lived in a big old house which was stylish and pristine. I shook hands with the family and handed over my gifts. Marie looked as nervous as I felt. Her mother was a gracious, petite lady with stylish grey hair, she welcomed me and served refreshments. Her father, an affluent businessman, studied me and invited me for interview in his study. We were under no illusions, this was a male inquisition. Her father wanted to know my story plus why I became a draft dodger. I told him about my family back in Allbrite, about hunting with Poppa, boxing, sport and my good grades at school. I told him about Poppa's furniture business and explained why as the eldest son, I did not want to take it over.

When it came to the draft, I explained my reasons for leaving the States. I explained how I met Marie over dinner and that she had captured my heart and soul at first glance. I realised I was not affluent yet, but I promised to take care of Marie and cherish her for all my days. My business was growing, I would soon need to take somebody on to manage the demand. As I had established a good reputation, I was planning to train up staff and perhaps a few apprentices to learn the trade. At present I had a bedsitter in Westmount and was investing my earnings into the business for future growth.

Marie's father was a self-made man and understood where I was coming from. He explained that Marie needed to be married in the Catholic church, would I be willing to convert? I had not considered religion, it did not play a part in my lifestyle, but I was able to agree that our children could be brought up Catholic. We agreed that I would make an appointment to see the priest. It seemed that I was not yet a suitable match for Marie, but I would be allowed to see her.

I asked for her hand in marriage, it was not given but not denied either. Her father would follow my progress. I was not ideal son-in-law material. Despite my lack of credentials, Marie's happiness was at stake and her father wanted her to be protected and provided for in comfort. It would be up to me to convince him that I was up to the task. When I shook her father's hand, I told him that I loved Marie the most in the world. I would never do anything to hurt her. Marie accepted my probation and glowed in my presence. We went to see the priest and I accepted instruction. I would have done anything to advance my marriage.

With my workload spiralling, my French improving and my religious instruction, I did not have enough hours in the day. Celia kept the work coming and unbeknown to me, my future father-in-law kept an eye on my progress. I took on two young apprentices, Dean and Pierre, one from each community so we were bilingual. They accompanied me on all the jobs, gradually picking up skills as I had done, for a minimum wage.

Both were eager to learn and were grateful for the opportunity. I made sure they worked reasonable hours and got overalls for dirty jobs plus protective eye coverings. They took training courses at their own expense. I gave them time off for courses and exams. When they passed their exams, I refunded the fees with a bonus. We all got along well and work flowed in. I was so busy, I rarely had time to see Marie, but I telephoned her regularly and thought about her at night.

One day I was given the opportunity to bid for a local government refurbishment project. I went to see the premises and calculated the budget at home. It would need specialist equipment which I could hire. It also meant that the regular jobs would not be covered. My two apprentices were fine at maintenance, but I would need to recruit more professional staff if I were successful. Marie's father was behind the contract, he wanted to test me. He had sent a private eye to check out my family, my history and my work without me suspecting.

When I was successful on the project, Celia found me two established professionals, a plumber and an electrician, Dave and Pete, who worked alongside me until they retired. The apprentices carried on with the local work, learning on the job, we refurbished the project to a top-quality standard. Celia decided we needed a regular office and rented a place near her house. She designed flyers and advertised our services in the local media. Work flowed in, Celia was my right-hand manager, I paid her the salary she requested, though she was worth triple. When we needed to recruit again, Celia found the personnel and I trusted her implicitly.

My future father-in-law was delighted with my progress and called me for a drink in the city centre. He admitted he was behind the refurbishment process, that he had checked out my background and felt that I had a bright future. I was not indignant, it seemed fine with me that Marie had a caring father. This meant that I could now officially court Marie and an engagement party would be planned. It seemed that I would need to think about the future with a wife and potential family and start preparing for it. I was so overwhelmed with gratitude that he was trusting me with Marie, I felt tears in my eyes and hugged him.

At the engagement party Marie looked radiant. Dave and Pete came with their wives. Dean and Pete came shyly along with girlfriends. Celia looked amazing, she came with her husband and had dressed like a queen. I did not invite my family because I could not reveal my location. I missed Mama sorely because she would have loved to be there. Both my parents would have been impressed with my in-laws. I had to put the pain to one side and focus on the future. Marie had chosen a simple ring and I had proposed on one knee. I was now a Canadian immigrant and fully prepared to stay put.

As a wedding gift, my in-laws provided us with a small property on the outskirts of Westmount, in a good area convenient to local facilities. Marie and my mother-in-law enjoyed shopping to furnish it. I did not interfere as long as it was comfortable and not too stylish to feel like a home. I spent little time there often returning to eat and sleep as the business was growing rapidly. It was not all work though, I made sure there was time to take Marie out on dates or accompany her on special occasions. I lived alone in the house until we were married.

The wedding was a large affair although I had very few guests. Marie was the most beautiful bride in the world in my eyes, her bridesmaids wore pale blue, the guests and event passed by in a dream. I could not take my eyes off Marie. When she threw her bouquet to her squealing girlfriends, we ran off to change for our honeymoon.

We caught a flight to Mauritius in a special honeymoon luxury resort where we had two weeks of private paradise, part of our wedding presents. It was a dream, I have never been happier. A chef made us personal special meals (another present) and we had massages and treatments (presents) and went fishing. It was bliss and we felt like the luckiest people in the world.

When we returned it was painful to leave Marie behind to go to work, but I vowed to do everything in my power to make her life happy and content. I opened another office in town and work snowballed. Celia recruited more staff most of whom stayed, we hired more apprentices and kept busy all the time. In time, we ran four offices in different districts with competent staff. I hired a retired professional builder to teach the apprentices how to work. He proved so successful, we advertised courses for professional qualifications. Money was flowing in and I felt fulfilled. I could not ask for more.

Marie told me she was pregnant, and my heart overflowed with joy. She would not let me fuss over her. I was so overprotective, she had to tell her father to speak to me. I was so nervous. Our beautiful daughter Sophie was born first, followed by Chloe two years later. Sophie looked like a feminine version of me, Chloe looked like her mum. I now had three beautiful girls to care for and protect. I wanted to get in touch with my parents to tell them, but I discovered they had moved and I didn't know their address. I intended to try to look them up somehow but was not sure whether it would be advisable, so in the end I did nothing.

Celia hired somebody to look up my family and report back to me. I learnt Poppa had stood for mayor. My parents had a different address in Allbrite; Mama, now grey-haired, looked older but dignified, Dan was running the furniture business. When I read about Marshall losing half his leg, I felt bad for him. I suffered pangs of shame that I had not gone to war but only momentarily. It seemed that Marshall was an accountant, married with kids. I had missed all the family events just as they had missed mine.

With Jimmy Carter's amnesty in place I rang home for the first time. Mama answered the call and speaking to her felt wonderful, I almost cried. We talked about our families and I invited her to Montreal. Mama had never travelled, I offered to collect her. She asked if I had plans to visit, I hadn't thought about it. We left the topic open-ended and finished the call reluctantly.

I mailed photos of my family over and sent my love to all the extended family. It seemed a different world away. The farm boy I used to be disappeared years ago into the entrepreneur I was becoming with my father-in-law's help. He enjoyed coming up with money-making ideas and schemes. I provided the muscle. We got along well together. Marie tended to buy my clothes, my weight did not vary much as I was not a heavy drinker and the physical work burned the calories, so I began to look smarter and with regular haircuts I was well groomed.

The idea of taking my family on a trip to meet my parents and siblings began to grow on me. They were all curious and looked at photos of their other grandparents. Marie thought it might be an adventure for them during the main summer vacation. We could travel around and spend a bit of time getting to know them. It seemed a promising idea to me. I was so proud of my girls, I could not wait to show them off. All my siblings had found different careers, so it would be interesting to catch up and see how we had all turned out.

Marshall's story

I am the second son in the family and spent my early years tagging after Ryan. He was my big brother and hero, I tried hard to keep up with Ryan's accomplishments, but he was always too quick for me. Ryan and I resembled Poppa, although I was a more faded version. Mama always told Ryan to look after me and I am sure I was a nuisance tagging along after him and being a cry baby when he was mean to me. Until Matilda came along as the new baby, I enjoyed the limelight. Both my parents worked hard and led busy lives so as kids we had to amuse ourselves. In the summer we played outside, in the winter we played indoors and got into squabbles.

From an early age I was always into numbers. Words could be misinterpreted but numbers were constant, they did not let you down. I enjoyed symmetry, order and patterns. Give me numbers to crunch and I am happy. As a conventional person I enjoy law and order, I don't often do spontaneity or surprises. I prefer analysis and planning. Competitive sports and latest trends do not interest me. Quizzes, puzzles and problem-solving suit my reserved nature. At school my favourite subject was maths, the more complex the better. Science was interesting but only in the equations and theories. I helped all the family with their homework.

I had a happy childhood with siblings to play with, home cooking and baking, plus home-sewn clothing passed down. We had enough to live well and were expected to contribute to the chores and house maintenance. There were no luxuries and we made our own amusements. Due to the distance between home and school, we got a lift to catch the school bus midway. My friends would probably be called nerds today. We were serious boys seeking to expand our mental horizons in the midst of redneck jocks. When teams were picked for sport, we were always the last, but we didn't care. We admired the pretty girls from a distance but enjoyed conversations with the bright girls. Our set of values was different from the mainstream.

With the development of computers, we came into our own. We learned all the technology as soon as it came out, read technical data and built our own computers at home. Whilst most of the family and neighbours put great store on social events and occasions, we enjoyed being creative with the latest gadgets and devices. Most people tended to ignore us. My family tolerated me and did not expect much interaction as long as I did my share of tasks. Poppa saw I had no craft skills so he knew I would be no good in his business. Mama insisted we all learned basic cookery and sewing. I participated without enthusiasm, though it did prove useful in time.

I rode my bike everywhere, checked out nature and weather predictions and swam in the summer, there was always something to do or somewhere to go. Life seemed promising and full of potential. The four kids who followed me grew up around me and looked up to me when Ryan was gone. I had more patience and tolerance so they would hook up with me and vie for my attention. On the whole, we were obedient because Poppa had boxing skills and a bad temper. To be fair, Poppa worked hard, rarely lost his temper and was entitled to some peace when he came home. If we broke or damaged household property our allowance was withdrawn to pay for it.

Poppa taught us how to handle money. He explained about money coming in and going out. We were taught that everything comes with a price and that we get nothing without putting something in first. We were taught not to be fooled by smooth talking salesmen with exclusive offers. Life had to be evaluated and to live well, we needed self-control. All the boys were taught self-defence and how to be assertive without being aggressive. Drugs, drink and tobacco would damage our bodies and our minds, Poppa said, although it was acceptable to drink moderately on social occasions. There was nothing wrong with a few beers for relaxation, the art was knowing when to stop.

This made sense to me. Poppa said we would all be given chances in life. When we let the chances go by, we sometimes regretted it and then the body would sag and change shape. People who stopped trying started a steep decline. It was important to have a healthy diet, work hard and exercise to stay fit and well. Taking banned substances to get high resulted in chemicals poisoning the body and the mind. Most drugs were addictive leading to crime to sustain the hits. They led to an early grave. Poppa encouraged us all to live a good life and achieve our potential before making any commitments which brought on responsibilities. This all made sense to me.

Poppa was very strict about homework, we could not go out or have dinner until it was done. He checked our projects and made sure we visited the library when we were in town. We did not get many confectionery indulgences but if we did well in school, there would be treats like a visit to the ice cream parlour. Bad behaviour resulted in being grounded and sometimes doing dirty jobs. We knew our boundaries and lived within them. Our family was loyal because we had nobody else.

When Ryan disappeared, our lives changed dramatically. We had all been at his farewell party having fun. At first, we thought he had sneaked off early to avoid his goodbyes. We knew Mama would be upset. He left no note, his belongings seemed to be in place. His buddies had gone too so we assumed they had all gone quietly to avoid fuss. It was only when the police came around looking for Ryan that we understood what he had done. Poppa was mortified and turned pale with shock. Mama nearly collapsed, we kids fell silent, uncertain whether to feel shock, horror or shame. We couldn't understand why Ryan had not confided in us.

We didn't know where Ryan was nor what to do. The law assumed he was a draft dodger. When a year passed by and we hadn't heard anything from Ryan, Poppa hired a private investigator to track Ryan down. He did this to appease Mama who constantly fretted and worried about Ryan. The investigator told us Ryan was living in Toronto, Canada and working in the building trade. This eased Mama sufficiently. We all knew as a renegade Ryan would not be able to return without getting arrested.

When it was my turn to be called up there was no farewell party. Instead Mama made my favourite meal, we all ate it together and I was escorted to the call-up bus. I had no intention of evading my duty. I could not understand Ryan's mindset, he was fit, active and used to hunting. Ryan seemed to be patriotic so why he fled from his duty seemed out of character to me. I knew Ryan was not a coward. So, as the second eldest son, I was determined to salvage the family honour. I hugged all the family goodbye and set off proudly with the other new recruits.

Army life discipline suited me. I enjoyed the routines and order. Among the other recruits I made friends from around the States. It was interesting comparing life styles and interests. For once I was not a geek but part of ongoing teams. We had team spirit and thought going to Vietnam would be tough but a new adventure. The humidity hit us first, we sweated and scratched. Our quarters were basic with plain rations and vacuum-packed pouches when away from base. We were hot, sticky and always thirsty. It was hard doing our training exercises or concentrating on lectures.

On active duty there was no time to explore or admire the scenery, we had to be vigilant. The natives seemed to be small and slightly built, the girls had delicate features, the men seemed to be lithe and wiry. These were my general impressions. I felt no antagonism towards them until some of my unit were killed in an ambush. Sentiment was replaced with a hardened heart. I knew the Vietnamese were defending their land from invaders, I realised the families were afraid and just wanted to live in peace, but the turmoil and uncertainty tainted the air. Off duty many soldiers drank themselves to sleep.

The day I lost half my right leg started off on patrol, my colleague stood on a land mine which knocked me sideways and took my leg below the knee with it. I was fortunate to survive with the rest of me intact, mainly due to the bushes and scrub surrounding me. I did not regain consciousness until I awoke in a field hospital. Shock made me speechless and distress hit me when I learnt about the demise of some good friends.

I felt so sad and helpless that life had come to this hopeless state of affairs. I was glad that Ryan had escaped the carnage and madness prevailing. Depression hit me deeply and I thought life as I knew it would be over for me. I had always taken for granted that I had a fit body and could choose how to deploy it. It seemed now I would be crippled.

Painful therapy began in earnest, I was too lethargic to co-operate. A false leg was made to suit my requirements. I could not wear it until the wound healed, but the measurements took account of my height and weight. I felt my life had been ruined and my future seemed dim. I was young and had not started to live or achieve all my hopes and dreams. It seemed wrong to be cut off in my prime. I realised I was lucky to survive but resented my predicament and felt sorry for myself. It seemed to me that women would not want damaged goods. Despair and dejection haunted me.

My transfer to the States was affected and I was sent to a forces' hospital for wounded veterans. My family were informed but were not allowed to visit me when I arrived. I knew they would be concerned about me but lacked the energy to comfort them. If I had continued brooding my decline would have been swift. My appetite for food and life had disappeared, I could not see any hope. The idea of strapping a false leg on was abhorrent yet using crutches or a frame seemed worse. I refused all offers of communication or commiseration and withdrew in a downward spiral.

One day a wheelchair was driven into my room, the door closed, and I barely noticed. In the chair was a veteran who had been badly wounded, he had lost both legs and one arm was strapped to his body. He had scar tissue on his face and was undergoing plastic surgery. Jordan introduced himself then told me about his injuries, his therapy, his plans for the future and his intentions for his career. I looked at this guy who was barely holding himself together and probably looked sceptical.

This was what Jordan was waiting for. He scoffed openly at me, he told me what a disgrace I was to myself and all the service personnel around me. He told me to curl up and die if I wanted to, not to clutter up the bed which could be used for someone more deserving. If this was the sum total of the life I had lived, it left plenty to be desired. Jordan lectured me without mincing his words. He shamed me and woke me up from my stupor. I was shocked and appalled at the way he saw me. Tears poured out of me and I shook. He left me crying and went away silently. Every day for a week Jordan visited me and either remained silent or else reiterated his progress and his intentions for the rest of his life.

Something inside me awoke and I discussed my options with the doctor and therapist. The implication was that I would be fitted with my artificial leg and would be able to lead a full, normal life in time. I would be able to walk and probably run, work, raise a family and do most activities. My mindset and determination would affect the timescale of my recovery. It would not be easy or without pain, the opportunity to recover was available to me, the rest was my choice. I was scared, I withdrew and wondered if I had the strength and tenacity to succeed. Jordan looked me in the eye and asked me when I planned to get started.

Recovery was a long, painful, arduous process. At first, I was afraid to fall and do more damage, my balance was lopsided. I did not like to look at my stump and was afraid to try my artificial leg on, afraid to put weight on it, afraid to try to walk using it, afraid of every movement. Giving up was not an option, but many times it was a temptation. Jordan refused to let me, he glared at me, swore at me, challenged me and kept me trying. Pity was a dirty word and never used, sympathy was for sissies and empathy was unspoken. Wounded veterans were constantly being admitted and treated, many far worse than me. I was a moderate case and due to be shipped home as soon as I was able to walk independently.

All the patients had consultations with a shrink who encouraged us to talk about our experiences. I did not want to talk, I wanted to put the past behind me, plus I was fortunate enough to have been unconscious when wounded so I could only remember being on patrol. My war service ended after nearly 18 months, although it took many more months to tie up paperwork and be released. I did not feel like a wounded hero and had to think about my future when I went home. Meanwhile, I needed to learn how to use the leg, which hurt when kept on for long. I had to wear it for increasing periods and adjust to the pain.

When my time came to be sent back home, I could barely manage to support myself, but my bed was needed. Jordan came to see me off and wish me well. We hugged and I felt bad leaving him. I could not express my gratitude to him, it was too emotional. He knew and told me to let him know how I progressed, it would suit him to have some correspondence whilst waiting around. I promised to write.

Whilst the nurse accompanied me to the taxi, she told me that Jordan was living on borrowed time. His injuries were incurable and had resulted in a slow decline. I was shocked and asked her if Jordan knew. "Oh yes," she said, "that's why he is so hard on the survivors." I cried for most of the journey and made a pledge to Jordan to succeed.

My parents came to the airport to collect me. They looked smaller and older than I remembered. I had a folding wheelchair and wore my artificial leg which still gave me pain when I walked. Appointments had been made to continue my therapy at a local recommended clinic. It took over a year until I felt able to walk and act normally wearing the leg which had been adjusted for comfort. At home I took it off, in public I appeared normally, if a trifle slower than before.

Whilst I was healing, I began studying, doing a correspondence course in elementary accounts. Once I felt confident, I obtained a clerical job in Allbrite working for a Government revenue subsidiary. I attended night school classes to study accounting and continued step by step to become an accountant. It was not easy working full time and studying for all the exams, but my love of numbers kept me going. I looked for patterns and logic to balance equations and situations.

It was also through my work that I met my lovely wife Linda. My clerical role produced information to be compiled into monthly reports which Linda processed at the library. She used to contact me once a month with the statistics. Her library was part of a selected trial regarding usage and facilities. We used to chat whilst waiting for the information to be processed, at first making polite small talk, then slowly we became telephone friends.

We carried on for months without meeting but having pleasant conversations. Once when I was not available owing to a hospital appointment, Linda said she had missed me. I was surprised and found myself explaining about my injury, something I tried to avoid. Instead of revulsion, Linda said sincerely how brave I had been and how impressed she was with my studies and job to pay my way. She offered to help me with books from the library if I advised her what I needed. It would be cheaper to borrow books instead of buying.

I was delighted and we decided I would visit the library, check out the accounting section and perhaps have a coffee when she finished her shift. We described our appearances to avoid confusion. I envisaged Linda as tall, dark haired and sturdy. She was medium height, blonde short hair, grey-blue eyes and had a lovely warm smile. We shook hands and were suddenly self-conscious initially.

Our easy conversation was stilted for a brief time until we relaxed, laughed and set off to explore the accountancy section. Being a small-town library, it had a limited supply of suitable books, but Linda offered to check the records for books from other libraries which we could reserve. Linda was warm, helpful and made me feel like a normal man. I thought she was very attractive, but I lacked the confidence to invite her out.

We continued to talk, and I visited the library inviting her for drinks and occasional meals. All the time we talked we discovered how much we had in common. Our views tended to be similar, we were not trendsetters and we did not want to conquer the world or seek power. Linda thought she might become a teacher, she was taking some courses. Her aspiration was to marry, raise a family and enjoy a simple, comfortable life. Linda enjoyed being outdoors, she loved nature in all its glory.

The more I got to know Linda, the more I admired her until friendship was not enough. I needed to know whether we could ever be more than friends. Although my manhood was fine, I was afraid of losing Linda's friendship if she would be repulsed by my injury as I still felt incomplete. I agonised over taking a chance and withdrew from our conversations. Linda was concerned she had done something to cause offence.

Finally, I plucked up courage and asked Linda if we could be more than friends. With tears in her eyes, Linda hugged me and said she thought I would never ask. I introduced Linda to my family and saved up for an engagement ring. She cried when I proposed. I made sure she saw my injured leg in case she changed her mind. Linda kissed my stump and I knew she was the girl for me.

My family adored Linda for her warm personality. She had two older brothers who checked me out thoroughly before I was allowed to meet her parents. Her father questioned me about my future and having served in the forces in his youth, gave me his approval. Linda's mother fussed around me and was unsure until she got to know me.

We had a two-year courtship because we were both students, saving our small salaries for a down-payment on a house. Poppa and Dan made us some beautiful bedroom furniture, a dining table and six chairs for a wedding present. Linda chose the designs, I left the furnishings to her. Mama, Matilda and Linda's mother made all the soft furnishings. Linda's father and I left them to it.

When our two sons were born, Hal came first then Jake, both families were ecstatic. Our little family was complete. I was earning decent money in my probationary accountant role. Linda was a qualified teacher so we knew it would work out well during school vacations. We wanted our boys to have the best education we could provide and encouraged them to enjoy playing outdoors and learn extracurricular skills. They gave us joy and pride as they grew questioning everything, getting dirty, making mischief and giggling. My boys thought I was a special bionic daddy because I could take my leg off. We loved every part of their childhood and tried to make it a happy one.

Matilda's Story

Everybody called me Tilly, I've even been called Matty and Millie, whatever was easiest for the younger children to manage. With two big brothers to follow and disturb, I tried to be like them in the beginning. It was clear from the outset that my temperament was unsuited. Boys drifted around making messes, they seemed to focus on sports, fishing and dens. I liked to be creative, to talk about life's whys and wherefores. Whereas boys were interested in taking things apart, I enjoyed mixing things up to be creative. I also developed a tendency to boss the boys because they never seemed to listen to me.

When we had the old place, I loved helping out on the land, I would have made a good farmer. I didn't mind getting my hands dirty, I enjoyed the smells and tastes of food grown on the land. Each process pleased me, I planted, watered, watched them grow, picked, packaged or pickled, thrilled by the experiences. Even as a very young girl I enjoyed active participation. When I was old enough, I helped Mama in the kitchen. She taught me to bake, cook, pickle, display and arrange dried fruit and groceries attractively for sale on the markets. I cried when school intervened and she would not let me accompany her to market.

At school my grades were above average, and I majored in chemistry because I enjoyed figuring out compositions and formulae. My parents were keen for us all to have careers and offered me a chance for further study, but I knew my future lay in food. I enjoyed experimenting with recipes and was never happier than when I was busy in the kitchen. My cookies were the best, my cakes the lightest and most delicious and I constantly devised new mixtures. I tried vegetarian and vegan meals which tasted good, but our menfolk enjoyed their meat. When I got tired of familiar home cooking, we had Mexican,

Indian, Chinese, Italian and Mediterranean dishes. I had no truck with fast food ready meals which were full of additives and preservatives.

I felt very strongly about food and reckoned this generation would be harmed by all this instant food. People preferred convenience to health and opted for easy options disregarding the alien nature of all the added contents. Supermarket produce could not compare with home-grown. Food was stored in refrigerators until all the flavour dried out.

It was interesting to discover new vegetables and herbs imported from other countries which led to more experimentation. Mama continued with familiar home cooking whilst I brought new dishes to the table. I reckoned there was room for both, and the family tolerated my experiments giving me valuable feedback. Nobody held back on my feelings, they gave it to me straight, surprised when it tasted good.

Growing up I ran around and played, swam, made good friendships at school. We used to get the school bus with the Millers and the Taylors, both families were our nearest neighbours in opposite directions. We all got lifts to meet the bus and waited to be picked up after school when we were dropped off. The girls talked together whilst the boys kicked a ball or chased each other around. The girls were usually neat and tidy whereas the boys were a mess by the end of the day.

We all lived in fairly isolated areas, so we enjoyed meeting up to discuss social events and exchange news. Sometimes the boys teased the girls, who ignored them. Likewise, the boys ignored the girls as much as possible. We were like an extended family without living together. Very little escaped our attention and we grew up in unison expecting it to remain that way. When our land was sold and we moved to town, the relationship remained but became more distant in time.

The move upset me deeply, I had delighted in the open vistas, the clean air, the peace and working the land. I helped take everything down and packed up the remaining seeds and crops to sell or relocate. Of all the family, I was the most affected. Poppa was dismayed, Mama worried about everything, my siblings felt it would be more convenient and a new adventure. I felt traumatised and cried at night in secret. Our new home seemed confined and small to me. I never really liked it. The kitchen compensated for the move, it was wide and spacious with a big old range. There was plenty of storage space with a big pantry and cellar.

When the time came to think about careers, I knew mine had to involve food. I was prepared to study catering or food related science, but I had no wish to waste years of my life trying to get qualifications. I knew how to cook and bake well, I needed to understand how to cater and about food composition and hygiene. This would serve me well, so I enrolled on a couple of correspondence courses and took books to study from the library. In the meantime, I catered using seasonal produce. My creativity kept the fascination building, I was always making something new. My dishes were well received, and my baked goods always sold out quickly at the market with orders for more. Allegedly my cookies were the best in the area.

Socially, I had some good girlfriends to hang out with. We went to the movies, the ice cream parlour, barn dances and dedicated events like Harvest Suppers or Thanksgiving. We went swimming in the summer and picked fruit and crops for extra cash. It was a friendly community where we tended to know everybody. When it came to romance, I tried a couple of times with local boys, but perhaps having brothers ruined it for me. There was no finesse, no excitement, it was all so predictable and stereotyped, I preferred to stick to food where the reward was enjoyable. This did not stop me taking an interest in all the romances taking place around me.

One afternoon whilst I was rushing across town, loaded up with baked goods to take to the local coffee shop, a voice called out: "Matilda O'Brien where's your manners? Don't think you can ignore me."

I turned around surprised to see Phil Taylor approaching. Phil had been away studying for a pharmacy degree in California. He was Ryan's age, the second oldest Taylor offspring. Secretly I had always admired him. Tall, dark and handsome was appropriate with his athletic build, dark curly hair and liquid brown eyes. I knew the family from school bus days and also being our former distant neighbours. The captain of sports teams - a real stud - cheer leader girls and glamorous types hung around him.

I suddenly felt conscious of my scraped back braids, my old comfortable clothes and lack of any feminine charms. Unfortunately, I was a faded feminine version of Poppa and missed out on Mama's good looks. I had mousy hair always tied back and green eyes. I rarely dressed up and never knew any trends or fads. Not having seen Phil for a few years apart from at a distance one Christmas, I suddenly realised how grown up he seemed. He carried some of my load and we walked across town together.

I asked about California where he said the girls were really hot. I imagined he would have been successful in any environment. Phil told me he had just returned home and was being apprenticed in Old Man Foster's pharmacy with a view to taking over when the old man retired. I wished him well and we parted company. With confidence and at ease he strode back down the street. My heart seemed to flutter but I put it down to rushing carrying a load.

Poppa's furniture business had grown with Dan's input of modern designs and techniques, so a furniture showroom was opened in the high street. Mama and I helped to dress the windows and added homely touches to the displays inside.

Before long an expansion to the property was required. A partnership was established between the owner of the building and Poppa. When the partner died, he left the building to Poppa thanking him for allowing him to prosper to enjoy a comfortable old age. Poppa was grateful and invested the money to pay off his mortgage as well as extending the premises.

At home, in front of the barn-like shed where the furniture was made, Dan built me a cabin with a wide window shelf where I could display and sell my baking. News got around and I often had customers queuing. This inspired me to suggest opening a coffee shop in a corner of the furniture store. Poppa was perplexed and thought about protecting his furniture from spills and crumbs. I told him that customers would take more time in store if they had a place that served refreshments. They could view the furniture over a coffee, use the convenience and mull over visualising the bespoke pieces in their homes. This would stop them rushing off unsure.

Dan took my side and created a narrow coffee shop alongside the smaller side window. I made it look inviting and installed the latest coffee maker in the business using my hard-earned savings. After a slow start it really took off and became a good earner. When queues of shoppers formed, Poppa decided to take over the adjacent store which had recently come onto the market, to expand the coffee shop and make it part of the offer.

I was rushed off my feet with customers and take-away sales, particularly for breakfast, so I had to hire extra staff. Dorothy, a housewife mother of two, came along from early morning until school finished, she was front-of-house and a real asset. Conscientious and scrupulously careful about cleanliness and hygiene, Dorothy was pleasant and reliable. To help with the food preparation I took on two apprentices, Sean did the evening shift assisting with the bread, buns and morning goods.

Ellie came early morning and left in the afternoon to attend her courses. She gained more hands-on work experience with me than in all her studies. With ambition and determination Ellie applied herself and offered innovative ideas and trends to the equation. A slip of a girl to look at, Ellie learned quickly and had great stamina. I could leave her to takeover when I needed to. We all got on well together and built up a great relationship. I spent more time with my staff than with my family. Mama suggested I took my bed into the shop to save me the journey.

I hired Millie Taylor to run the cabin for me. She was a student and needed the money. At 7 am she called at the shop to collect goods for sale. Poppa or Dan ran her to the cabin in his truck. She would open up, put the coffee on and present the goods for sale. Millie prepared all the regular orders and rang me to advise when stocks were getting low. Gradually, we established a good routine.

When Millie moved on, she passed the role on to Susie, her younger sister, who was equally reliable. So, I kept abreast of the Taylor family news and gossip. It seemed Phil was enjoying his work in the pharmacy where he seemed to be a hit with the local ladies. This did not surprise me as he did not have to try hard to get attention. Phil called round to the shop one day and hung around munching. I called out "Hi," as I went to load the van with extra supplies for the cabin. After making inane small talk for a couple of minutes, I told Phil brusquely that some of us had work to do.

Phil flushed and asked me awkwardly if I wanted to go to a charity event with him the following week. I thought he was probably on a wager to set me up and I would not be made a fool of, so I brushed him off telling him I was sure there was no shortage of willing females he could take. He flushed and shrugged saying, "I thought it might be more fun taking you," before walking away. This startled me momentarily, then I thought I would ask Susie what was going on.

Susie told me girls flocked around Phil as they had always done. He was being hotly pursued by two society belles but had been concentrating on work and sport so had not been bothering with any girlfriends. Any free time he had was spent going for beers or pool with his buddies. I said I thought Phil had asked me out for a wager. Susie thought that would be unlikely with her working for me. She did not think he would risk any upset.

I asked her why he would ask me out when he could take his pick. Susie thought the fact that I did not pursue him meant that he could relax and be at ease with me. Neither of us imagined Phil actually wanted to be with me. We left it like that and did not mention it again. I saw him occasionally around town or during weekends in the distance.

The church was having a fund-raising barn dance and having found cover at the bakery, I was persuaded to go. I set off with Candice who inherited all the good genes of the family past and present. Candice was the beauty, and she was devious with it. I felt like the dowdy old maid sister alongside her, but I planned to enjoy myself, so it did not bother me. I wore a green blouse to highlight my eyes, left my hair down and wore a swishing skirt good for twirling. For once I put on make-up and perfume and felt feminine.

On arrival I linked up with my girlfriends arranging to meet Candice at home time. We stood around gossiping, sipping soft drinks. At intervals we were invited to dance by local acquaintances. It was hot, thirsty work, and just when I decided to go outside to get some air, Phil appeared in front of me holding out his hand.

"I was just going out to get some air," I snapped.

"Fine, count me in," Phil said walking beside me.

"It's too hot in there, they need to invest in air con," I said.

"Maybe that's what the fundraising's for," Phil said teasingly.

"How's the pharmacy functioning with you working there?" I asked.

"Still standing and actually very interesting, I get to know everybody's secrets," Phil joked.

"So, are you enjoying it?"

"Very much so. Do you enjoy your baking?" Phil asked.

"For me it's as natural as breathing. I'm thinking of new things to try out all the time," I said twinkling.

"I'm happy to be your guinea pig," Phil said patting his flat stomach.

"You don't look like you need feeding up, I heard your Mama is a good cook," I said.

"She is, but there's room to try out modern styles to compare how they match up," Phil said hopefully.

"If I need a guinea pig then I will let you know, so far my supplies don't last long enough to try out - which reminds me, I need to go back to the store to see how Sean is coping," I said suddenly anxious to disappear.

"Sean will be fine, Mandy is helping him," Phil said confidently.

"Who is Mandy?" I asked alarmed.

"Mandy is his girlfriend and I paid her to give Sean a hand, so don't worry."

"You did what?" I exclaimed suddenly furious. "How dare you interfere in my business? How would you feel if I took over in the pharmacy? I have studied chemistry you know," I spluttered red with indignation.

"Calm down Tilly," Phil said taking hold of my hands to prevent a smack. "It was the only way I could think of to get some time with you. I tried asking you out and you turned me down."

"Are you serious?" I asked, astonished.

"Deadly," Phil replied coming closer to me, looking into my startled eyes.

"Why me? You can have any girl in town. I'm not your type."

"How do you know what my type is? That's for me to decide. You are certainly the most difficult one to persuade," Phil sighed, moving closer.

"You will not persuade me to do anything Phil Taylor, just keep your distance," I snapped pulling my hands free, intending to go away.

Phil Taylor swung me round into his arms, leaned over, kissed me and took my breath away. My knees actually trembled whether with fear or ecstasy was uncertain. I was shaking when he let go, I nearly fell, so I tried to say goodnight and fled to the safety of the shop. There I saw through the window Sean and Mandy beavering away chatting harmoniously. I left them to it and slunk home forgetting about Candice. Fortunately, one of her admirers accompanied her home.

I decided to avoid Phil Taylor and not mention him again to his sisters. Work would be my salvation and I would bury myself in my endeavours. I was already planning a new sandwich range where folk could pick out the fillings from a display counter. I worked out pricing for an offer of a sandwich, soft drink and chips. We stocked yoghurt and I devised a new offer for yoghurt with self-picked toppings including fruit, confectionery or nuts. We already offered milkshakes, so I added fruit shakes or exotic vitamin shakes. Ideas were bursting out of me, so I had little time to brood.

Phil came to the bakery, I told staff I was not available for social calls. I busied myself in the oven, but my staff betrayed me and gave him admittance. They seem to side with Phil, and I threatened them all with dismissal. The more resistance I put up, the more persistent Phil became. He even gave us a hand with the work when he had free time. I made sure he scrubbed up. I realised this state of affairs could not continue indefinitely, particularly as he was affecting my disposition. Involuntary shakes and trembles, beating heart and feeble mindedness was disturbing me whenever he was around.

In order to settle the confusion, I allowed him to walk me home but not to touch me. I questioned his intentions. Phil nodded and said he would like to court me with marriage in mind if we bonded. He said this calmly and smoothly. I nearly fell down.

"That is the most ridiculous thing I have ever heard," I said. "Anyway, you are like my brother, we have known each other for ever."

"I have two sisters," Phil replied, "and don't feel brotherly at all to you. You have no shortage of brothers yourself and I refuse to be added to the list."

"Anyway," I stuttered, "that is the worse proposal in the world."

"Would you prefer this," Phil said getting down on one knee in the street, hand over heart gesturing dramatically: "Matilda O'Brien will you do me the honour of becoming my lawful wedded wife, providing we can manage to get along?"

"Oh, get up," I said giggling. "Are you serious?"

"You keep asking me that Tilly, I assure you marriage is a serious business unless you prefer to have a hot passionate affair instead?" he raised both eyebrows suggestively.

"Phil Taylor will you stop teasing me. I'm very confused right now and can't tell if you are serious or joking. Give me some time to consider the matter. I don't have an answer for you."

"Don't take too long Tilly, I am longing to start our lives together. I have a good future ahead of me. You can stay here, bake and cook as much as you want, just allocate some time for me into your schedule and make me the happiest man in the world. I can follow my interests, you can be your own woman but the time we spend together has to be magical and exclusive. What do you say Tilly?" Phil lifted my chin and placed a delicate kiss on my lips. I automatically stretched up for more, but he just laughed and left me at my front door.

Naturally, I thought I would not sleep all night, but the excitement knocked me out. In the morning I wondered if I imagined the whole thing, but then the flowers arrived by courier followed by treats every day. My family were more excited than me and begged to know who my secret admirer was. Poppa told me to invite him for supper and an interview. Mama asked if she needed to put together new outfits for the family. I was mortified and remained silent. In the end Phil showed up after church and walked along with Poppa in earnest conversation. Mama, who was normally so observant, did not notice my consternation. The entire family had no idea that Phil was my mystery beau. It was not very flattering.

Mama invited Phil for dinner with us.

"His folk will be waiting on him," I said.

"Thank you, Mrs O'Brien, I would love to join you," Phil replied smiling pleasantly.

"Lay an extra plate Matilda," Mama instructed bustling around enjoying extra company.

The dinner went well for all the family. I squirmed and kept my head down not speaking throughout the meal. Unbeknown to me, all the family knew that Phil wanted to marry me. They were all waiting for me to accept and giving me every encouragement. Throughout the meal they enjoyed my discomfiture after years of my bossing them around and maintaining order and discipline. We all knew the Taylors and got on well. Phil was a favourite right from the start, so although I had no plans ever to marry, it seemed that our wedding was settled all around me. I continued working hard in a daze wearing a shiny fancy engagement ring which I removed for work.

All the Taylor family were delighted to welcome me. If they were surprised by Phil's choice of bride, they did not show it.

They were happy to have a top rate baker and cook in the family they said. Mrs Taylor teased me saying I was welcome to take over feeding her brood, she had done her best but would welcome a break. His sisters wanted to be bridesmaids. I stood back and let everybody plan everything around me. Mama made my wedding dress which was simple and elegant. She also made me an exquisite headdress using an antique hair accessory she inherited from her grandma. By the time I was primped and made up, I did not recognise myself. For once I looked beautiful.

Phil was radiant with delight, he could not stop admiring me and insisted on holding my hand all the time. I felt too embarrassed with all the attention and flattery to think of our wedding night. Our photo appeared in the local paper. We were whisked away to go on honeymoon to a secret destination. Mama had packed for me. I was happy to get changed into my departure outfit and sit down in the limo which lulled me to sleep. For years afterwards, Phil told everybody how his bride nodded off before we even got started. Our romance did not match the movies or the best sellers. Inside I felt excited and happy, I just did not know how to show it.

We honeymooned in the south of France staying in a romantic hotel in Nice. It was colourful, picturesque and I fell for French cuisine in a big way. We toured the area in a hire car. When Phil wanted to go for a round of golf or do sports, I arranged to visit the kitchen to study with the chef, Monsieur Leclerc, who was very enthusiastic and courteous. In the intimacy of our boudoir, Phil released all my inhibitions and I was enthralled by him. Perhaps all his experience had been training for my benefit because I had the most handsome desirable husband in existence. He captivated my heart, my soul and became my lifetime partner. Each time he came near me, I felt a thrill of delight. This never wore off, in my eyes he remained as handsome and virile as on our wedding day.

Phil wanted a family, I wasn't fussed but to make him happy along came Eithan, a dreamy sweet natured boy, followed by Scarlett a couple of years later, a temperamental bundle of energy who would have exhausted a saint. Fortunately, Grandma Rose Taylor was an active hands-on support who delighted in taking care of the children. I took advantage of her kindness, so I could continue working even though I had hired permanent competent staff to run the business. If I did not bake or cook, I felt twitchy. Creativity made me feel complete. Phil was happy when I was happy and was always prepared to hire help to do the housework or tasks I disliked.

The children enjoyed staying at both sets of grandparents and seemed happy with or without us. Eithan was not interested in sport and despite Phil's attempts to bond over different activities, it was Scarlett who determinedly shone at everything. Whilst Eithan's head seemed to be in the clouds, Scarlett seemed to know instinctively far too much way too soon. He was angelic, she was a minx. I decided that I didn't want any more children. With one of each Phil was content. We looked like an advertisement family. We lived in a large detached house in the suburbs where I grew herbs, had a vegetable patch and little orchard. I enjoyed getting my hands dirty.

Eric's Story

As one of the middle offspring, I don't resemble any of the others. The first two sons took after Poppa in looks, the younger members looked like Mama, I am different. My two older brothers were too busy to bother with me when I was small. When they needed one extra for ball games or tasks, they remembered me. I was not much use in sport, never felt the competitive urge to conquer. My co-ordination was not as sharp as they wanted either. Although Poppa taught us all carving skills, he gave up at my clumsy attempts. Matilda bossed me about, Dan looked up to me and Candice wrapped me round her little finger. I never minded being ignored or overlooked, my mind was occupied elsewhere.

One time when I was recovering from chicken pox Mama found an old box camera which had belonged to my grandpa. She gave it to me to play with to distract me from scratching. I was fascinated and persuaded Poppa to install a film inside it for me to try. It seemed magical to me to capture images through the lens. I used my meagre pocket money to get the prints developed. From this early age I was hooked on photography. It became my passion and I wanted to learn everything I could about it. The family thought it would be a passing hobby but I knew it would shape my life. Nothing else could compare to it.

Growing up in Allbrite with scenic views surrounding us, I practised taking landscapes, then people going about their lives. Most residents knew each other plus all the business and personal issues, so did not perceive me as a threat. As I grew older, I learnt to ask permission to take photos. Our family was large and varied enough to capture but they were not my aim. I used them to learn how to focus. They refused to pose so many shots were hit and miss. I also made myself a black room in the attic where I taught myself to develop film. There was an old blackout curtain there from the war.

Having exhausted the library books on photography, I saved up and did odd jobs to earn money so I could enrol on photography courses. I wanted qualifications to show Poppa that I was serious and planned to make photography my career. There was so much to learn including photo journalism, black and white photography, wildlife, architecture and so much more. I showed Poppa an advertisement for an MA or Post Graduate Diploma in Photography Studies which offered studying with talented practitioners on an international scale, being part of a global community of like-minded professionals, being taught by and engaging with experienced industry professionals and the opportunity to demonstrate your creativity and photography skills with an international qualification.

Poppa was not impressed but he knew how serious I was, so he told me to take a loan for the expense. I could study and pay him back with my earnings. This seemed fair to me. I learned to drive at Poppa's expense and was happy to accept his offer. Mama worried initially if I would succeed in earning a living. Poppa assured her that I would learn to do so. I was pleased to hear he had faith in me until I realised that he meant I would learn to earn a living, not necessarily doing photography. I had always been different, when the others wanted to climb hills, I wanted to reconnoitre the landscape. If they swam in rivers, I wanted to see where the river went to or came from.

Instead of spontaneous action man, I was Mr Curious always seeking answers as to how, why and where. What was the motivation behind things? How did things work? Why did people behave in mysterious ways? Did something happen by chance or was it fate? Was fate something real? If there was one God, how come there were so many different religions? Why did each religious sect believe they were the right one? My head buzzed with unanswered questions. At home I annoyed my family by questioning everything, so I learned to keep my thoughts to myself. Mainstream trends and celebrity culture passed me by. I cared nothing for fashion or gossip or TV game shows. I needed more input.

One of my major attributes in my profession is my ability to blend in. I am tall but do not stand out in a crowd. I am neither handsome nor plain, somewhere in between. At school I did above average but never came top or bottom. Nobody noticed me which served me well. Often in my work I had to sneak into position or have moments to capture something special and I escaped notice. When it came to romance, I knew all the local girls, who was hot, who was easy, it was too familiar. I could not pursue any of them knowing their families and backgrounds. A few came along to try to pursue me, but I diplomatically helped them on their way. I had no intention of making any commitments. There was a wide world waiting for me.

Fortunately, by the time I was old enough the Vietnam war was over and so was compulsory conscription. Ryan had long gone, Marshall married Linda and was very happy. Tilly married Phil but still spent her life around an oven. Before anybody could try to matchmake me, I took off. I had sought advice from professional photographers, had lists of international agencies and contacts. I had created a portfolio and entered national competitions. Whenever I had free time, I would seek out compositions to photograph. Eventually, I won a nature competition for my picture of an eagle feeding its young. I also became runner-up in an international major competition showing a scene of end of term timeout snapped at precisely the right moment.

I felt I should explore the States before venturing further afield. It seemed a promising idea to enter the calendar market to raise funds. A buddy of mine had connections in the media and promised to help me with the end product. So, my plan was to work in bars or do casual labour whilst photographing twelve states featuring every day scenes. Wherever I went I spoke to people as I was genuinely interested to learn about their lives and views, what it was like living in their location. People tend to open up if they feel you are a good listener and are sympathetic. Some of my best shots exposed emotions and raised my profile globally. This stimulated me, I could never get enough. I was not after glory or trophies, I just wanted to reflect the lives of everyday people living in our land.

Sometimes I tended bars, I waited tables, washed dishes, serviced pools in affluent areas, did some gardening and whatever I found I did with a good heart. I smiled and refused to be hurried or bullied. So many confidential tales were told to me without my asking. Perhaps my demeanour was non-threatening, or perhaps it was being listened to properly, but I felt humble and grateful for my own upbringing and the freedom to move on when I wanted. I made sure to ring home periodically so that Mama would know I was OK. Away from home I missed nothing and nobody. At Christmas or festive times, I would remember my family, but I felt no desire to join them in what seemed a very distant world.

I thought about specialising in one form of photography. It had been drummed into me that before going abroad, I needed to research the customs and prohibitions of the country. There were specialist war photographers, but I wasn't sure whether I wanted to live in conflict zones. Africa was a missionary offering with charities trying to raise funds to improve life. I felt that scene was not for me. Wild life and nature made for interesting pictures but I did not feel the buzz. I enjoyed snapping people unawares, scenes of daily routines, life in the raw. Politicians seemed full of hot air and empty promises to me. Media held some appeal, so I introduced myself to photographic agencies offering my availability to go on assignments at a moment's notice.

Whilst they were receiving my offerings I worked hard for the local press, entered more competitions and sent in shots of local scenarios. In this way I slowly began to be noticed. Eventually, I received a trickle of assignments starting with Mexico and the shot that launched my career. I noticed a would-be migrant struggling across the scrubland carrying a small child covered with a blanket. The sadness and heat on his face combined with the innocence of the little face peeping out of the blanket was haunting. It went global, from then on offers came my way.

On an assignment in Morocco, I had finished work and was relaxing at a beach bar when I met Rachel, a South African world traveller. We got talking and found we had a similar outlook on life. With much in common it seemed natural to continue our conversation and we ended up travelling along together. Rachel was tanned and vibrant, living life each moment. She had seen far more of the world than me but was open to new experiences and was ready to learn about everything. She was attractive rather than beautiful - charismatic and sparkling. I enjoyed her company more than any other, we bonded and in time began a love affair.

Rachel helped me with my work, she encouraged the agencies, did good public relations and wrote captions or little stories to accompany my shots. We made a good team. Whilst all was going well, Rachel told me that she was living on borrowed time. It seemed she had an inoperable tumour. I felt devastated particularly because I felt so helpless. Rachel knew how much I cared and told me she did not want me to witness her death. I refused to leave her to die alone. She did not want me to be broken hearted and said if I cared about her I had to promise to live the life we wanted for both of us. She vanished without trace one night when I was asleep. I never saw her again nor found anyone else who meant as much to me.

Marriage and children held no appeal to me. Sometimes I had liaisons with women I met on my travels. There were opportunities I declined, I lived one day at a time. Whenever I saw somebody from behind who looked like Rachel, I was always disappointed. Time was a healer, but I missed the close companionship and partnership I had lost. I got on well with children in general but had no desire to perpetuate my line. My expectations were low, I tried not to anticipate or manipulate and drifted along from one job to the next. My only passion was for my work.

I did not dabble in drink or drugs - Poppa's warnings still rang in my ears. A few beers, or an occasional whisky, would make me drowsy. With my valuable equipment in mind I maintained self-control at all times. Travelling around like a nomad showed me only too clearly the ruination drugs and alcohol caused. I did a successful project showing the ravages of addiction. Smoking also turned me off. I tried weed a few times, but it also made me sleepy, so I just carried on without stimulants. The nomadic life suited me. I travelled light, my equipment and a few changes of clothing plus something to read seemed enough to carry around. Possessions tied people down.

On my travels I sometimes met foreign journalists and cameramen. Other photographers were usually found in bars frequented by the media. They were glad to exchange stories for booze, so I was accepted most of the time. Some were egoists and I dismissed their tall stories, a few were surly and unsociable having seen too much tragedy. Whilst on assignment in Slovenia, I met Katia, a media correspondent and Gunther, a German cameraman. Gunther suffered from reoccurring bouts of malaria. One afternoon Katia sought me out and asked me to accompany her to Gunther. He was unwell and asked me to take over filming later that night as he was shaking too much to go.

I had no experience behind film cameras, but Gunther gave me need-to-know crash training and begged me to go. His job was at risk, Katia would accompany me. I worried I might ruin his career but finally agreed to have a go. We went to film some unpleasant footage of persecution and intimidation witnessed behind some ruined buildings on a hill. It was a disturbing and distressing situation, but my focus was on controlling the camera. I resolved to learn how to use it professionally to expand my skills when this was over. Katia helped me and pointed out details with background knowledge of the players. She also got the filming transmitted for Gunther who had to return to Germany to be hospitalised.

I was moving on and to my surprise Katia wanted to accompany me. My next assignment was in Laos where I expected to take magnificent shots. Katia taught me good media skills and techniques to get ahead. She introduced me to a cameraman who taught me in depth about using the latest television and movie cameras. I needed to understand how they functioned and what limitations they had. Once I mastered the technique, I added it to my resources.

We had a long tiring journey to the Mekong Delta which looked incredibly scenic and peaceful in the sunshine. It had a dreamy quality on first viewing and I found it hard to believe my country had bombed it extensively. If the natives resented me as an American, I would understand. Instead, I found the natives friendly and helpful and the girls were exquisite. Katia left me as she had her own agenda to complete. I took time to adjust to the climate and explore. During my assignment I was given an interpreter called Kalaina which I was told meant exotic, mysterious. Kalaina was intelligent, smart and enchanting, she took my breath away. When she smiled it was like sunshine. I was smitten.

Always professional and polite, Kalaina must have been used to guys falling for her. She handled me diplomatically and kept her distance. I felt huge, awkward and a real clumsy American oaf next to her. Besides no language skill, I knew nothing about the food, the culture or the customs. Normally I read up about countries I visited but this assignment came up just before I left. I planned to buy some books and swot up. When Kalaina came onto the scene I asked her lots of questions. At first, she distrusted me as if I were a spy, then when she discovered my genuine interest she opened up, shyly at first.

I walked around taking endless pictures, everything fascinated me. Life was so different from anything I was used to. It seemed simplistic and the people seemed poor, but many looked happy. They had very little and used everything carefully. Most were slim and fit looking. I was dazzled by everything and begged Kalaina to guide me to books about their philosophy and beliefs. I could not get enough. I invited her to accompany me for meals to explain to me what I was eating and drinking. She took me to meet her family when I decided to stay on, as she explained that it was important for them to see that my intentions towards her were honourable. I took gifts for the family and bowed down saying the few words Kalaina had taught me.

Despite the humidity I fell in love with Kalaina, her family, her country and felt a sense of coming home. This surprised me because I was always thinking about moving on. I had no desire to go any further. The thought of not seeing Kalaina did not bear thinking about. I taught English to the locals to earn some money and sent off some of my best shots to international magazines and agencies. I developed a series entitled *Daily Life in Laos*. It met with moderate success and kept me solvent. It seemed I needed to assess my future.

I also needed to understand whether Kalaina had feelings for me. I would not force myself upon Kalaina nor would I offer her a marriage of convenience. Kalaina had a good job as an interpreter and helped to support her family who were small farmers. She had ample opportunity to mix with foreign nationalities. Her family had made sacrifices to give her a good education, she always looked immaculate and kept up to date with current affairs. In addition to her own language, she spoke fluent English and French. There was no way she could be compared to 'mail order brides'.

By her own admission, Kalaina was patriotic and reasonably content with her lifestyle. She had not been looking for a husband and felt a strong duty to take care of her family. Her married brother also contributed to the family budget. The fact that I was obviously smitten by her charm was not unique in her experience.

I tried to learn the language, which was difficult for me. The sounds did not stick in my head, I tried tapes and enrolled for lessons, but there was nothing familiar in the writing or vocabulary. Over time I hoped I would be able to grasp it. As I had led a nomadic life for many years, I had no home of my own and few possessions. My work took me travelling regularly. I needed to decide whether I was ready to settle down, what I had to offer sophisticated Kalaina, where I wanted to live and how I could make a sufficient living.

My heart wanted to rush in, my head felt confused and afraid that I had nothing to offer. Fortunately, work intervened, and I was sent to China. I used the time to meditate and think about my life.

Meanwhile Mama told me she and Poppa would like a visit from me. They were both getting older and she thought I should see the family I had left behind whilst they were still around. Feeling reluctantly guilty, I sought out an assignment in the States for one of my photographic agencies. The States seemed an alien world to me. I was accustomed to foreign shores, exotic food, tropical climates, alien experiences. I wondered if I would fit in back home. There were also new nephews and nieces to meet.

I wanted Kalaina to join me but had still not plucked up courage to approach her and her family until I felt certain that marriage was for me. I knew I could be happy with Kalaina but all my life I had struggled with commitment. The idea of being responsible and tied down depressed me. Convention suited most people. I was not materialistic and mortgages, steady jobs and sucking up to advance seemed abhorrent. Being able to support myself and discover the world was invigorating.

Women wanted security, families to raise and someone to support them. Even the women's libbers seemed to appreciate the solid traditional qualities I seemed to lack. Although my heart was overflowing with love for Kalaina, I could not bear to disappoint her. It was better to love her eternally in my heart and allow her to find somebody more suitable. I felt gutted at this realisation but could not fool myself. Some sort of selfishness inside me prevented me from making a conventional commitment.

Dan's Story

As the youngest son in the family I favoured Mama in looks but became Poppa's apprentice because I had the gift of capable hands. My interest in creating furniture and masterpieces expanded into design and pattern cutting. I kept abreast of trade journals and international trends in furniture all from my doorstep. I never felt the urge to go off gallivanting like my older brothers. I was always a homebody, enjoyed my home comforts and being familiar with all and sundry. It sure made it easier to do business. There may be better places to live but I ain't complaining, Allbrite has been good to me.

As a boy I remember helping out on the land, the big open spaces that stretched to the horizon. Waiting for the school bus in the cold winter months was no picnic and we had to travel long distances to get anything. I guess that made me self-reliant, I learned to take care of myself and to plan ahead if I needed something. I enjoyed sports and baseball games. Poppa taught us to box, later I took up wrestling and judo. I tried to keep fit and active and went for runs early or late when I could. I liked action, contrasting with the stillness and patience I had using my hands. There were always plenty of chores to do at home and no excuses to evade them.

My folk were big on education, so I did my best and usually came in the top five. I did my homework as fast as I could. I was always in a hurry to be off to do something. My bike was handed down from my brothers. Mama always instructed me to watch out for Candice. If you ask me, I needed protection from her. Eric used to monitor me, but he was easy going and easy to fool. I tried to be a good boy, but I was not averse to drinking cider with my buddies or sneaking out at night sometimes when I was older. On the whole, I behaved and saved my allowance for things I needed. In season I earned extra money helping with harvests, packing, lifting or markets.

There was a group of boys I hung out with from school, we got up to mischief, eyed up the girls, played pool and hung out together. We swam, fished and took part in sports in the summer. In the winter we hung out in various venues. Four of us even started a rock group using Johnny's dad's garage. We got a few local bookings, but I think our enthusiasm was more than our talent. I played drums and used to tap in the house on surfaces which annoyed the family. The family had a policy of encouraging us all to find our talents and see where they led. There was no shame in trying and not succeeding. Shame lay in not trying.

Because I became Poppa's apprentice it meant I had to miss out on social occasions which interfered with my training. In addition, I had to study techniques and processes to have an all-round knowledge of carpentry and design. There was never much time for socialising. By this stage in my life only Candice and I remained at home. This gave us additional chores to add to our commitments. Candice used to try to buy favours to get out of stuff, but I enjoyed being mean to her and always refused. That girl was so egoistic and self-centred, you wouldn't think so to look at her, but I knew her inside out.

My friend Frank's mother May invited me to her 50th birthday party which was held in the community hall. I went along and helped lay out the provisions. His sister Claire was home from college, and I was surprised to see how mature and attractive she had become. I don't like skinny girls, I like curves on a woman. Claire had curves in all the right places and a pretty face. Something had changed from the little girl who was Frank's sister. I helped her sort out the silverware and glasses and we got chatting. It seemed as if we had just met instead of knowing each other all our lives. I was reluctant to part from her, but Frank called me over.

I told Frank I was surprised to see how grown up Claire appeared now. He shrugged, said she had some boyfriend at college who couldn't come to the party. Frank was more interested in baseball scores and bets on coming fixtures. My concentration was focused on watching Claire prepare for the party, so I zoned out. Later in the evening when the booze had relaxed the crowd, speeches and presentations were made and dancing started up, I waited until the floor was busy then invited Claire to dance. Just after we started dancing the tempo slowed and I found myself holding Claire in my arms. It felt like she belonged there, I wanted the music to continue forever. I asked Claire about her life as a student and if she had a boyfriend. Claire was doing scientific studies. Her boyfriend was not serious, just a colleague she hung around with on the same course. To my surprise I told Claire he must be foolish to let her out of his sight. I told Claire she felt good in my arms and how I wished she could stay there. Claire asked if I had been drinking but when she leaned back to look in my eyes to see if I was serious, I saw her expression soften as she realised I was smitten. This was unexpected and I was not sure how Frank and his family would feel. The rest of the evening was a blur as I would not be parted from Claire's side.

Frank asked me if I was interested in Claire or if it was just the drink taking over. I had only had a couple of beers and had never felt more sober. I asked Frank if he minded if I courted Claire. Something had happened to me that evening and I felt I needed to watch over her and protect her. Frank grinned and said Claire did not need looking after but he realised I was serious. He told me to speak to his father after the event. We both forgot that Claire would need to be consulted if my intentions were leading to marriage. Fortunately, with Claire's consent and the approval of her family, we began a two-year courtship whilst we both advanced our careers.

When Mama was robbed on the day I was out delivering finished pieces, she became edgy and insisted on moving to a new house. Poppa gave in and bought a small property on the outskirts of town. The home and barn used for construction 'was passed over to me. Candice had gone to college by then and the rest of the family were settled. I brought Claire over and asked her how she felt about living there when we were married. She made me get down on one knee to propose properly then walked through the place room by room listing the alternations and modernisations she insisted on to bring it up to date. There would be no wedding until all the refurbishment was done to her satisfaction.

This entailed a communal effort with family friends and neighbours lending a hand when time permitted. I had a couple of apprentices working for me who were recent school leavers, so I trained them to keep the business ticking over whilst we practically gutted my parents' place. Mama came around with refreshments and snacks to sustain us. Claire found work as a lab assistant in an environmental place outside of town. She gave the orders and had to wait until she finished work to inspect the progress. The aim was to let in more light and equip the house with modern appliances, low maintenance and minimalist style. If Claire was happy, it was enough for me. I liked her ideas and was happy to go along with her plans.

Poppa developed early signs of Parkinson's Disease, his hands shook. Early diagnosis meant he had access to the latest medicines. It was all to be tried and tested. This meant that the business rested in my hands. I didn't mind as I already did most of it. With Poppa only able to advise and the rest of the family mainly indifferent, I thought we ought to discuss the future of the business. At present we had the barn style workshop, the showroom in town and received orders from surrounding districts. My aim was to expand the business, open up another showroom in the neighbouring district and to eventually run a mail order offering. This would require recruiting more staff and larger premises.

Modern furniture could be mass produced on specially adapted equipment. It was an investment initially, but the potential was unlimited. Poppa felt we should go to see our bank manager to discuss the matter. Employment opportunities in our region were limited and as I felt we could recruit trainees from school leavers locally, it seemed like a good offer. Poppa was worried that my youth and comparative inexperience may go against me. Mr Dawson, our bank manager, had known our family for many years, he'd seen us grow up, so was prepared to consider our proposals when we had worked out our financial plan in detail. He told us how to figure out in detail what would need to be submitted. Marshall would be able to help us to do it professionally.

When the house was finished, Claire, her mother Rose and Mama had many excursions excitedly turning it into a home. I was tasked with making and creating the basic furniture requirement based on illustrations from magazines that Claire had found. It was a learning curve for me, and I used the experience in our new production ranges. Styles, colours and fabrics changed regularly so our ranges had to keep up. I was fascinated by the constant changes just like women's fashions, colours were favoured for a short time only. It seemed sensible to feature neutral colours that could be enhanced by soft furnishings. Candice was good at trends and helpful at displaying the ranges to catch attention. Women seemed to have the knack of adding little touches creating welcoming rooms.

My wedding day was one of the happiest of my life. Claire looked a vision, the smiles and goodwill of both families plus friends teasing made the day special. Apart from Ryan, all the family were there. We had a great time and left to go on honeymoon to Florida Keys where we toured and chilled out in a romantic secluded resort on a beautiful beach front. I felt that Claire and I were made for each other. If all the movie stars lined up and begged me, I would only ever choose Claire and felt so happy she had chosen me. Our honeymoon flew by and we enjoyed every moment. If I ever feel downhearted, I just look at the photos and feel happy again.

We visited both sets of parents regularly, they were all getting older. Mama kept busy and active finding interests she had never had time for before. Poppa had the shakes to contend with but met with his cronies regularly. They were both impressed with our home. Mama wished it had been ready sooner, so she could have enjoyed it.

Privately, Poppa declared it was too modern for his taste, he liked dark colours and heavy furniture. I reckon each generation gets used to styles in vogue in their time. Poppa still kept an eye on the business and often had good advice regarding techniques and offers. He insisted we stick to a quality finish rather than cheaper materials which would not last.

I suggested to Poppa that modern furniture was not built to last. People liked to change their furniture every few years. If we priced it too high for quality, they would look elsewhere. Poppa disagreed, styles would change but quality provided good value for money and would carry families through lean times. We never argued and I listened to Poppa, ultimately reaching a practical compromise. Chipboard was not a feature in our workshop. Vinyl had limited application but was useful for kitchen and beach commodities. We were open to all ideas and visions for all uses. What we could not do immediately, we studied and found methods to adapt. This stimulated me and kept the business growing.

When Claire told me that she was pregnant I was over the moon. Leo arrived in April, screaming, red faced, little legs kicking, big mop of hair. He was a big baby and Claire was exhausted. Ollie arrived just over two years later completing our family. Being a father to two beautiful boys invigorated me and kept me busy. I wanted the best of everything for them and was determined to keep fit and active so that I would be able to play with them. Rose, Claire's mother, enjoyed taking care of the boys. My Mama also enjoyed her role as Grandma but led a busy social life. Claire missed work and went back part time when both boys were out of diapers.

Allbrite had expanded and changed a great deal since my childhood days. Coffee shops were replaced by fast food outlets, ice cream parlours and specialised bars offered foreign food, smoothie drinks and yoghurt treats, it was all new. A few traditional bars and coffee shops were still around including Matilda's which was very popular due to her baking. She opened three branches in different parts of town, all of which were continually busy. Tilly recruited a large staff working shifts but was constantly glued to her ovens. She liked the personal touch.

My friends had all settled down. Frank was married to Shirley Miller, one of our former neighbours, so we were all close friends. Claire and Shirley had always been friends. We saw my family on occasions, they sometimes dropped in but without Mama's influence we were all too busy to get together much. Life moved at a fast pace. When the children arrived, we were constantly chauffeuring them around, always picking up and dropping off, kids came for sleepovers and then there was shopping and fixing things. I have never been so busy in my life. At night I would fall in bed exhausted. Kids always woke up early ready for action all year round. I don't remember my family being so lively first thing.

When Mama had her conversation with Ryan, it seemed she wanted to visit him in Canada. I was uncertain about it. Mama was entitled to a vacation for sure. It seemed to me that Ryan should bring his family over to visit us. I don't know how I feel about Ryan. When he left, I was only a young boy, I don't remember him much. Why he avoided the draft seems strange to me, I heard he was ace at hunting and made a name for himself on school teams. Ryan had been captain of the baseball team, he played sports and knew how to box, so it seemed odd that he would avoid defending our country. I don't know how I would have reacted, but I was glad I didn't have to find out. Ryan was no coward but he did not seem like a hero to me.

Marshall had recovered from his injury and was raising a beautiful family. They lived across town in the suburbs, we caught up with them periodically, the kids played well together. Eric was another surprise, he was always travelling, never putting down roots. Growing up with Eric ahead of me meant that we were fairly close, although very different natured. Eric was unconventional, laid back - almost horizontal - yet very caring and loyal. We only heard from him via Mama's occasional telephone calls. Time was moving on swiftly and we were all racing along trying to keep up.

Candice's Story

As the youngest in the family, I got the best looks and the most indulgence. From a very young age I used my looks to get what I wanted. I fluttered my big blue eyes and looked sad or cried until most people submitted. There's no point being modest, I have always been noticed and if I don't look out for myself who will? As a child a photographer wanted me to model for magazines, Poppa refused permission.

Mama dressed me well to enhance my eye-catching appearance. My big brothers were a doddle, Matilda had her head buried in ovens, Mama was always busy, and I knew I was the apple in Poppa's eye. I did not always get my way. Always interested in fashion and design, I customised my dolls' clothes then as I grew older, I customised my outfits.

Allbrite was a bit of a let down on the clothing scene, it catered more to a matronly bygone era. Sometimes market traders would bring interesting clothing onto the scene. Mama felt it was cheap and not likely to last, so she would not buy it for me. She missed the point that fashion was not meant to last. Neither Mama nor Tilly cared a hoot about fashion and it showed. I knew I had to cater for the girls and women who cared when I grew up.

In my childhood I tagged along behind my older siblings, often annoying them by getting in the way. If they bugged me, I told tales when I got home to get them into trouble. I constantly told them how to behave, what was right and wrong, but they paid little attention. When the boys were courting, they consulted me regarding their outfits and for buying presents. Dan used my expertise to display his showrooms to advantage. It amused me to see what a diverse family we turned out to be. We all had our talents and our uses.

It was important to me to always be part of the in-crowd. From kindergarten onwards I set the trends, where I led others followed. Most people were pushovers, especially boys. If I was bossy it was because I did not like to waste time. I knew the right way to do things, what to wear, how to dress, it was important to look good, so why waste time repeating and waiting for the dim ones to get the message. Telling me how pretty I am is irritating, it is useful for manipulation but hardly original. I would not be overlooked or classed as ordinary.

Allbrite was too provincial for my ambitions but I had to bide my time until I could be independent. My self-belief ensured me that I could be anything I wanted. Feminism and women's lib did nothing for me. I reckon that individuals make their own way with grit and determination, irrespective of the gender. Also, men were such pushovers when presented with a pretty face and sexy body, it's useful but so conventional. Behind my feminine frame lurks a karate expert so nobody messes with me. Poppa also taught Tilly and me some defensive and attack moves.

I could pick and choose my friends, I always picked the society princesses so I could learn tips from them. Living remotely had its uses and I got to stay over in some smart houses. When we moved into Allbrite it was convenient, but our new place needed a complete make-over. Mama settled for a coat of paint and some soft furnishings. Claire came into the family with vision and brought the place into this century, but I was gone by then. The rest of our family barely noticed what they wore or how the world advanced. As long as they were well fed and comfortable, it seemed to be enough.

My ambition was to make my name as a fashion designer. I wanted to be famous and mix with real celebrities and stars. Once I had the training and gained some exposure, I knew I would be successful. Allbrite certainly needed some upmarket ranges. Like many small rural towns, styles were endlessly repeated, suitable for old people with conservative taste. The same old dated clothing appeared adapted to suit each season. Whilst I approve of classical lines, there were limits. I subscribed to fashion magazines and watched shows and videos of the latest creations.

Poppa proved difficult to persuade about my choice of career. I needed to study to get professional skills. It was costly and no suitable courses were to be found in Allbrite. I needed to move away and the courses were expensive. Poppa wanted me to do correspondence courses or go to night school. He didn't understand that this would not cut it. It took long and hard negotiations until I managed to get sent off to study.

Being Poppa's youngest meant that I was his eternal little girl and he was over-protective. I wanted to go to New York or California, but I was allowed to go to Boise, Idaho which was the furthest Poppa would agree to. In my mind this was step one, so I figured it would be a learning curve. Once Poppa saw I could manage alone out there, it would make the next stage easier.

Mama let me use her old sewing machine and I started creating garments and customising tee shirts from an early age. I used to sell them in school and even took some to the markets when my family were selling there. Many were too radical for Allbrite but I built up a following. I knew I was talented, but I needed to learn techniques to expand my skills. The more I learned, the more I desired to run my own brand. Everything was open, I could mix, match, dye, blend and create endless possibilities. This excited me more than anything else.

Marshall accused me of being materialistic and shallow, I think it is good to aim for self-improvement, to be one's best. We all have potential, but many miss their opportunities and seem content to vegetate. Grazing and gazing get a person nowhere. Look how many people are out of shape and out of time. Obesity is a major epidemic, that's where all that eating and sleeping gets you. To achieve and advance requires effort and hard work.

I could always take my pick of boyfriends but found the local boys dull and predictable. From the star jocks to the creatives, they disappointed me. Self-centred and hoping to score turned me off. I could always find an escort to important functions but not one of them was worthy to pop my cherry. I was saving it for a real man. My future would leave Allbrite behind so there seemed to be no point in getting involved with anyone. Whilst girlfriends talked about guys they wanted to marry and how many children they would have, I dreamed about how many stores I would open in how many States.

From childhood we all had to help with the chores. Mama taught us to cook simple meals and some sewing and home skills. I could make a mean stew but knew that I would employ somebody to run my home for me when I had one. Domesticity was not my scene, life was too short. Besides I would help somebody with employment. I could never fool Mama any of the time, no pouting or tantrums worked on her. She said I was a spoilt brat, but she still loved me anyway. We got on well and managed my brothers between us.

Going to college was a real eye opener to me, I had so much to learn including dressmaking and design, fashion and pattern cutting, industrial sewing, corsetry and so much more. I signed up for the couture tuition programme which was expensive, so I got part time work in a local bar to help with the finances. I shared a house with three other girls on different courses, but with varied schedules we rarely crossed paths. My time was spent on campus or working, fortunately I got fed at work because I begrudged spending my hard-earned money on food.

As usual there were plenty of boys willing to share their rations or take me out. My new best friend at college was a gay man called Henry, we often teamed up. Some of the girls resented me because I was obviously pretty and talented. They had no time for me and I returned the favour. I courted the truly talented gifted people who had plenty to offer. Their favour was hard to come by, but my persistence paid off. I learned a great deal from them just by listening and watching.

I had to call home regularly to maintain my allowance. Mama did not worry about me much, she knew I was a survivor. Poppa fretted if he didn't hear from me. For my part I was happy to escape and be my own person. Allbrite seemed another world away, small-minded and limiting. Friends kept me up to date with all the uninspiring home news which made me more determined to stay away.

Allbrite was scenic and maybe good for retirement. I hoped when I reached that stage, I could live somewhere better suited to me. Ryan and Eric had the right idea moving away. Ryan was a hazy memory in my mind, I vaguely remember trailing after him. Eric could be useful when I launched my collections. The future looked bright.

I enjoyed my courses there were so many techniques to learn and I tried to absorb everything. As an extra I took a communications course to understand how to market myself. I needed to understand how to use the latest technology to generate interest worldwide if I was smart enough. At first it overwhelmed me, but once I got the hang of it with help from some of the guys on the course, I figured it would serve me well. Everything changed so fast it was hard to keep up, but I made sure I did. I could not rely on anybody else to sing my praises.

An important charity fashion show was coming to Boise, Idaho featuring Roberto, the Italian designer who clothed the rich and famous. We were all very excited and wanted to go but the tickets were out of reach. I dressed smartly and went along to the hotel telling them I was a fashion major assigned to the collection to get experience for my course. I blagged the fashion crew that the hotel had assigned me as extra staff to assist them back stage. I knew they would be busy and from past experience of modelling in Allbrite fashion events, an extra pair of hands would be welcome.

Roberto cruised in later giving commands, folding the material and checking the models. I watched him surreptitiously whilst making myself busy. He did not notice me. I studied the stylist, how they pinched and pulled the material, draped the models, arranged the hair and make-up for maximum impact. The finish on the clothing was perfect, the garments had been hand sewn, made to measure and looked so classy, it was awesome.

After the show and bows before Roberto left, I dashed over to him and thanked him for the show, gushing how fabulous I thought his garments were. Roberto brusquely said thank you and made to go, I sensed he had heard his praises many times before.

"I am a fashion major," I said anxiously, "Can you give me any advice for the future?"

"Be original," Roberto said, "You need to offer something different. Now I don't have time to look at your designs and if you are after my body stand in line. Pretty girls are ten to a penny in our profession. Buena sera signorita."

He swept away followed by his entourage leaving me with burning cheeks feeling humiliated. Whilst I admit he was very masculine and sexy, I had not intended to offer myself to him. It occurred to me that I had fallen into the same pattern would-be suitors used when chasing me. Shame rose through me. I went hot and cold, gathered my coat and departed thinking about originality. One day my name would appear in big letters and he would know who I was. First, I had to work on my design and figure out what I had to offer. There were many good dressmakers, but the top designers could be counted.

To pay for my studies and supplement my meagre allowance from Poppa, I still worked in the bar. With the night school and various projects on the go at college, I was scraping by and always tired. At Christmas I was glad to go back home for a rest. It felt luxurious to be back in my own bed and only have chores to do. I took some finished garments to sell on the market and could have made a killing if I'd had more. It showed me the demand was there. The new generation in Allbrite wanted something different.

Seeing the family again was fun catching up, playing with my nephews and nieces. I caught up with the town gossip, helped in the kitchen, went shopping with Mama and had a cosy time. Some of Allbrite's eligible bachelors were introduced to me, but I was not interested in forming liaisons. My life was too busy for relationships. When I needed escorting Henry would take me places, I did the same for him. We were like brother and sister. He would tell me about the men he fancied, I listened and made him laugh. I talked about my ambitions and Henry encouraged me. He understood my passion and drive. I did not need to impress Henry, he accepted me the way I am.

Before I left to return to college Mama spoke to me about visiting Ryan and his family in Canada in the summer. She wanted me to accompany her and would pay for me. I had not thought about visiting Canada and asked why Ryan and his family did not come to visit us instead. Mama said her 60th birthday was coming up and the family wanted to treat her to a scenic memorable trip by train to take in amazing scenery and visit Ryan in Montreal. As the rest of the family were married with young children except for Eric who was abroad, Mama asked me again.

I have to say my heart sank, I had planned to work during the summer and start producing products to sell. Canada seemed to be going backwards somehow. I needed to get myself known in trendy areas with cool dudes. Mama sensed my reluctance and told me to think about it. The rest of the family put pressure on me, told me to stop being selfish and think about Mama for once. As I was a student they would pay my fare and not expect me to contribute to their collection. They expected me to help Mama with her holiday wardrobe instead. My wishes and opinions were irrelevant.

Back at college I became engrossed in my courses and extra activities and forgot all about Canada. The more I learned, the more I experimented. I learned about fabrics, dyes, accessories, fancy stitching, crochet, knitting, tapestry, embroidery, handling delicate fabrics, cleaning and stain removing techniques, jewellery, fur, lace. It seemed I could never learn enough. I was often to the last one to leave class, out of hours I could be found making something. Eating and sleeping became secondary. Some of my tee shirts and sweatshirts were on sale around the campus under the brand *Candice*.

As soon as I graduated, I planned to set up a small workshop in Allbrite and start production in multiple categories. I would produce items for market, student wear and my smart designer wear would be feminine and classy in an original way. I was still working out how that would look. It was therefore a surprise when Mama rang me to tell me the tickets were booked for Canada. She sent me a passport application to complete. I filled out the form and sent it back to Mama with photos because I felt I ought to have a passport for my foreign markets.

When term finished, I returned home and assisted Mama with her holiday clothes. Mama's figure did not vary much, she kept too active to put on weight. Busy feeding all the family, she ate little herself. Perhaps she was slightly smaller, or it could be me overtaking her. Anyway, once I had her measurements it was easy enough to conjure up outfits for every occasion. She had plenty of coats and jackets to choose from. I was the shabby one, I had to run up a few outfits last minute as I tended to dress in student fashion.

Mama sent me some information about travelling. She did not want to fly and thought going by train would be scenic. It seemed we could board at Whitefish station and take it from there. She sent me a railroad leaflet saying that on average, a train trip from Montreal to Whitefish would take 60h 36m to make the journey and that Amtrak had the fastest advertised travel time for the journey.

It was typical of Mama to get the journey back to front, but it seemed a long time to travel. Mama refused to fly. I looked up Whitefish which was the busiest station on the Amtrak route. It had links to buses, car rental and handled more passengers than all the other Montana stations. Apparently it is the busiest station between the Pacific Ocean and Midway Station, St Paul Minnesota. There was more information, but it made me tired, so I left Mama and Marshall to handle the arrangements.

I was not enthusiastic but thought I might find inspiration for my original lines by travelling further afield. I would broaden my horizons and check out the fashionistas en route. That cheered me up and I began to look forward to the trip.

We had a big family dinner the night before we left. Marshall drove us to Whitefish station. I was reading about it in the back whilst Mama chatted to Marshall giving him instructions about Poppa and family commitments. Althea was a Filipino nurse who had moved in to take care of Poppa. She had become a member of the family and was totally reliable. Marshall already knew what Mama wanted but humoured her. I read the official leaflet saying:

"Whitefish provides great options for train travellers looking to hit the road. This train stop is served by Jefferson Bus Lines s and Amtrak train schedules. It has popular train routes to many nearby cities."

When we arrived at the station Marshall helped us out with our luggage which he put on a trolley. Mama insisted he departed immediately. She hated goodbyes and would not move until she had waved him off. As we were still very early for our trip, we decided to visit the restroom in turns. Mama went first, I followed leaving her minding the trolley. I admit I fixed my make-up whilst in there and touched up my hair. I felt it was important to appear my best.

When I came out of the restroom, I told Mama I would go to the news stand to pick up some magazines to read on the train. I asked her what she wanted and left her waiting for me. I was not gone long even though there was a small queue. When I returned Mama was gone. This did not make sense. I retraced my footsteps and searched the entire station including the platform for our train. Panic set in, I informed station personnel and even called the police. There was no sign of Mama and she had not boarded the train. Sick with fear and apprehension I froze as our train pulled out of the station. The family would never forgive me.

I got the train personnel security searching for Mama, we studied camera footage and I saw our arrival. Mama was standing where I left her with the trolley, then she leaned forward to speak to somebody just as a big party of travellers entered the station and blocked the view. When they had all passed by Mama and the trolley had disappeared. Due to the numerous passengers and equipment traversing the station, we could not locate Mama again. I had lost her before we even departed, and I did not know what to do.

Mama's Disappearance

I was standing with the baggage trolley waiting for Candice to return when a slim little old lady with tears in her eyes tugged at my sleeve.

"Please can you help me?" she asked tearfully.

"What's the matter?" I asked, alarmed.

"I need to get on my train and I can't find my way, will you help me?" she begged.

I looked around for some railway personnel but in the crowds, I couldn't see anyone, and the service desk had a long line waiting.

"Where do you want to go?" I asked her, wondering who could help.

"I need platform 5, my train will go without me and I don't know what to do," she sighed looking despondent.

"Don't you have somebody travelling with you?" I asked, surprised.

"No," she replied. "Please help me, I don't have anyone."

As she spoke her bag opened and the contents spilled out. I bent down to help her retrieve the contents explaining that I was waiting for my daughter to return. Before I got any further, I was shocked to see the old lady rushing away pulling my baggage trolley. I grabbed her bag with its contents stuffed in hastily and rushed after the trolley which raced along the platform, down a slope, along a corridor and up the other side. Platform 5 had a long train with the guard outside. I saw the old lady hand tickets over to the guard and beckon to me. To my consternation the guard loaded up my trolley contents onto the train and beckoned to me to hurry.

Breathless, I tried to explain that this was a mistake, I was only trying to help the old lady, but the guard spoke over me bundling me on board saying:

"Ma'am that's really cutting it fine, another minute would have been too late."

He slammed the door shut, blew a whistle and the train moved off. I was horrified, the old lady studied me cautiously over my baggage which she handed back to me. She then led the way forward to her carriage with dignity. Almost speechless with shock, still catching my breath, red faced, I slumped down opposite her.

"Are you crazy? What's the matter with you? My daughter will be so worried. Do you know what you have done? Where is this train going? I want to get off," I spluttered indignantly.

We seemed to have the carriage to ourselves, nobody passed through.

"Allow me to introduce myself," the old lady said looking calm and serene. "My name is Lilly Saunders, I appreciate your help. We have a long journey ahead of us. I will be happy to explain everything once we have some refreshments. Take a few deep breaths, relax then if you still want to go back, I am sure it can be arranged."

I vowed to get off at the next station and call home. Candice would be alarmed and I could not contact her. Guiltily, I realised that Candice had not wanted to accompany me. I would have gone alone but the family insisted I was accompanied so I bamboozled poor Candice into joining me. She had lost her mother, her baggage and I had our tickets in my purse so she would miss the train we were supposed to be on.

"How dare you ruin my life?" I yelled, "This is my special birthday present from all my family and you have spoilt everything. My family will all be so worried, I don't even know where you are taking me."

I felt like crying with frustration.

"We are on route to Chicago but that's not our destination," she said calmly.

"Chicago! Are you nuts? I'm going to see my son in Montreal. I haven't seen him for many years. I want to get off this train," I said standing up looking for a cord to pull.

"Sorry but you will just have to hear me out then you can get off at a station. It won't help you stopping in the middle of nowhere," Lilly said pulling out a thermos and pouring coffee into two plastic cups. "Sorry, I don't take sugar," she said passing me a cup.

Reluctantly I drank it and found I was very thirsty. I put the cup forward for more.

"This had better be good," I said settling back in my seat.

"If you are ready, then I'll begin," Lilly said.

Lilly was one of three daughters all named after flowers, her sisters being Daisy and Violet. Her parents emigrated to the States from Wales in the United Kingdom. Her father was a coal miner in Wales but on arrival in New York, he did manual work until he heard he could get land out west. Leaving his wife with the girls and some money, he travelled ahead to pave the way. He was intending to go to Oklahoma but ended up in Massachusetts on account of some fellow called Burt whom he met while travelling.

Burt and Lilly's father set up a small business turning out food to go. Her father remembered how to make Welsh cakes and tasty sandwiches. Burt took the money, wrapped the food and displayed it. Boston was a busy developing place, people in a hurry appreciated their food to taste good and to be ready quickly. The Welsh aspect proved popular because the offer was different. Scones, buns, Welsh cakes and cookies appeared.

The two men lived upstairs above the shop. As business grew, they expanded and opened another shop across town. They recruited extra staff training the bakers. Before long they were thriving. Lilly's father sent for his family to join him and rented a modest little house in town. Burt rented a house nearby and sent for his fiancé Stacey to join him. Lilly's family attended their quiet little wedding. All went well until Lilly's father started getting sick. It seemed the mining had damaged his lungs. This had not been apparent when he arrived in the States, but the cold winters affected him.

Lilly's mother learnt how to do the baking. The girls served in the shops out of school hours. Violet also learnt how to bake. Their father deteriorated and before they were able to contemplate moving to a warmer climate, he died aged only 38. The family were devastated. Burt had started a family and became fed up of the early starts and long hours baking. He wanted to sell the business and move on to California which sounded a good prospect. Lilly's mother was confused. She did not know what to do without her husband's guidance. When the business was sold, she took the money and started a small bakery. All the girls helped her to run it, cutting short their education.

The girls made friends at school and got to know many people in the neighbourhood by serving in the shops. They went to local dances and social events. Violet was the beauty of the family and married well moving to Connecticut with her husband. Rose married a legal man who later became a judge, so she also married well and moved into a brownstone property now worth millions. Lilly married a handsome, smooth man she had met at a charity event. With charm in abundance and sophistication, Tony made Lilly feel special. Tony was visiting the area so pursued Lilly relentlessly and a quick wedding followed.

The wedding had all the style and trimmings of her sisters' events with numerous dark suited guests from Tony's side. Lilly was totally enamoured and waved goodbye to her family as they left for honeymoon in Mexico. Their home was in Columbia and married life was blissful. Tony worked for a large organisation, Lilly was too naïve to realise she had married into a drugs cartel. She felt safe and protected by the enclosed environment and became friendly with the other wives. There was always something going on, swimming, shopping, events, Lilly was always escorted and was aware something was unusual but felt pleased to be protected.

In time she gave birth to a large baby boy they called Carlo and later her daughter Gloria came along. After lavish celebrations Lilly was fully occupied taking care of her family and trying to keep Tony happy. Once the children were born, Tony became more demanding of Lilly's attention. When she was occupied he was moody and if he took offence at her tone or lack of attention, he hit her. Shocked, Lilly retreated and felt frightened. She dared not say anything to her family or colleagues. Tony worked all hours, she never knew when he would turn up. She smelt perfume on his clothes and even found lipstick on his shirt a few times, but she never said a word.

Lilly felt trapped, she tried to be a good wife and mother, her children were adorable. The strain of trying to be perfect made her feel ill, she lost weight, her clothes hung on her. Tony was annoyed and insulted her making her shrivel inside. When he married her she had a good body, now she was turning into a hag. She was not keeping her side of the bargain. Tony warned her to shape up. Lilly thought Tony was using drugs, she suspected cocaine but realised it could have been anything. So, her husband turned out to be a womaniser, boozer, drug user and bully. When he was high, he turned to violence with regularity. It seemed to turn him on to see her cringe. Tony never hit her face, she wore long sleeves and trousers, scarves draped round her neck, but she knew she could not continue.

As soon as the children were old enough for schooling, Tony sent them to exclusive boarding schools. Lilly protested they were too young, Tony shrugged and said they would grow up with high society kids. If it was good enough for the rich and famous, their kids would be equals. It was never too young to get ahead. Their kids would be champions and make good lifelong connections. Lilly cried herself to sleep longing for the vacations. After a shaky start both kids seemed to settle down and when they returned home they were always eager to go back to school.

Life seemed empty without the children. Making a big effort to be pleasant and appease Tony, Lilly tried very hard to keep the marriage going. Tony became very critical and her confidence sank. Verbal abuse was wounding, physical abuse was frightening and Lilly didn't know who to turn to. She did not know who was listening. When she tried to speak to one of the other wives, the wife stopped her with a finger to her lips and shook her head.

Security was internal as well as external. It seemed there were secret devices in the houses. The telephones were tapped, monitoring took place constantly. Lilly asked Tony for permission to visit her family with the children to show them off, or without them whilst they were at school. To her surprise Tony agreed and arranged an escort to accompany her to visit both her sisters and her mother. He told her to take lavish gifts and photos of the children. Tony warned her not to speak about their marriage or any intimate details. He grabbed her by the throat and insisted she wore a single pearl on a chain which would always monitor her. She was never to take it off.

The visit was a success, both sisters had lovely families and were delighted to see her. She explained her bodyguard saying that in Columbia everybody had protection, it was a way of life. The guard stayed in the background the whole time and if the family thought it was strange, they did not comment. Lilly was very circumspect during her visit, but her sisters suspected that something was amiss. There was no private conversation as Lilly conveyed to both sisters she could not talk and for her sake they refrained. They noticed Lilly was thin and sad so tried hard to feed her and cheer her.

Lilly's mother had met an older man called Jeff in the grocery store. He was a widower with grown up children. They became friends, companions and eventually got married. Lilly's mother moved in with Jeff and they were very happy. When Lilly visited, she felt like she was playing gooseberry. Seeing her mother so happy made Lilly even more reluctant to return to her own unhappy home. Once the trip ended Lilly returned home subdued with presents for Tony. He was absent for two days after she returned. When he finally came home, he told her to sit down, he had something to tell her.

Tony had found a replacement for Lilly. He said he would make sure Lilly was provided for. The children would stay in school and he would ensure Lilly kept up to date with their progress. Lilly would have a divorce settlement and could live wherever she pleased. She would need to keep the pearl necklace on and would have to agree to confidentiality regarding family affairs. If she stepped out of line or took the necklace off, it would be the end of her. Tony said they had had a good run but were not a team any more. Lilly was not a suitable wife for him, he knew she had tried but a man in his position needed more.

Lilly sat listening head bowed shocked and terrified. Tony got up telling her to get her things together and tell him where she wanted to live. When she stammered about the children, he told her he would handle it. Tony would always make sure their happiness and welfare came first. It was because of the children and their future that he was making a new start. When Tony walked out of the house Lilly crumbled and cried heartbroken. A maid came over from the big house to help Lilly pack, she took some of her clothes, a few bits and pieces and told the maid to tell Tony she would return to Brooklyn. A car drove her to the airport where she boarded a plane to New York. She did not see Tony or her children again.

Lilly kept her necklace on and was escorted by an estate agent to a two-bedroomed apartment in a central location on the first floor. It was fully furnished in a conventional style and, numb with grief, Lilly unpacked, shopped for basics and tried to settle in. A bank account had been opened in her name, there were cards and some flowers on the coffee table. Lilly felt her life was over and she was a failure.

In the beginning she hoped she would be able to see the children in the vacations. It never happened and she was too afraid to ask. She did not know what Tony told the children or whether life would be worth living without them. The woman who replaced her with Tony had her work cut out. For months Lilly lived in isolation afraid to contact her family or friends, unable to hold a conversation. The stress and hurt combined with lack of regular meals and care made her run down. A chance meeting with an old school friend led to Lilly taking a tonic and taking up exercise classes to use up her frustration.

Gradually, Lilly came to terms with being single. She followed her children's activities in society news items. Lilly hoped the new Mrs Tony would be kind to her children. Despair still overwhelmed Lilly but she realised she needed to find a purpose in life in case the children needed her. She wanted to communicate with them to tell them how much she loved them but she did not dare. Sometimes she was tempted to remove the necklace and let them kill her.

Lilly volunteered to help homeless and unfortunate people. With flexible hours to fill and good listening skills, Lilly was a popular attribute to the organisation. Without revealing her own history, the people she helped sensed Lilly's suffering and respected her. The years passed and Lilly began to suffer headaches and feel unwell. When they did not pass, she went to the doctor who diagnosed an inoperable brain tumour. It seemed she was living on limited time.

Somehow Tony found out and had Lilly put into a hospice. Lilly was only 64, she had kept fit and active and found the home well-intentioned but tragic. It depressed her and once again she felt trapped by Tony. She devised an escape plan. If she was going to die, she would enjoy herself first. So far, her life had been difficult, and Lilly decided to end it pleasurably to suit herself. The train tickets had been booked for Chicago for Lilly and a female nurse hired by Tony to accompany her. Lilly had removed the tickets from the nurse when she was distracted with the baggage. When Lilly saw Mama at the station, she saw a kind face and knew that she had found a helpmate.

Mama was shocked and uncertain. Lilly paused to offer the remainder of the coffee.

"You have a choice now, I don't even know your name," Lilly said handing over the cup.

"Rachel O'Brien," Mama said, "I don't know what to say. Are you certain about your diagnosis?"

Lilly took out some medical notes and showed Mama who sighed.

"Do you have a plan?" she asked Lilly.

"Yes of course, are you in or getting off? I wouldn't blame you," Lilly said.

"How will you manage to escape?" Mama asked.

Lilly removed the grey wig, took her coat off and turned it into a jacket, stepped out of her baggy skirt revealing body fitting jeans, then fiddled in her bag for a long auburn wig, sunglasses and a knitted hat. In seconds she changed from an old lady to a middle-aged suburbanite. Mama was impressed.

"My family will be looking for me," she said.

Lilly said: "When we get off you can call at the station before we leave and tell them you are safe. We will then go on the next stage. She took off the pearl necklace placing it in the baggage rack above.

"From now on we will not mention any place names or destinations. I don't think we have any devices monitoring our conversations or surveillance apart from the necklace. So, Rachel are you joining me? I don't think it will be for too long, but I have plenty of money and I promise you adventures and fun. What do you say?"

With tears in her eyes Mama nodded. All business-like, Lilly told Mama to go to the toilet and change her clothes. Mama returned wearing a different coat, Lilly put a curly wig on Mama and a hat with spare sunglasses. Lilly told Mama to sort out the baggage and leave anything surplus in a station locker. Mama said she would put Candice's case in and some of her stuff which she had planned to take for gifts. As she had no idea of her destination, Mama felt she would keep her case. Fortunately, Mama had her passport, cards and money in her purse.

Lilly left the flask and cups in the trash, signalled to Mama to get ready and they got off the train. Mama followed Lilly's lead, paid for a locker, loaded it up and the ladies walked out of the station boarding a long-distance bus to New York. The train containing the necklace continued on to Chicago. Mama's case was placed in the bus storage. She rang home and told a startled Althea to tell the family she was sorry for the upset but had run into an old friend unexpectedly who needed Mama's help. Mama said she was safe but was on the move, she did not know when she would be back and they need not worry about her. Mama said she would be in touch when she could, then hung up.

On the bus Mama snoozed and relaxed. Life moved in mysterious ways she thought as she dozed. Lilly also slept with her head lolling on Mama's shoulder. With pit stops they ate, drank and exchanged life stories. Mama had always put her family needs first. She rarely had time to indulge herself. Only recently with all the children flown the nest, Mama had begun to please herself. Poppa had Althea to care for him and his cronies to socialise with.

Mama had been looking forward to her reunion with Ryan and meeting his family. She supposed it would happen sometime in the future. After all these years, a bit longer would not be a problem. Mama felt internally excited at the unknown adventure and spontaneity. Lilly removing her necklace had brought home to Mama the brevity and uncertainty of life. Caught up in the spirit of making the most of the time Lilly had left, Mama decided to help her enjoy it. It would be a grand adventure for both of them.

Lilly was adept at reading faces, she saw Mama's inner turmoil and appreciated the sacrifice Mama was making to accompany her. Inwardly frightened, Lilly appeared calm and knew she had struck gold approaching Mama. Instinctively Lilly knew she had found a true friend. Talking about growing up, the two women found they had much in common. Encouraging Mama to tell her life story, Lilly asked if Mama had nurtured any unfulfilled aspirations. Mama hesitated, in her day girls just wanted to get married and raise families. Without thinking, Mama had gone from girlhood into marriage and done her best to meet expectations.

They discussed women's equality issues and speculated what they could have achieved with the freedom modern women took for granted. When they married women relied on their husbands for support. Women could not open bank accounts or get loans or mortgages without male approval. Men earned much more even doing the same jobs. Some women managed to study at university for professional qualifications, but they were a minority and often well heeled. Modern women felt equal to men and were independent enough to manage their lives without them.

Mama reflected on her daughters. Matilda was always cooking and baking, Phil encouraged her but laid down the law when he wanted attention. It was Tilly who submitted to Phil because she appreciated his co-operation and flexibility to ensure she was fulfilled. Tilly could not be tied down to house and family raising, Phil accepted that and accommodated her.

Candice was headstrong and ambitious. Mama had no doubt she would achieve great things. Strikingly beautiful, Candice could have thrived on her looks alone, but her way was to strive for notice to display her talent and creativity. Mama had persuaded Poppa to allow Candice to study sewing and knew how passionate she was.

Although men flocked around Candice, until now she had not shown interest in any of them. Mama thought that one day Candice would meet a man, not a boy, with maturity and wisdom to handle her. Candice would not appreciate admiration or fawning over her, she needed a strong character. Mama felt Candice would be hard to pin down. Women today wanted more than marriage and children, they wanted to have a career and enjoyment off duty. Men were expected to participate in running the home and family. Mama chuckled to think how inept Poppa used to be when he had to help. Expectations were higher now and couples lacked staying power, when it went wrong they tended to give up. It was an instant gratification, throwaway society.

Lilly said how pleased she was to have reached an age where she became invisible. She could suit herself regarding her activities and had no time constraints. If she had her time again and knowledge, naturally she would have done things differently. Bursting into tears suddenly, Lilly revealed that her daughter was getting married shortly to a high society man and that Lilly had not been invited.

The endless hurt and pain of Tony's cruelty knew no limits. Lilly assumed both her children thought she was dead. Mama felt hurt and distressed for Lilly and passed her tissues. When

Lilly was all cried out, she fell asleep again. For once Mama was helpless and prayed silently for guidance to help Lilly.

By the time they reached New York it was evening and very busy. Lilly found a phone booth and dialled a number.

"Ciao Saskia, is that you sweetie? Have you conquered Time Square yet or are you stuck in Grosvenor Place?" there was a delighted outpouring from the phone.

Lilly told the recipient not to mention any names or places. She asked if there was room for a friend and herself to stay over for a few days whilst they were in the area.

After a delighted response, Lilly said they were on an adventure and it was important they remained incognito. If anybody made contact asking about them, they should be told they had not seen each other for years which was true. Checking the address had not changed, Lilly said they would jump in a cab and be right over. Stopping at a stall to buy some confectionery and a bottle of champagne, Lilly led the way to the queue for cabs. Both ladies kept their hats on and pulled their coats around them as there was a chilly wind. Lilly told Mama not to converse in the cab, from now they needed to be bland and anonymous only speaking in private.

The cab pulled up at a brownstone in a smart neighbourhood. Tired and dishevelled the women pressed the buzzer and thankfully entered the building. A dazzling redhead rushed to meet them, enfolding Lilly in a big embrace, hugging Mama too. She reminded Mama of Bette Midler. Whilst Lilly caught up with her friend, introduced as Saskia from the old neighbourhood, Mama took a soak in the tub and nearly dozed off. Putting on her nightdress and a towelling dressing gown, Mama staggered into the living room in time for a takeaway meal delivery.

"I hope you like Chinese," Saskia said.

"I'm so tired anything simple will do," Mama replied.

"Well eat up and get some rest, we can make plans tomorrow. Lilly has told me you need somewhere safe to stay so consider this your home for as long as you want. I am a widow and my kids have all flown, so this place is too big for me now. In fact, whatever you are planning, count me in. I need to get out of here."

"We will talk about it tomorrow," Lilly said spooning her food onto a plate. "Thank you Saskia, you are an angel. You look so good," she added, yawning.

Mama and Lilly had separate comfortable rooms and slept deeply. When they awoke mid-morning, Saskia made them breakfast then they sat round the table whilst Lilly explained about her illness and intention to go out in glory. Visibly upset Saskia vowed to help Lilly have fun. They discussed their options. Lilly wanted to revisit her childhood neighbourhood, their old school and areas. Saskia said the old school had been pulled down, the neighbourhood had changed considerably, but she was game to go investigating. Saskia had a chauffeur at her disposal so it would not be a problem.

Mama said this was her first trip to New York. Instantly Lilly decided they would go sightseeing as tourists. They giggled and realised that neither of them had ever done that so looked up tours. They settled for a NYC best attractions tour which allowed them to skip the lines and see more. With so many options to choose from they decided to do the first main tour then go it alone to selected highlights.

It was hard to say who was most excited about the plan. Saskia had an extensive wardrobe and invited both ladies to help themselves from it. As she was fuller figured than Lilly, Mama was the main beneficiary. They got on so well, giggling like teenagers, they felt they had known each other for years.

Lilly wanted to go to Coney Island where they strolled along the beach, saw the New York Aquarium, checked out the rides, ate junk food and admired the bizarre sights. Mama enjoyed herself so much and her thrill at everything she discovered enhanced the experience for the others. They were both wealthy women and would not let Mama pay for anything. Using your cards would give away our location, Lilly told her. Mama remonstrated with Lilly until she revealed she had new cards in a different name. Lilly would not reveal her source but said if asked, her name was Marianne. Saskia had no reason to hide her movements and acted as front when paying.

They visited Central Park to see what was happening, Mama was impressed by its size and vibe. They ate well in the vicinity and tired themselves out. Nightlife was avoided except for meals. Going to clubs or popular bars was too risky, so they watched movies or talked, played cards or amused themselves having make-overs or beauty treatments.

New York was buzzing, congested, the stores were enormous, the food and offers with street entertainment were something Mama had never experienced. She began to understand Candice's ambition more. Allbrite could not compete with so much excitement. Mama also noticed the down and outs, the beggars and the homeless.

After visiting Lilly's original habitats and most of the boroughs, the ladies decided to pamper themselves and choose where to go next. They rested for a few days, closely monitoring Lilly who revived refreshed and announced that she would like to visit California and Florida, Martha's Vineyard, all the fancy places she had never seen. "Hang the expense," Lilly said, "I've got money to burn, I can't take it with me."

Saskia found a route advertising 13 incredible stops on the Pacific coast highway, the leaflet stated that over you could see stunning coastal views, seaside villages, untouched forest and could travel through some sunny wine making districts.

Before they left, Mama Left a long telephone message to the family assuring them she was well and having adventures. She apologised to Candice and told the family they were not to worry about her, she would explain when she returned. At present she was constantly on the move so they could not contact her. She did not know when she would return and hoped they were managing well.

Lilly seemed to have a collection of accessories and wigs in her bag. Mama and Lilly wore big sunglasses constantly. They also wore wigs or hats for disguises and dressed to blend in. At their age they passed unnoticed. Saskia recovered her joie de vivre. After her husband died of cancer, Saskia felt lost. She had been married for 45 years and done everything with him. Adrift in the apartment she could not bear to move for sentimental reasons. Her kids kept in contact by telephone, but Saskia felt lonely and unloved.

Being with Lilly and Mama rejuvenated Saskia. Lilly was ecstatic, each day was a new adventure. They tried different food, studied the crowds for the latest trends, enjoyed people watching over coffee or beer. All three had the time of their lives. There was so much to see and do. They found hotels along the route. Saskia registered them in her name with Marianne Foster and Suzanne Clark accompanying her.

Mama did not understand how she could pass for Suzanne Clark but was happy to go along with it. Lilly scanned the newspapers for society news and was distressed to see her lovely daughter's wedding photo in the press. The article mentioned businessman Tony proudly giving her away. Saskia found pictures of Tony's wife and Lilly's son but tactfully hid them. Lilly was inconsolable for about 24 hours. They let her grieve and hung around the beach and pool in case she needed them. Lilly suggested they should continue their trip so that if she did manage to see her daughter again, she would have plenty to tell her.

'Travelling to Martha's Vineyard by bus from New York can be convenient and you don't have to worry about parking your car' said a tourism advert, so they booked and set off. Lilly sat with Saskia, Mama sat beside them gazing at the views. They checked in a quiet place behind the mainstream and decided to stay awhile to chill. All three loved the vibe. It was delightful, laid back, simple, oozing with charm, they felt healed and restored. Lilly said she would be content to end her days there.

Saskia had a close friend living in Sarasota, Florida who offered to loan them her summer holiday home. Mama looked up tourist information on Sarasota and read aloud: 'Sarasota is a city south of Tampa on Florida's Gulf Coast. It's also the gateway to miles of beaches with fine sand and shallow waters, such as Lido Beach and Siesta Key Beach.'

Although reluctant to leave Martha's Vineyard, Lilly agreed it was probably not smart to stay too long in one place. They flew to Florida and took a cab to the house where they located the keys with the hired caretakers. It was a traditional wooden shack complete with a wide veranda overlooking the bay. All three said "Wow," dropped their bags and sat in spacious chairs gazing at the stunning white beach and calm turquoise water. This house seemed like paradise, they barely moved the whole time apart from getting provisions.

They bathed, swam, ate simple healthy meals, snoozed in the sun and mellowed. Lilly said she could stay forever and what a privilege it was to be there. Mama felt sorry for all the folk who could not experience such bliss. They spoke to the neighbours on occasion and joined in a few barbecues. People were friendly but not intrusive. It was understood that people came to unwind so no questions were asked. The three ladies asked no personal questions and accepted each day as it came.

In the midst of their bliss, Lilly became lethargic and suffered pains. She didn't want the doctor or any fuss. Saskia wanted to get help, but Lilly pulled herself together and said it was time to go back to Brooklyn. Her intention was to die in the apartment Tony had assigned to her. She did not care if somebody else inhabited it. Lilly still had the key and she hoped it would inconvenience Tony.

Silently and anxiously, Saskia and Mama packed up and escorted Lilly back to New York. Saskia's driver was waiting for them and took them to the address Lilly gave him. The apartment was empty and chilly. They put the heating on, tucked Lilly in bed, she refused food, drank a little water, groggily thanked them both for the best experience in her life. During the night she groaned and left them. Saskia and Mama were devastated and clung to each other in grief.

Saskia arranged for the funeral and sent messages to both Lilly's children. Lilly had left letters for both of them. They both turned up at the funeral accompanied by Tony and his henchmen. Mama and Saskia were too upset to be intimidated and ignored them. Lilly's son and daughter told Saskia they thought their mother had died long ago. When she handed over their letters, they both sobbed uncontrollably.

Tony's painted wife glared at Saskia and Mama as they walked away. One of Tony's henchmen attempted to threaten Saskia and Mama, but they turned their backs on him mid-flow and walked away. Mama and Saskia spent a few weeks in seclusion at the home of her family friends until they were able to resume their lives.

A tearful Mama hugged Saskia and promised to keep in touch. She rang her family saying she was on her way home. Mama knew she would not be able to explain herself for some time, it was too upsetting. The journey back seemed lonely on her own. Marshall arranged to meet her at the airport and drive her back. Mama was uncertain of her reception when she returned and expected an inquisition but was too sad to care.

She was surprised to find that in her absence Poppa had deteriorated rapidly. His new medicine was not helping him much. Poppa was clearly going downhill. Mama held his hand and sat reading to him. Althea told Mama to call the family together including Ryan to say their farewells. Mama was shocked that her partner for so many years was going to leave her. She couldn't handle it. Matilda called Ryan and Eric who came as quickly as they could.

Poppa's Demise

When Poppa left us with all the family around him, Mama did not cry. She seemed to shrivel and age suddenly. From a vibrant active woman, she stayed home and seemed to diminish. At the funeral she stood stoically and shed not a single tear. When Ryan arrived, she told him he was too late, he should have arrived sooner. She nodded to Marie, tapped the children on their heads and ignored them all. Eric said she was in shock. Her behaviour had been strange since her return. All she would say was that she had found her best friend unexpectedly and helped her to die from a terminal illness. We did not know who this best friend had been. All our lives Mama had been a homemaker, she had left her friends behind when she married Poppa.

Marshall looked through the Christmas card list and could find no mention of a Lilly. Mama said if Saskia rang her at any time, they were to get her immediately. We wondered if Mama was losing the plot. She was not interested in anything or anybody, so we just had to wait and watch. Tilly took care of the feeding arrangements sending something over.

Althea left us for a new role in the next state. Candice, who was the most tormented about Mama's absenteeism, returned to college after the funeral and did not return home for the next 18 months. Mama drifted on aimlessly, we hired a cleaner for her house. Tilly and Eric helped to clear out Poppa's clothes for charity and blitzed the house contents throughout.

Eric decorated most of the house in cream emulsion to freshen it up. All Poppa's medicines and equipment were removed. Some of Candice's cushion covers were used to brighten up the living room. Mama made no move to co-operate or object. Our doctor advised us to leave her to grieve in her own quiet way. Sometimes the bereaved needed a long period to overcome the loss. We all kept an eye on Mama throughout the winter. By spring she seemed to emerge slowly back into the world. A telephone call from the mysterious Saskia seemed to revive Mama's will to live. We all heaved silent sighs of relief and waited to see what would happen next.

Mama took a computer course and started writing a story on our home computer. We thought she was writing her memoirs, but she said she was paying tribute to a dear friend who had been very brave and worth remembering. Dying without a trace was normal for most people, but Mama thought her friend's Lilly's story was worth celebrating. Saskia came to stay with us for a few months to help Mama. Marshall updated the home computer to speed it up. We were all impressed with Saskia, she was warm and friendly and took a genuine interest in the family. Saskia suggested Mama could write a story about the family next, but Mama pulled a distasteful face at the idea.

Whilst Mama drifted, Dan introduced new stylish furniture to replace the old worn pieces we had grown accustomed to. When Mama made no objection, Dan craftily brought a new comfortable pair of sofas and coffee tables. He told Mama she should try out the furniture as a guinea pig for a new line he was introducing. When Ryan came he updated the white goods and bought a new TV. By the time Saskia arrived, our home was looking fresh and presentable. Linda brought flowers regularly which she arranged strategically to add to the new set up.

Gradually Mama joined her fitness classes, went out with a walking group and devoted hours to writing. When she looked after her grandchildren she spoiled them and kept them busy inside or outdoors, seeking new experiences and adventures to teach them. All the children adored her and she loved them all equally. They loved hearing tales about when Mama was young or their parents. Mama was far more indulgent with her grandchildren than when we were young. She played with them and talked to them as equals. When we were young she was always busy.

Mama's Homecoming

I got home to find my husband fading away. He seemed to have gone downhill rapidly in my absence. I felt too drained and exhausted to take it in. Briefly, I wondered if my absence had caused him to decline, but the doctor assured me that after coping with the disease so many years, Poppa's mechanisms had depleted. The doctor suggested I called family members together to bid him farewell. This was beyond me, so I delegated to Matilda who dutifully informed everybody. I wanted to take to my bed and do a Rip Van Winkel, instead the house was invaded by family and friends visiting. There was no space to be private or quiet.

When my husband passed away, I felt a sense of relief rather than grief. I could not cry or feel regret. The man I married had ceased to exist a long time ago. My family mistook my silence for grief. There was no energy left inside me to cope. Once the funeral was over - which was an ordeal with the girls sobbing, people fussing, gushing platitudes and getting under my feet with a desire to be helpful - I hoped normality would be restored and I would be left in peace. There was no chance. After years of neglect and indifference, my sons took it on themselves to renovate my home. To be honest I didn't care about changes, I let them get on with it in the hope that they would finish up and go away.

Michael and I had a long marriage, we had our ups and downs like most couples, we raised our family best we could. With different interests and temperaments, we managed to get along and gave each other space when required. I would say we were happy rather than unhappy. Products of our time, we married young and settled down. Michael was always good with his hands. I focused on home and domestic comforts. Women from my era did not expect to have careers. Men were the bread winners and women were expected to snare one then do their duty. If I had had the opportunities modern girls enjoyed, I expect I would have studied and made something of myself.

Even then, although it was unusual, I made sure all my children knew how to take care of themselves. Boys and girls had to learn basic cooking and needlework. I gave them all chores which had to be done after homework and instilled in them a work ethic. I told them a home does not run itself and in order to enjoy the comforts, they needed to put something in. I also took them to the library as soon as they could read and insisted they spent time reading. We used to do general knowledge quizzes en route to places or games that made them think. It seemed important to me to open their minds while they still soaked information in like sponges. Interestingly, they all chose different paths in life.

When Ryan returned with his family I felt disappointment that he arrived too late to make peace with Michael. Despite appearances, Michael had fretted internally for years over the absence of his first born. Michael and Ryan had been inseparable until Marshall was about four. I knew how Michael would have enjoyed a reunion with his favourite son, I remembered him sending the private investigator to find Ryan. Once he knew Ryan was safe, Michael did not mention his name again, but I knew he always missed him and hoped Ryan would return of his own accord. So, when Ryan arrived, I did not embrace him, just told him he was too late.

Ryan chose a lovely wife called Marie, she was French Canadian and had a gentle soothing disposition. She did not say much but I felt empathy with her and enjoyed her presence. The two little girls were cute, one like each parent. All my grandchildren are beautiful, these two included. Fortunately, they all got on swell and it was a pleasure to see them all running around playing together. My house overflowed with visitors and well-wishers. Matilda saw to the catering, I was lucky to be able to make a drink in my own kitchen.

Eric removed all Michael's medicines and equipment. He decorated the room where Michael had stayed plus the nurse's former room which reverted back to the dining room. I chose cream as a neutral warm background. When the decorating was done it made the rest of the house look bad, so Eric ended up painting the entire house. He enlisted the help of some family members and friends, I left them to it and went out for walks or to tend the garden. When that was done along came Dan who replaced almost all the furniture telling me I was trialling his new range. I am sure they think I am simple. Candice got busy designing soft furnishings.

As if all that intrusion was not enough, Ryan came along, renovated the bathrooms and replaced all the white goods. This created more mess but to be fair, he did clean everything up. I came home one day and there was a big fancy television in front of the living room wall. I began to wonder what all this modern splendour was for, were they trying to get rid of me? It was impossible for me to work up any enthusiasm because I had not requested any of this change. I understood they were trying to make changes to give me a new lease of life without Michael, but it was not doing it for me.

First Candice left, she was still hurt by my abrupt departure and had borne the brunt of family disapproval. Of all the children, Candice was the best looking and most determined. Whatever she set her mind on, she would conquer, I had no fears for her. People taken in by her looks alone would be in for a surprise. We did not see her again for a couple of years, she was too busy getting established. Eric left to go on assignment on foreign shores. He was still footloose and fancy free, enjoying his freedom with no plans to settle down. Ryan and his lovely family left next and I felt sad to see them go. I gave Ryan a hug and looked deep into his eyes and forgave him.

Once they had all left, I only saw Dan and Marshall. Linda came by with flowers which she arranged around my fancy new house. Claire also dropped in when she could, bringing casseroles, baked goods or little treats. They were good girls and were raising delightful grandchildren. My boys knew how to pick good wives, so I must have done something right. I didn't miss Michael much unless there was something on TV or in the paper that I would have shared with him. During the day I kept myself busy, at night I was glad to sit down. To be honest I felt too tired at night to be lonely. I chose the programmes that interested me, but I often fell asleep before they ended.

Somebody suggested I find a replacement man, perish the thought. I had spent the main years of my life servicing one man and a large family, the last thing I wanted was an old man to take care of. Thankfully, Michael had provided well for me plus I had my pension. It was not a fortune but more than sufficient for my needs. With Michael's death coming so close behind Lilly's, I felt down and lethargic. I wondered what the point of existence was. It seemed like an endless merry go round, by the time you had some freedom at retirement, you began to wear out with old age. All the repetition, do this, do that, turn around and begin again. Who actually cared if perfection or chaos prevailed? Did it matter when choices were made? Women seemed to become invisible after a certain age. Lilly had embraced life before she left it. Since her demise my spirit had nosedived in her wake.

Saskia rang regularly and I enjoyed our conversations. We were both still grieving for Lilly when Michael died. Saskia wanted to fly over to be with me. I told her to wait until they had all gone, so we could be ourselves. The kindest thing she could do would be to visit when I got rid of them all. Saskia sent a big wreath and waited for an invitation. I think she understood more than all of them, my need to be alone and my frustration at all the well-meant intrusion. As a widow herself, Saskia understood and let me be. During one of our conversations Saskia said it was sad that Lilly had gone without a trace. Inspiration hit me full force, I would write a story about Lilly and record her life. Saskia could help me and we could improvise on the missing bits.

I immediately enrolled on a computing course to learn all the basics. Marshall upgraded our home computer and I was off, typing like my life depended on it. Saskia came over to stay for a few months while we developed Lilly's story. She got on well with all my family who loved her warmth and sincerity. When we reached a big gap in the early part of Lilly's life, Saskia returned to New York to do research. I focused on the Lilly I had known. Having grown up with Lilly, Saskia had contacts from their past. This project gave me a new lease of life. With my energy returning, I went back to keep fit classes and joined in on a few communal activities or talks that appealed to me.

The family seemed pleased to see me active again and kept in regular contact to check up on me. I wanted to tell them I was not planning to disappear again, but decided it was more fun to keep them guessing. I joined a walking group and had some good hikes. There were more women in the group than men, we had some good discussions and usually went for a meal afterwards. Some of the group had travelled extensively and I enjoyed hearing about their experiences. I thought it would be fun to go on vacation with Saskia at some point. Saskia would know where to go. I just had to get around to organising myself.

Whilst the family home was being renovated, I blitzed the contents of years of accumulated unused hoardings. I told the kids to choose anything they wanted. We held a yard sale and donated the rest to charity. I tended to wear the same few clothes and used the same dishes and pans endlessly. It amazed me how little I actually needed. I donated good sets of tableware to the family as they entertained regularly. This enabled me to be comfortably unsociable. I felt pleased with myself for getting rid of so much, it was like a weight had been lifted. The kids seemed to think I was having a late midlife crisis, which secretly amused me.

Candice wanted me to go to stay with her and model some clothes for mature ladies. I thought she could find better models. Although slim, I was not graceful nor particularly feminine. I dressed in old jeans and sweatshirts, my hair was tied back and I rarely wore make-up. This made Candice more determined, she said I would not cost her anything and she would smarten me up. At this stage Candice was in Los Angeles getting known for her casual wear.

I asked her why she wanted an old woman to model. This excited Candice, it seemed she had identified a gap in the market. Older ladies could choose between haute couture or chain store bland clothes, otherwise they tried to dress too young. Candice had developed a unique range taking young styles adapted to older ladies. I would be fine to start with. Candice suggested Saskia should join me and anybody else who was old enough. Different heights and shapes of older ladies were needed to show Candice could suit everyone.

Saskia was excited when she heard, and we arranged to fly out together. I also brought along one of my walking group called Sandra, she was tall and lean. Saskia brought her neighbour who was smaller and dumpy, so we were a diverse group giving Candice a challenge. We booked ourselves into a Holiday Inn and enjoyed the warmth and bright light, but not the pollution. Candice and her team kept us standing around being measured, pinned and primped for days. She had us manicured and groomed with pampering treatments.

Ultimately, she took us to her hairdresser friend who snipped and colour treated us beyond recognition.

A fashion show was being staged at one of the main department stores in the area. It was sold out so a second one was booked. Candice was one of the exhibitors. On the big day we were visited by the hairdresser again and a make-up artist. By the time we were ready, having previously been taught how to walk and display the clothing, we were buzzing - especially after the secret tipples Saskia had slipped to us for courage. It was a gas, we were stars and felt like a million dollars. What fun we had parading and being changed at express speed behind the stage. We enjoyed ourselves and it showed. The audience were buzzing with excitement.

I like to think that we helped Candice start her career big time. The reality is that Candice was really talented and determined to succeed. In addition, Candice was photogenic and her angelic appearance helped her get noticed. Her designs took off big style and were posted globally; women of a certain age wanted her clothes to make them feel good. Later Candice developed ranges for different age groups and her label, simply called *Candice*, became famous. She was invited to all the top shows, interviewed on television, featured in magazines and propositioned by celebrities. Candice always enjoyed being top dog, she loved the 'in' crowd. I wondered if fame lived up to her expectations.

Famous names were linked to Candice although she never brought anyone home. Most of the magazine pictures were publicity orientated. Candice did not seem to want or need to be partnered with anyone or care to reproduce. When she could take her pick, she lost interest. If anybody would pierce the armour surrounding Candice's emotions, it would be somebody unusual. All her passion was directed at her work. It was as though she was driven to design clothes and soft furnishings. Trends were launched by her initially and copied worldwide even by royalty. I felt proud, but Candice was never satisfied and was always self-critical.

After all the excitement of modelling, life seemed a bit flat when I returned home. Reading the weekend newspaper, I saw an advert for a charity walking challenge called 'Beyond the Grand Canyon' and involving seven days of moderate walking. Intrigued, I sent for more information. The programme, aimed at raising money for charity, invited participants to trek through Arizona's mountains, enter into the ancient homelands of the Navajo Indians, explore the Sedona area and Monument Valley and celebrate in Las Vegas. The advertisement stated that we had the opportunity to visit the Grand Canyon, one of the wonders of the world. We would walk through winding canyons, paddle in blue pools and follow the ancient footsteps of the Navajo Indians.

There were different challenges every day, instructions about how to prepare for the trip, what kit to bring, temperatures and levels of difficulty. The walking challenge was fundraising for cancer in an organised camping group. The itinerary was listed in day order and the Walk for Charity brochure quoted:

Day 1 in Sedona

Our 7 km trek takes us through rock trails and back roads developed by early ranchers and minors. In the evening dinner will be around a camp fire.

Day 2 The Dead Horse State Park

We will drive to Monument Valley to do the 11 kms hike to the Dead Horse Ranch State Park. Some of the terrain will be uphill. Our evening campsite will be in Flagstaff.

Day 3 Monument Valley

Red sandstone buttes, ancient ruins, pinyon trees, dramatic canyons with scenic rock formations, we will find at the Grand Canyon National Park. As this is the spiritual heart of the Navajo nation, we will learn about the culture around the campfire over dinner.

Day 4 Mystery Valley

Over 600 years ago the Anasazi Indians lived here. We will view artistic remains and sandstone arches. In the evening we have dinner at a ranch.

Day 5 Zion National Park

In Zion Valley at Weeping Rock we see water seeping through sandstone walls making hanging gardens. We will climb to Observation Point, look at Echo Canyon rock formations with white cliffs.

The final day was for preparing for departure home in Vegas. I read through the advertisement, checked the cost was plausible and then went for a walk. It would take place in just over three months, which was ample time to prepare. I called Saskia to tell her about it. Saskia was not keen, she did not walk much and had got out of the habit living in New York. She knew somebody who may be interested if I wanted company. Instead Saskia would sponsor me. I left it with her but it played on my mind.

It occurred to me that Sandra, who modelled with us, was part of my walking group. I thought I would discuss it with her. She would be ideal to go with on this adventure because we were both locals. In fact, I could see if any of the walkers would be interested in this adventure, raising money for a worthy cause. I became so excited I couldn't sleep. We may even get a special rate if there was a group of us going. The trip included a whole bunch of stuff with expert advice and guidance. I couldn't take it all in.

At the next hike I called a meeting at our drinks pit stop and read out the Challenge advert asking if anybody was interested. We decided to discuss it over dinner. Our leader Glen said he would circulate it to all our members to generate interest. Glen also said he would check out the hikes and the fitness levels that would be required. With regular training preparation, Glen thought we could probably be able to manage it. My heart started beating fast, I worried that at 60 I may not be fit enough, but I wanted to try. What would the family think of me now?

Ryan's Story

When Mama and Candice failed to arrive, we were very worried. We checked at our end and there was no sign of them nor their baggage. Even before Tilly called to say Poppa was dying, we planned to go over during the school spring break. Despite our good intentions Poppa died just before we arrived, so I never got to see him again. Mama turned to me and said I was too late, I should have come sooner which made me feel bad. She didn't embrace me or welcome me, I put it down to grief and shock, but I am not sure.

All these years I had been busy establishing my business and was hesitant to visit earlier because I dreaded the disapproval of Poppa regarding my evasion of service. Poppa had always expected more from me as I was the eldest. The main reason I had avoided returning home was because I felt too cowardly to face Poppa. I couldn't bear him being disappointed in me. In the end I didn't have to.

Mama thanked Marie for looking after me, holding her hands and welcoming her into the family. She adored the girls and sent them into the kitchen for cookies. Until Mama told me that Poppa had sent a private investigator to search for me, I hadn't realised how anxious my parents had been. When she told me, I felt ashamed and very small. As a parent myself, I realised how thoughtless and inconsiderate I had been to the good family who raised me. In all the years that had passed, I had put my family out of mind whilst joining Marie's family instead.

I told Mama I was a successful businessman now and asked how I could help her. I told her I knew it would not make amends, but I genuinely wanted to contribute. Mama shrugged and said she had all she needed thank you. Looking around the house I replaced all the white goods plus bought a new modern TV and stand. Even the microwave was old, so I bought a new one with simple controls. Mama accepted the new appliances without enthusiasm, Tilly taught her how to use them. Eric had redecorated the whole house in cream so it looked fresh.

Apparently, Poppa had lived downstairs and the dining room had housed his nurse. There was no trace of medical history now. The dining room had fresh flowers, Mama's bedroom had a smart accent wall with lots of cushions and a throw on the bed. Only a few souvenirs of Poppa remained like his pipes and collections. It seemed very peaceful in the house and strange that he would not be appearing.

Whilst in Allbrite I took Marie and the girls around town to show them my old school, where we played, the library, the community centre, and drove us out to our original land which was farmed as far as the eye could see in all directions. I could barely tell where we used to live. Allbrite had grown and expanded considerably. There were new shopping malls, suburban housing estates, cosmopolitan eating places, a multi complex movie theatre. My old school barely remained as new buildings had sprung up around it. Whilst it was small compared to Montreal, it had a quiet suburban charm. We introduced the girls to their cousins and after that we hardly saw them. Our girls grew up bilingual speaking English and French.

Marie liked Allbrite and my family. She greatly sympathised with Mama and chastised me for neglecting her. Whenever she could, Marie would quietly assist Mama in cooking, laundry or just sitting with her. Marie didn't speak much but managed to say volumes in empathy. I could tell Mama was very impressed with Marie. Tilly was always rushing around and welcomed us with meals and visits. All the family went out for excursions and picnics like the old days.

Candice was only around for the week after the funeral. She quizzed Marie about Canadian fashions and thought Marie was very chic in a French style. My girls had beautiful bone structure Candice said, she hoped to pay us a visit one day. Candice said it had not been her fault that the trip had not happened, yet the family acted as if she had been responsible. I could tell this really bugged Candice which is why she ran off for about two years to develop her career. Marie was impressed with some of Candice's designs and said she was very talented. Claire and Linda took Marie out with them a couple of evenings and introduced her to the local scene.

I met up with my old buddies for drinks and pool. We laughed to see each other as family men and no longer cool dudes. Each day I kept in touch with my company, everything was running smoothly or else they were keeping quiet. It was tempting to stay in Allbrite and carry on. The lifestyle and town were so different to ours. Maybe because the community was smaller and more familiar, it seemed slower, laid back and old fashioned in a genteel way. It could have been the vacation spirit made it feel that way. We took a big family group photo before we left. I had it enlarged and framed on my living room wall. Marie said it would be a reminder not to forget my family again. We were all sorry to leave, the girls kept hugging their cousins.

Back home we returned to our regular routines, but I felt unsettled. A recession seemed to be taking place, the economy was shrinking and various companies were cutting back. This seemed to be happening on a global scale. My business was always busy because people were spending less and repairing or refurbishing more. Houses always needed repairing or updating as climate, age and disintegration took their toll. I had a talented crew, reliable and competent, so I made sure I treated them well. They earned top dollar as long as they performed well. I told them I wanted no shortcuts or quick fixes, if they could not do the job well, they were gone. I hired people who took pride in their skills and we often became friendly with their families.

Sometimes I worried about the future for my children. Youth unemployment was not yet serious in our area, but it was becoming increasingly difficult to get established and onto the career ladder. We lived in a cosmopolitan society with migrants trying to gain entry from many countries. I watched the news where migrants struggled to get into Europe. Even in this age there were conflicts, violence, discrimination and all the old evils I thought had gone. Most people just wanted to raise their families well and live in peace. It seemed many didn't, and bombs were exploding in major cities killing innocent people. I worried about my family.

Although I only worked on selected jobs, I made sure I kept my skills updated. Whenever there were new trade developments or technological improvements, I attended courses, bought the manuals and then trained my staff. We also devised our own strategies and equipment to aid us. Marie nagged me about diet and exercise, so I went running to keep fit and played basketball with some friends once a week in the local gym. Our house was full of healthy fruit, vegetables and salads, so any junk food had to be indulged in secret. If I gained love handles from beer, Marie would take me in hand and give me grief until they were gone. I loved her looking after me and often teased her until she gave up.

Our girls were very different in appearance and nature. Sophie was fair with blue eyes and took after me in appearance but in a pretty version. She was very athletic and sporty, got good grades in school and was always aiming high. Sophie wanted to be included in everything, she got bored if she had nothing to do. Chloe was like a mini version of Marie, dark hair, elfin face, brown expressive eyes. Happy being creative, Chloe did above average in school. She could amuse herself for hours and enjoyed crafts. Both girls had their own friends and mostly managed to get along. Sophie raced around like a whirlwind creating mess, whereas Chloe helped Marie in the house and kept her room tidy. As a proud father I thought they were both perfect.

The visit to Allbrite disturbed me. I had not considered future planning. Having gone to Canada to avoid the draft, I lived in Toronto and drifted into Montreal where I stayed because I found Marie. I wondered whether I wanted to stay in Montreal indefinitely. With a flourishing business, a growing family and a smart modern home in a good district, it seemed I had everything going well. It would be easy to continue this lifestyle and drift along. The girls enjoyed school and were receiving a good education, Marie enjoyed her part time work, she chauffeured the girls around, enjoyed activities with her girlfriends and looked after us. It was idyllic if a bit too predictable.

Whilst I did not have much time for introspection, something within me resisted the nesting instinct. I wanted a challenge, stimulation, a new adventure. This feeling grew inside me. It was no longer enough to be a good provider. My siblings had all taken different paths in life with determination to succeed. I was good with my hands and felt the need to use my skills for something more than home improvements. My staff could run the business without me, with Celia at the helm. I cast around for a project and found a scheme to build a school and accommodation in a remote part of Guatemala.

I researched information about Guatemala which is located in Central America. It is bordered by Mexico to the north and west, the Pacific Ocean to the southwest, Belize to the northeast, the Caribbean and Honduras to the east, and El Salvador to the southeast.

Historically, the Maya people flourished there building palaces, pyramids, important cities and observatories. They were advanced in mathematics, astronomy, literature and art. In the tenth century Mayan society declined but descendants still exist in Guatemala. Although they are a majority in the country, they live in poverty where they are a repressed minority-majority.

Spanish conquistadors defeated the weaker Maya forces. Aggressive colonization began with the establishment of large farms where the remaining Indians were forced to work. Spanish colonial powers exploited and persecuted the remaining Maya for 300 years, ruthlessly trying to erase Mayan culture from world history.

Guatemala City is the capital with a population of over 15 million with different indigenous peoples. Mestizo people are the biggest group of mixed race and European ancestry. Spaniards locally born are known as criollo. 18% of the population are white.

Indigenous groups include the K'iche who live in the highlands: the Kaqchikel with their own language: an aboriginal group in the Western highlands called the Mam: and the Q'eqchi who were dispersed through migration, persecution and land displacements.. Most of the other indigenous groups live in the Eastern end of Guatemala.

Smaller groups of Arabs reside in Guatemala City along with Jews who migrated from Germany and Eastern Europe during the 19th century; and Asians mostly of Chinese and Korean descent whose ancestors came to Guatemala to work during the 20th century. Guatemala has a variety of races, cultures and languages.

After reading about it and discussing the project in more detail, I felt excited and knew I needed to talk to Marie.

Marshall's story

Life was busy, centred around the family with work occupying too much time. When Mama returned she often helped with the kids. I was relieved to see Mama back to herself again. Her disappearance caused us all great anxiety then her bereavement made her withdraw from family life. We all rallied around and tried to make life easier and more comfortable for her, but Mama did not pay attention until her friend Saskia talked her round. It's strange how none of us remember Mama mentioning Lilly or Saskia before her disappearance. I think we would have remembered the name as it was unusual in these parts.

Linda visited Mama regularly taking her flowers and helping her with the garden. When she had time Linda had green fingers, she had taken a flower arranging course and enjoyed gardening programmes. As a teacher, Linda had the convenience of school vacations but since the boys came along, she took a part time role in charge of the school library where she also taught reading and specialist courses. Each year Linda had to take up a new topic to update her qualifications. She didn't mind the learning, but it took up time which she would have preferred to use elsewhere.

When our firstborn son Hal was a baby, Linda used to play classical music including Brahms' lullaby when he went to bed. This must have influenced him because as soon as he could run around he would tap out tunes. He climbed onto a stool in my den area where I left my keyboard and managed to make up simple tunes after a short spell of tinkering. We were amazed as neither Linda nor anybody in my family was musical. Whenever he could, Hal would play on my old keyboard in preference to playing outside. We decided to get him tuition when he was older.

We had visitors and social occasions when somebody would play guitar or musicians would be involved and Hal would watch them fascinated. A toy guitar was not good enough, he wanted to make real music. All musical instruments appealed to him. By the age of four it was obvious we had a gifted child. After seeking advice at the school, we signed up to enrol him in music classes after kindergarten. We were told to encourage him so we bought Hal a small guitar and traded in my old keyboard for a second-hand piano. Before long we were serenaded. Hal was taught to read and write music before he learned the alphabet.

Once Hal went to school he seemed to pick up topics quickly and retain knowledge. He was a really smart little boy at the top of his stream, he made friends easily but music rather than sport was his passion. With high intelligence Hal got bored waiting for others to catch up to him, so would often compose music as a side line. Linda and I hoped we could provide him with everything he would need to succeed if music became his future aspiration. We were proud of his accomplishments at such a young age, but uncertain whether to encourage him. Hal kept us busy and was the centre of our world until our second son Jake came along.

Jake was a totally different natured boy. Fair haired, with a lovely smile, he was placid and happy to amuse himself. As he grew, he was slower than Hal to crawl, sit up, stand and finally walk. Everybody was different we thought. Whilst Hal enjoyed picture books and quickly grasped reading and colouring-in, Jake had a short attention span. Jake adored Hal and enjoyed listening to his music, yet he did not try to emulate him, he preferred doing puzzles. I played ball games with Jake and we watched sport on TV together.

It was only at kindergarten prep school that we were advised to get Jake tested for dyslexia which proved borderline positive. Jake may struggle with literary skills, concentration, with personal organization, time management, and short term memory. This really shook up Linda and myself. We worried about his future.

We read as much as we could on the topic imagining the worst-case scenarios. Our doctor gave us helpful literature and advice. It seemed that school had a team that met on a regular basis to discuss problems a specific child might be having. Parents could arrange a meeting at any time.

Fortunately, because Jake was diagnosed early, he was able to proceed in his classwork with the help of extra tuition and monitoring. Linda spent time with him assisting his development. Between the two boys' needs, there was no spare time to do more than strive to keep everything functioning. Hal was very protective of Jake and always supported him in public. At home the boys would argue and wrestle at times but usually got along.

I always felt guilty that I had not waited with Mama and Candice until they boarded the train. Mama had insisted I left because I had a meeting to attend. When my brothers Ryan and Eric returned for Poppa's funeral and began renovating the house, I felt obliged to do my part in assisting when I could. I also upgraded the family computer.

For years I had been the acting eldest big brother and felt protective of the family. When Ryan returned with his lovely family, it was a shock to my system. His little girls were cute, I was pleased my boys got to hang around with girls for a change. They all played really well together. Dan's boys joined in when they could. It was a pleasure to see all the kids having fun.

As the sensible conservative member of the family, I led a rather predictable life. I was an accountant in a local firm and moved up the ranks to be second in command. When my boss reached retirement age, he sold the business to a big conglomerate based in Boston with offices in Chicago. Employment was guaranteed provided we relocated. This was a blow as I had no intention of moving. The news broke just before Christmas when it was impossible to make any moves. My only option was to resign without knowing what to do next.

After updating my CV and scanning the media for opportunities within the vicinity, I came up with zilch. My pride took a fall and despondency set in. Here I was in my prime with commitments and despite my qualifications and experience, there seemed to be nothing out there for me. Linda suggested I opened an office by myself in town to cater for the clients who had lost their local accountant. I thought about the idea and researched about becoming independent. I registered for a course on setting up a business and tried to work out expenditure.

Never impulsive, I proceeded with caution. All the family put out feelers and discovered an old-fashioned drapery store was closing down due to retirement. It was located in the centre off the main square, consisting of three rooms downstairs and in need of decoration. I confidently negotiated the lease for a fixed term contract whilst inwardly quaking. All the family pitched in to help decorate it. Dan furnished it and provided comfortable chairs for waiting around. Candice got somebody on her team to handle the press release and marketing. A photographer took a shot of me and there was a write-up in the local paper.

Linda found a young mother called Sam who would be my part time receptionist and assistant. Her mother Nora came along to learn the ropes and offered to fill in if Sam couldn't make it at times. As Nora could type and had good computer skills, I gave her a list of potential clients and we composed an introduction mailing to invite them to use us.

After a slow nervous start work came in. It seemed folk preferred to deal locally and be able to make personal contact with their affairs. There were at least a couple of other accountants in Allbrite, but our family name was well known and trusted, largely due to Poppa's reputation. We also made the office look modern and inviting.

Candice instructed Linda about décor enhancements. Linda and Nora set up a filing system and office practices to ensure everything ran efficiently and smoothly. As we became busier, Sam made an attractive receptionist whilst Nora took on the brunt of the work. Being my own boss suited me, I worked hard and became engrossed in doing things my way. In time we took on Ruth who was studying for business qualifications and wanted to gain experience. For ten years Ruth worked with us and as far as I knew, she never seemed to progress with her studies. Her parents had told her to get qualifications so that she would have skills to fall back on.

Ruth worked conscientiously, occasionally making innovative suggestions to improve the role. I think she was happy to leave the studies behind. I offered her a bonus upon graduation but although she thanked me, I was not taken up on my offer. I tried to pay my staff a decent wage and accommodate them when they needed time off. We all worked comfortably together.

I was approached by the high school to ask if I would talk on opportunities in finance. They also asked if I would be interested in marking maths examination papers which would necessitate attending a training course. After giving the matter some thought and researching on line, I agreed on both counts. It was not good for me to be too set in my ways, new challenges would be stimulating. Finance could be considered dull, but I wanted to show the kids how fascinating numbers could be, so I went over enthusiastically. At first the kids slumped looking bored, but I involved them and intrigued them so by the time I left, I had them hooked.

My kids were always busy with activities, parties, games, sports, play dates. There was always something going on. Hal was involved in music and played solo at school concerts. The principal suggested he applied for a musical conservatory in Idaho. We felt he was too young to leave home as a boarder.

Jake was making good progress but we kept an eye on him as common sense was not his main feature. To keep our sanity, Linda and I agreed to have one night a week to escape with our friends. On special occasions such as birthdays or anniversaries, Mama or our next-door neighbour's daughter would babysit for us.

As I entered my late thirties I thought about the future. Politics seemed uncertain with global unrest, recession had dominated many markets, immigrants poured out across the world, prejudice still attacked minorities, there were fewer opportunities to get onto the job market or property market. I worried about my children and hoped life would improve by the time they grew up. Linda also bullied me into regular exercise sessions to maintain my health. We tried to eat healthy food and she was strict with the children regarding sugary drinks having watched a documentary showing kids with teeth extractions at a young age.

I did my best to call round to see Mama regularly, she was often out somewhere. In retirement Mama seemed to have a busy social life and kept active. She told me not to be boring, to make the most of my life. Once she had done her computer course, she started writing a story based on her friend's life. I didn't see how she could write a story about somebody she had known for such a short time. Mama said Saskia was helping with the early days. They had decided to improvise when they reached unknown parts. Mama said life was for living and I should get on with it while I could. She always knew how to provoke me even though I was the main one looking out for her.

Matilda's Story

My problem was that there were not enough hours in the day to do all I wanted. I could never say 'no', so when requested to bake for school, the retirement home, charity events, fairs or something connected with the church, I could not refuse. Being part of the local community meant that everybody knew I baked and expected me to help on every occasion. Apart from running two shops and the furniture shop, there were the family commitments like keeping mine fed and watered, checking up that Mama was looking after herself and maintaining harmonious relations with my wonderful staff. It made each day disappear before I got started.

Phil joked that he needed an appointment to see me. I often fell asleep on the sofa or as soon as my head hit the pillow. So, it's no wonder we had a regrettable incident which could have destroyed our marriage. I knew Phil was still handsome and had good rapport with people. He tended to accompany Scarlett to her activities and picked her up. When he could, he stuck around to watch her or wait for her. In between, he often went running to keep fit. Unbeknown to me, one of the high school kids had a major crush on Phil. The girl Carly hung around Phil and tried to chat him up and entice him. To be fair Phil was flattered and polite.

Therefore, I was surprised to receive a poison pen letter implying that this Carly had been seen giving Phil a blow job. It came during one of my busiest periods with Easter approaching, staff shortages due to a flu outbreak, I virtually slept on the job. I was too busy to even speak to Phil. The issue stayed at the back of my mind whilst I carried out my duties. Two days later I managed to get Phil alone when the kids were in bed. Silently I handed him the note and watched him turn pale.

"Is this true?" I asked him, shocked.

Phil nodded, looking uncomfortable yet defiant.

"Are you having an affair with a high school kid?"

"I am not having an affair and it was a one-off occasion when she caught me unawares," Phil said.

"What do you mean unawares? Do you know you could lose your license if this got out? Have you taken leave of your senses?" I stammered close to tears.

"Tilly this happened accidentally and I didn't mean to upset you."

"Well you have, and I want an explanation," I sat down crumpling with shock.

"It happened in the men's changing room when I had showered and was getting changed to pick up Scarlett. I'd had a shitty day with everything going wrong. You never seem to make time for me these days. I felt really low and suddenly this bright young thing who adores me - I can see it in her eyes - came along, stroked my shoulder and said: "I know what will make you feel better." She offered me a massage. I declined at first and made to move but she insisted saying she had special skills."

"I bet she does, the strumpet," I interrupted. "Go on."

"Before I knew it, she had me laid flat on my front across the fold up bed opened up of course. She rubbed something smelling good all over me and I started to relax and feel better. When she said turn over I realised I had a hard-on. I was drowsy and forgot it was not you, to tell the truth. She was very talented and I felt amazing until I realised this was not my wife. I jumped up immediately and told her this was an accident and could never happen again. I was horrified."

"I don't know what to say," I murmured.

"Saying is not the issue, it's the doing that is the problem. Tilly, we have a good marriage, brilliant kids, you have your baking, I work hard but I feel you are neglecting me. I try to help out, you have a cleaner, I chauffeur the kids, but I feel I always come last in the pecking order. Tilly I am a good man, still young and I won't come last. Life is too short. I love you Tilly I always will, but unless you start paying attention to your wifely duties we will be going downhill. Now I don't want that to happen. You need to think on about this conversation. I am sorry this incident happened and now you know my shame, I feel it has cleared the air. The rest is up to you." Phil finished and walked out.

A range of mixed emotions ran through me, shame, hurt, jealousy, complicity, guilt. I realised Phil had a valid point, I could not remember the last time I gave him priority. He was a good husband, an excellent father. Our marriage agreement was based on the fact that I could pursue my catering career provided I allocated time to being a good wife. Phil deserved my attention, I needed to fine tune my lifestyle if I didn't want to lose him. This upset me, I could not imagine a world without Phil. The thought of Phil with someone else hurt too much, I couldn't handle it.

Being methodical, I adjusted my calendar and diaries marking out clear periods to devote to Phil. I wanted to be a better wife and mother. Too upset to stay in the house, I asked the girl next door to babysit for an hour while I popped round to see Mama who was home doing her writing.

"Mama," I burst out after a hug, "Phil is accusing me of neglecting him. How can I be a better wife?"

"Have you had a row?" Mama asked.

"Sort of, but tell me what to do."

"You are too obsessed with your baking and such, always have been. If Phil were a recipe, you'd be all over him. Nobody works the hours you do. You need to put your home life first; the baking comes second. Men are easily pleased, you keep them well fed, perform your wifely duties to stop them straying, listen to them or pretend to when they ramble on. Result: one satisfied husband," Mama said sagely.

"What if they have strayed already?" I asked upset.

"Are you saying that Phil is having an affair?" Mama asked, appalled.

"No Mama but he could unless I sort myself out. You make it sound so easy," I sighed.

"It takes patience and diplomacy but it's not rocket science. Men have needs and it's your role to fulfil them, otherwise why did you get married? Phil has always indulged your career, he provides you with home help and he's so good with the kids. I think Matilda, you need to sort yourself out fast. No other man would be so tolerant.

Look at the state of you, old clothes, your hair needs washing and styling, you hardly look an attractive female to come home to. Day after day there are attractive young women looking for a handsome man to latch on to. It's time you woke up and made yourself desirable again."

"Oh Mama," I cried "I'm such a fool."

"There there," Mama said hugging me, "It's not too late to start over. Book yourself in at the hairdresser, get some highlights and style, throw away these old clothes and treat yourself to some modern gear from this century. Try a bit of make-up and perfume and I will babysit for you so you can go out on a date with Phil. In fact, why don't you introduce a date night every week to have quality time together? I can babysit," Mama suggested.

"Mama you always know what to do, you inspire me, thank you so much," I said kissing Mama and hugging her. "I can't wait to tell Phil."

I rushed off, paid the babysitter, took a long fragrant shower, washed my hair, sprayed perfume, found an old sexy nightie and tried to stay awake until Phil returned. Apparently, Phil returned after midnight drunk, rolled into bed snoring until the morning without noticing my efforts. We laughed about it much later when we had salvaged our marriage. I made it my business to maintain good relations with my husband so he never felt the urge to stray again.

When my brothers came home for Poppa's funeral, we had such a good time fixing up Mama's place. Ryan looked a bit older but otherwise the same. As a kid I used to follow him around and worshipped him. He always let me bug him until he had enough when he was adept at disappearing. I loved Marie and those little girls are the sweetest in the world. They wanted to help me bake. Candice made them outfits in different colours, but their features were so delicate, they could have worn a bin liner gracefully. We all bonded well, and I felt sad when they left. Eric stayed a bit longer before taking off on one of his international assignments.

In school vacation we took the kids to the Walt Disney World Resort an entertainment complex in Florida. We booked packages to include the Magic Kingdom famed amusement park. It had six themed lands with rides, costumed characters and parades. The kids were entranced, Phil and I were impressed too, especially by the firework display and hologram experiences. We paid extra so we didn't have to queue. During our visit we also managed Epcot, Disney's Animal Kingdom and the Hollywood Studios tour.

There was so much to see and do we couldn't manage it all. We did our best but there were limits to our stamina. We were all exhausted at the end of each day. The kids said it was the best experience of their lives so far. They asked if we could go back again to do all the rest. Phil and I felt we needed another holiday to recover when we got back. The kids ran out to catch up with their buddies and show off their vacation souvenirs. I was left with the unpacking, dirty washing and restoring routine into our lives. For once I felt happy to assume the domestic mantle, I felt tanned and ready for anything.

Over time I learned to delegate. I still supervised and felt in charge of all our operations. When family commitments or circumstances intervened, I let my deputy Hilary take over. We had extra part time staff and ran courses in baking and confectionery for apprentices. Our operations were welcomed in Allbrite where unemployment was higher than it used to be. Linda's school sent groups over to see how bread was made. We always encouraged the kids and gave them something sweet to take home. Our kids took no interest in the business unless they wanted to eat from it. They seemed to think they had a divine right, so I had to ration them. I did not want to overload them with sugar.

Eithan was a delightful boy, even tempered, a good student, content to go along with mainstream opinions. He rarely complained and was always ready to lend a hand with a big friendly smile. Scarlett, or Miss Impatience as I nicknamed her, was too sharp for her own boots. She favoured gymnastics and entered competitions, winning medals and cups. At school she joined all the sports events she could and was always picked first. There was even the opportunity to represent our state in a national gymnastics event which meant she had to focus on one thing in case of injury.

I called round to visit Mama most days, usually trying to feed her. Often the house would be empty. It looked like a furniture showroom most of the time as Mama did not use it much. She tended to eat in the kitchen, do her writing in the study and sleep in her bedroom. If she watched TV she didn't talk about any shows. I had to admire Mama for her vigour and the intensity she brought to all her endeavours. All the kids admired and loved her greatly, the fact that she indulged them all and told them stories helped. I don't remember Mama being so soft with us.

Allbrite offered opportunities for fitness, leisure and social groups. As I contributed to most of their events, I knew most of the people and often caught up with my friends that way. When the kids were small we had sleep overs, play dates, parties and many shared experiences. When they needed help with their homework I referred them to Phil. I did my best, but systems seem to have changed since my school days. They did everything differently with new terminology that confused me. If there were emotional issues or they hurt themselves, Phil sent them to me. We made a good team.

My home was comfortable and was maintained by a cleaner and gardener. My cleaner Maria also took care of my laundry and grocery shopping, she was irreplaceable. I was alarmed one day to find out she was an illegal Mexican immigrant who had lived in Allbrite for over twenty years. Her children had been born and raised in Allbrite, but unless legislation changed, Maria could be deported. Phil and I took legal advice to see if we could help. It seemed Maria came into the States with her family when she was five and stayed, being educated, married and had her children in the States.

We engaged a lawyer to help with the red tape. This was not an easy process. We vouched for Maria's character, her hard work, her family. Life without Maria was unthinkable, so we took an active role in her case and tried not to rock the boat. I appreciated the help and support of being surrounded by a caring family and tried to smarten my act. At times I felt suffocated but waited for it to pass.

I looked into nutrition following an article I read about convenience food and the decline in home cooking. It seemed families were opting for convenience meals and take away options ignoring the chemicals and artificial contents, not to mention the sugar and salt contents. Previous generations had always cooked and baked from necessity. As a result of this new diet populations were becoming obese, children were losing teeth, cancer was increasing and diabetes and life-threatening illnesses like dementia were rising.

It seemed to be a new lifestyle choice but one that had not been tested on previous generations. I was concerned about my family. It seemed even fruit and vegetables were not immune to chemical sprays. I worried about our future prospects if this continued. My resolve was to teach all the children in the family about wholesome healthy diets and planned to make it fun.

Eric's Tale

My next briefing concerned the under privileged from the poorest nations. This group included people fleeing war torn countries including the Iran-Iraq conflict, who were asking for refugee status. I had to find an angle to express human suffering and misery. My interest lay not in politics but in the resulting conflicts. My task was to link up to a journalist called Ed and accompany him to photograph the difficulties people were facing.

I was given some facts to read before I set off. It made grim reading. After a long flight I was very tired so following introductions, I left Ed and hit the sack. Ed hired a jeep and we set off early the next morning to a troubled border area.

Locals had mixed feelings about foreigners: some considered us unwanted invaders: others were sympathetic and tried to help with clothing, water and snacks for people fleeing. Although many were helped, people kept arriving. Through no fault of their own they arrived dirty, smelly and with virtually no possessions.

Many people had been robbed on the way by unscrupulous gangs. Children and babies were used as ransom to obtain secreted wealth. We saw exhausted people falling to the ground crying, trying desperately to get up and walk on. A camp centre was set up to house homeless people which was quickly overwhelmed and unsanitary

Frustration had mounted amid donor fatigue and growing difficulty accessing funds to meet the increasing need for humanitarian aid on the frontline. Processing and progress was slow and in some cases non-existent. We found some English speakers who seemed to be a mixture of professional families forced to flee their homes. From middle class established backgrounds, they found themselves unwelcome on foreign shores. More worrying was the number of minors.

We then travelled around the Mediterranean investigating the poor deprived under classes. Heart breaking stories of ruthless authorities caused misery and distress. This affected me very deeply. When my task was complete, I could not return home. Whilst I did not have a solution for the wars, the hatred and the prejudice, I felt that people had a right to be treated with dignity. Travelling light after having given away many of the clothes and items I had left home with, I decided to explore the more remote parts of the world to see if people fared better there.

Ed told me about an American ex-pat called Mike, a former sound engineer from Texas, who was building a backpackers' hostel in the Guatemalan jungle. We decided to check it out. After a long journey we found Mike with his hippy volunteers who helped with building and chores in return for bed and board. The site was spread out containing rickety bridges. Mike showed us how to catch fish with machetes. There were lots of ongoing projects and good ties with local Mayan people. I took pictures which Ed carried back when he departed. It was adventurous but not really my scene, so I moved on.

It occurred to me that trying to live in a remote area and fend for myself might be an interesting project. I did not know if I had the requisite skills or ability to provide for myself to survive, but I felt I should give it a try. With a scenic view tucked into a hillside with an overhang, I built myself a shelter and scouted around for salvage materials to use for basics. There was a small town a few miles away so I knew I could buy provisions and basics if I decided to stay. I had a couple of books to read and time to think. My family did not expect to hear from me too often, I did not need to be anywhere. Now I had my total freedom I had to decide what to do with it.

Poppa had taught us all to fish and hunt and I was based near to a stream with a river lower down, so I got off to a good start. I had a blanket and used grasses and rushes for shelter and fires. For the time being I felt comfortable and at ease. If I wanted to stay for any length of time, I would need something more stable. I decided to go exploring and met some locals who shook my hand warmly. I helped them with their crops and joined in with their activities despite not having a common language.

They invited me to eat with them and I befriended the whole family. I remembered a few tricks I had picked up on my travels to entertain the children. By sign language I told them I was exploring the region, how beautiful it was and that I did not know how long I would be staying. I really enjoyed their company and ended up staying overnight as darkness fell suddenly and I didn't have a torch to find my way back. They invited me to accompany them to the local market the following day, so I learnt a good shortcut to the town.

I wished I had brought my camera to this colourful, remote market. My camera and goods were buried discreetly on site but separately from my dwelling. Caution made me hide anything of value. The market supplied locals with all their needs and different ethnic groups participated. Stalls were set up with local brews, food and unknown offerings. I vowed to return the following week and spent my visit investigating sites and angles for the best shots. Most of the Mayan people tended to be shorter than me and some of the women were beautifully dressed in colourful costumes.

When I finally returned to my simple dwelling, I felt lonely for the first time and decided to seek out somewhere proper to stay near to the town. Having decided I went fishing and enjoyed a succulent meal. The angst I had arrived with following the refugee crises began to ease away slightly. I realised I had spent the last few years hurtling from crisis to emergencies with little joy in my life to compensate. Perhaps I needed time out to discover what I really wanted. I seemed to have lost myself somewhere.

I rented a small place just outside town. The landlord sent his daughters to clean the place out and make it ready. I went shopping and met my friends on the market. They allowed me to take some shots which I cherish. I treated them all to something to eat and drink in a small kiosk. They came back to my new house to see it. I think the former tenant died as they all crossed themselves. The little town was beginning to look familiar and I felt comfortable being there. I bought some new warm clothing for early and late when there was a chill in the air, so I looked like an overgrown local. I stopped shaving and tied my hair back, wore hats and my own Mama would not have recognised me.

To earn a bit of money I began whittling away using the woodwork skills Poppa had taught me long ago. Although no match for Dan, I could produce household and ornamental simple items which bought me provisions and a few home comforts. Overseas telephone reception was not always available. I managed to call Mama and tell her I was safe. To my surprise she told me Ryan would be doing some work volunteering in Guatemala but she did not know where. I asked her to get the details and thought it would be interesting to see where he was headed. Meanwhile, this new lifestyle was the complete opposite of anything I had been used to and I enjoyed it.

Dan's Tale

In Poppa's time, people valued hand crafted furniture which was bought to last a lifetime and was looked after with pride. Times had changed and modern houses were built with smaller rooms. Fashions also varied with people changing their styles every few years. As a result, our business began to decline and the recession did not help the situation as people were prepared to make do, refurbish or some even made their own. Action had to be taken if we were to survive.

I invested in a factory in the Allbrite industrial zone which was spacious enough to encompass specialist equipment to create lines of laminated furniture. Poppa would have been horrified. By studying the trade magazines, I learnt the best sellers and created storage units of various shapes and sizes which could be stained and arranged collectively or separately in any size of dwelling. They sold like hot cakes. Allbrite was expanding with new housing developments springing up on the outskirts in every direction.

Flushed by success, I opened a new line selling flat pack furniture for bedrooms and dining rooms, there was also a line of self-assembly garden furniture. In addition to our furniture shops, we started up a mail order catalogue. We could barely keep up with demand and had to expand several times. As this meant more recruitment, the mayor was delighted with us. We still manufactured craft handmade furniture but mostly to order. Candice kept me informed of each season's colours and styles. It was useful having a fashionista in the family. She often sent me décor accessories for displays to complement our ranges.

My boys were always busy. Leo was keen at sport, he was in the baseball team and enjoyed basketball too. Ollie liked to kick a ball around and followed his favourite teams avidly but did not choose to be a team player. Whereas Leo needed to be constantly active, Ollie could play by himself forever if we didn't stop him. When I was not working, I would take a ball out in the yard and play with them. In summer we went fishing or swimming. I tried to teach them self-defence, but they were not very interested.

Claire and I shared our duties, we made a good partnership. We each had time out to spend with our friends or do activities. As we both worked full time, we had some home help. I tried to keep the house in good shape and regularly updated it. First impressions on visiting our place was to my mind an endorsement to the business. By maintaining a good impression, visitors would be more likely to call on us when they wanted new furniture. I made most house decisions, Claire supervised the boys' education and social calendar.

One day when Claire was at work, she received a phone call from Mr Mathews who ran the grocery store near school. It seemed Ollie had gone into the store, helped himself to some chocolate bars and ran out again without paying. Mr Mathews was unable to catch Ollie and wanted to speak to us before taking any action. Claire was shocked and told Mr Mathews she would deal with the situation and refund him. She apologised profusely and told Mr Mathews that Ollie had never done anything like that before. I was equally shocked and appalled when Claire rang me to tell me.

After school I came home early and we sat Ollie down between us and asked for an explanation. At first Ollie just shrugged, eyes down, but glanced at me and said, "The guys said I had to."

"Which guys?" I asked sternly

"The guys in my class, they are always picking on me and said if I didn't do it they would get me on the way home."

"Have you told the teacher about this bullying?" Claire asked upset

"You don't snitch, it would just make it worse," Ollie said, getting upset.

"Do you think it is acceptable to steal from Mr Mathews?" I asked

"It was just a couple of chocolate bars, I didn't want them, I gave them to the guys," Ollie sniffed.

"Well if you didn't pay and ran away that amounts to stealing, you could go to gaol," I told him.

"I didn't want to do it, they made me," Ollie said tearfully.

"Well after you have told me who these guys are, you can just take your piggy box round to Mr Mathews, apologise and pay him what you owe. Mummy or I will go with you," I told him.

"I thought we brought you up better than this," Claire said angrily. "Don't you know the difference between right and wrong? Mr Mathews works hard all day in that store to make a living. Imagine if everybody went in and just helped themselves."

Ollie cried but we gave him no let up. Once he promised never to do anything like that again, Claire accompanied him to see Mr Mathews who graciously accepted Ollie's apology and payment from his savings box. The next morning Claire had a word with the teacher who gave the class a lecture about bullying and honesty. Mentioning no names or exact punishments, the teacher made it clear that no bullying would be allowed in their school. The teacher also had a quiet word with the culprits and assured them that if they wished to remain in school, they had to make amends to Ollie. Leo hung around the playground at breaks for a while to observe Ollie but there were no further incidents.

When Claire went for a routine check-up some abnormal cells were found in her womb. This necessitated an overnight hospital stay for a dilation and surgical removal of part of the lining of the uterus by scraping and scooping. We all worried until she got the all clear. Claire disliked fuss so it was hard to try to look after her, but she seemed to be ok again. It made me realise how important she is to me. We didn't tell the children, they thought Claire was having a sleep-over like themselves.

One of the most annoying aspects of running a business is getting rid of waste in an environmental way. I always complied with rules and regulations, recycled the maximum, paid to clear extra and tried to keep packaging down to the minimum. Therefore, I was angry to find illegal dumping near my factory. I cleared it once but noticed it began to occur regularly, so I installed CCTV, snapped the culprits and had them fined.

I ran the warehouse, three furniture stores in Allbrite and surrounding areas, plus we had the mail order business. My staff were instructed to be vigilant to anybody loitering or dumping waste. It seemed to be a modern phenomenon when something was discarded to just drop it anywhere. I drilled my family about picking up and taking their trash with them, so I was not willing to carry other peoples.

To let off steam I went running either before work or in the evenings. I played baseball with the guys, occasionally we played golf or pool, and just hung out putting the world to rights. My buddies and I went back to elementary school, most had married and were raising the next generation.

I enjoyed vacations as much as the next guy, but never felt the urge to explore the world. For me the world was within my family and Allbrite was my comfort zone. I agree that Allbrite would never set the world on fire, but I liked that. When I had to travel to Chicago or New York, I hated the chaos, the congestion and surging crowds. Allbrite was picturesque in an old-fashioned way and there was room to breathe.

I remember one of my buddies telling us about a road-rage incident he had witnessed. We were all astonished at road-rage in Allbrite where people drove at a comfortable pace. It seemed some traveller guy was angry because an old lady cut him up.

She was driving sedately and he was in a hurry. The guy let down his window and shouted abuse. The old lady had a hearing aid and drove on oblivious, the guy had not noticed and got really mad because she ignored him. My buddy crossed the street and asked the guy what his problem was. The guy had got lost in the one-way system and was unable to find his destination. My buddy sorted him out, told him to calm down or to leave town. As my buddy is a big fella, the guy took notice and drove off meekly.

One of the good things about small town life is the feeling of wellbeing, taking time to greet folks, knowing your boundaries, being supported in your endeavours and knowing most of the folk surrounding you. Class sizes in school are good and teachers take an interest in their students. Kids are encouraged to use their talents and have a good chance to get onto sports teams, play an instrument or explore sciences and technology. I hoped our kids would thrive and find their way. Neither showed any interest in following in my footsteps. However they turned out, I hoped they found happiness and satisfaction.

Mama's place was on my route home so I often called round to check up on her. These days she had a full calendar of social events, I could not keep up with her. She allowed me to stage her home like an advertisement for a showroom because she tended to use the kitchen, her office den and the bedroom. We had always got along well, although we did not tend to go in for conversations much. Mama knew she could depend on me. Ever since she went missing, Mama had returned more confident and determined to make the most out of life. I liked that and always backed her up. For my part I said: "long may she continue" - as the Mama who never gets old.

Candice Rises

From leaving Allbrite to go to college, I knew my future lay elsewhere. My courses led me to skills, and worlds brimming with style and glamour. I could be as creative and daring as I wanted without anybody saying: "You're not going out like that are you?" I absorbed the courses like blotting paper, I was always the last to leave classes. With talented students who also wanted to hit the big time, I knew I would have to stand out. I needed a unique brand, I would create one but first I needed to absorb maximum knowledge. I always knew I would be successful.

My brother Dan could design sleek lines in modern contemporary furniture with the best in the business, but he was clueless about décor. I practised my home furnishing skills by producing soft furnishings and décor each season to complement his ranges. I continued that long after I found fame, it kept me grounded. When I lived at home, I used to take regular garments and customise them for sale on Allbrite market or in school, they always sold out. Pretty though it was, Allbrite was too small-town for my ambitions.

My lucky break started innocuously enough, I was in the powder room at the Beverly Wilshire Hotel in Beverly Hills after having dutifully met a relation my mother sent to check up on me, who was travelling around the area. We had just parted company after taking afternoon tea. I had slipped into the powder room to touch up my make-up. I was in Beverly Hills with Henry, networking and pushing my portfolio for a forthcoming fashion show. Henry was off doing his thing. Suddenly the fire alarm rang out and I heard people moving about outside.

I thought I had been alone in the powder room, but a washroom door opened and somebody hissed at me. A little face peeked out and I recognised Valerie, one of the latest pop princesses. Hiding my surprise, I halted with my mascara brush in hand and asked her if I could help her.

"Gee is that alarm for real do you think?" Valerie asked me.

"I guess so, it hasn't stopped and I can hear people moving about," I said.

"Holy shit, I can't go out there like this, I'm not even supposed to be here," Valerie said. "I'll get mobbed."

"I can help you if you like," I suggested nonchalantly.

"Can you?" Valerie asked eagerly.

"Sure, but it will cost you," I said seizing the moment.

"You want money?" Valerie asked

"No, better than that, if you let me dress you for some major event where you will be photographed, I will make you stand out like a true star," I said confidently.

"Dress me? Are you some kinda pervert?" she asked backing away.

"Course not, I'm the best dress designer you will ever have, and I will transform you given the chance. So how about it?"

"Shit, you'll help me get out of here if I agree to see your designs?" Valerie asked.

"You let me transform you from a pop princess to a glamorous Hollywood star," I said, "and we'll go together right now."

"Ok," Valerie said, "but if I don't like your style, I'm not going out in it."

"You will love it, now come on," I told her.

In my bag I had my version of a baseball cap which had a wide flowing brim shading the face, I gave Valerie my sunglasses, we exchanged jackets and bags in case anybody noticed her going in. I linked her arm and we walked along through the crowds, out of the front door where people were assembling on the courtyard. We kept on walking and chatting, out of the drive and around the corner until we reached a quiet area where we hailed a taxi. By then Valerie had relaxed and was busy filling me in on her private life while I studied her measurements and complexion.

I accompanied Valerie back to the apartment she was renting and was sworn to secrecy about our meeting. If anybody asked, I would pretend to be an old friend. We talked style, I told Valerie that she was not making the most of herself. At first, she was indignant as she employed a stylist to make her look good. I knew that celebrities always felt insecure and needed to boost their confidence in a competitive world.

"Your stylist is making you conform to current fashion images. All the up and coming starlets look the same, it's like an unofficial uniform, boobs out, skin-tight skimpy costumes, skinny bodies, the only difference is skin or hair colour. OK, your music is your own and is obviously successful, but in a crowd of celebrities you just blend in. Is that what you want?" I asked, fired up.

"What do you have in mind?" Valerie asked, hesitantly.

"Well, for a start get me one of your favourite outfits," I said.

Valerie brought out a skinny sequined number. I teamed it up with a long flowing top and skinny leggings, with a chiffon scarf to complete the outfit. Approaching Valerie, I scraped back her hair, which covered her face, pulled it tight like a ballerina and made side ringlets. When she put the outfit on Valerie was surprised at the transformation. It would not have occurred to her to put the ensemble together.

"Do you want to replace my stylist?" she asked, admiring herself in the mirror.

"No, that's nothing to what I can make for you," I promised.

"Well, I have a nomination for an Academy award coming up next month. I already have a designer outfit but let's see what you come up with," Valerie suggested.

"Fine, on the condition you put yourself in the hands of my hair stylist and make-up artist to complement the dress I will design exclusively for you. I guarantee you will not only be noticed, but you will be the belle of the ball. Nobody will ever find out how we met, but you will launch my career. I can't say better than that," I said.

Valerie was excited and decided to take a chance, figuring she had her original gown and staff as fall back. We exchanged numbers, I measured her and when the time came Valerie was the best dressed female in the event. Whilst others bared all or displayed their assets, I covered Valerie from head to toe in an eye-catching rust silk fabric which concealed her body until she moved when it rippled suggestively tantalising all who saw her. Valerie was suggestively alluring and stood out amongst the crowd, who were wearing predictable colour-coordinated numbers. We plaited jewels in her hair which sparkled in the lights and kept her outfit very simple and classic.

The fact that Valerie won an award for best female artiste helped but the publicity wearing my dress opened the door for my career. I was inundated with requests especially when demand for my services exceeded supply. Henry and I decided to link up and start our own business in a small rented office. He would do menswear, I would look after the ladies. Our brand name was *Candice*. Students begged to work with us for experience, we picked the best and gradually grew. Once we became known we were invited to all the best parties and gigs. At first this was exciting, especially when we recognised famous celebrities.

I noticed how much drug taking took place with lines of cocaine being snorted openly, inhibitions vanished, people drank, got high and tried to avoid eating in case they got fat. The models were the worst, rail thin and starving, they tried to escape with various 'highs'. Poppa had drummed into us kids about the harm drug addiction could cause. As a control freak,

I had a fear of letting myself go, if I took an occasional drink, I would make sure I watched it being poured. Henry told me about people who spiked drinks, so I only used bottled water.

In this heady new world, there were many gay people enjoying the liberated atmosphere. Henry enjoyed himself but was always circumspect. With my style and looks I attracted more than my share of male attention. Nothing was more guaranteed to turn me off than admiration, compliments or patronisation. I was not a pet to be paraded and given accolades. My passion and attention were reserved for my work. Although I loved my nephews and nieces, I did not wish to go forth and multiply, nor did I need a man to provide for me. My indifference often inflamed my would-be suitors, so I stopped attending functions unless it benefitted the business.

I kept in touch with the family and always made sure Dan was well stocked with up to date décor pieces. Mama and I spoke regularly, she seemed to keep busy and told me how proud she was of my success. From Mama, I kept abreast of all the Allbrite news and scandals, it was another world. There were not enough hours in the day to do all I wanted, so I was not planning to go home again in the near future. In the fashion world a designer was only as good as their last showing. I ensured that my style did not reflect trends and I always remained unique.

My research covered smocking, tapestry, lace, silk and satin in various contemporary styles. Lengths and designs varied along with accessories. We had hired a young designer of purses and accessories who complemented our ranges. We made fashion shows in working class areas which were always packed to capacity. Magazines sent photographers along to try to gauge what we were up to. Because we heard of garment theft, we stored our finished stock in various secret places only known to limited staff. I was still young and upwardly mobile.

Life did not stand still, we had to prepare seasons ahead of time. I researched into ethnic costumes and came out with some stunning lines. Henry mentioned the changing seasons, so we interpreted them into a clothing range. People travelled all year round these days, so we made sure our range suited all seasons instead of being packed away each season change. We catered for all sizes, we encouraged curvy figures to dress well. I told Valerie countless times that she was too skinny, she would look better one dress size larger, but she would not listen.

It seemed in the fashion world a girl could never be skinny enough. I was aware of eating disorders and obesity at the other extreme. Fortunately, I was born with a slender frame but often I was too engrossed in my work to remember to eat. My assistant brought me food and drinks reminding me to eat. Healthy eating and exercise were lost on me. My intentions were good but I begrudged the time. Mama was always trying to feed me up, I was always too busy. Henry belonged to a gym and ate healthily. He watched out for me and was my best critic. Men snapped up Henry's clothes as soon as he produced them, yet he never chose independence.

I gave media interviews, helped various charities, opened local events and tried to smile appealingly. This brought me fan mail and even threats, so Henry hired a bodyguard. The security around the workplace was beefed up. I pitied my security because I led such an introverted predictable life. If I needed to go places, I had a chauffeur. My assistant handled the mail. My interest lay only in the creating, I was not involved in the rest. Sometimes if I heard a sad tale or somebody deserving having a bad time or illness, I would secretly create something to be handed to them discreetly with the label removed.

The lifestyle I had dreamed of living had finally come true. It was fulfilling and rewarding, but the desire to achieve had strengthened and I never felt satisfied. Henry told me I needed a good sex life to get balance. He was always suggesting fit looking suitors. Handsome young men left me cold. I preferred the company of mature men who had experience of life. I liked confident men with sophistication who knew how to handle life and were not afraid to take charge. Young men were vain and egoistical in general, they wanted trophy women to display.

I had a secret that not even Henry knew, at the age of 28 approaching 29, I was still a virgin. My body was a temple and although it had needs and desires, I had not found anybody worthy to go all the way with. There had been hot guys and near misses, but I would not give in to the wrong guy. I must have been one of the last virgins in America, so I never discussed my private life. Speculation and rumours may have existed about my single status, but I cut out when issues got personal. I decided to remedy my situation before I reached thirty.

My problem was finding a suitable man. In my neighbourhood there was an abundance of fit guys, would-be actors filling in as gardeners, pool attendants, tennis coaches, personal trainers etc. I wanted a man, not a boy and did not know how to find him. It was impossible for me to use dating agencies, I had a bodyguard each time I went out and usually had a professional escort provided when I attended functions. Most people in my business had their own agendas, so I had little contact with normal heterosexual men. It occurred to me to go home and try Allbrite again, where I was known as Mama's daughter.

Mama was pleased to see me but carried on with her own busy life. The rest of the family called round and hugged me. Henry had equipped me with suitable gifts for my four nephews who were shooting up like beanpoles, they had earnest innocent faces and long thin arms and legs. Everyone was pleased to welcome me home but they all led busy lives, so I settled into my revamped former room and did some work on the computer. I agreed to stay for Thanksgiving and carried on working from home which felt very relaxing. Henry delegated at the office and we kept in regular contact.

Linda rang to ask me if I could look after Jake for a couple of hours. She had to accompany Hal to a recital in Portswood, a neighbouring town which was hosting an event. I agreed wondering how much looking after an eight-year-old needed. Once I drove over to their place, Jake asked if I would take him to watch a baseball game at school. He wanted to watch the seniors go through their paces. This seemed like a good solution for both of us, so we drove over. I sat on the steps whilst Jake hovered over the edge of the field. He seemed to be fully absorbed so I did some work.

Towards the end of the game the ball soared over towards Jake who put out his hand to catch it. Unfortunately, the ball hit his hand against his middle finger on the right hand. Jake's finger turned blue and swelled up immediately. He came to show me. I was horrified, what would Linda say? This was my first ever supervision of a child and I didn't know what to do. The coach came over and told me to take Jake to the hospital across the way to get an X-ray. Coach said it was an unfortunate accident, but Jake would be fine.

Jake did not complain or cry, he said he was OK. I panicked and rushed into the Outpatients Drop-In. I held off calling Linda until I knew the outcome. Besides, Linda would be in the middle of Hal's recital. Jake's hand was X-rayed and we were asked to wait in reception as doctor would call us when the result came through. The nurse called us in.

Dr Martin Wood was sitting behind his desk, writing when we entered. A thick head of greying hair with a side parting, large dark bespectacled eyes and a welcoming smile greeted us. I caught my breath, he appeared to be just the type of man I was looking for. It seemed Jake had fractured his finger which would need to be strapped up and he would not be able to play sport for a few weeks to give it chance to heal Jake was more disappointed that he couldn't play than bothered about his injury.

I explained to Dr Wood that I was Jake's aunty on a visit from LA. This was my first supervision of a minor I revealed, and I felt terrible. Dr Wood said that as a father he could vouch that accidents happened all the time. Jake would be fine. The doctor told me he had studied medicine in LA and enjoyed the experience. I asked what brought him back to Allbrite? He told me his wife was from Allbrite so when they graduated, she wanted to return to her roots. Disappointment filled my mind, so I thanked Dr Wood for his prompt service, and we made our way out.

"Get in touch if you have any problems," Dr Wood said, escorting us out.

"Thank you," I said, going out.

Linda and Marshall thanked me for taking swift action and assured me it could have happened to anyone. I mentioned the kindness of Dr Wood. They told me that the good doctor had settled in Allbrite with his wife and young daughter only to discover his wife developed multiple sclerosis. He could not save her and had been left with his young daughter to raise alone. Linda thought his daughter was in Jake's class at school. All the women in town had flocked around to aid the doctor, but he was fiercely independent and showed no interest in anybody. This had been about 18 months ago. Doctor and daughter were seen about town together. A rota system had been established to help him in term time with picking up and dropping off.

This gave me plenty to think about. I understood how off-putting unwelcome suitors were. I thought Dr Wood had a pleasant manner, a warm smile and tried to figure out how I could justifiably manage to meet him again. I most certainly did not want to be added to his list of wannabe admirers. For once my scheming brain stopped functioning, putting it down to trauma, I decided to sleep on it. In the morning I had an idea. I enquired about Dr Wood to the family and decided to invite him for a drink to thank him.

I told Dr Wood that I was from Allbrite originally but had only just returned on a visit after an absence of more than two years. As I had no children of my own, I had been traumatised by Jake's accident. Jake was doing fine now thanks to the doctor's prompt attention and his parents had forgiven me. I wondered if I could buy Dr Wood a coffee or drink to say thank you. I thought we could compare our LA experiences. If this request seemed out of order, then I apologised in advance. I said since my return Allbrite had changed so much and that most people were too busy to socialise. It was unusual for me to have some free time. I thanked him again and signed off with my name in full.

Nothing happened for a while so when I had abandoned all hope, I got a message saying the doctor had limited free time but would be happy to join me for coffee and cake at the Bakehouse the next morning at 10.30 am, his treat. This took my breath away and I did a full manicure and hair treatment. For once I did not know what to wear or how to be myself. I had butterflies and needed to take deep breaths to calm down. After waiting an extra five minutes to be cool, I strolled into the Bakehouse realising the doctor's time would be limited and that he was probably on his break.

Mama's Charity Hike

Since Lilly's demise my outlook on life changed dramatically. Instead of saving for a rainy day or being thrifty, I decided that life was too short, and I would take opportunities when they came along. The hike tour filled my head, I did not know if I could do it, it might work out to be expensive and I had never done anything like it before, but I decided to try. Several members of my walking group were interested but some had family commitments, others could not afford the outlay, a few lacked the confidence, so ultimately, a group of six including Glen our leader and myself opted to do it.

We were three men and three women. There was Glen, a widower called Jed and a pensioner called Wes. In addition to Sandra and myself, a single woman called Mary joined us. We were an eclectic mix with more enthusiasm than fitness, so Glen took over the organisation and started fitness training to get us ready. He called in a Fitness Trainer to talk to us about preparing for the trek. We all listened avidly, it helped that he looked like a fitness advert and was very personable. I wished I was much younger. I made notes of his talk along the lines of:

Before we start.

Do not underestimate the importance of training even if active and exercise regularly. Training should be adapted to build strength, stamina and endurance for the challenge. I should identify the type of exercise I would do, the duration and intensity.

I needed to establish realistic fitness objectives and goals. It should be achievable but challenging. I should not aim too high and it was important not to overdo it to avoid injury.

I should begin training gradually then review and adjust my programme as necessary.

We were advised to book a training weekend. These took place in parks led by highly qualified and experienced leaders. They offered treks or exercises to monitor fitness levels. There were talks on suitable clothing, equipment, expedition health and wellbeing, basic first aid.

Before he finished, the trainer gave us some Top Tips telling us to:

- Get up an hour earlier for a brisk walk or walk to work where possible.
- If commuting get off earlier and finish the journey walking.
- Walk or exercise during lunch breaks.
- Take the stairs instead of the lift
- Swimming, squash, badminton, cycling or other sporting activity will increase your fitness level.
- Walk wearing your rucksack and boots
- Join a training weekend

We all mulled over his talk over coffee and decided to set up our own training programme. The instructor consulted with Glen on appropriate fitness regimes. We did not feel ready to join a training weekend, but if necessary we could do our own in the local park. First, we needed to get ourselves fit. Meanwhile, Marcie, who was not joining us, wanted to get involved so she volunteered to handle the publicity fundraising side. She had good connections.

Marcie set up a plan to raise funds and liaised with the local press to personalise our story with photos. We didn't need to handle any money as providers would send any funds raised straight to our charity. Within a short time Marcie had contacted local newspapers, television, radio, schools and all the socialites explaining our aim and worthy cause. She told them our average age was 59, and we were starting a training programme. She asked for help to fund such a worthy cause, and said it would put Allbrite on the map.

Fundraising events were planned and Allbrite town was invited to get involved to help. Photos of our team in training were circulated and updated regularly. Marcie called us The Allbrite Goldies and circulated an instruction sheet to us:

- Tell your story why you are fundraising for your charity. People will be more interested if they know your motivation.
- Explain briefly why you are doing the challenge.
- Tell people your fundraising target and how their contribution will help your charity.
- Treat your fundraising as a work in progress by adding updates, photos and reports whenever you can.
- Communication is important. Keep everyone updated. People who sponsor you will be interested in how you're getting on. It's a reminder for those who didn't sponsor you to donate.
- Whilst you are building up to the challenge, bring your family and friends on this journey with you. Take photos of you training when it's cold, dark, raining, before work or at weekends. These will demonstrate your commitment and inspire people.

Marcie spread the word socially. She asked for help providing kit, equipment and clothing. Where possible we could hire but we needed suitable camping gear, decent sleeping bags, etc. Team tee shirts and sweatshirts were designed and donated by Candice in eye catching orange. We publicised Candice handing them over. A detailed kit list was provided by the trek organisers which we published, resulting in generous donations from the Allbrite town folk.

We left it to Marcie. It was all most of us could do to get up and keep training. One of the disadvantages of aging is the creaks and aches in the joints, particularly the knees. Without warning something would seize up or make itself known. Symptoms we had never heard of like Baker's Knee would occur. Waves of fatigue would sweep across us. Although the programme was designed to build up strength, there were times we felt uncertain that we would get through it. This is where moral support from the others would help us to carry on.

My family offered financial support and were wary about encouraging me. They tried to protect me but knew better than to fuss. I reckon it was hard on them having a Mama who refused to grow old gracefully. Eric and Candice were genuinely supportive. Whenever I felt tired or disheartened, I remembered Lilly and thought how she would have loved to get involved. Saskia kept in regular touch and was a generous sponsor.

When the time drew nearer, Glen arranged for Dr Martin Wood to give us a talk regarding our health. Dr Wood warned us about overdoing it, we were fit for our age but not as nimble as we used to be. If we felt tired or anxious, we should stop until we recovered. We should not feel pressurised into over achieving. He warned us about heat and to be aware of dehydration and heat-related conditions, especially when exerting ourselves. He advised us to drink three to four litres of water per day and add extra salt to our food.

Sunburn was a risk and Dr Wood warned that it can have long-term effects, including skin cancer and premature skin ageing. To avoid it, he suggested wearing a hat, using 50+ sunscreen and wearing 100% ultra violet protective glasses.

As biting insects can spread disease, Dr Wood advised us to use anti-bug sprays, and to cover up at dusk and in wet weather. He told us to always wash our hands thoroughly after going to the toilet, before handling food or eating, carry anti-bacterial hand gel, drink bottled water and avoid ice unless it is made from treated water, eat freshly cooked food and ensure it is piping hot.

When all the warning was over, Dr Wood told us how much he admired us and wished us every success. He gave us his emergency number in case we needed him. He would be avidly following our progress throughout.

In Allbrite sponsorship activity was hotting up. There were cake sales, games, sweepstakes on sporting events, coffee mornings and dress-down jeans to work days. Employers were requested to match money raised by their employees. Nearer the time there was a ball and dinner to which certain local restaurants offered to donate part of the cost, car boot sales thrived, some brave souls decided to shave their heads, bar quizzes, raffles and challenges to go sober for a month.

Perhaps interest flourished because Allbrite was a quiet sleepy town where not much happened, so we gave folk something to get hooked into. It made our team determined not to let them down. We gave our all to the training and hoped that it would be enough. Everywhere we went people recognised us. We became minor celebrities.

Before we departed, we invited Allbrite to join us in a hike around Peasom Park where fundraising activities would be set up. The weather behaved and it was a perfect day out. Families streamed around the trail we set up. Tilly set up a refreshments booth and stalls, Candice offered some designer sportswear, Dan sold wood carvings and Marshall arranged security and took care of the money. Local singers and aspiring groups played their hearts out hoping to be noticed. The media turned out in force.

Finally, it was time to go. We said our last goodbyes and were driven to Billings airport for a flight to Sedona. We had discussed and planned this trip for so long, it seemed surreal to actually be doing it. I sat with Sandra and we chatted about the campaign and what may lie ahead of us. In a movie we would all find romance and live happy ever after. In real life we were half excited and half fearful to face the challenge.

Upon arrival we were transferred to a community hall where we found refreshments waiting. As we had a few hours to fill until the remainder of the travellers arrived, we went to explore Sedona centre. The scenery was awesome with gleaming mountain ranges. We saw several shopping malls and interesting outlets. Holistic and esoteric centres appeared to flourish. The street furniture and statues were interesting, and people appeared happy to be there.

We saw a fleet of pink jeeps offering off-road tours and rugged adventures. Place names were fascinating. There seemed to be so many choices of activities and venues, we wished we had longer. One of the highlights of being in Sedona was the sunset. We were told to look out when the sun went down as the mountains glowed beautiful shades of pink and gold.

After an hour transfer, we hiked across the rock trails and back roads developed by early miners and ranchers. The temperature was pleasant, so we walked slowly along admiring the majestic scenery. I thought of spices because the colours of the rocks went from turmeric, cinnamon, paprika then pepper with off white parts. Wild vegetation flourished with some flowers and shrubs appearing unexpectedly. It was beautiful in every direction, I was in heaven.

In the evening we made our first desert camp at a ranch in the Dead Horse Ranch State Park. Our baggage was being transported ahead. We were all given bottles of water and told to use them. We reached the ranch at dusk and as the sun started to set it was breath taking. Cameras snapped but I just drank in the splendour. It was awesome and so peaceful, worth coming just to take this in.

Our hosts had a campfire going with huge barbeques. We were invited to use the facilities and allocated tents with camp beds already set up. I shared with Sandra. We washed up and explored the ranch house facilities before settling down for our supper. While we ate heartily, we were serenaded by cowboys with guitars, harmonicas and mouth organs. It was a real-life adventure. Full and content, we fell into bed too tired to talk.

After an early start we had a long trek of 11 kilometres to the Dead Horse Ranch State Park in Arizona. It was a tough climb uphill leading onto some gently undulating terrain. After trekking we would transfer to Flagstaff where we would camp for the night. The rest of our party seemed a mixed bunch of varied ages and abilities. We were not the oldest party. There were some young students, mixed ethnicity groups and numerous guides were scattered throughout the trail. The pace was steady but not too exhausting, with stops to drink.

I found it tough going and the climbing up a steep hill caused me to stop regularly to catch my breath, but I was determined to make it. The view from the top was worth it. The man climbing beside me introduced himself as Will, he said: "I wanted to challenge myself to get fit whilst being treated for cancer. Having a training plan to work to was brilliant." He made me feel humble and grateful that I could enjoy this opportunity and raise money to help people like him. I vowed not to complain.

At the end of the trek refreshments were set out and a fleet of jeeps transferred us to Flagstaff. On the outskirts of Flagstaff we saw pine trees and snow-capped mountains. The scenery reminded me of how I imagined Switzerland to be. It was very pretty and quiet. We by passed Flagstaff centre and were dropped off at a campsite sheltered among the hills. This was our first night setting up our tents and equipment. Our guides circulated to assist if required. I had a little tent which just had room for my sleeping bag and rucksack. Sandra camped beside me. Dinner was cooked on a communal campfire with a selection of barbecued fish, chicken or burgers, accompanied by buns and salads. There were vegetarian options.

After the meal I felt too exhausted to linger, I could not keep my eyes open and had to go to bed wearing my clothes. The clean fresh air or the exercise wiped me out. Next morning Sandra woke me up and we headed to the showers to wash away the sweat and grime. I thought somewhere along the way I would need to wash some clothes but figured I could survive for now. My legs felt stiff and ached a bit, my body needed to loosen up too. Sandra also felt the same. We reckoned the climbing had been hard going and hoped there would not be more.

Ryan's Experience

I spoke to Marie about volunteering to go Guatemala. Marie was shocked.

"What brought this on?" she asked.

"I feel the need to give something back," I said.

"Back to who? Can you not do some good here?" she asked.

"We live well here and there are plenty of charities and organisations to help people, I want to sacrifice my comforts and go where I can do some good," I replied.

"What exactly do you want to do?" she asked, frowning.

"It's a project to help build a school house and dormitories for poor kids. I could be a real asset," I said enthusiastically.

"How long would you be going for?" Marie asked.

"That would depend upon you," I replied.

"What do you mean? What about the children and me? How will we manage if you disappear?"

"I won't disappear for long, it's just something I feel I can do to help poor unfortunates that don't have a chance."

"What about the business?" Marie asked.

"The guys are competent enough to run it without me. Brian would be around if you had any queries," I suggested. Brian often deputised for me, he was my second in command having started with me at the beginning.

"What would I tell people?"

"Tell them your husband has volunteered to help unfortunates build a school in Guatemala."

"Won't they think we are estranged or something?" Marie asked upset.

"Honey, you know that I adore you, I always will."

"You seem happy enough to leave me now," she said.

"My darling girl," I said wrapping my arms around her, "I would never leave you for long. This is something I feel I should do and it would be a big sacrifice being without you. I will think of you and the girls constantly."

"How long do you think of going for?"

"A week or two wouldn't hack it, I reckon about a month?"

"A month?" Marie echoed distressed.

"Just think about it for now," I said, "If you really don't want me to go, I won't."

"It may be dangerous there," Marie said.

"There's danger everywhere these days," I replied.

"I don't know," she said, "let me speak to Maman."

"Fine," I said, and we left it like that.

Maman told Marie that if she interfered with my desire to go, I may resent it and turn against her in later life. Marie suggested that my place was with the family. Her mother said I would not be leaving the family for long. It seemed that Marie could benefit from having more time to herself. She would not need to make meals, the laundry would be less. Marie could socialise with her friends and family if she was lonely. I only heard about Maman's support after Marie gave me her consent.

There was a telephone number on the article I read about Guatemala volunteering, so I called and arranged an interview. I drove out to Raynes Creek and was given a leaflet to read which informed me that more than half of all Guatemalans lived in poverty. Spending on health and education was low with minimal social assistance. Combating crime and drug trafficking was taking up resources along with disaster relief due to climate change.

Many children lived below the poverty line especially in rural areas. Malnutrition stunted growth among children under five, especially in rural and indigenous areas. Illiteracy was high with an average of only three and half years of schooling at primary level. Girls in poor areas tended to receive less education. Secondary education was low in disadvantaged groups. Many schools did not have enough books and teaching materials. It was difficult to recruit qualified teachers in rural areas. Children from poor families often have to leave school to help their families or could not afford to attend due to the cost for uniforms, books and transport.

I had just finished reading the leaflet when a middle-aged buxom lady came to shake my hand and lead me into a cluttered office. Introducing herself as Hetty Parks, she asked me about myself and why I felt I should volunteer. After my explanation Mrs Parks asked me if I still felt the same after reading the article. I told her I had the skills to help these people and felt glad a school would contribute to the wellbeing of the children.

Mrs Parks told me that throughout much of its history, education in Guatemala has been traditionally reserved for citizens, a status not fully extended to women or the indigenous population until 1945. She explained that more than half the Guatemalans lived in extreme poverty and many could not afford to buy basic food. Home could be a damp shack with a corrugated iron roof, no windows or running water which can sleep five or more people on two beds. When it came to possessions, they may have a few clothes hanging on string, a couple of blankets and plastic buckets on the stone floor. Chickens or animals may roam around.

Overcrowding and poverty can lead to violence, sexual abuse and family breakdown. The families who have education gain the opportunity for households to improve their standard of living. Improvements in public services and education are taking place gradually. The most disadvantaged group are rural indigenous girls who have limited education. Many get married young, have large families and live in chronic poverty. They are expected to leave school to help with the family.

Mrs Parks paused and asked if I still wanted to go. I was stunned by the information she had just imparted and felt how important this mission would be. My life was luxurious in comparison. I wondered if a month would be enough. Any time I could spare would be appreciated, Mrs Parks told me, there were no limits. She suggested I took out small stationery items for use in the school. Thrift shops would be a good source. I would need to distribute them to the school principal to lock away so that they would not be sold.

Accommodation would be in a remote village in the Highlands where the weather could be extreme. Conditions would be basic but running water had been installed and the building work was underway. I should prepare clothing for extreme weather conditions due to the height. A convoy of aid would be leaving in the next month and I would be welcome to join it. My return journey could be arranged on site. Did I have any questions?

My mind was whirling. I told Mrs Parks I ran a successful building and maintenance company and I would be willing to train locals whilst over there. Mrs Parks thanked me and told me any training would be enthusiastically received. She suggested I put my affairs in order and be ready to leave on the 19th. After exchanging phone numbers, Mrs Parks handed me paperwork to complete and accompanied me to the door.

I drove home in a dream thinking about the poor under-privileged kids and the lifestyle. When I got home, I showed Marie the leaflet Mrs Parks had given me to read. Marie felt upset to hear about such poverty. She told me to contact Mama and ask for family donations. Marie intended to raise awareness locally of the plight of the children and ask for donations of school supplies and clothing or used games.

At the same time Marie put together a medicine and first aid kit to cope with any emergencies. She worried there would be nothing suitable on hand. Marie also sorted out my winter wear and packed for me with secreted snacks and a small bottle of whisky wrapped in some socks.

Mama told me Eric was also in Guatemala so she would pass on my contact details. Candice offered to run up some school uniforms if I would advise her what they wore. Dan sent patterns for simple desks, chairs and beds as well as storage units. He offered to get a cheap supplier for provisions. I told Mama to tell them all to contact Mrs Parks for details. When the time came to depart, I felt very emotional and clung to Marie and the girls. I could not wave goodbye just marched off, it was the hardest thing I had ever done. We had not been parted before.

I was dropped off at Mrs Parks' building where a pickup truck took me to catch a flight in a rickety old cargo plane. There were a few other passengers who seemed to be Guatemalan, so I could not talk to them. We all sat sideways along the plane. It was dark when we landed, and I was tired. A jeep was waiting to take me and some cargo inwards. The driver introduced himself as Carlos who had lived in the States and spoke good English. As we had a long journey, I asked him to tell me about life in Guatemala and if there were things I should not do. He gave me detailed advice:

"Don't take photographs without permission, especially of children. This is particularly important in remote areas. People may ask for a small sum of money to have their photos taken. Fears of child kidnapping or theft of vital organs by foreigners have led to lynching. Carry a photocopy of your passport for identification. Make sure your passport is valid with unused pages or you may be fined."

As the rainy season in Guatemala runs from June to November, coinciding with the hurricane season in the Caribbean, we wanted to get building work completed in time. I was advised to avoid travelling on public buses which are repainted US school buses. Private inter-city coach services are safer. I should avoid demonstrations which occur with little or no notice causing traffic disruptions.

Guatemala was a macho society where often women needed permission to leave the house. Violence to women tended to be condoned and society often blamed the women. Apart from elections when politicians wanted their votes, women were not important. Many indigenous girls don't go to school and are likely to be illiterate, sick, poor with unplanned families. Sometimes they are subjected to rape, violence and forced into the drug trade. They face discrimination because they are poor, indigenous and women.

I asked about the size of the population and was told that eight million indigenous people live in Guatemala, mostly descendants of the Mayan civilization. They earn less money than non-indigenous people, often working in casual jobs picking crops or selling street food. Their life expectancy is 13 years shorter, and the maternal mortality rate more than twice as high. They often speak one of more than 20 native languages rather than Spanish.

This was depressing news, so I asked about food in daily life. Carlos told me: "Corn is made into tortillas or tamales, black beans, rice, and wheat in the form of bread or pasta are staples. People also eat chicken, pork, and beef." He explained that people living near water eat fish and shellfish. Seafood is becoming popular due to improvements in refrigeration and transport.

Carlos also told me that Guatemala grows vegetables and fruits, including avocados, radishes, potatoes, sweet potatoes, squash, carrots, beets, onions, and tomatoes. Lettuce, snow peas, green beans, broccoli, cauliflower, artichokes, and turnips are grown for export and are also sold in local markets. They are eaten more by Ladinos than Indians. Fruits include pineapples, papayas, mangoes, a variety of melons, citrus fruits, peaches, pears, plums, guavas, and many others.

The main meal of the day is eaten at noon. Most stores and businesses in the urban areas used to close for two to three hours siesta to give people time to eat at home and rest before returning to work. Transportation problems due to increased traffic are changing this custom. In rural areas women take the noon meal to the men in the fields, often accompanied by their children so that the family can eat as a group.

Tortillas are eaten by everyone especially the Indians usually with chili, sometimes with beans or stews flavoured with meat or dried shrimp. The poor may drink anato for breakfast, a thin porridge made with any oatmeal, , cornmeal, or ground fresh corn. Others may only have coffee with sweet bread. The evening meal is always lighter than that at noon.

On 1st November, the Day of the Dead, families congregate in the cemeteries to honour and share food with deceased relatives. Codfish cooked in various forms is eaten at Easter. Christmas is a time for gourmet tamales and ponche, a rum-based drink containing spices and fruits. Beer and rum, including a fairly raw variety known as aguardiente are the most popular alcoholic drinks."

"Carlos, you are a font of knowledge, I am so glad I met you. What about work opportunities?" I asked him.

"Agricultural products are produced for sale within the country and for export. Handicrafts are made and traded to tourists. Ladinos and Indians make them in small workshops or at home. The best are sold to museums and collectors. There's textiles and clothing; baskets; ceramics; carved wooden furniture, jewellery and hand-blown glassware.

'Maquilas' which are like factories produce clothing and items for export using imported materials and semiskilled labour with relatively high wages for many Guatemalans. There is also work processing locally grown products like chicken, beef, pork, coffee, wheat, corn, sugar, cotton, cacao, vegetables, fruits and spices. Beer and rum are big employers. We also produce paper goods.

Business, professionals and academics tend to be upper classes. Ladino and Indian teenagers tend to work as domestics. Children work at household tasks and in the fields in farming families from aged four. They sell candies or other small goods on the city streets or 'watch' parked cars.

All children must attend school between ages seven and thirteen by law, though many don't. Sometimes there is no local school or the child is needed at home. Sometimes the family is too poor to send them, but the situation is improving."

There was no time for more discussion as we had arrived, and I felt exhausted. It was night and I was given a key to a room and was pointed in its direction. I fell into bed after taking my boots off and was out like a light.

Marshall's World

My business was faring well. It seemed the good folk of Allbrite had their regular share of financial matters to sort out. I expect I could have expanded, maybe opened up elsewhere but I felt it more prudent to be a big fish in a small town, than anonymous in a big one. We lived comfortably and kept up with all the kids' demands, so I was not complaining. It was comforting to be near all the family and convenient when we forgot something or needed to be somewhere. Life was too short to spend in traffic jams.

When I was not working, I often had to ferry the kids around. I had a calendar on the kitchen door marked with all the family commitments and activities. These kids had a better social life than their parents. If it wasn't a party or ball game, it was a trip or play date. Linda's mother had been in hospital being treated for cancer. When she came home Linda moved in to help care for her. I really adored my brave mother-in-law and wished her well. In the meantime, I was glad I ran my own business. Dropping the kids off for school was fine. I booked them into after-school activities when I could, or I arranged for them to be looked after until I finished work.

Linda's sister Katie came home from Missouri to help. When Linda returned, she sat me down and said we needed a holiday. I figured she was tired and entitled to a vacation so asked her where she fancied. To my surprise Linda became agitated and said her mother's cancer had brought home to her that our time was limited. Linda had always wanted to travel to see the world and she had never been anywhere. I had expected Linda to choose an American vacation, as there were so many states to choose from, but Linda insisted we have a foreign vacation. I told her to see what she fancied and that we would all need passports.

"Well you had better get the application forms off," Linda said firmly. Shaken, I obeyed.

Linda wasted no time and presented me with a cruise going to the British Isles stopping in Bermuda, the Azores, Lisbon, Bilbao and Le Havre before reaching Southampton for London. It would then go to Guernsey in the Channel Islands, Cork and Dublin in Ireland, Belfast in Northern Ireland and Glasgow, Invergordon and Edinburgh in Scotland – before the ship returned. It seemed like a lot of travelling to me.

Linda felt we might be able to trace our roots as both sets of parents had emigrated to the States. She said she would ask Mama and her own parents to see how far back they could go. Any hesitation or doubt from me was quashed instantly. Linda was serious and would not be thwarted. It seemed the ships catered for active boys, there were facilities for sport, entertainment and leisure. We could choose whether to go ashore or not. Our memories would last a lifetime. It would not be cheap, but we could afford it. My hesitation was down to my reluctance to leave my nest. I have always been a homebody, but the business would run efficiently in my absence.

The 27-day British Isles Grand Adventure left from Fort Lauderdale. I began to research places on the itinerary and talk to the boys during dinner to prepare them. They already knew the names of capitals, so we moved on to sport, money, food and drink. I told them about the English royalty and explained that my grandparents had emigrated to the States. The boys related to soccer teams which the English called football. They also wanted to try English fish and chips. I hoped the vacation would be interesting and educational for them. Linda wanted to be waited on - endless meals she would not have to prepare.

Mama said she would root around in Poppa's old papers to see if she could come up with anything. O'Brien was an Irish name, but she didn't know if it stemmed from Belfast in the north or Dublin in the south. Mama said she would keep an eye on the house and the business for us. I think she wanted to join us, these days Mama was ready for anything. Fortunately, she was busy preparing for her big hike. I had not thought about my ancestors, how they had made the epic journey across the sea. I imagined travel had been less comfortable in steerage and marvelled at their bravery crossing to a foreign land, their future unknown.

Linda said that in the past there had been widespread unemployment in Ireland. Looking at the financial news it seemed there was a global downturn and many companies were facing uncertain futures. If modern technology replaced humans, it would lead to job losses. Third World countries were copying products and exporting them cheaper. China had a huge population working for a fraction of the cost of our workers. Pollution was spreading throughout the newly industrialised world, but determination to succeed ignored it.

At school the teachers suggested the boys kept a journal about their trip. On their return they could tell the class about it. Linda decided to write an account each night with them. Everybody was excited about the trip. The UK was small compared to the States and full of history. People we knew were full of suggestions and advice even if they had not been themselves. We were offered names and addresses of ex-citizens living abroad who may be useful. I reminded people we were going on vacation not emigrating. Linda said people meant well and were trying to be helpful. I figured I would be better off withdrawing from society and tried not to think about the departure.

Once Linda had shopped, packed and prepared everything for the whole family, we just had to close the house, leave keys at our neighbours for emergencies, then say our farewells. We flew to Fort Lauderdale to board the ship The Majestic, which was very impressive. We shook hands with the captain and some crew members. There was a maze of corridors, but we found our cabin which was well kitted out. The boys had twin beds. We even had a small balcony with a little table and two chairs. Linda was delighted. The boys raced around the cabin opening everything. They picked up a leaflet and read out information about the ship.

Our ship offered three main dining rooms, an ice cream parlour which served crepes, a café and snack bar, a tea shop, wine bars, a pizzeria and 24 hour room service. There were showrooms, theatres, lounges, nightclub, cocktail bars and television studio as well as the pools. A daily programme of social events was issued including movies, spa and fitness, casino, sports, kid's and teen centres, art gallery, shops and medical centre. There were detailed statistics concerning the accommodation and build of the ship.

Linda told the boys to keep the leaflet as part of their journal, so they could tell the class. She then read out to me enthusiastically:

"The Majestic offers a relaxing adults Sanctuary and a light and water show. Chefs bake, grill and cook delicious fare to suit all tastes," Linda paused and said: "Oh my, I will be so fat after this, but let's make it worth it. I can't wait to try it all out."

I had to admit that the ship was magnificent. It made me wonder about maintenance and running costs, plus the cost per person. Savvy enough to keep thoughts to myself, I was happy to go for an exploratory walk to get our bearings. It was much larger than I had envisaged and was well signed. I hoped we would find our way back to the cabin because we seemed to walk for miles, stopping and starting to exclaim new discoveries. When the ship siren sounded our departure, we all stood on deck watching the land fade away.

Our boys joined the Kid's Club and disappeared from morning to late afternoon, unless we had plans to disembark. They quickly made friends and had evening discos, shows, and their own entertainment. This suited Linda and me, we could not remember having time to be together and I found it very satisfying. My Linda was still a lovely woman to me. We held long interesting conversations without mentioning home or kids. It reminded me of our courtship and Linda caught me under her spell all over again.

When the boys returned to us for meals or to change before going off again, they were bursting with news and stories about their escapades and new friends. They were obviously loving it. There was so much to do, Linda enjoyed the shopping centre, it reminded me of a mall, so I left her to it. I enjoyed the international newspapers and tried English lager and beer. When it came to food we were spoilt for choice. We could indulge from morning until night, but we tried to get some exercise on deck in between meals, morning coffee, afternoon tea, late night snacks. I told Linda we had to stop eating like this. She agreed but we both loved it. Linda beamed constantly, I kept smiling. We made friends with other couples we shared tables with. Everybody was friendly. If we had drinks or visited areas on board, passengers were welcoming and we felt very comfortable.

After two days at sea we arrived at Bermuda where we disembarked and had a day to explore. We did not book an organised trip because we thought it might be too much for the boys. They needed some time to run around freely so we set off leisurely around the seafront area, indulging them with ice creams. The dockyard was modern with tourist attractions including a National Museum, beaches, art and craft centre, restaurants, pubs and a shopping mall with boutique shops etc. Island and boat tours were on offer with water sports, golfing and fishing tours.

The Snorkel Park and beach were a five-minute walk from the cruise pier and the Clocktower Mall was a few minutes away. Three Visitor Information Centres offered maps, brochures, bus schedules, information etc. They sold bus and ferry passes to get around the island. The Dockyard used to be an outpost for the British Royal Navy when they lost their ports in the American War of Independence. It has become the busiest passenger ship port in the island. Built by thousands of convicts from England and slaves from the island, along with Kings Wharf pier in 1809, many workers died from yellow fever. The Kings Wharf and dockyard operated for over 100 years and the naval base remained in operation through the World War II as well.

As cruise passengers, we did not want to stray too far and risk getting back late. This was our first excursion, it was picturesque and busy. We enjoyed the scenery and the buzz but felt relieved to go back on board in familiar territory. There had not been enough time to visit Hamilton City, the capital of Bermuda, or the historic town St George's. We had enjoyed our visit and felt satisfied. The boys liked exploring and looking for souvenirs.

The next days were spent at sea enjoying the entertainment programmes, swimming, sunbathing, eating and drinking. It almost seemed a shame to arrive at Ponta Delgardo, Portugal where we would do our own thing. We decided to book a tour when we got to Lisbon. We read on a tourist information sheet that Ponta Delgardo is the capital of Azores with arched city gates and the Gothic Church of St Sebastian near the harbour. Nicknamed the 'Green Island' it is a gateway to the crater lakes of Sete Cidades in the northwest. There were old churches, a fort and a museum.

At the harbour we booked a mini-expedition to catch sight of whales and dolphins. The boys were riveted at the side of the boat when we were joined by three whales. We also managed a trip to the Lagoa das Sete Cidades, a twin lake in a volcanic caldera. The walls rose steeply around the shore rich with conifers and ferns. There was a divide between the two bodies of green water and was stunning.

We returned to the ship tired but happy after an exciting day out. How fortunate we felt to experience such wonders. The boys were making notes to tell their friends. I had to admit that travelling abroad was exciting, but my joy was watching the faces of my family having fun. Linda looked relaxed and content, the sea air was doing us good. I hoped the remainder of the trip would be as pleasant.

Matilda

Just when we thought life was running smoothly, I had a phone call to go to Willie's Drugstore in town where Scarlett needed me. It seemed there had been an incident and she had gone to the drugstore for help. Alarmed, I left Hilary to deputise for me and dashed off. I didn't understand why Scarlett would be in town by herself when school was out, she usually got picked up or had after-school activities.

Scarlett's year at school had recently had a talk, 'Say No to Drugs', detailing the causes and effects drug taking had. She told me enthusiastically why it was bad and how she would not be tempted. I chose the opportunity to tell her to guard her drinks when she went out as some bad people slipped drugs into drinks. Scarlett said she had heard that, and she was going to be careful. With her gymnastic ambitions, Scarlett looked after her body. Later she told me she had told her teacher she had seen some high school kids dealing behind the bike shed.

After school the workout Scarlett attended was cancelled at the last minute, so she decided to take a walk through the town centre before heading home. She refused a lift and walked into town stopping to look in Benson's Jewellery shop window. Suddenly somebody grabbed her from behind, put a hand over her mouth and dragged her into the alley alongside the shop where he pushed her against the wall, roaming his hands over her body.

Scarlett froze with shock and fear, she tried to scream but the hand was still over her mouth. She heard a zip and made herself go limp, his wandering hand propped Scarlett up and she kicked as hard as she could. Her attacker moaned and dropped his hands and she ran fast into the nearest open place she could find which happened to be the drugstore, crying, shaking and in distress. Willie called me and the police. Unfortunately, Scarlett had not seen her attacker, she could describe his height and that he wore old jeans. Willie ran out with a rolling pin but could not find anyone.

When Bernard, the cop, arrived he told Scarlett how brave she had been. He filed a report saying they were on the lookout for a man who could not walk properly. There was very little to go on. Fortunately, Scarlett had escaped unharmed but her confidence was shattered. I held her close and rocked her like a baby. Phil went ballistic and wanted to send out a search party. The mayor got in touch and the press, this attack was unprecedented in Allbrite. We pleaded for anonymity although people knew. At school the headmistress addressed the entire school and told them to be wary and not to go about unaccompanied.

Immediately afterwards I arranged for a Self Defence course to be set up at the Civic Hall and circulated its existence. I ensured all our family kids joined regardless of whether they wanted to. I wanted all the town kids to know what to do. Pep talks were included about drugs, safety, security devices. Scarlett was hesitant to go out for a while unless she was chaperoned but gained confidence gradually once she mastered self-defence techniques. Apparently, it was Poppa who told her to kick somebody in the goolies if attacked. Poppa taught us all self-defence, I wish I had paid more attention.

Once Scarlett had scrubbed herself clean and thrown away her clothing, she became withdrawn for a time and reluctant to resume her sporting activities. She began to take an interest in local affairs. She asked Marshall to explain how the budget and resources were allocated. For a time, Scarlett took an interest in politics and was a keen supporter of causes she validated.

"Do you know that women get paid less for doing the same job as men?" she asked me one day.

I explained that it was often the case. In the past women could not open bank accounts, obtain mortgages or do many of the roles open today, I told her. Scarlett was indignant.

"In many parts of the world even today women cannot leave the house or do anything without the permission of their men. Women are often treated as second class inferior beings," I said. "In Saudi Arabia women were still not allowed to drive. We are fortunate to live in a modern open society where woman have equal rights."

Scarlett fumed and joined marches for liberal causes. Eithan was very supportive and accompanied Scarlett when she allowed him to. He accepted all her orders and listened to her rants and raves. Phil would have wrapped Scarlett up in a security box if he could. Scarlett was medium height, slender and athletic, she usually wore her hair in a ponytail and looked younger than her age. I worried she may be scarred from her escape as she took no interest in boys and did not like to be touched. Her grades continued to be top or close to, she kept her girlfriends but socially she turned down invitations and stayed at home. We encouraged her to go out with her friends and offered to drive her, but she was not interested.

I drove my kids to the Self Defence course and collected them. Most parents accompanied their offspring. Eithan was learning to play the keyboard, Scarlett had her gymnastic classes. Sometimes there were school events to attend or trips to link up with. All the parents worried about their kids' safety, however, there was no repeat of Scarlett's attack and nobody was caught. We thought it could have been a druggie or somebody passing through town. Scarlett wondered if it happened because she told her teacher she had seen dealers behind the bike shed. Allbrite returned to its slow sleepy way of life, but Scarlett had lost her innocent joy. We told ourselves we were grateful it hadn't been worse.

All my family were doing exciting things. Mama was planning her hike for cancer relief, Ryan was in Guatemala volunteering. Eric was also in Guatemala and hoping to meet up with Ryan. Marshall, my staid older brother, had taken his family on a terrific sounding cruise to the UK. Candice mixed with the jet set and seemed to be based in California somewhere enjoying success with her designs. I was lucky to find time to keep up with my baking which now included teaching. It was hard to dream up new lines when I was always rushing around.

Maria our housekeeper and lifesaver had been granted leave to stay thanks to some string pulling. I could not manage without her. For everything she did for us I was eternally grateful and gave her annual rises. It was thanks to her that I managed to do so much. Phil also kept busy and I made sure not to neglect him or myself. Each week I scheduled in a massage, manicure and hairdo. Thankfully, I remained slim because I rarely ate my own baking. It looked good and sold out regularly so it must have been delicious. I was my best critic.

America had an epidemic of gun crime particularly in schools. Our school introduced drills of what to do in the event of danger. I suggested security measures on the doors where they would pass through an alarm like in airports. There was no budget for that. It was too easy to purchase guns and I worried. Some kids carried knives for protection. I wondered what the world was coming to. In my school days we walked miles to get the school bus and bad asses cussed or wrote graffiti. It never occurred to us to carry weapons. Poppa took the boys hunting but always locked away his guns and ammunition.

Phil decided we needed a family vacation, he wanted to go camping, I wanted the ocean, Scarlett fancied Hollywood and Eithan said he would be happy to go along with wherever we decided. I wanted some home comforts, not cooking over a camp fire or endless barbecues. We argued about it and as usual let it slide. Maria came up with a helpful suggestion to go south where bigger is better. The south was famed for hospitality, barbecue and creole cuisine plus Elvis, jazz and country music. Phil said he would look into it. I preferred Florida where those beaches turned me on.

I found a sensational self-drive journey to Florida featuring Orlando water parks, theme parks including Universal Studios, Miami's beaches and sunny islands in the Florida Keys.

We seemed to be a two-split family, the girls liked Florida, Phil and Eithan preferred the South. Neither child wanted to go to summer camp. Once we reached stalemate, we dropped the idea and carried on with our routines. Phil came home one evening looking pleased with himself. He had booked us into a vacation with a difference offering plenty of adventures for the children and luxury for us. We would be going on a luxury camping vacation in California. Despite our questions Phil would not tell us more. He said we would love it, we would see when we arrived and told me to pack for every occasion.

The kids and I were unsure whether we would like it. I was irritated that I hadn't been consulted, yet relieved the decision had been taken. Truthfully, my mind was occupied on daily matters. I had to organise a rota for all the baking and cooking requirements while we were away and ensure Mama would get regular checks. There was so much to do, I really didn't have time to go away. I hoped Scarlett would benefit from this excursion and realised the kids were growing up so would not want to accompany us much longer.

We flew from Billings to California where we hired a car and headed off to our site. The scenery along the way was majestic, picture postcard perfect, the climate was pleasant. We all enjoyed the route, Phil drove, looking very smug. On the way we played old family music and had a sing song. We stopped to eat and use the facilities. Located off the scenic Pacific Coast highway, five miles from Topanga Beach, we arrived at our destination and received a warm welcome which included a delicious cool drink and some fruit.

We were shown to our luxurious private camp site. Our host told us that their version of camping was to experience the splendour of the outdoors with creature comforts including a hot shower, continental breakfast, complimentary wine and a hot tub under the stars!

We were close to trendy shops and a choice of beautiful local beaches. There were mountain bike tracks and horseback riding trails. The advertisement poster said: 'Rise and stroll with the sun or challenge yourself to a walk to the sunset with stunning views of the ocean! Try hiking, horse riding, or spoil yourself with some pampering or spa treatments in Malibu, a half hour drive. You will also find yoga and Pilates sessions.

Our accommodation had everything we could ask for. Breakfast was provided and we could order picnics. Meals were available to order or eat in, but Phil said we should be flexible and eat when we needed to without time constraints. I accepted somebody else providing my food even when it was substandard. This was my vacation and I planned to make the most of it.

With hiking, horse riding, kite surfing, nature walks, paddle boarding, surfing on beautiful local beaches, we explored and paced ourselves, one day at the coast, one day around the site hiking or having adventures. The kids made friends and played ball games or chilled in the evenings. There was local entertainment after dinner if we wanted it, or we could relax and listen to the evening sounds over a glass of wine. We loved everything and settled into the lifestyle.

I fell for Phil again, he looked fit with his tan and curls. As a family we had never been so relaxed and content. Scarlett made friends with the son of a neighbouring family and we were pleased to see her hanging out with him. A couple of girls took a shine to Eithan and called for him when we were at home. Some of the parents were friendly and we ate together on a couple of occasions. The scenery was spectacular, the sunsets dazzled and the sea sparkled. We did not want to go home.

Camping has turned off some adventurers who would enjoy this upscale version. It was delightful to go on adventures in breath-taking places then return to a cosy bed with a real mattress. We could order gourmet meals and have a roaring campfire prepared in advance if desired. Alternatively, we could enjoy the privacy and romance of our own secluded world. A family could get used to gracious living but all too soon we had to go home.

It was hard to settle down again, I had forgotten how much effort was required to meet all the demands. My staff also had leave scheduled so it was my turn to work extra hours. After a few hours I felt ready for another vacation. I told Phil to buy a winning lottery ticket, but he kept picking the wrong ones. Scarlett had decided to do a project about Lawrence Allbrite, the town's founder, so she was busy with her research. Eithan played keyboard with some friends in a garage trying to form a group. Phil played baseball with his buddies and I baked and cooked as usual.

Eric's Reunion

I made friends with my landlord's family who were a great help to me. Maybe because I didn't quibble over the rent, paid regularly and gave them a hand with the crops, they invited me for meals, looked after my belongings when I travelled and gave me good advice. My place was my base. I had to move around to get decent shots to earn my living. I was building a portfolio of shots showing life in Guatemala for a potential book. If anything interesting was happening in the region, my new family told me.

When Mama told me that Ryan was volunteering in the highlands of Guatemala building a school, I admit I was very surprised. I wondered what Marie thought about it. My new family asked me where my brother was. The contact Mama gave me, a Mrs Parks, told me the address which I showed to the landlord. Ricardo, the teenage son who spoke pidgin English told me it was very far, on the other side of the country.

"You want go see your brother?" Ricardo asked me.

"Sure, if it's possible, how do I get there?" I asked.

After some rapid-fire discussion, Ricardo offered to drive me there for a sum if I paid for the gas too. To my surprise Theresa, his very attractive sister, wanted to come with us. She needed her father's permission. I really fancied Theresa but I was very careful to be a perfect gentleman in her presence. In their custom I would have to court her and marry her, so I kept my feelings circumspect. Theresa said she would come and help the volunteers with the cooking. The landlord agreed provided Ricardo chaperoned her. We shook hands and I got excited at the prospect. They told me to bring my warm clothes and keep my hat on.

Although most of Guatemala was safe, there were areas where gringos were not popular and I could get kidnapped or into trouble. Some groups did not like Americans. At night I avoided going far or wandering alone. Ricardo said I would sit next to him in the truck with my hat pulled down, Theresa would be by the window. If we were stopped, I should remain quiet. We were not expecting any trouble, but Ricardo took a rifle and ammunition just in case. I kept my passport and permit documents on me. I paid for provisions to take with us on the journey.

Theresa said it was her first trip away from home and she was so happy her father had agreed to let her go. I told her in my country women did not need to ask permission, men and women were equal.

"Not here," she said, "women here have no freedom. You go to school for three years then you help the family, get married and produce children. If you are lucky the husband treats the woman good."

"Do you choose your own husband?" I asked.

"Sometimes si, sometimes the girl's father chooses. Is not like movies no?" she smiled.

"Will you be getting married soon then?" I asked her innocently.

"Are you asking?" Theresa smiled her eyes flashing good humour.

"I think you can do better than me," I said smiling.

"I lucky because my father say I get married when I ready because my father special man," Theresa said.

"How old are you?" I asked

"Nearly 18, so I must be getting married soon."

"Don't you want to do something first like work or career?" I asked puzzled.

"What is career? Ah you mean like teacher or something? No, I cannot do studies for working. I have to help my family, so I stop school after third grade."

"Would you like to do something different?" I asked.

Theresa shrugged her shoulders and smiled enigmatically.

"Here woman does as her father then her husband says," Ricardo said.

"It is very different in America," I told him.

"Yes, your women are like men, like to boss and make trouble to get their way," Ricardo said.

"Not all of them," I said thinking I should change the subject.

We drove along viewing the countryside, watching people working in the fields, admiring the landscapes. It was lush fertile land with crops flourishing. I imagined it was back-breaking work, but the locals were used to it. At meal times we ate simple food and slept under the stars rolled in blankets. The old battered truck was our shelter and shade. We had a few boxes of corn in it to look like country farmers. If we didn't sell the goods on the way, we would give them to the volunteers. Ricardo said he would look around when we arrived to see the work potential.

After two nights camping, having taken a scenic route the land became hilly then mountainous in the distance with lush vegetation and tropical growth. It was also cooler the higher we climbed. Finally, we arrived at the village where the building was taking place. I could not visualise Ryan there, it was very basic. It seemed that several buildings were being constructed in various stages. Ricardo spoke to a village elder who pointed where we were to go. It was like a scene from an exotic movie, I bade them wait while I stepped out to take a few shots.

Ryan was in the mess having his evening meal when I walked in and slapped him on the shoulder. He nearly fell off his chair with astonishment. Mama did not tell him I would be visiting him. I introduced him to Ricardo and Theresa, and he invited us to pull up some chairs and join him. We were all tired and hungry, so we set to.

Before we could catch up on family news, I told Ryan I was there to help him, Theresa offered to help prepare the food, Ricardo was looking for paid work. We had some corn to donate and some to sell. I could see Ryan was impressed, especially when I spoke in my basic Spanish. The first evening felt surreal. I bunked down with Ryan in his room. The other two went off with the supervisor to find digs. Ryan and I caught up on the family news as best we could and had a late night.

Next morning, after breakfast Ryan took me round the buildings explaining what they were doing. He was involved in the furnishings and fittings, I said I would assist him as Poppa had taught us both. In addition to the school there were dormitories, a health centre and a civic hall, plus toilet blocks for both genders. Ryan had only been there for a few weeks and found the locals friendly but reserved. He thought it was because of the language barrier. I told him that the people needed to get used to foreigners and feel they could be trusted. After all they had suffered, it was natural to be reserved.

Before the project started people lived in meagre huts which were often overcrowded, and many were without electricity. Children and adults were getting sick but there were no vaccines or medicines because there was no refrigerator to keep them. At night they were burning kerosene. The charity raised money to purchase solar panels which allowed villagers to expand their access to electricity. A solar powered water pump was installed generating clean water from underground. One water pump brought water to seven villages as it flowed up to four kilometres. By bringing clean water and power to the village and providing education, we were helping to break the cycle of poverty.

Children were able to go to school and the villagers were healthier. They could grow vegetables and their own food all year round. Some sold vegetables and fruit to the local market. Women were able to sell their handicrafts to become financially independent. I realised how much we took for granted in our safe comfortable lives and felt proud of my brother for volunteering.

Candice had supplied school uniforms in various sizes. Dan had sent patterns for basic furniture using simple designs. Marie had rallied round with clothes, toys and bedding from her area. These were waiting with the uniforms until a convey could be delivered from Mrs Parks. In Allbrite our women had appealed for warm clothing and goods to be collected for Guatemala, so more would follow.

The weather varied and when it rained it was torrential and flood-inducing. It could be very cold or baking hot. I found it hard to adjust when I first arrived and got insect bites. Ryan had also been bitten but he seemed to cope. It reminded me of our youth, me following Ryan's lead. As kids I used to copy him the best I could. He was my big brother. I asked Ryan if he ever thought of moving back to Allbrite, but he said his business and his life were in Canada now. Marie still had her elderly parents to look after. Canada had been good to him. His girls knew English and French, it was very cosmopolitan there.

Allbrite held fond memories for Ryan. He asked about my future plans and if I thought about settling down. To be honest, I did not know how to answer. My passion remained photography. When I was focused on my work, I lost sight of everything else. I was my own worst critic, always aiming for perfection. Travelling around like a nomad suited me. I disliked possessions and routines, they made me feel trapped. The thought of living in one place with a repetitive lifestyle depressed me. I did not feel fulfilled and kept an open mind. I had not discovered my reason for being yet.

Ryan asked about women. I told him I had been close to marriage with a beautiful woman but could not commit myself, so I moved on. He asked if I did not regret it. I said I did every day, but she deserved more than I could give her. We worked, ate, drank bottled beer, made good progress and Ryan's month was up. He rang home to say he would be away for three months to finish the task. Marie was upset but Ryan talked her round. I reckoned Ryan felt stimulated by the challenge and understood his need to complete his part of the task.

We took photos and I rang home. Ricardo had found himself some work and Theresa seemed happy to work in the kitchen. They were waiting for me to decide when we would return. I felt I would hang around until Ryan left. Although we worked long hours and it was physical, there was satisfaction and teamwork. On a Saint's day we had celebration food and a party with music and folk dancing. The locals got dressed in their finery. Spirits were passed around and a good time was had by all. I picked up some of the local dialect although they spoke too fast for me.

I liked Guatemala but knew I would not be staying. Whilst I was there, I missed work opportunities. In my profession I needed to put myself out to get the best jobs. I planned to go back to Allbrite to see Mama, but I got an opportunity to go to Columbia. Ryan told me I picked all the best places to visit and warned me to be careful. I promised to avoid the drugs.

When our work took shape we stood back to admire it. Good carpentry skills meant low maintenance and durability. Whilst we had to make do with tools and equipment, our work was not shoddy. We were proud of our achievements and hoped they would stand the test of time. Ryan and I were given a celebratory meal and party send off with grateful thanks. We hugged and left simultaneously, he went his way, I left with Ricardo and Theresa to finish up at my lodgings before flying to Columbia. It seemed that Theresa had attracted an admirer who was going to ask permission from her father to court her. Her eyes sparkled whilst she told me about him. Ricardo had vetted him and pronounced him as acceptable.

On our return to the village I took small gifts for the family, collected my stuff, gave some away, then caught a flight to Columbia where I used discreet equipment to take my shots. Fortunately, I had to focus on flowers and fauna, it was a nature assignment. I was conscious of invisible surveillance all the time and felt relieved to keep the trip short and fly out. I decided to go home to Allbrite for some rest and recreation. Some souvenirs from my travels would make little gifts for my nephews and nieces who must have grown in my absence. I had travelled widely and made some good friends, now I needed to touch base in my home town.

Allbrite seemed to spread each time I returned. There were new housing developments and shops. Street cafes and fast food outlets seemed more numerous and our furniture stores looked very stylish. I reckoned Candice was still involved in the décor. I couldn't wait to see all the family. To my dismay I had missed Mama who was on her hike. I decided to wait until she returned so she could tell me all about it. I had enough money to live on and no tempting work assignments to call me away. It was time to play with the kids, flirt with my sisters-in-law, look up my buddies and generally annoy everybody by remaining footloose and fancy free whilst they were hunkered down with mortgages and families.

I was having dinner at Dan and Claire's one evening with a group of their friends including a firecracker called Betsy Levine who worked with Claire. This woman was opinionated, irritating and a political activist. On hearing about my travels this Betsy challenged me with imagined conceptions that bore no resemblance to reality. I am easy going most of the time, but this woman really bugged me. My meal with friends turned into a stand-off so being well brought up, I conceded the point and bid everyone farewell. I don't know what was said after my departure but I was annoyed to find the woman on my doorstep bright and early next morning.

"Eric I know you are in there," I heard as I stumbled downstairs.

There was Betsy Levine, dressed for work and obviously in a rush.

"I just wanted to apologise to you for last night," she said breathlessly. "I had too much to drink and I was out of order."

"Yes, you were," I agreed rubbing my stubble and conscious of my old night attire.

"OK let's put it behind us and then we can be friends," Betsy said smiling.

"I have enough friends, I don't need more," I replied.

"Oh, Mr Grumpy in the morning, huh? I was hoping you would tell me all about your travels, I really am interested," she said shuffling her feet.

"I don't think so," I told her.

"Oh, I don't mean now silly, ask me for a date."

Flabbergasted I staggered backwards and shook my head.

"OK I have to go to work now, I'll be in touch and we can sort something out," she said waving gaily as she sprinted off to her car.

"Don't bother," I told her, retreating, seriously tempted to take off myself.

I had not been pursued by a woman for years and was out of touch. Normally, I called the shots when I was interested in a woman. I felt on the defensive with this female harridan and planned to enlist Claire to put her off. Claire was no help at all, she was amused and told me Betsy was very attractive.

"She may be attractive, but somebody ought to tell her it is not seemly to chase a man. If he's interested, he will make a move," I said indignantly. "Especially first thing in the morning before a man is dressed."

"It depends on the man," Claire giggled.

"Claire, I need you to put a stop to this, you know I am a nomad …"

"Maybe Betsy can go with you, she can carry your camera case," Claire suggested.

"That is so not funny," I said.

"Come on Eric, be flattered she fancies you."

"Tell her I am not a free agent," I replied.

"Tell her yourself," Claire said moving away laughing.

With Mama away I had the house to myself and planned not to open the door. Family members had their own keys and I was not expecting anyone else. I kept the blinds closed and tried to keep a low profile. During the day I felt safe as I knew Betsy would be working. Allbrite is not the largest town so I expected Betsy would manage to find me eventually. I thought she would come by the house so took to parking cautiously. Ms Levine caught me grocery shopping late one night and cornered me in the dairy section. She flushed and kissed me on both cheeks before I could escape.

"Can we start over?" she asked me. "I really loved the pictures you took on the flowers and fauna of Columbia."

"How did you see them?" I asked, surprised.

"I enquired about you and checked out your recent work plus the family showed me stuff."

"I'm very flattered," I said.

"So you should be, when you're done with your groceries how about we go for coffee?" she asked.

"Didn't your momma tell you not to chase men?" I asked.

"Phew if I wait for you to chase me, we'll get nowhere," Betsy said scornfully.

"Where exactly do you think we will be getting?" I asked her nastily.

"Eric my dear, just wait and see, now are you done?" she asked smiling.

"You are a pain in the ass, why don't you leave me alone?" I said annoyed.

"Stop playing Mr Grumpy again, I know you don't mean it," she said playfully.

"How do I get rid of you? I don't want your attentions thank you," I said moving away.

"Have coffee with me, we can chat and then I will go away," she suggested.

"Is that a promise? You will leave me alone?" I asked.

"Of course," Betsy said leading the way to the supermarket café.

"Can I have that in writing?" I asked following her, admiring her pert behind.

"Eric sweetie, you have met your match and you just don't know it yet," she said calmly.

I didn't know whether to laugh or cry, I wanted to run but my feet seemed to be glued to the ground. Maybe this was a family set up to try to ground me. Suddenly in need of coffee, I thought I would sit this one out, let her talk and figure out what was going on. Betsy Levine could certainly talk and some of her conversation was thought-provoking. She was an intelligent woman, ambitious, well read and when she wasn't in pursuit of me, quite an interesting person.

I asked why she was chasing me. She told me I lived out of the box, she liked that. She was unconventional and found my lack of commitment stimulating. I told her she would not change me. Betsy said she did not want to, she wanted me to show her how to be more like me. This lady was dangerous.

Dan the Man

My life seemed to be divided into three main parts: my family were the most important, work occupied most of my time, and then sport. I loved sport and encouraged our boys to join me playing or spectating. We tuned into the sports channel and went to matches when we could. Claire had her own TV and girlfriends, she was not enthusiastic especially when all the dirty kit needed washing. She said it kept us out of mischief, so she did not complain.

Business was thriving, we got two big contracts which meant expansion and more recruitment. One was to furnish all the show houses and apartments in and around Allbrite. The second was more lucrative concerning municipal buildings and refurbishments. Our range expanded to cope, Candice kept us updated on trends and décor pieces. We also had a work experience segment with local schools and a few young apprentices.

The shed Poppa had carved his original work in had long been discarded for more modern factory accommodation. I told Claire we were able to move to a bigger house if she wanted. We thought about it and went to see some houses. In the end we preferred the high ceilings and spacious rooms in our current home located in a convenient place that suited us. We decided to stay and replace the old shed with a guest/games extension to our home and to landscape the grounds. I drew a plan and got a team assembled.

We had a pool table, TV, sofa, bar, bathroom, bedroom and even a computer facility. A sound system was installed and fancy lighting for parties. The guest suite was comfortable with patio doors overlooking the yard. Claire was pleased to get all her men out of the house. It meant we could have guests or people staying over. The boys loved it and showed off with their friends.

Claire told me Eric was being pursued by Betsy Levine. I laughed and told Claire she was heading for disappointment.

"I wish her luck," I told Claire.

"Yes, but I think she is serious, she told me Eric was the one for her," Claire said.

"Have you ever seen Eric make a commitment with a woman?" I asked.

"No, but he's still here," Claire replied.

"Yes, because he's waiting for Mama to return," I said.

"Betsy seems very determined," Claire stated.

"Eric's a big boy now he can handle it, if she bugs him, he will take off," I said confidently.

"She's very attractive," Claire said.

"Not very feminine though is she, Eric usually goes for the gentle type."

"Let's wait and see."

Ollie had food allergies which caused him a range of symptoms including mild rashes, hives, itching and swelling. We had him tested and found he was allergic to cow's milk, so we had to watch his diet and gave him something to carry around with him to show when eating out. The doctor told us that people he was missing the enzyme lactase which breaks down lactose, a sugar found in milk and dairy products. As a result, Ollie was unable to digest these foods which caused him to experience nausea, cramps, gas, bloating and diarrhoea. It was not a life threatening condition.

We were lucky there were so many lactose-free products on the market. It meant reading the labels on all the foods, but we adjusted and Ollie maintained a healthy diet without feeling deprived. I imagine in the past it would have been difficult.

Both boys had healthy appetites. Claire said they needed horses feeding bags round their necks as they could eat non-stop. I said they were growing active boys and needed their fuel. I was proud of them and wanted them to grow up strong men.

As stand-in coach at school matches and supervising the apprentice scheme at work, I had regular contact with the school. My boys seemed to be doing OK in different directions. Leo seemed to be aiming for a sporting scholarship and wanted sport to become his career. Ollie was artistic and had a flair for design. I had visions of him designing our furniture ranges because he had a unique style. We would adapt to cater to his designs. Ollie was more like Poppa, he was a stylish craftsman. He wanted to become an architect. I told him that had been my Poppa's dream but he had never had the opportunity to pursue it. It was early days for both, they could change their minds. I just wanted them to lead happy fulfilled lives.

Instead of a fancy vacation like other members of our family, Claire and I toured Montana and went camping and fishing. Claire caught up with her reading and sunbathing. We all went swimming, hiking, had barbecue suppers and went to a few line dances and hoe downs along the way. It was relaxing and the weather was kind to us. Our free time was limited because Claire had commitments to her parents. Her father had been diagnosed with early stage dementia, so Claire wanted to keep in close contact in case her mother needed help. We were saddened by the news as we all got along well.

In the summer when families went on vacation, I planned new lines for the following year. Christmas was a time for refurbishment, so I kept abreast of furniture trends and liaised with Candice who actually came home, hung around and seemed to be planning a return. This was unusual, Candice did not get homesick she could not leave Allbrite fast enough.

Perhaps age was making her sentimental, although she still looked about 20 tops. Maybe the fancy jet set she mixed with was too shallow and she needed some genuine hometown experiences to set her straight. We were certainly an assorted bunch. In our family everybody was different.

Claire worked hard and looked after her parents as well as taking flowers round to Mama's. Each week she met her girlfriends in town and they had fun. People liked Claire, she had a very warm pleasing personality. Charities targeted her because she was a soft touch. The boys adored her and I knew I was a lucky man. We got on well, Claire did not shout or nag, we didn't always listen to her but fell in with her requests because we wanted to please her.

Most nights we kept up with the news and saw the Berlin Wall crumble, were shocked by the Challenger explosion and Chernobyl. Britain had defeated Argentina in a war about the Falklands identity. Astronaut Sally Ride became the first American woman in space. Mikhail Gorbachev became the Soviet leader. Indian Prime Minister Indira Gandhi was assassinated by two Sikh bodyguards. There was the Exxon Valdez Oil Spill and a new disease called Aids which had no cure. Mount St. Helens erupted and John Lennon was assassinated. Ronald Reagan was elected. President. From 1980 to 1988 there was the Iran-Iraq war. Iraq used illegal chemical weapons to kill Iranian forces and against its own Kurdish populations.

In different parts of the world there were bombs and violence. There were a series of terrorist attacks on airplanes and a cruise ship. Terror could strike anywhere at any time. It was a war where the enemy were disguised as fellow citizens. Nothing was sacred, there were no age limits. Vigilance was called for at home, in school and we tried to be cautious.

Another aspect of modern living was the number of paedophiles being reported in churches, boarding schools, scouts' groups, it was a plague. We told our children to be wary of strangers. I told my children that for safety they needed to connect with people they knew or had requested information from. They should not accept lifts or go off with strangers however tempting.

Modern living was more luxurious than when I grew up but fraught with dangers that didn't exist before. There was little privacy and more surveillance. I imagined it must be hard being famous as celebrities were on show and watched wherever they went. Claire told me I was getting old. I heard about identify thefts because people were too open and free with their belongings and trash.

Meanwhile famine raged in Africa, viral infections spread in new countries, terrorists kidnapped people for ransom, floods, earthquakes and natural disasters were reported, ice caps were melting. I was grateful to be alive and leading a comfortable life in the assumed safety of Allbrite. There were more exciting places, more challenging lifestyles but Allbrite offered enough for me. When I had to travel for work as we expanded the business, it always felt good to come home.

We didn't win the lottery, we didn't mix with high society, we dressed comfortably, sometimes we over indulged, our house was clean and homely, we led simple lives. Occasionally, I did some woodwork carving to keep my hand in. It was useful to create unique presents. I had always fancied trying my hand at extreme sports, but with a family to protect I kept that to myself. If I had my time over, I would probably do the same again. Not many people could say that.

225

Candice Yearns

Dr Wood was very easy to talk to. He made me laugh and I found myself talking more than usual. I asked him to tell me about his daughter Zoe who was in Jake's class. He was obviously very proud and protective of her. I told Dr Wood that I was going back to LA shortly for work commitments, but I would be returning to visit Mama after her hike. Perhaps Zoe could suggest a movie to go to, I could take the boys for a treat and maybe he could take Zoe. I figured if he accepted, it would be a good ice breaker if I met Zoe when I was with our boys. Dr Wood said he would mention it, made his apologies and left me.

This was a new experience for me. Normally men ran after me, asked me out or wanted to sleep with me. Dr Wood made no moves at all, he was courteous, polite and showed no reciprocal interest or curiosity. This bugged me, had I lost my touch? Why didn't he want me? Did I come on too strong? Was I losing the plot? I returned to LA, but I could not get Dr Wood out of my mind.

When I returned to work, I was inundated with designing for the new season, updating our catalogues, new suppliers, sample materials, it all needed my attention. Henry was thriving, his designs were selling as fast as he could produce them, he had a new boyfriend he wanted to tell me about in detail and my office manager had documents to sign and queries. I didn't have time to daydream and thought I must have had a holiday meltdown. Despite my activity, I still thought about Dr Wood before I went to sleep.

All my life I had been noticed, often wooed and pursued. To be ignored was a new experience and indifference was unusual. Perhaps my interest in the good doctor was the novelty of me making the moves. I remembered he had lovely eyes with long lashes and a warm kind smile. He was probably still in love with his late wife. I could not hope to attract him by chasing him, plenty of other women had tried. To get his attention I would need a careful plan. If he really didn't care I would lose, but first I needed to try. It hurt my vanity and upset me to know that there was one man I couldn't attract. I found that I wanted his attention and that hurt.

My work kept me busy all hours, there were fashion shoots, a show to prepare for, end of season ranges to put on sale, and hours flew by. If my staff forgot to feed me, I carried on regardless. Sometimes I slept on the office sofa in reception because I was too tired to go home. My theme for the Fall was nostalgic and made me think of firesides and cosy evenings.

Once Mama returned, I would book my flight back home and tackle Dr Wood face on. I would invite him and Zoe to the movies, in fact I would call and ask to speak to her first. Zoe could recommend something, and I could invite her to join us. She may want her father to accompany her.

Mama decided to stop off on the way home for a few days, so I had the house to myself. Eric planned to return after his latest assignment. The evening I settled in I rang Dr Wood. He sounded pleased to hear from me, I asked if Zoe was in. He called her and passed the phone over.

"Hi Zoe, my name is Candice O'Brien, aunty to Hal, Jake, Leo, Ollie, Scarlett and Eithan. Your father kindly helped me when Jake hurt himself recently."

"Hi," said Zoe shyly.

"I was wondering Zoe, if you could recommend a good movie? I want to treat the kids to a movie as a surprise outing, but don't know what's good."

Zoe suggested a popular new film.

"Is it playing right now?" I asked her.

"I think so," she said, "I can check."

"Ok that's good, would you like to come too, with or without your father of course?" I suggested.

"I'm not sure, I'll ask him, hold on a moment please."

I heard her asking her father.

"When do you want to go?" Zoe asked me.

"I'll have to check their schedules and call you back. I do hope you can come and not leave me with all the boys. It would be cool to have some female company," I said.

"Ok, I'll wait to hear from you," Zoe said and put the phone down.

The movie theatre was showing the film on a regular sequence so I rang Linda who told me Jake could go, but Hal had music stuff to go to. Claire said Ollie could go, Leo was going with scouts. Finally, I called Tilly who said to check with Phil. Scarlett could go and Eithan wasn't home, but they could meet us in the foyer. I rang Zoe back and told her Scarlett could come. There was a pause and Zoe said:

"I don't really know Scarlett well, she's one of the cool girls, she may not want to go with me," Zoe said shyly.

"Of course she will," I said, my heart going out to Zoe in her wistfulness. "You are similar ages and Scarlett is a good girl, a bit bossy but she has a good heart. Please say you will come Zoe and you can choose your own ice cream."

"Daddy doesn't let me have much ice cream," Zoe said.

"Is daddy there? Put him on and I will ask his permission. Will you come then Zoe?" I asked.

"Ok what time will you pick me up?"

"I'll arrange the time with your father, can you put him on please?"

"Bye" said Zoe handing over to Dr Wood.

"Hello Candice," said Dr Wood with a smile in his voice.

"Hello Daddy Wood, please may I take Zoe to the movie with my nephews and niece?"

"Are you sure you can manage them all?" he asked.

"Please feel free to join us if you want to," I suggested.

"I'd love to but I have evening surgery, it's my turn on the rota. I can meet you outside to pick Zoe up afterwards," he said.

"Ok then. One more thing, can Zoe choose an ice cream at the theatre because I will be getting the others?"

"Yes she can, allow me to pay for the ice creams for them all, it's the least I can do," he said.

"I wouldn't hear of it, this is my treat," I told him.

"With so many children having dental treatment very young these days, I try to be careful with Zoe's teeth, so I restrict her input of sweet things. Are you going to buy big tubs of snacks or packets of candy?" he asked.

"Just the ices, it reminds me of my youth. If we were good we got a lolly or a tub as a treat when we went to the movies," I said sighing.

"Me too from the lady in the front stalls carrying a tray," he laughed.

"How times have changed," I said. "Ok I had better get a move on, shall I pick Zoe up at yours?" I asked.

"Ok, how about 6 o'clock?" he asked.

"Sure, just tell me your address," I said, pretending I had not checked it out and memorised it.

I called for Zoe who looked excited and adorable, obviously trying her best to look cool. We were meeting the others in the foyer so we travelled down companionably. Scarlett smiled at Zoe and engaged her in conversation immediately as if they were old friends. The boys followed behind the girls and I sat at the end. When I picked Zoe up, she was waiting with a neighbour who sometimes looked after her, so I hadn't seen her father. I couldn't wait until the movie finished so I could see Dr Wood again. I wanted to see if he really was worth all the fuss I was making. Inside I had butterflies. This had not happened to me before.

We came out of the theatre to find Linda talking to Dr Wood. I hugged Linda and wished I could hug Dr Wood who pecked me on the cheek. Linda was taking all our family home and I felt redundant. Dr Wood invited us all to stop off for a drink on the way home. Thankfully Linda had to be somewhere, so she declined. I arranged to meet Zoe and her father in a Diner car park down the street. My heart was beating fast and I wasn't sure I could drink. This felt very strange and unusual. In my teenage years I had always been confident.

I took a deep breath before getting out of the car. We walked inside together like a family of three, I thought as I saw our reflection. Zoe was telling her father about the movie. I found myself unable to look the doctor in the eye. My cheeks felt flushed and I wanted to hide. Dr Wood was asking me polite questions about my work, how long I was staying, how my mother enjoyed her trip etc.

I swallowed and mumbled short responses like an idiot. This was torture, I wanted to tell him I thought he was very special but couldn't. Thankfully Zoe was a regular chatterbox and kept the conversation flowing. Dr Wood was scrutinising me so I drank up, stood up abruptly, thanked Zoe for her company and fled.

When I got back to Mama's I had a shower to cool down, sat in my night attire and was unable to move. Dr Wood rang me about an hour later to thank me for taking Zoe and asking if anything was bothering me. He asked if his company had spoiled the outing for me. Shocked I blurted out that his company seemed to have the opposite effect on me.

"What do you mean?" he asked anxiously.

I was so hyper I confessed that since I met him over Jake's accident, I had been thinking about him. This had not happened to me before, so I could not understand why he kept entering my thoughts. I know women had pursued him because he was a good catch, but I had never chased a man in my life and did not mean to do so. I apologised but seeing him again this evening had disturbed me so much I couldn't handle it so had to get away.

There was a brief silence before he asked me: "Well Candice, what do you suggest we do about it?"

"You're the doctor, you should know how to handle foolish women," I said.

"I don't know any foolish women," he replied.

"Well maybe if you just ignore me, I will go away again," I suggested.

"I don't want you to go away Candice. I thought your life was in LA with the jet set. I imagined you inundated with guys, I never imagined for one second that you could even notice me. I'm just a humble widowed doctor."

"I didn't notice you, I feel like I absorbed you into my system, isn't that strange? What's your diagnosis?" I asked him.

"I think some TLC may be in order but tell me Candice, are you planning on sticking around? Whilst I can handle absences it would not be fair to Zoe if you came into our lives then just took off one day. Please think carefully before you reply. We have said enough for tonight. This is too important to be hasty. Think about the type of future you want. If you decide to stick around, I am ready to get to know you and perhaps take this further. I am not speaking lightly, if you take me and Zoe we will offer you commitment, so this is serious. Goodnight Candice."

"Goodnight," I said putting the phone down.

The conversation left me stunned. I had no idea what I wanted. My career had taken off because I made sure to be in the right places at the right times. True I could design anywhere these days, but being successful meant being seen and active. Would I be content to return to Allbrite? My business was thriving and I could target the States and do global business without being based in LA. Could I maintain my allure from a distance? Did I want to settle down? Could I form a serious relationship? I didn't even know the doctor yet, but I knew that he would not fool around. I would consult Mama when she returned, she would know.

On impulse I called Henry but remembered he had gone on vacation with his new love and probably switched off his phone. I couldn't speak to any of the family. In a few days I needed to return to LA. Meanwhile, I needed to get on with the new designs pending a big fashion show. It was hard to concentrate. Dr Wood had not propositioned me or flirted in any way, he did nothing to contact me, I was the one who made all the moves. Why couldn't I let the poor man carry on in peace? What was so special about him? Just the thought of him made me shiver, perhaps I was ailing. I had never felt so obsessed about anybody before and I didn't like it.

Work helped but did not distract me enough. I had no answer and tried to think about my future but could not focus. Did I want to be this independent career woman all my life? Was success worth the effort? Could I see myself as a potential wife and mother? This frightened me because part of me responded favourably. This was so out of character, I couldn't handle it. If Mama did not return in the next two days, I would be off again. In LA I may be able to focus again and get my priorities. In Allbrite I hid in the house, afraid to go out in case I saw him again or the family noticed.

Mama did not return so I flew back to LA where I was restless, I could not settle and annoyed all my staff for being vague and inconsistent. When Henry returned bronzed and loved up, I hugged him and burst into tears. We were both astonished at my tears.

"Candice I didn't know you had it in you," Henry said patting my back.

"Had what?" I sobbed.

"I didn't know you could cry. What's happened?" he asked anxiously. "There, there stop wetting my new Ralph Lauren shirt," he said hugging me.

"I can't think straight anymore. I don't know what I want," I sobbed.

Henry sat me down, poured me a brandy and asked what the problem was. When he heard it concerned a man, he heaved a sigh of relief. The business was safe, the designs were taking shape, so man trouble seemed a relief.

"Candice O'Brien in all the years I've known you, I've never seen you upset about a man. That's usually my stance," he said smiling. "Who is he and what's he done?"

"It's not funny," I sniffed, "He's a lovely kind man, a doctor widowed with a daughter and he doesn't mess about."

"So, what's the problem?" Henry asked.

"He hasn't made any moves, I've been chasing him and using his daughter to get to him. She's a lovely girl by the way. When I see him I melt. Anyhow he's told me he won't get to know me unless I stay around."

"You mean he's not swooning at your feet or behaving like your admirers so that bugs you? Do you want to move back to Allbrite? You could work from there and fly back for events, it's not so bad," Henry said reflectively.

"I don't know what I want," I said angrily.

"Drink your brandy and take some time out, he didn't give you a deadline, did he?"

"No, he didn't give me anything, no promise, no attention just courtesy," I complained.

"Hah lady Candice must have found that very confusing," Henry said smiling.

"Don't you start," I said rising.

"Chill Candy girl and get on with your work. Let a solution find you," Henry suggested.

"Do you mind, I've got work to do," I said settling down at my studio desk.

"Just tell me his name so I can look him up," Henry said leaving.

I gave him the finger, he chuckled and went away. He offered me sound advice, so I focused on my work and stayed around the clock until my staff told me to go home to sleep and shower. They said I smelled and looked like a tramp. If any business came snooping, they would think I was a bag lady. Reluctantly, I went home and crashed for about twelve hours. The 'phone woke me up mid-morning, it was Mama home again, sorry to have missed me and full of excitement about her trip. I let her ramble on until she ran out of steam.

"Candice are you ok? It's not like you to be so quiet," Mama eventually asked.

"I think I've fallen in love Mama and it hurts," I said woefully, wanting a hug.

"Wow that certainly beats my news," Mama said excitedly. "Does he feel the same?"

"I don't know but he doesn't mess about," I told her.

"So what's the problem you don't sound happy?" Mama never missed a trick.

"I would have to live in Allbrite again," I said.

"Well it's not such a bad place to live," Mama said loyally.

"He lives there and would not take me on if I kept coming and going."

"Ooh is he anyone I know?" she asked me puzzled.

"Maybe, it's Dr Wood," I sighed.

"Dr Martin Wood the widower with the daughter in Jake's class?"

"That's the one"

"But he's a widower, he's not been dating, all the single women tried, how did this happen? Are you seeing him?"

"Hardly, I'm in LA. I met him when Jake hurt himself. We get on really well, we had coffee and I invited Zoe, his daughter to see a movie with our gang."

"Very slick manoeuvre," Mama interrupted. "So?" Mama waited.

"He makes me feel alive and like a woman, he looks inside me, I just can't stop thinking about him."

"Has he made any moves on you?"

"No, he's been courteous and the perfect gentleman, that's the trouble," I confessed.

"Well honey, he's been married once and he's gonna be mighty cautious about taking on a second wife, especially one as glam as you. You are not exactly small-town material."

"Oh Mama, I don't know what to do. I don't know what I want or where my future lies. Work has always been so important and success, my whole lifestyle resolves around it. Somehow the thought of not seeing Dr Wood or being near him is unbearable. I don't know why this is happening to me. I didn't set out looking ..."

"Could the attraction be that Dr Wood is the one man who has not fallen for your charms?" Mama asked.

"No, it's because he looks beyond the exterior. When we talk it's dialogue between two people, my looks don't matter."

"Don't sell yourself short Candice, your looks could alight a movie screen," Mama said.

"What should I do Mama?"

"Take some time to think about what really matters to you. Don't do anything until you have decided. If it's meant to be, he will wait for you. He's not going anywhere. You know what he wants, so take as long as you need to know what you want. If you want to come here your room will be waiting for you."

"Don't tell the family Mama please"

"Of course not my angel, this will just be between ourselves," Mama promised.

We talked about other things and I felt marginally better. Mama and Henry both told me to weigh it up and think about the future. I absorbed myself in work with a busy couple of months and let the matter calm down. This all disintegrated when I had a call from Doctor Wood who was attending a medical conference in LA. I immediately flipped with shock and agreed to meet him for dinner at his hotel miles away. Simple things like deciding what to wear or how to put on my make-up became impossible. I wanted to look good and could not stop shaking. I called a professional make-up artiste we used to come over to fix me up. Henry offered to drive me, but I said I would not be able to get back.

"Honey you may not be coming back," he joked.

I smacked him on the back and drove myself using a highlighted map. My knees trembled when I walked into the bar. Martin was sitting there nursing a beer, his face lit up when he saw me. I wobbled over in a trance, he hugged me briefly and kissed my cheek. My breathing speeded up and it was hard to speak. Any sense I had left me. This felt so strange yet so right, it was as if we were the only people in the world.

Doctor Wood had asked my mother for my number and told her he was coming over for the medical conference. He asked Mama if she wanted him to take anything for me, so Mama dutifully complied and gave him a small packet to give me. Inside the packet was my childhood good luck locket on a gold chain that Poppa had given me. I felt emotional to see it and thanked him for bringing it.

"No problem Candice, it's a pleasure to see you again. How are you?" he asked quizzingly. "You look a bit flushed."

"It's the effect you have on me," I said trying to joke but it came out earnestly.

"Really?" he asked astonished. "Do you still feel the same way?"

"I've been trying very hard not to, but it won't go away no matter what I do," I shrugged helplessly.

"Candice, I think we need to talk," he said taking my hand and leading me out into the garden where he found a secluded bench with a spectacular view.

It felt lovely being led instead of always taking the lead. I would have walked anywhere.

"This is confidential but important. You know I have been married before. My wife was a lovely person, gentle, kind and a devoted mother. She was raised in Allbrite but originally came from Kansas, we met as students. We moved to Allbrite because it was a good career opportunity for me. I felt happy and fulfilled doing a job I enjoyed. My wife gave up her career to look after me and eventually Zoe. She wanted to act and had already been chosen for some key parts in LA. Backstage she knew all the ropes and could manage all the equipment and techniques.

In Allbrite there was not much scope then she fell sick. As a doctor there was little I could do to relieve her symptoms, I watched her worsen. It was a relief to us both when she passed. If I am honest, I can say that she was not happy living in Allbrite which is why I would never force that decision on you. Zoe was only young and was upset of course, we comforted each other. Zoe likes you and your family, she's shy and doesn't have as much freedom as other kids, so it was good of you to include her," he stopped hesitantly.

"Dr Wood..." I began.

"Martin," he interrupted.

"Martin, there's something confidential I have to tell you, something nobody knows. It's hard to say ..."

"Go on," he said taking my hand and squeezing it.

"I have had lots of admirers and escorts, would be boyfriends but I have never had a proper relationship. My career has been my focus and all my energy has been channelled into fame and fortune. Men were always available for escorting me to important events. I am tired of being told how beautiful I am, etc. it is a big turn off."

"But you are stunning, I thought you would be well out of my league," he said.

"What I am trying to say here," I swallowed staring straight ahead, "is that I am still a virgin. All these years I have saved myself for someone special. I did not want to go through the motions unless it meant something. Truthfully, I never gave anybody a chance to mean something, nobody mattered enough. Now for the first time you take my breath away and it frightens me. I don't know how to handle it," I stopped upset.

"Oh Candice," he said pulling me to my feet, gathering me in his arms and then he kissed me, gently at first and then desire flowed between us and I trembled. He had to hold me upright. It was then I knew the decision had been made, despite my attempts to ignore it.

Mama's Adventure

I was loving my adventure and bonding well with the others in the group. We sweated and struggled, moaned and strived, the banter and wit were sparkling. This experience was amazing! For me, it really was life changing and exceeded all expectations. I made a group of friends for life, pushed myself physically and mentally, but more importantly raised money for a great cause. I wanted to challenge myself and motivate myself to get fit. I tended to hang around with a guy called Frank and a woman called Sarah from Texas, as we moved at a similar pace. I slept with Sandra or with others.

At the start of the trek after breakfast we drove to Monument Valley stopping at Grand Canyon National Park for a view of this natural wonder. I felt myself leaning over as if drawn downwards. We were warned to exercise caution. Trek highlights included the scenic and spiritual heart of the Navajo nation with stunning red sandstone buttes, ancient ruins, desert sage and stately pinyon trees. We trekked across open desert paths into side canyons with dramatic rock formations. We hiked through amazing sandstone buttes and arches, stopping for a taco dinner where we learned about Navajo culture around the campfire. It was like something out of a movie. We camped that night exhausted and exhilarated.

Next day was a 12 km trek. After breakfast, we transferred to Mystery Valley to explore ancient ruins of stone dwellings, rock arts and sandstone arches from the Anasazi Indian culture over 600 years ago. In the evening we transferred to a Ranch for a dinner. The colours and scenery were stunning and the art was amazing, after so many years it was still visible. I reckoned modern art would not survive as well as this. At the ranch we were pleased to hose ourselves down, wash a few clothes and eat a delicious barbeque.

Our trip was passing too quickly. Next day we transferred through Zion Valley. Our hike took us past Weeping Rock, where water slowly percolated through sandstone walls creating lush hanging gardens. A steep ascent led to Observation point where we saw spectacular views. We viewed the valley below and glimpsed Echo Canyon with its beautiful slick rock formations and white cliffs. It was tough climbing but the view was worth it. The formations were incredible. I kept my diary record and took photos so I could remember it all. The atmosphere of the area felt special, timeless, awesome.

It was our last day, time to say goodbye to the desert and head to Las Vegas. There was an option to take a limo tour of some of the city's more iconic highlights including Freemont Street, the Las Vegas sign and the famous Strip. I went because it was my first visit to Vegas. After the serene beauty of the desert, I found it brash, artificial, busy, in my face. I guess it was interesting but I felt too old to appreciate it. A special dinner was held to toast our achievements. The following day we would all depart. I could not bear to go straight home so accompanied Sarah who was visiting her daughter in New York for a few days. I needed space to adjust.

I hugged Sarah goodbye, we promised to keep in touch. My sponsorship needed to be collected and sent in within four weeks of the end of our challenge. Once I returned from my challenge with photos and stories of bravery, I had to send a thank you to all those who had sponsored me plus a final request for support from those that had not yet got round to it. I hoped we had raised a tidy sum to benefit the charity. I sent a message to the organisers saying I had always wanted to visit the Grand Canyon, I had eaten rattle snake and taken amazing photographs. I thanked them for the most amazing adventure I have ever undertaken.

Tilly met me at the airport and filled me in whilst driving me home. She told me about their camping adventure and how it had helped Scarlett to relax. Once she explained about luxury camping it sounded ideal. I was glad they had managed to get away. Our winters were severe so it would set them up. It seemed the rest of my family were busy. I thought Tilly looked tired and hoped she was not overdoing things. She said she was always busy, she was used to it. Phil and the kids were also occupied doing their own things. Tilly always complained that there were not enough hours in the day. I told her to utilise them more carefully.

Allbrite seemed small and familiar, it was welcoming but seemed static after my nomadic existence. I returned home to a few surprises. Marshall and Linda were away on a cruise, Ryan and Eric had linked up in Guatemala. I worried about them both because it sounded a dangerous country to be in. It seemed that my two unwed children were both getting involved in potential romance.

It seemed a female colleague of Claire's was pursuing Eric with persistence. I was amazed he had not run away. It seemed he was on an assignment at present but planning to return to my house afterwards. This woman must be something special if Eric was staying around.

Candice was even more astonishing, she told me she had fallen for our Dr Wood. He seems a very pleasant man with a daughter he dotes on. I am surprised because although I like the man, I thought that Candice with her fancy lifestyle would have gone for somebody rich or famous. I cannot imagine Candice settling down in Allbrite again.

Dan and Claire had gone camping so I had no welcome home. Ryan called to make sure I was back, but we only spoke briefly because it was long distance. After being surrounded by people, I felt quite alienated to be on my own. I caught up with my laundry, rested and thought about what to do next. It occurred to me to go back to my roots and catch up with the family I had left behind. Apart from Christmas cards and birthday cards, we did not maintain contact and had few family occasions to meet at.

I made a few calls and decided to visit my sisters in turn. It was years since I had been to Idaho and wondered if our old house was still standing. I expected many changes had taken place. I thought I would wait to see the kids first, so we could catch up and compare trips. My sisters offered to accommodate me, but I decided to wait until I had firm dates. I could stay in a Holiday Inn or similar, I needed to decide how much time I wanted to spend with my sisters. It would be interesting to see how we all fared. In my head we were all girls not women in their 60s.

Candice came back first glowing and obviously in love. She barely spent any time at home and told me she had found the man of her dreams. It seemed Candice had plans to work out. I asked about Dr Wood's daughter's reaction. Candice said Zoe and she were good friends and she was a great girl. I couldn't get any more from her. I had never seen Candice besotted over anybody before, it softened her. I hoped Dr Wood would be able to handle Candice and not let her walk all over him. My daughter could be very assertive and imposing.

Next came Eric followed closely by this Betsy woman. I scrutinised Betsy to see if she was in with a chance. Eric usually fancied gentle girls. Betsy had long black wavy hair, dark almond shaped eyes and a very strong determined manner. I watched Eric with her but could not detect any romance. They conversed and Eric seemed to accept her presence as he would one of his sisters. When they left the house, they walked side by side with no close contact or touching. Eric planned to stay in Allbrite for a while to compile a book of photographs. Perhaps I was missing something.

Marshall and Linda returned glowing and relaxed. They had enjoyed their cruise and all the stop-offs. In the UK they had traced some family members and explored ancestral haunts. We exchanged photos and itineraries and had an enjoyable evening swapping experiences. Dan and Claire joined us to report on their trip and said although it was modest in comparison, they were lucky with the weather and had fun too. Tilly was always too busy to join in but sent us delicious refreshments.

Once I heard that Ryan had got home safely and knew Eric would be home, I booked to go to Idaho for a week spending half with Theresa and half with Stella. It was difficult to choose presents to take for both families, so Candice advised me. I took clothes Candice decided would be appropriate, sorted out some recent family photos and Eric drove me to catch a bus. One of them would pick me up when I returned. They all sent best wishes, I realised that my nieces and nephews had not grown up with my brood, so they were all virtual strangers which seemed sad.

Theresa met me at the station and it was good to see her. She looked the same but an older version. We had shared a bedroom and grown up together, she was a widow like me with two grown up children who had fled the nest. Her son Noah was doing something in computing in Silicon Valley; her daughter Mandy was in Nebraska involved in a social programme. I asked her if she got lonely.

"Not really, I keep busy and active," Theresa told me.

It seems Theresa did charity work and played golf. I commiserated on the loss of her husband Norman two years ago. To my surprise Theresa told me it was the best thing that happened to her. He used to hit her and abuse her, he drank and became violent. All the housekeeping money went on drink, she had to work and hide her earnings to ensure she could feed the family and pay the bills. Norman was a bad man and because of him both kids left home as soon as they could. I asked Theresa why she had not left him or asked me for help.

"In those days he was the wage earner, women weren't free like today. I depended on him, where would I go with two kids? I tried to leave but my kids needed educating and supporting. My earnings were low, I had no profession, so I was stuck. I could not ask for help for marrying a bad man. Anyhow, eventually he drank himself to death and good riddance. It made the kids more resilient and I am proud of the way they turned out."

Theresa showed me photos, they were both good looking young people. I asked if our parents had helped her. She told me they did what they could and helped with the children. Our parents did not interfere in marriages, they felt you made your own bed etc. I remembered them clearly when she said that. We reminisced en route to the small one bed apartment Theresa called home. It was simply furnished, clean and minimalist. I told her Candice would approve. I would be sleeping on the sofa, I refused to allow Theresa to give up her bedroom.

We talked non-stop, catching up on years of history. Theresa took me to my parents' graves where I left flowers. Our old house had changed almost beyond recognition. It had been expanded with new windows and doors, and had been cladded throughout with landscaped gardens. I would have walked passed it. The town centre had expanded and modernised but seemed to lack the charm of Allbrite. I told Theresa to come to visit me to meet my family. It seemed she and Stella had little in common and did not make much contact.

To visit Stella, I dressed smartly and caught a taxi from town. Stella lived in a smart suburb of Boise. She opened the door and I caught my breath. From an ambitious aspirational young girl, Stella had turned into a faded old woman. Despite her facelift and cosmetics, I saw a sad discontented expression and the beginnings of midlife spread which seemed constrained by corsetry. Stella hugged me and brought me into her show home where an old white-haired man waited on the sofa. He rose and hugged me too.

"You remember Laurence?" Stella said.

"Hi, Laurence, how are you? Thanks for having me," I greeted him, smiling.

"It's a pleasure Rachel, long time no see. Can I get you a drink?"

"Coffee would be fine but there's no rush," I said.

Stella went to get coffee, I sat down and looked around, everything was immaculate and looked unlived in. When Stella returned, I asked how their only son Bobby was.

"Robert married a Chinese girl and lives in Switzerland now. They have a daughter Poppy nearly one year old," Stella said proudly showing me a photo of a cute little girl.

"Oh lovely, so do you manage to see them?" I asked cautiously.

"They come over once or twice a year, we try to visit," Stella said.

"We keep in touch regularly," Laurence said.

"I feel lucky to see mine except for Ryan who lives in Montreal. He has two cute little girls and a lovely French speaking wife Marie."

"Isn't he the one who avoided military service?" Stella asked frostily.

"Yes, but he had his reasons," I said defensively.

The conversation was stilted, and I wondered how I would endure a few days in their company. After v they had showed me to my room, we went out for a drive whilst they showed me their locality, told me about their achievements and lifestyle and the atmosphere defrosted. Over dinner at a smart restaurant in town, we talked about how times had changed since we grew up, our former aspirations and Stella became my big sister again. Afterwards we managed to get on well enough. Laurence was always courteous and polite to me, a real gentleman.

My impression was that Stella had achieved her goal of moving away and living comfortably, she had made a career for herself as a dental nurse before her marriage, yet she seemed to be disappointed. I am not sure what she had expected but perhaps her life felt empty without her son and grandchild to keep her busy. We were never close growing up, I understood Theresa much better. Stella said she rarely saw Theresa. I felt glad to have made contact again and left it like that. I told Stella and Laurence they would be welcome to visit Allbrite to meet the family. It may be imagination, but I thought Stella gave an involuntary shudder.

Once I returned to Allbrite I decided to stay put and bond with my lively family, reunite with my friends and volunteer to do some charity work. I was a lucky woman to have such a good family on my doorstep and I really appreciated them. I also had romances to catch up on with my two single offspring. If any weddings developed, I would hopefully have more grandchildren to look forward to. My grandchildren were the joy of my life, I spoiled them, indulged them and played with them in ways I never did with my own brood. I was indeed a fortunate woman.

Ryan's Family

When I returned home and had hugged Marie until she protested, swung both girls in the air, I sensed something was wrong. Marie shook her head, so we made small talk, I gave the girls souvenirs to play with. We caught up on local news and events. After the girls went to play in their rooms, Marie told me that Chloe was being bullied. I asked her what she meant. It seemed one day when Chloe was taking her books out of her locker, Chad Jordan, one of the school jocks, accidentally bumped into Chloe making her drop all her books. Chad apologised, bent down and picked everything up with Chloe who blushed with embarrassment. He introduced himself, said sorry again, waved and went on his way.

Chloe thought nothing of it but that evening she got a message on her locker warning her to stay away from Chad Jordan. It was printed saying Chloe was a lowlife and not worthy. At first Chloe thought it was a sick joke, so she ignored it. Messages kept coming full of verbal abuse implying unpleasantness without overt threats. Chloe had no contact with Chad who was in the senior year, captain of the baseball team and good at all sports. She thought about reporting it in school but felt afraid it may make it worse.

One day when she was queuing for lunch Chad waved to her. Chloe looked around to see if he meant someone else. If he passed anywhere in Chloe's vicinity he said "Hi." Alarm bells rang in Chloe's head, she avoided eating in the school canteen, kept a low profile but despite her efforts, the messages kept coming and getting worse.

Marie noticed Chloe was pale and subdued so questioned her until she burst into tears. Unbeknown to Chloe, Marie went to the school head and complained. The head said that this abuse was a modern phenomenon, he suggested that Chloe kept close to family and friends. Chloe could come to the head at any time she felt concerned.

The head had a discreet word with Chad Jordan who was indignant and very angry, he felt protective of Chloe. He was warned not to contact Chloe again. A counsellor had a session with Chloe and suggested she wrote everything down to clear her feelings. She could start to write it all down under an anonymous name. Chloe called her story *Detresse* which was French for distress. Once she wrote down exactly what had been happening to her without mentioning names, Chloe felt lighter.

Chloe's teacher asked her permission to send her story to the local newspaper under Detresse, the teacher explained it may help other kids experiencing the same problem. A visiting journalist read the article and took it back to New York where it spread with feedback from kids suffering abuse. To Chloe's surprise people responded, and she discovered she was not alone. Many victims had fallen foul to anonymous bullies.

As Chloe's father I was enraged. Both my girls were slim and delicate, Choe was shy and quiet. How dare somebody insult her and the honour of our family. I was ready to go and knock somebody over. I told the entire family to be on lookout for any bullying. Marie calmed me down and mentioned how successful Chloe's writing had become. Apparently, by dealing with her feelings this way, Chloe was coping and comforted to find she was not unique. Indeed, her story spread and she was inundated with positive responses.

I hated the fact that this coward was going unpunished and asked the Head if I could speak at the school assembly. Chloe begged me not to, she cried and pleaded so I withdrew but the anger did not leave me. I did not blame the young man but told Chloe to hold her head up high and be proud of who she was.

I told Sophie to watch out for Chloe and to travel to school and back together if possible. Sophie should not tell Chloe that it was my request. Fortunately, both girls were close. Chloe became popular in school due to the success of her story. She was very unassuming and modest. Her writing flourished and she decided to study journalism. I figured Chloe would need more confidence in that endeavour, but always encouraged her.

At this time Marie's father died. He had been suffering from dementia and it was sad to see him decline. Sometimes he recognised us, eventually he didn't seem to. In the end he was moved to a nursing home because he was a big man who sometimes became irate and unpleasant. Marie had always been a daddy's girl, so she was very upset. My father-in-law and I had got along well, establishing a male bonding among the women. He was a decent man who had done well by his own efforts. I had admired him and promised Marie we would look after her mother.

The funeral was well attended. Mama came with Eric, Dan, Marshall and Candice. They did not stay long but paid their respects and I was touched. Mama and Marie's mother empathised well, they were both widows. Our girls were subdued and upset because their grandpa always spoilt them, they never knew Poppa. Our house was gloomy and sad, Marie was constantly popping over to her mother's. Suggestions were made for us to move in with her mother who was left alone in a big house, or her mother to move into our place. The girls could share a room. I had other ideas but decided to wait for a favourable time to say them.

I managed to talk to Eric who was still being hounded by this Betsy person. He told me she had become part of his routine, he didn't notice her any more. It puzzled me why he put up with her if he didn't want her. Eric said she was OK for conversation and she was intelligent. I asked if he was involved with her. The look of contempt Eric gave me assured me that he had not changed.

"Why does she persist when you are so not into her?" I asked him.

"Put it down to my irresistible charm," Eric replied.

I slapped him on the back and pitied the girl. Still, Eric remained in Allbrite so this Betsy must have something going for her. Allbrite was on my mind, I was thinking about opportunities there compared to Montreal. Montreal was a big beautiful city with opportunities. Sometimes I felt that perhaps we could do better in a smaller community like Allbrite. My business was well established, I could find demand anywhere. People always needed things fixing or building.

The trip to Guatemala had shown me that happiness did not depend upon possessions and being cool. With Chloe's experience in mind, I wondered if both girls could flourish better in Allbrite. I kept my thoughts to myself.

Candice rang me and we had a long conversation. She was planning to get married to an Allbrite doctor and move back home. This was amazing news and I congratulated her. She brushed aside my good wishes and told me of her plans to open a department store. In a way she was already working with Dan in the furniture business providing him with accessories and décor pieces. She planned to start a range of home furnishings.

Her plan was to have half a floor featuring room settings with all the accessories found in modern homes, the other half would have the products to make a house into a home. One floor would be divided into clothing with Henry her friend catering for the males. Candice would offer clothing to suit females of all ages. Tilly would run a coffee shop and sell food to go on another floor. Candice was offering me a chance to join in and offer maintenance services. I could also advertise in all the catering and furnishing outlets the family ran.

This was exciting news, I had money to invest. I told Candice I would be interested but needed to think about it. I asked her not to mention anything to Marie yet because she was still grieving for her father. I decided to take the whole family to Candice's wedding and rent a house for the summer vacation. Marshall could find me a decent place with an extra bedroom for Marie's mother and the family could try out life in Allbrite. Hopefully, living in the place would grow to suit them. The girls had cousins to play with. I just had to present the idea to Marie and her mother as a change of scene would do us all good.

Marie was thrilled for Candice and looked forward to meeting her groom. Candice wanted me to give her away and said our girls could be bridesmaids with Scarlett and Zoe, the doctor's daughter, so that went down well. I suggested we go down to Allbrite, rent a house and spend the summer there. Marie looked puzzled, I told her the family were considering a new venture and I may be part of it. The girls needed fittings for their bridesmaids' dresses, Marie and her mother needed to get away. It seemed an ideal opportunity.

Marie queried why we needed to stay the whole summer. I said it would be fun to get to know all the family better and explore the region, which had plenty to offer. I knew Marie was suspicious and that she wanted to support me, so she persuaded her mother to join us. In my heart I think Marie was afraid that I would go off without her if she refused. With her mother accompanying us, Marie had no worries in Montreal. My business affairs were delegated to Pete and Celia who could hire and fire. In fact, these days everything ran regardless of my presence.

It would be good to get my hands dirty again. I needed a new challenge. My girls were excited to be bridesmaids and see their cousins. I told Marshall to choose a good place, expense should not be spared, I wanted them to enjoy living there and it should be central, not out in the wilds, comfortably furnished or, if empty, to get Dan and Candice to do it tastefully in modern style.

For my part I was ready to take off immediately, but we had to wait until school ended. Marie's mother settled her affairs, arranged power of attorney to her brother and we all departed loaded with gifts and clothes for all seasons. I told the ladies to cater for all occasions, even the odd spell of cold which meant they brought some warm clothing.

My hope was to remain in Allbrite but I couldn't say so. We were all in good spirits with a wedding to go to. We sang in the car to the airport. Dan met us in a van and drove us to a spacious detached modern two storey house. Inside it was minimalist but tastefully chic enough to win approval from the ladies.

Dan drove me round to the proposed department store site and then to all the existing furniture places including the massive warehouse. I was very proud of his achievements and Candice's success which enabled them to do it. Tilly also had food outlets throughout town and was still virtually attached to her oven. They had all done well.

I told Dan about my business thriving and virtually running itself. Dan suggested I join the family and open in Allbrite which included neighbouring areas. I said I was interested but not to mention anything to my family yet, let them get used to living here. Dan smiled and understood why I had chosen the most expensive property to rent.

I rang around the women in the family and asked them to take Marie's mother under their wing and get her involved in town activities, so she could make new friends. Mama told me she would take Marie's mother to the women's groups and social events. All the girls agreed to include Marie and her mother as much as they could. Marie's mother gave Tilly some baking ideas and went into the bakery to show her some French techniques. From the bakery they went out for a meal where Marie's mum was introduced all round. Our girls were involved with their cousins so we hardly saw them. Marie was cautiously pleased if a little anxious.

Claire took Marie to her flower arranging group where to her surprise, Marie thoroughly enjoyed herself and made new friends. Marie also met a few French speakers who lived in Allbrite and invited her to go out with them. I was busy investigating business opportunities. I found a cleaning lady to maintain the house and do the laundry. She didn't have to work too hard as we were all out more than in.

Marie's mum found some ladies who played bridge, she also got involved in a local charity committee, so she found herself busy socially which relaxed her. There were no sad memories in Allbrite which she found charming.

I did not push my luck, so I said little and watched everybody settling in. Sometimes I caught up with my former buddies, we played a game of pool, had a beer or two and talked about old times. Compared to the young crowd, we were the older guys now which amused me.

It was easy to fit into old references and Allbrite ways. I felt myself relax and unwind. Montreal was familiar but Allbrite was home. My family had not complained so far but they expected to go back to Montreal. I exploited all the goodwill of my entire family to make my family feel at home too.

Marshall's Fatigue

On our cruise the next day was spent at sea, which was lucky for me because a wave of exhaustion swept over me. My head felt heavy and I thought I was coming down with something. Perhaps I had picked up a bug somewhere. Linda was very good and kept the children busy so that I could rest up. I slept like Rip Van Winkle but it did not refresh me. My legs felt wobbly so I ate in our cabin, Linda insisted I had something. I drank a lot of water and waited for it to pass. All the rest of the family felt fine, so it did not seem to be contagious.

We had booked and paid for a tour round Lisbon, Portugal so I forced myself onto the tour bus where I remained when the others got off sightseeing. The driver found me a café to rest in which was shaded. I encouraged the family to enjoy the day and not worry about me. They could fill me in on their return. Truthfully, I was relieved to be left alone, I felt feeble and just wanted to relax and nod off. Linda insisted I went to see the doctor when we returned to the ship. I am sure Lisbon was very interesting, but I just remember the waterside café and warm sunshine.

When the family returned in high spirits they joined me at the café where the boys ran around, we had a drink and waited to return. Linda called the doctor and marched me off. The boys went to the kids' club. After the doctor examined me, he thought it might be a viral infection. He advised me to rest and drink plenty. If I did not improve in a few days, I should return. My vital signs were normal and I was not in pain, just lethargic. Doctor said it was a signal to rest, I had probably done too much without realising. Sometimes changes in temperature and water can affect people.

I fell into bed determined to get my strength back. The next day we sailed so I managed to get on deck to laze in the sunshine which seemed beneficial. We arrived at Bilbao, Spain after that. As we had not booked an official tour, we left the ship and while Linda took the kids to see the Guggenheim Museum, I parked myself with my book in a street café. We headed for Casco Viejo, the Old Town, which looked fascinating. There were too many steps for me, so I waited. We all had lunch somewhere flat and enjoyed people-watching. Linda was worried about me and very sympathetic. I enjoyed the ambience and sunshine.

We saw a beautiful old building called the Arriaga Theater, everything was vibrant and lively. I really liked the place. Somebody from the ship recommended we visit the Alhóndiga which was one of the city's most iconic buildings. It used to be Bilbao's wine warehouse, today it's a cultural and leisure space with exhibitions, concerts, lectures, cinema, children's workshops, a gym, a swimming pool, a library and a place to have a coffee or eat lunch. We caught glimpses of some colourful appetising food. It was eye-catching and the boys enjoyed the visit. We caught a taxi back to the ship, once again I needed to rest.

I had a full day to recover until we reached Le Havre for our trip to Paris. The resting helped and I felt marginally better. I was pleased to have booked the official tour because it meant we would be taken to places, so I just had to sit and look. We were all excited. Paris was spectacular, just like the movies without the berets and striped jumpers. The Eiffel Tower was much bigger than we imagined, the artistes sold their pictures along the river side. We admired the shops, buildings and sights. Our tour bus drove us around the main sights. There was so much to see, we tried to absorb it all. Adrenaline kept me motivated to keep going and I managed until we returned to the ship where I went straight to bed.

The next day we arrived at Southampton, but I had to stay in bed. Linda called the doctor who visited me in the cabin. He gave me some tablets and advised rest. I told Linda to take the boys and explore. She was reluctant to leave me, but the doctor said he would keep an eye on me. We were in England and I hoped to be well enough to visit our family's ancestral homeland. The day passed swiftly, I dreamed strange things which I forgot when I woke up. I awoke briefly when the family returned then slept through the night.

Linda and the boys had gone on a trip to London where they had a whirlwind tour around the sights. The boys loved the guards outside Buckingham Palace and tried to make them laugh at Horse guards Parade. They had a quick look at the Tower and whisked around Piccadilly Circus, strolled around Trafalgar Square and bought some iconic souvenirs for presents. I was sorry to miss it as I felt sure it had been a highlight visit. They brought me a miniature bottle of brandy to buck me up. I knew that it would have been too much for me.

At Guernsey the family set off while I sat on deck wrapped up admiring the island's coastline. It looked white and pretty. The crew brought me drinks and refreshments. I think I dozed a few times and felt it was beneficial. As long as the family were having fun, I was content to stay put. I had to conserve my energy for Cork and Dublin. It seemed a bit cooler, so I went back indoors and sat in the lounge reading newspapers, talking to some of the other passengers until they returned. The next day was Cork and after that Dublin, so I was determined to go forth.

Linda's family had connections with Cork, she had traced some of her family ancestry so when we disembarked some of her distant family were there to greet us. It was very exciting for Linda and the boys. This welcoming family were warm hearted and generous. They took us in two cars on a tour around Cork, with lunch in an old-fashioned pub with live music and generous portions of food. Linda and the wife exchanged photos and information. The husband sat with me and explained about the craic. Our boys were given puzzle games to solve which kept them busy. Apparently, Hal looked like one of his cousins.

We had a lovely day and returned to the ship happy. I felt echoes of my former self. I took my tablets and we sailed off to Dublin. The O'Brien's hailed from the outskirts of Belfast but had a branch in Dublin. I had contacted them and told them of our arrival. We had an invitation to visit for afternoon tea. After taking a local tourist bus ride around the city, we took a taxi to the Logan family who made us very welcome. Everybody was pleased to meet us and plied us with food and drink. Time flew by and we were sorry to depart to get the ship. The husband drove us back.

Our next stop was Belfast where we had tried to make connections but had not had success. We travelled to the area the O'Brien's originally lived and asked in the local pub about potential connections. The landlord was very friendly and explained that in Poppa's day many people had left because of famine and lack of jobs, never to be seen again. Those who remained had moved on to seek a living. It was unlikely that any of the original O'Brien's were still around. He remembered an old customer called Sean O'Brien and called him on the phone. The old fella was now in a nursing home, but he may remember our family if we cared to visit. With limited time we took a taxi and managed to see him. He turned out to be remotely related and could recall Poppa as a boy, so we took photos and left him to snooze.

Belfast was a modern city which had settled down after all the troubles. We saw a few murals on the way. We just had time to take a tourist bus guide to see the sights before we had to head back to the ship. Both sides of Ireland had welcomed us, and we felt warmth and an affinity. We took photos of some funny names and unusual places. I had managed fairly well, I just felt tired but relaxed. Our trip was nearly over, we just had to explore Scotland before we went back home. We bought whisky from the distillery for presents for the guys.

Our final trip was the visit to Edinburgh which thankfully I felt well enough to enjoy. It was beautiful, the sun shone, we saw bagpipes being played in a variety of Highland kilts. The castle loomed in the centre with a 'Can You Believe' attraction next door which fascinated the boys. There was a dungeon experience and so much to do and see, we ran out of time and did not want to leave. It was one of our best days. We all returned to ship exhilarated and had to start packing for our return home. We were flying back. I left Linda to supervise the packing and suddenly had to lie down again.

The return journey passed in a blur as I stumbled along, Linda handled the luggage. I pulled myself together with an effort to get through controls and into my window seat, then conked out. Linda left me to sleep. She had bought things for the boys to do on the journey, so they were kept occupied. When we returned Linda insisted that I went to see Dr Wood right away. We didn't know then about Candice and the wedding. Our car was parked at the airport and Linda drove us home. We were all shattered, so we went straight to bed without unpacking.

Next day Linda woke me up and drove me to see Dr Wood as an emergency appointment. Apart from the jetlag, I felt vague but no worse. I explained my symptoms and how it seemed to go away then return. It made no difference how much action I had taken.

Doctor Wood gave me a thorough examination and said it could be ME. We asked what ME was. Doctor Wood explained that chronic fatigue syndrome is a medical condition that limits a person's ability to carry out ordinary activities. The cause is not understood and diagnosis is based on a person's symptoms. The fatigue is not due to strenuous exertion and is not relieved by rest. Fatigue is a common in many illnesses, but the unexplained fatigue and severity of functional impairment is comparatively rare. There is no cure, with treatment being symptomatic. No medications or procedures had been approved in the United States.

Dr Wood explained that in some patients a gradual increase in activity suited to individual capacity can be beneficial. ME mainly leaves the patient feeling extremely tired and generally unwell. Symptoms vary in each person from day to day, or even within a day. It can make it difficult to carry out tasks and activities.

It was too soon to ascertain if I had ME, so Dr Wood proposed I keep a diary for a month initially, to see how I went on. We could then extend it to three months. Perhaps now I had returned home my condition could right itself. He told me not to worry too much, he would monitor my situation.

Dr Wood asked how we had enjoyed our cruise then dropped the bombshell that he and Candice were engaged. We both forgot about all my symptoms with shock. I had expected Candice to remain a single tyrant. Dr Wood was such a kind gentleman, I hoped he would be up to living with Candice. We wished him congratulations and left the surgery stunned.

Matilda's Family

Life seemed to get busier as time went by. If I was not making food, I was ferrying the kids to various places. Phil helped and had his own agenda. I needed to slow down but couldn't seem to manage. We were both watching Scarlett covertly. She still did her gymnastics but was also turning into a political activist. If a new cause appeared my daughter would be there behind them. In addition, Scarlett was researching religious beliefs and ideologies which she announced she wanted to major in. We wondered whether this was in response to her escape but made no comment. Both of us just wanted her to be happy and fulfilled.

Eithan seemed to have inherited the carpentry gene. When he started woodwork in school, he made a few nifty pieces which he took to show Uncle Dan. Once he mastered a few techniques, Eithan asked Dan to show him how he made the furniture. Dan was delighted because his kids were not interested. Whilst Dan showed him flat packs and master carpentry, Eithan suggested using technology to make original specialist designs for discerning customers. Dan could not believe his luck, he gave Eithan homework to come up with some designs. We only found out later when we got together with Claire.

As Eithan was a whizz on modern technology, he took his homework assignment seriously and went back to Uncle Dan with a folder full of designs. Dan sat him down and they studied each sketch seriously. Dan pointed out possibilities and obstacles and told Eithan if he was seriously interested, he would need to do a draughtsman's course which included master carpentry, upholstery, etc. It was not a simple case of whittling. Eithan told Dan he was very interested and wanted to make it his career, he hoped to be part of the family business one day.

Dan spoke to Phil who knew nothing about it. We both sat Eithan down and questioned him. Eithan told us he wanted to learn with Dan and take over the family business one day. He told us enthusiastically that he was full of ideas and plans to modernise. People always needed furniture so if he could apprentice with Dan, Eithan reckoned he would do well. Phil and I looked at each other, Eithan was obviously keen and determined, we decided to wait and see.

The furniture business was jointly owned by all the family. Poppa left everything to be divided equally. Dan had grown and developed the business so obviously earned his living from it deservedly. We all had shares in it. Candice was planning to open a big store featuring opportunities for all the family to partake. A meeting was planned next month to discuss the venture in detail. Ryan was bringing his family over for it before the wedding. It was all very exciting and I was intrigued. Most of my outlets were run by dedicated loyal staff these days, I made sure they were amply rewarded and encouraged.

I thought Scarlett may enjoy the company of her girl cousins when Ryan came. She had grown up with all the boys playing basketball, soccer and baseball. Her circle of friends was close, but Scarlett often preferred to stay home rather than socialise. We were not sure about her future career which changed regularly. I rather expected something socialist or political with her interests. She had no interest in baking or cooking, so I hoped she would find a good man who would cook for her, when the time came. She could always be a fitness instructor although I sensed her interest was waning.

My body was thankfully lean because I rarely had time to indulge. I made delicious things for others to enjoy. At home we stuck to lean healthy cuisine supplemented by pizzas and burgers occasionally. There was plenty of choice available these days to eat well. Phil did regular sport and kept active so remained fit and handsome. We understood each other and could communicate without words. He still aroused passion in me and sometimes we got each other little surprises. I was grateful we had a good marriage and lovely kids. My nephews were cool dudes too and I always indulged them when they visited.

School kept me busy, if it wasn't fancy dress occasions, they ran campaigns like Civic Clean Day where the kids went out clearing litter and waste with pick up sticks. These days people tended to drop their trash, or the disposals overflowed and it scattered. Allbrite had always been a clean town, now it was getting fouled with trash and plastic that could not be recycled. Scarlett was campaigning for a cleaner environment. As for tipping, the mayor introduced big fines for anyone caught.

I sent food donations to a homeless shelter and residential care home for the elderly. Scarlett volunteered to help at the shelter as her community aid project. She enjoyed unpacking goods, filling shelves and meeting people. The regulars who went there were often friendly people who had fallen on hard times. Many worked in low paid jobs or had extended families to feed. Some had to care for elderly relatives.

With her welcoming smile and helping hand, Scarlett was much appreciated. It gave her an insight into the struggles people had to make a living. We had always made our kids do chores in return for pocket money, but we had provided for all their needs. The shelter showed Scarlett another world. People used it to fill the gap between income and necessity.

When Eithan had to do community aid he volunteered to teach residents in the residential care home how to use computers. I was very proud of his patience and devotion. Whilst Eithan taught basic skills, the old timers told him stories of their past and of Allbrite. This fascinated Eithan and he used the information in his designs when possible. Both kids still kept up with their homework and other activities. We often had kids visiting or staying over. I never knew until I got home who I would find.

Ryan came back with his family, it was lovely to see them again. Marie's mum came with me to the bakery to teach us how to do French delicacies and had such fun, we invited her to join the team as and when she wanted. I took Marie with me when I had some social event to go to. Their lovely girls soon made themselves at home and were a calming influence on the boys. All shyness soon passed and they were often chucking a ball about or off swimming.

Allbrite held a Race for Life in aid of cancer. Ryan, Phil, Dan and the kids all signed up. I provided bottled water and snacks for the racers. Most of the family took chairs to the park to watch. Fortunately, the weather was good, not too hot. Some of our kids appeared on the evening news bulletin. We had a picnic in the park afterwards and sat around talking. It was lovely to be together as a family. In Allbrite we had volunteer surveillance and were pleased all went well.

Scarlett, Sophie and Chloe took part in a women's walk for breast cancer. They were all believers in women's rights and took equality as a norm. It did not occur to any of them that there were men's jobs or women's jobs. They believed each person should be judged on merit. When I told them that in some parts of the world women were treated as second class, they had to have permission from men to even leave the house, the girls were incredulous. I told them women in Saudi Arabia were not even allowed to drive. Our girls could not understand how it was possible. I warned them to be careful where they went travelling.

I made sure Ryan's girls had self-defence training. They knew the facts of life. I warned them about spiked drinks, leaving their bags unattended, getting lifts home, communicating with strangers who could be impersonating teenagers, then I stopped. I did not want to frighten them. I wanted them to feel safe leading regular lives. They were all pretty girls still young and hopefully innocent. Chloe told me about her bullying story. It seemed cruel that girls could not grow up freely without taunts or insults.

Sophie asked me if I could help her to promote gluten-free food which was tasty and tempting so that she could spread the offer. We spent some serious time in my home kitchen experimenting and came up with some tasty bakes and meals calling it the *Sophie* range. The girls gave out samples in town and we got publicity in the press and on radio. As a result, our *Sophie* range took off and we received requests from across the States. It made me aware that food allergies and special diets could be a big untapped market. I decided to look into it more closely and make it a feature in the new store. Everything about food fascinated me.

Linda, Claire, Marie, Betsy and I all got together to discuss Candice's wedding. We needed to organise a hen night without going too far away or being too outrageous. Betsy was not seeing Eric any more, but we included her because she felt like part of the family. We expected them to reunite at some stage because she was obviously still carrying a torch for him. Playing hard to get seemed to be paying off because Eric looked miserable these days, so we told her to keep it up.

Our girls would be bridesmaids, our boys would be page boys escorting the girls, Candice was designing all their outfits which were secret. Claire said her floral arrangement group were going to handle the flowers according to secret instructions given by Candice. We ladies needed to look for smart outfits. There would be dancing in the evening, so we all decided to go for glamour and hire a make-up artiste and hairdresser to fix us all up together on the day. Marie's mum could be included too and Mama.

Surveillance cameras were introduced all over Allbrite. Marshall increased surveillance at Mama's place and at Dan's factory. It seemed crime statistics were on the increase although compared to big cities, Allbrite was quiet. Identity theft was also increasing so we were all advised to be vigilant especially at cash machines. Trash needed to be shredded if it contained our names or addresses. People tended to use cards for transactions rather than cash.

Different states in America seemed to be struggling with race issues, black people were being shot and riots ensued. The world was an ethnic mix that merged together. Most people wanted to raise their families to do better than themselves and live in peace with their neighbours. I just wanted everybody to be treated equally with dignity. It was too bad agitators caused unrest in power struggles.

Eric's Dilemma

I had been approached to put together iconic shots of interesting places I had visited for a book. Also, I wanted to put together my own book featuring historic moments captured in time. To do this successfully I decided to remain in Allbrite and arranged with an ex-school friend to use his photographic facilities for developing. I had to research and prepare proposed images. With all my archived stash, I spent hours trying to catalogue my work. Betsy offered to help me and I was impressed by her efficiency and patience.

Betsy Levine kept appearing in my life. I stopped thinking about it or her. If she could not find better things to do, I accepted her presence. I gave her no encouragement, there was no romance. Sometimes we had interesting conversations, other times we got along comfortably and silently. Whatever I did she would advise me or manipulate herself into accompanying me. I got used to her hanging around, but she was still very lippy, which I tried to ignore because I couldn't be bothered arguing with her.

When I was going on an assignment Betsy told me that I would miss her.

"You wish," I said.

"We could make beautiful children," she said deliberately trying to aggravate me.

"In your dreams," I told her.

"You know what your trouble is?" Betsy asked.

"I'm sure you are going to tell me," I sighed.

"You just don't want to grow up, look at you, mid-thirties living at home with your Momma. You don't want responsibility because you still have the mindset of a boy."

"Maybe that's just your opinion," I said thinking she was accurate, "But maybe it suits me."

"Huh, will you still be hanging on to your mother's apron strings when you are 40? Why don't you make a base of your own somewhere? You don't have to stay in it all the time. You make good money, you could afford a place to call home."

"Next you will be propositioning me," I said grumpily knowing she talked sense.

"You could do a lot worse, I at least understand you," Betsy said smoothly.

"You think you do. Why don't you find someone else to marry you," I said unkindly.

"Maybe I will, go and stuff yourself, mummy's boy," Betsy told me, flouncing off.

I went away the next day on assignment in Burma where Aung San Suu Kyi was in the news with her house arrest status. There was plenty of free time to think. Hanging around made me think of Betsy telling me what to do. I didn't exactly miss her but realised she had a point about getting my own place.

Betsy had become an integral part of my routine without my realising it. She was the most irritating female I had ever met and I was well shut of her. I wished her well at somebody else's expense. In all the time I had known her I had never once given her any encouragement. She was not my type, life with her would be hell, she would try to programme me from morning to night.

Nevertheless, when I flew back home Betsy was there to meet me. To my surprise she greeted me with a big passionate kiss that shocked me. She threw her arms around me and actually fitted under my chin rather well. I did not understand what had brought this on. Before throwing her off me, I allowed a brief cuddle as she felt warm and soft. If she could only keep her mouth shut, I could enjoy the experience.

"What's happened to you?" I asked moving away.

"I missed you so much," Betsy said taking my free hand.

I didn't know what to say or how to release my hand, which she held in a firm grip.

"Why are you kissing me?" I asked lamely.

"Huh," she said in disgust, "Because I am in love with you, I want to marry you and have your children. I will make you the best wife and we will be happy."

"Are you for real?" I asked horrified.

"Of course I am, you are just too dumb to see it."

"You know I do not want to get married, I hate commitments apart from work. I just want the freedom to live my own life. I don't want another person to take care of."

"More fool you then," Betsy said and walked off leaving me stranded. I took a cab.

The conversation replayed in my mind for several days. I had my share of girlfriends and relationships. If I didn't marry Kalaina who I genuinely loved, Betsy Levine had no chance. Nevertheless, I was flattered to know that somebody cared about me enough to want marriage and my offspring. I always felt children were cute to play with, but it was always good to return them to their parents. I thought I would tell Betsy thanks and brush her off more kindly next time I saw her. For once she did not return. I thought she may be sulking and looked out for her, but it was like she had never been. Claire told me she was still in work.

I did not intend to contact Betsy and slowly realised that I did miss passing comments to her, getting feedback and advice and even abuse from her. She was not my type but had been supportive and a good friend. Being alone meant nobody was interested in my comings and goings. If I wanted an opinion, I had to find a member of my family who was usually not interested. I expected this was Betsy's way of being irritating and she was succeeding. Claire told me Betsy had a date. I sympathised with the poor man but also felt annoyed she could be so fickle. I was better off without her.

A month passed and I was busy working hard from home. I was planning to check out places to buy because then I could spread out and not inconvenience anybody. I had just left the photographer's and was going in search of something to eat when I saw Betsy going into a healthy food outlet across the street. I followed her into the premises, tapped her on the shoulder and when she turned around in surprise, I found a ridiculous grin on my face. I was pleased to see her.

"Hi Betsy, long time no see. How have you been?" I asked pleasantly.

"Fine," she said coolly turning her back on me.

"Do you want to hang on while I get mine and we can eat together and catch up?" I suggested."

"No thank you, I have to get back to work now, see you," she said disappearing.

As she swept off, I noticed she wore a figure-hugging blue outfit that made her look quite fit. I had not thought about her being female before. She obviously did not want to make conversation or hook up with me now. I wondered why that did not make me happy. When she had chased me, I took it for granted, now she was ignoring me it hurt. I had tried to be a nice guy, had not taken advantage of her so she had run after me of her own accord. Perhaps her date suited her more. I felt agitated by her coolness. I waited for normal cool calm behaviour to return but the agitation grew, and I became jealous of her new suitor.

For peace of mind I went to visit Claire to ask her advice. She sat me down in the kitchen and asked me what I wanted. I did not know except I kind of hoped Betsy could be my friend again. Claire told me Betsy was a popular lady, she didn't need any more friends. I fidgeted and confessed hesitantly that I missed Betsy being around.

"So, tell her," Claire said.

"You tell her," I suggested.

"Eric be a man for once, if you want to be with Betsy, you need to make the moves," Claire said annoyed.

"What do you mean for once?" I said picking up on a sensitive issue.

"You swan around all over the world drifting through life, expecting to come back and your mother will still look after you. It's time you took control of your life."

"Betsy said something similar," I said surprised.

"Well how old are you now? What do you have to show for your existence apart from some fantastic pictures? Is that enough?" Claire asked me brutally.

"No," I said sadly and got up to leave.

They couldn't both be wrong. I realised that life had gone on abstractedly with me drifting from place to place. I enjoyed being a nomad, I had little to show for my life but a healthy bank balance as I lived modestly. Did I want more? I needed to think so took a low-key assignment in Texas to consider where to go from here. Somehow being solo did not seem so appealing, nor did loose women or booze. I rang Betsy on a whim, she did not hang up immediately, so I reckoned I still had a chance if I got my act together.

"Hi Betsy, it's Eric," I said stupidly.

"I know," Betsy said, "What do you want?"

"It was good seeing you the other day," I said lamely.

"So, why are you ringing Eric?" she asked coolly.

"I guess you were kind of right, I do miss you being around," I said.

"You had your chance and you blew it," Betsy said hanging up.

I was shocked at her dismissal. My ego came crashing down. What exactly did I want from Betsy Levine? Bedding her would probably be fun but not enough. I wanted her back in my life, under my feet, making me laugh. The problem was how to make amends. I realised that Betsy would not be interested in having a fling, I did not dare think about marriage, I was too scared. If I did nothing, Betsy could take off with someone else. The situation overwhelmed me, so I got drunk and fell into bed. With a hangover next morning, I decided to wait until I returned to Allbrite to see Betsy in person.

Dan Can

When Candice told us that she was getting married to Dr Wood we were all surprised. He seems to be a pleasant man, I hoped she would treat him well because Candice has a strong will and can be argumentative when she doesn't get her own way. Before we could absorb that surprise, Candice told us about her plan to open a family department store in Allbrite. To explain her proposition, she called a full family meeting. It seemed she had premises in mind, so Marshall, Ryan and I went with her to check it out.

On the outskirts of town there was a row of old dilapidated buildings which used to be small shops. Candice wanted to demolish and rebuild a three-storey modern department store involving the whole family. Everybody had a role to play. I was to design and fit out the store, Ryan could help to build it. There would be a café run by Tilly, clothing ranges for young people – Scarlett, Sophie and Chloe were tasked to spot trends and fashions. There would be a range for women by Candice and a range for men by Henry. Accessories, shoes and purses would be supplied on a small scale by Candice's favourite designers.

The middle floor would be divided into two parts. One part would have room settings in three categories: one would be classical, one minimalist, one traditional. I would change the settings every month. All the furniture would be provided by me. The other side would be full of home furnishings designed by Candice: décor, accessories and bed linen. Candice would put her designs into my room settings. A limited range of lighting would also be stocked. Each month would change according to seasons and festivals.

I immediately thought that Ollie and Eithan could help with the modern designs. Both were computer literate and had strong ideas for design, they could make a name for themselves. There could be a competition in school to design pieces for the store. My head was buzzing with ideas. It would be a challenge to keep coming up with new styles every month, but I was up for it.

Marshall could negotiate the contract with Candice who would sweet talk officialdom into the famous names she would invite. She planned to use her name and spread the word in high circles. Eric would take some scenic shots of Allbrite accompanied by Candice and some props to make it look desirable. Claire and Linda could spread the word at work and in their social groups. Mama could pose by some home cooked food. Publicity could be generated in local press and in the media and Candice would get somebody famous to open the store.

Discussion centred around the name. O'Brien's made it sound like an Irish bar, so we tried Candice, Candy World, Candy's Allbrite, It's All Brite at Candy's, Candy Land. Ryan said that because Candice had made her fame using her name as her brand, we should simply call the store *Candice*. She agreed and told me to put her in touch with our promotional people. It seemed Candice planned to expand her catalogue shopping to include the store. Henry would provide all the men's ranges including cool gear for young men.

"Can Allbrite afford your prices?" Mama queried.

Candice said she would modify her range into cheap, medium and high-end. There would be something to suit every pocket. She would also create jobs in Allbrite and planned job share for people who could only work part time. Candice planned to entice Betsy away from her personnel role at Claire's work, to be the recruiter and personnel officer to run the role. Work experience opportunities would be created for high school kids and perhaps some apprenticeships later.

I had to admire the ambition and determination Candice had shown. Despite being the youngest O'Brien, she was a leading light. She must be well-heeled to afford such a big venture. Candice asked us all to invest in the company which would be a family concern, like my furniture business which could run separately or incorporated. We all needed to digest so much information. Marshall would accompany Candice once a surveyor's report was received. Nothing would happen until after the wedding. I imagined it would take a long time to accomplish, but Candice said we all had to start planning how to fulfil our briefs.

As a successful furniture outlet I was doing ok, but most of it seemed to be routine. This project stimulated my imagination and I was willing to participate. I told Ollie to use his potential architect skills to draw up plans with Candice as to how the store could look. He agreed to consult with Candice and get busy. Eithan wanted his school to have a shot at making contemporary wood carvings for the store. I agreed, saying the best entries would be submitted. Candice could judge. The girls in the family became would-be fashionistas studying their favourite pop stars outfits.

I decided to increase my skills and enrolled on two courses, one was portable furniture which folded away and could be quickly assembled in multiple ways; the other was boat building. Although we were inland, I wanted to build a boat that we could use for trips and adventures. We could always sell it. A decent boat on display would cause interest and could be a new avenue. We also included bespoke furniture solutions upon request for additional fees. I felt we had a good offer and that Poppa would have loved the family venture. Poppa was always proud of his family and gave us all encouragement to be our best.

While we waited for the wedding date to draw near, we set up ball games with Ryan, Phil, Martin Wood and Eric. Our boys joined in when available. Hal usually had music activities to do but Jake, Leo, Ollie and Eithan often joined us. The women seemed to talk clothes and slimming, so we left them to it. There was a buzz in the air as news leaked out about our prospective plans. Dr Wood was a popular man and was congratulated and teased by the community. I reckon there were some disappointed ladies, but nobody could compete with Candice who was even more radiant in love.

I taught our apprentices and took them camping over a long weekend. We discussed over the camp fire how they saw their futures. Allbrite did not have many job opportunities so some planned to move away. A couple hoped to apply for jobs with Candice either in maintenance or construction. This made me realise what a good opportunity our venture would be for local enthusiastic talent. Without saying anything specific, I urged them all to undergo proper training to get qualifications. Local talent was familiar, settled, reliable and eager to learn, an ideal mix for recruitment.

Leo was still active in sport and planned to continue to make it his career. He was captain of Allbrite Warriors baseball team, played basketball and was equally good at water sports. I noticed girls hanging around our place sometimes. It made me feel old and tired that they were not there for me. When I sat down at night to watch a match or a movie, I tended to fall asleep and miss the ending. This bugged me and I woke up confused and dismayed. Claire also nodded off sometimes, so I figured we were getting middle aged.

Mama was always busy either socialising or helping with family duties. She didn't seem to age, she had looked the same since Poppa died. It was Mama who organised the kids' activities, who looked out for them when we were all busy. The kids adored her. She spoiled them all and welcomed Ryan's girls into her kitchen where she taught them all to make specialities to surprise their parents. I called around to see her regularly and fixed up any maintenance issues.

Finally, it was time for Dr Wood's bachelor party which we kept top secret from all the family. With some friends and colleagues of his, all the O'Brien men accompanied the good doctor for an adventure weekend in the hills and that's all I am saying about it. Dr Wood proved to be a good sport, we laughed, chilled, had a few spills and some top-notch entertainment. What went on was good old-fashioned fun fuelled by booze and good humour. Dr Martin Wood was welcomed into the family as a fully-fledged member.

Zoe, Martin's daughter, stayed with Mama for the bachelor weekend. She got on well with Candice and took an active creative interest in designing fashion for girls. Candice encouraged Zoe and they bonded well. Scarlett, Sophie and Chloe included Zoe in all their activities so that she felt like part of the family, although she was still shy amongst the men. Our boys thought she was cute and felt protective of her. I was pleased we had all raised decent kids and hoped Zoe would enjoy a happy childhood. It must have been tough losing her mother so young.

As part of my business public relations endeavours, I had joined Allbrite Golf Club and played with leading community members. I picked up good contacts there who came in useful for developing our project. Candice encouraged liaisons with everybody who could help so I took her along to special golfing functions as my escort. Claire was happy to miss them as she found them boring. When I walked in with Candice all eyes turned towards her. Candice could charm anybody when she wanted, so I happily relaxed in the background and left her to it.

The mayor came to see me to discuss our proposals in confidential detail. We needed his support, so I welcomed him into my office, poured him a whisky and shut the door. Once we had discussed both family members and the town's affairs, we got down to business. When he heard how Candice planned job sharing, training, work experience, school competitions and potential apprentices, he was overjoyed and assured me he would influence the planning committee to raise no objections. The council owned the land the shops were sitting on. We parted on good terms.

School rang me to report that Leo had got into trouble fighting. I went round to see a sorry looking kid with bruises and a smouldering Leo in the head's office. It seemed the loser kid had been mouthing off about Zoe. Leo felt inclined to protect her honour. The loser kid apologised publicly for his loser mentality, Leo had to apologise for hurting the loser. Zoe's honour was redeemed and there was no more trouble. Martin came over to thank Leo. He hoped this would be an isolated incident. It was because Zoe was shy and kept a low profile. I was proud of my son but didn't let on.

All the women folk went with Candice somewhere for their hen party leaving the guys at home to babysit. We were not supposed to know where they had gone but I noticed something about Vegas in Claire's bag, so hoped they would not gamble too much. I didn't let on. My boys and I ate pizza, watched sport and a movie and I let them stay up late. In fact, we all went to bed at the same time. We didn't bother with house chores, left everything until the last minute when we had a whip round and got the hoover out. We finished all the ice cream and snacks and had a cool time.

I went with the men to get our suits for the wedding. Candice insisted everything be top notch. Apparently, high flying media would be coming to take shots. She had her dress and bridesmaids sorted. Meanwhile she was busy instructing

Marshall to prepare contracts for building services. Price was not the main criteria she told him. Contracts had to be given to local reliable contractors, they could be multiple to give locals a sense of involvement and pride. I was also lectured about furnishings and fittings in the store.

Life was busy but exciting. My boat building was progressing slowly but surely, I found it relaxing. I had not been sailing, so I thought it would be amusing if I got seasick. On the movies it looked good sailing through turquoise waters. Building my boat was my excuse to escape and chill. I was in no hurry to finish it, I liked the idea more than the reality. I thought the boat could be suspended in the store and decorated with home furnishings. It would be a focal point of interest.

Candice Reigns

Life was busier than ever as my head was full of plans, schemes and romance. Now that I was in love, the world seemed to be a magical place. I noticed colours, textures and felt joyful. Whilst Martin and I got to know each other, I decided to stay in Allbrite returning to LA when necessary to work. I stayed in Martin's house and tried not to interfere in their arrangements, domesticity not being my thing. Zoe and I got on like best friends. She enjoyed having female input and loved fashion, so I made her my junior apprentice and consulted her on my designs.

One day I got a call from Henry saying: "Candy babes I have something amazing to tell you. Are you sitting down?"

"What's wrong?" I said already seated.

"I'm settling down," he said.

"You've only known this guy for a short time. Are you sure?" I asked worried.

"Candy, I knew the moment I first saw him that he was the one for me. He is everything I have ever wanted and dreamed about."

"I haven't even met him yet," I said confused.

"You will next time you come back, we'll go for dinner or something. He can't wait to meet you."

"Well congratulations then, it just seems a bit sudden but if you are happy and this is what you want, then hey, nobody could be more pleased for you," I said with tears in my eyes.

"Oh, Candy that means a lot to me. We are so lucky to be born in this age. Years ago, homosexual men would have been locked up. This is for real and everlasting, we are for keeps. I'm so excited," Henry gushed.

"What does he do again?" I asked

"Gary is into robotics, he is a smart guy. His company also does state of the art sound systems which is how we met. I was doing the big Florida show and he was sent to install the sound system which was on trial. The beautiful thing is that we spoke as two people first rather than flirting or bar jibe. He is gorgeous Candy."

"What do your family think?" I asked.

"They are pleased for me and really like Gary."

"Great, will you be moving in together?"

"We are just making arrangements. I mean like when you know, there's no point hanging around," Henry said happily.

"Well give me fair warning, we should celebrate. Can I bring somebody?" I asked innocently."

"Candy have you met someone too?" Henry asked excitedly.

"Yes," I said shyly, "he's the family doctor in Allbrite, a widower with a daughter."

"Wow that's taking on a load," Henry stated cautiously.

"Zoe's really sweet and we get on like sisters. He's a really neat guy and I've fallen hard," I said.

"What's his name?" Henry asked,

"Dr Martin Wood"

"And does he feel the same?" Henry asked

"I think so, we are very happy together. I have moved in with them and we are getting to know each other better."

"Oh, and you call me fast, Candy this guy must be something special, I've never known you make moves before, I never thought it would happen. I have to meet this guy to check him out, make sure he's worthy," Henry instructed.

"Oh Henry, let's hope we will all live happily ever after," I sighed.

"What does this mean work wise?" Henry asked seriously.

"Henry my honey, I have BIG plans and I am going to fly over to tell you in detail. I hope you will come on board and we will have a brilliant future as a team. You are The Man and I will be The Woman, we will set the world on fire."

"When are you coming?"

"Next week, I get in on Tuesday afternoon, I don't want to stay too long because I hate leaving Martin," I said.

"Candy my girl, you've got it bad. I can't wait to catch up. Be happy babes, see you then."

"Congratulations again, love you," I blew kisses and hung up.

My trip to LA was action-packed. We had to plan next season's designs, colours, styles, themes and discuss the on-line site. I had big plans to open a family store in Allbrite with mail order catalogue shopping. All my family could have roles and I knew the perfect site on a derelict row of shops on the outskirts. Henry was dubious at first until I assured him that he only needed to contribute and make occasional guest appearances like at the opening. Henry would continue to run the LA set up, we would still be partners. If we both co-ordinated our efforts, we would spread style across the nation.

Gary turned out to be a lovely guy, I was impressed. Tall, fair wavy hair, clear blue eyes, amiable and smart, a perfect combination. To see Henry so happy made filled me with joy. Gary and I hugged and I felt I had known him a long time too. He obviously adored Henry and would treat him well. This was no fly-by affair or chat-up, I could tell they were serious and would sort themselves out. Seeing them together made me miss Martin more. I resolved to discuss my future in depth with Martin and my family when I got back.

Henry and I discussed our plans for the forthcoming season, instructed our staff then I flew home, called a family conference and included Martin and Zoe. Tilly provided refreshments. They were initially amazed at my plans, they thought it audacious, worried about funding and asked what Henry thought. I asked them all to invest so that they would commit and feel involved. Now *Candice* was a successful brand in the fashion industry, I had leverage and glamour. The family decided it would shake Allbrite up and give it kudos. Marshall cautioned about getting approvals and consents from local government etc. I knew it would work with such a diverse talented family behind me. Martin felt relieved that I had plans to stick around and Zoe was delighted.

I took Marshall and Dan to inspect the site and liaise with the negotiations. When I rang Ryan to discuss my plans, he was enthusiastic and told me to count him in. Ryan had started his own successful business and gave me lots of tips. When Eric was home I accompanied him around Allbrite, taking scenic shots using props to make it look appealing. I planned to use Allbrite on my catalogue covers and as background. On a beautiful day Allbrite could match anywhere for appeal. This meant extra work for me and I was frequently exhausted.

Martin was wonderful, he had his own career and routines, special time with Zoe. When he saw that I had no plans to interfere in his life, he relaxed and felt more secure. We did not argue, spoke frankly to each other and I totally respected him because he was not swayed by my appearance.

Martin treated me as an equal and made me feel special. The more time we spent together, the more addicted I became. Every time we parted company, I couldn't wait to get back together. One night over dinner in a smart restaurant, Martin got down on one knee and proposed. Candice O'Brien became the happiest girl in the world.

My family were excited for me and Henry flew over with Gary for our engagement family party. Ryan came promising to bring the whole family over for the summer. He hinted to me he would like to take a property for the summer vacation, bring his mother-in-law and check out life in Allbrite these days to see if his family fitted in. I could not mention it then, but I reckoned he had plans in mind to join in my scheme.

Fortunately, Henry, Gary and Martin bonded well. Zoe liked having Henry and Gary making a fuss of her, she blushed and giggled charming them both.

When time moved on and I had to think about the business and make wedding plans, I discovered I was pregnant. As I had not been promiscuous, I was rather lax about family planning and tended to leave it to Martin. I did not tell him and although normally this would have been good news, I figured my future depended upon maintaining a strong brand image to launch the business, and to be bride of the year.

It would have suited Martin and I to have a low-key small wedding. As a public relations exercise the publicity generated by the wedding would be an enormous stepping stone for the business which the family invested in. With a heavy heart I made secret arrangements to lose the baby. Through contacts I went to an abortion clinic and had the procedure. Nobody was told and I had to go through the distress and depression afterwards by myself.

I made sure I had good family planning afterwards. I thought that I would conceive again, so I despatched my chance at being a mother and suffered in silence for the rest of my life. If I had my time over, I despairingly think I would have done the same for the sake of everybody who depended upon me. It was something I was ashamed of.

Henry and Gary's getting together party was a wonderful showbiz celebrity bash. All the 'in' crowd attended. It was loud, colourful but tastefully show-pieced and the happy couple went off to a secret venue leaving me in charge.

Martin and Zoe spent a week in LA with me basking in the sunshine and touring. I worked and played with them when I could. We were all happy. It would be our turn next. As a designer all eyes would be on my wedding dress, it added pressure. It occurred to me to go retro to be a style guru, then everything fell into place.

My wedding inspired me to enter retro with a twist ethos to kick start the new venture. I would marry in a lace high-necked bodice with a long silk skirt. Allbrite would appear olde worlde, yet slick and inviting. The new ranges would reflect happy times with up-to-date fabrics and trims. My head was full of ideas and I settled down to get started while inspired. It occurred to me to delegate most of the business ideas as I had masses to do both at home and in LA.

When Ryan told me Marie used to help her father in his business, I called her and invited her to handle the requisition side. Marie said she had no experience, I told her to see Ryan and Matilda who would advise her on ordering from their suppliers. Ryan could help her with the maintenance side. Harry and I had a good PA in LA who could put Marie in touch with our suppliers. I would tell her to send Marie a chart detailing who supplied what. I told Marie she would be such an asset to start us off. Marie said she would be returning to Montreal at the end of the summer. I told her that gave us plenty of time to get started.

Martin stopped me from working continually and made sure I engaged in family time. We called in on Mama regularly, Zoe loved her and was spoilt like all the grandchildren. Zoe liked hearing all the family stories and adventures. Eric came and went. I was waiting for news from him about his future and if Betsy was included, but he was silent. Betsy was thinking about taking the human resources role in the business and had plans to do it her way. I was working on a recruitment list with her when I had time. There was so much to do.

Owing to commitments in LA, I had to spread myself between the two bases. Henry and I planned the new season, the shopping range and a catalogue circulated to our exclusive mailing list. Samples had to be made and viewed, some refinements were required. It was all time-consuming and essential. There were also fashion events we needed to be seen at. Now that my life was filled with Martin and Zoe, the glamour seemed to have lost its allure. It all seemed very artificial and contrived. I smiled and posed and couldn't wait to get back to Martin to kick my heels off and be free of cosmetics.

Mama's World

There was never a quiet moment in my house. If one child left another returned. It was like a station. Eric came and went almost silently. Candice moved in with Martin and Zoe who was a sweet child. Ryan brought his family over but rented a smart place the other side of town. My regulars Marshall, Dan and Tillie took turns to pop round to keep an eye on me. I'm not sure what they thought I may do, but guess I deserved it after my disappearing trick. For the time being I was content to stay put and observe.

Candice my beautiful daughter, was going to get married. I knew she would be an exquisite bride and stylish like a magazine cover. Dr Wood was a decent man and it would be good to have a doctor in the family. Always an overachiever, Candice seemed to be running two worlds, Allbrite and LA. I expected her to calm down after marriage. Zoe would be staying with me during her honeymoon. I think Zoe was pleased to be part of a big family after years of just Martin and herself. It's a pity her mother didn't live to see what a lovely girl she had grown into.

Betsy seemed to be around although less often. I told Eric to get a move on if he didn't want to lose her. Girls like her don't come around often I told him. Our Eric has always had a commitment phobia. He seemed to be busy working on his book and travelling less frequently. I told Eric he was not getting any younger and he told me that I was. He teased me mercilessly until I changed the subject. It would be good to see him settled, I worried about him travelling to the world's trouble spots.

Marie's mother was a pleasant lady, she volunteered to do baking demonstrations for Matilda and the school. I suggested she could do some events in the new store. I thought about having a notice board and leaflets advertising the range of activities available for seniors. Candice told me to start collecting literature and getting myself known. It made me think of tourist information in the area, if we were going to be attracting customers from far and wide, we needed to include local businesses and offers. My idea turned into a busy project and kept my brain ticking.

Poppa had been dead for a few years now, I still tended his grave and kept him up to date with the family news. He would have been mighty proud to see his family working together. It seems young Eithan may have caught the family carpentry skill. It would be good if he chose to continue the line. They were all growing up so fast, young, confident and ready for anything. I was slowing down a bit, I noticed that I tired more easily. These days I kept in touch with Saskia, my sisters and friends over the phone rather than visiting.

Candice encouraged all my grandchildren to take part in the family business. Chloe had a successful contact media page, so Candice told her to prepare a brief about what would be cool to attract young people to the store. Candice wanted a professional write-up but also told Chloe she could take charge of the young version provided she was up to the task. Sophie was given the task of checking out suitable sports clothing and gear. Hal was offered the opportunity to provide music for the opening, Jake could check out the hi-tech range for special effects. Scarlett was tasked with making sure there were equal opportunities and unisex ranges where appropriate. Eithan could produce some carved objects for sale.

I admired Candice for her ambition and drive to include everybody. Zoe followed her around and was already like her apprentice. Everything about Candice was full on, no half measures. It made her overpowering at times, but she was very sincere and believed only the best was good enough. Candice gave all the family girls plain white tee shirts to customise. They all had access to her trimmings and I arranged a session with snacks and needles at the ready. We played music and told jokes, it was fun.

Candice thought nearer to opening she would launch a competition to customise tee shirts to display in store. Scarlett said boys should be included so Candice gave all the boys plain tee shirts, but they were not interested. I told Scarlett that not everything was political. We discussed the wedding and outfits. It was a long time since we had a family occasion to attend and we were all excited.

Prior to the wedding the old shops were demolished and the foundations were laid for the store. Candice took along some champagne and posed with builders celebrating. She never missed an opportunity to get publicity. As Candice was now considered a celebrity, she featured on the local news channels. My daughter was never lost for a word or looked messy. Martin was a quiet low-profile man, he had lovely eyes and wore modern glasses. He was the type to pass by in the street without a second glance. Perhaps Candice fell so hard for him because he treated her as a person first and respected her ambitions. Most men only noticed her beauty.

I carried on my routine and was surprised when Eric invited me to accompany him to see a house for sale. He told me it was time he achieved some independence and thought it would be good to invest in a place to call his own. This suggested to me that somebody had influenced him. I enquired whether he was thinking of living alone. Eric said he planned to invite Betsy to move in with him, but there was no guarantee she would. I asked if they were reunited but he was uncertain, so I didn't push it. The house was compact with a pretty garden just outside town. It was lacking character but low maintenance. I thought he could do better.

Eric said he would look around and told me to keep my eyes open. One of my walking group was planning to move to a new house shortly to be nearer to her family, so I took Eric round on the way back. She lived in a lovely old house overlooking a scenic landscape. Eric was charmed by it, there were three bedrooms so he could use one as an office. I left them alone to discuss prices as I felt Eric's budget was his business. If Eric bought the place it would save my friend agent's fees and would be hassle free. Eric would need a surveyor and a mortgage. He asked if he could take Betsy to see it first and they made an arrangement.

My children all seemed to be settled except Eric. Betsy seemed to be important to him, especially if she had caused him to buy a place. I wasn't sure about their relationship. They were not romantic or involved like other couples. Eric seemed ambivalent towards Betsy. I was not sure if Betsy still wanted Eric either as she did not come around anymore. The situation was strange, and I steered clear.

I tried not to interfere with my kids and grandkids, it was not called for. Sometimes I found it difficult not to interfere, so usually distracted myself until the urge passed. It was interesting the way they all stopped at two children. Raising mine kept me busy all my married life. Now they were settled I could spend my time to suit myself and I revelled in the luxury.

My story about Lilly had been finished and sent to Saskia to edit before sending on to somebody she knew in publishing. Saskia had her own input to add. We had used her story but changed the real names of the characters. There was a dedication to Saskia in the back of the book saying she had been the inspiration behind the story.

I thought about writing a family history book and calling it Allbrite. It seemed to be a good project to get stuck into in winter months. As I aged I disliked the cold which I felt more. I could not hibernate but was vaguely looking for an escape route. Many older people travelled to warmer climates for the winter and were called 'snowbirds'. I understood their reasons and planned to look into options. Surely my family could be self-sufficient by now.

I read that a 'snowbird' is a North American term for a person who moves from the high places and colder climates of the northern United States and Canada to migrate southwards to warmer places in the winter such as Florida, California, Arizona, Texas, the southern United States, Mexico, and the Caribbean. Most are retirees who want to avoid the snow and cold northern winters. For the rest of the year they maintain their ties with family and friends by staying in the north.

It seemed that many own a motorhome to travel south in the winter. They often go to the same place every year and consider it a second home. Many parks get most of their income from the influx of snowbirds. Florida and Arizona have large communities that appear and disappear seasonally. Florida and Arizona have been the top snowbird locations in the past, but southern US states were experiencing a boom from snowbirds enjoying the climate.

This would be something to investigate after the wedding. Maybe Saskia had connections, or she may fancy the idea. Life was too short to be wasted huddled indoors. If I intended to play an active role in the new family store, that could restrict my ambitions. It seemed that the entire family had a part to play. I assumed something was waiting for me too.

Matilda asked me to sort out family photos to prepare a collage for Candice before the wedding. We had old albums and boxes of old photos that we never looked at. There were also family treasures stored up in the loft that needed trashing. The thought made me tired so I figured I would keep quiet.

Ryan seemed to have settled down well. I wondered if he planned to stay in Allbrite. His mother-in-law and family all seemed to have found active roles in the community. The girls were delightful, so fine and delicate, such a change to have pretty girls around. Scarlett was lovely too but couldn't stay still for long.

I wondered how Allbrite compared to Montreal which I imagine to be sophisticated and cosmopolitan. Now that Ryan's mother-in-law was widowed, perhaps she welcomed all the family activities and action. Maybe it kept her sorrow at bay. She certainly has class and refinement, a very gracious lady. Sometimes I felt like having a make-over because it seemed such an effort to get myself looking good. Most of the time I slouched around in comfortable old gear.

Dan and Claire asked me to babysit one afternoon. When I arrived I found Ollie poring over some work. I asked if he was doing his homework but he told me he was drawing up plans for Candice. She had given him a brief about the store requirements and asked him to show her what he thought. Ollie told me his thoughts and we spent the afternoon putting together our aspirations. We came up with some amazing concepts so when we were finished, I called Candice and insisted that she heard us out.

Ollie and Mama's Store Concept

First Candice, then the next day the Mayor of Allbrite, heard about the store concept created by Ollie, the potential architect and Mama, the matriarch of the family, an experienced shopper. Working on the idea that 'X' marks the spot, Ollie devised a huge three-story X-shaped complex with parking bays inside the spaces. The escalators and elevators would be in the centre part. He thought two elevators would be enough as most people could use the escalators. There would be a covered veranda area around each entrance.

There would be four entrances, one at each end with different focal points. We decided one entrance would have a cloakroom and umbrella deposit so shoppers could leave wet brolleys, bags, heavy coats etc. to shop hands-free. At one entrance there would be a stand with a noticeboard advertising 'What's On' in store and around the Allbrite area. It would also offer advice leaflets and information regarding courses and council business. The third entrance would feature flowers and plants supplied locally. The fourth entrance would be Ryan's maintenance service office where people could make appointments.

The ground floor would contain clothing in Candice's three styles: young, classical and special occasions. The adjacent part would feature shoes, bags, hats, gloves, umbrellas and costume jewellery. Similarly, Henry would offer the men's version. The remaining ground floor segment would feature coats, jackets, sportswear, beachwear and lingerie. Signs would indicate that if you can't find your size, you can order it at the 'What's On' desk. Every garment would feature a tag number for reference. There would be a limited range of beauty products and make-up by local specialist suppliers.

Ollie felt there should be no mannequins, instead shelving stacks and round displays should feature. We also felt it would be fun to do themed window displays e.g. using goods from every department, there could be a green window, or a blue one. It could show off seasonal impacts and having mixed displays instead of lifeless dummies would be more appealing.

On the first floor, there would be three segments displaying Candice's room settings of minimalist contemporary, classical and traditional. The fourth segment would be for home décor and accessories including lighting, linens and towels. Candice wanted the room settings to change on the first of each month to keep the offer fresh. We thought that goods could also move around to keep it exciting.

The top floor offered Tilly's café and cake shop on one side, one segment contained two banks of toilets for men and women with a powder room. There would be a hall in the third segment for classes, lectures, fashion shows, events and for hire. The last segment would feature Eric's gallery with a variety of prints and prices. There would be a feature on Allbrite with products and prints showing the town on calendars, serviettes, notebooks, cards, artefacts. Space could be rented to display locally made work.

We also thought the store should use paper bags and cups and offer hessian designer bags for purchase to customers. Where possible everything should be sourced locally. Schools, businesses and the local population should be invited to participate in keeping the store an active part of the community. It could be a meeting point for training courses and planned activities and the hire charge could help finance it.

Candice had sourced funding and agreed to name the floors after the main contributors so we had the Thomas Jenkins, Brad Longdon and Eve Carsham floors. The hall would be named Allbrite Hall. Once open Candice planned to invite celebrities. She also wanted to create competitions among the youth to submit their designs and ideas for display in the store. Plain white tee-shirts were offered to customise, and the best would be mounted in the elevator area.

For recruitment Candice offered some unique opportunities. She listed flexible hours and job share as important. Every employee had to find a stand-in for their role so that if they were on leave, ill or unable to attend, their stand-in would fill in. Stand-ins would be trained with role holders. Candice would liaise with a local nursery to build an extra room for staff children when necessary. This would be limited to employee working hours only at a subsidised rate, it would not be a full time offer.

Candice wanted to offer work training and apprenticeships. Once the warehouse and factory were completed on the industrial zone, Candice planned to get experienced machinists and specialised crafts experts to run training schemes for recognised qualifications. Anybody undertaking qualifications paid for by the store would need to work for as long as required to offset the cost. A contract would be drawn up accordingly. Shop floor staff and cleaners were all to go training for recognised qualifications. Customer relations training was vital, and everybody would be trained.

Each employee would be subjected to regular reviews and assessments. There would be a suggestions box and lockers for staff possessions while on duty. Security would be tight when entering and leaving, everybody would be subjected to random checks. There would be staff discount and free tea, coffee and water. Meals would be available at subsidised prices.

Every employee would be issued with two uniforms to enable them to remain smart at all times. Candice did not want tattoos or piercings on display. Long hair needed to be tidy and groomed. Floor managers would circulate and deal with any disputes. Anybody being rude to customers would be dismissed.

Candice wanted to issue a store bulletin highlighting 'What's new and what's hot' in store each week. This was in addition to her catalogue and shopping sites. To this end Candice hired the younger members of the family to seek out trends. The plan was to get established and offer services nationally. A 'can do' attitude was important to Candy, there were no limits for ambitious recruits.

Candice, the mayor and the family were stunned by the ideas and very enthusiastic. There had been nothing like it anywhere. We had a family meeting to discuss it all again. Ollie accompanied Candice to the professional architects and new plans were drawn up. The mayor agreed to meet with the planning committee to see if any extra space could be drawn up to cope with traffic and storage. He felt we would need to expand to keep up with demand once we started. It was good to have him on our side. Jobs and opportunities for the locals were the mayor's main concern, he would encourage the townsfolk to participate. It gave the young people a chance to stay and build the town.

Mama enquired how all these plans could be achieved and also where all the celebrities would stay on a visit. Allbrite had a few small hotels, a Holiday Inn and similar Motel style accommodation. The mayor suggested using school fields with specialist temporary facilities for the opening. He said he would invite tenders to build a new hotel but that would take time. Camping and chalet accommodation could be sourced. The mayor would check out facilities and costs.

Candice came up with a proposed delegated job list for all the family.

Marshall was to do all the accounting, and research wage costs, red tape, training costs, banking and security in store with the tills. All financial matters would be under his jurisdiction.

Ryan would cost out security, maintenance and building, plumbing, electricians and recruitment of a suitable workforce. He could have apprentices and would also need to recruit to run his own new business in Allbrite.

Dan would handle the furniture and would be responsible for the displays and moving the goods around. He could recruit apprentices and add to his successful sales site. Carefully crafted wooden articles could feature in Eric's gallery. Dan could offer competition prizes to schools for best entries.

Matilda would train staff to run the coffee shop and cake shop along with her other business interests. This would mean delegating to keep up. Menus needed to be refreshed periodically. Emphasis would be on healthy eating with low fat and low salt food and drinks. Candice wanted Matilda to source training courses for potential bakers and cooks to encourage recruitment. She would also need to maintain immaculate hygiene and ensure certification remained in place.

Eric needed to provide a range of Allbrite pictures at various times of the year. In addition, Eric could showcase his best work, arrange for inexpensive prints and room size pictures. If Eric wanted to add any write-ups or display his work in book form, he could hire help or do his own thing. Candice wanted Eric to devise a photography competition for young people. The best entry would accompany Eric as a trainee for a limited time.

Marie had helped her father run his business. Candice offered her an important role as business liaison manager. She could contact all local businesses to see if they wanted to rent space to display their wares. Marie would seek out teachers of yoga, Pilates, diet and nutrition, keep-fit and anything that did not require much equipment, who may wish to run courses in the hall generating revenue. Demonstrators for special events needed to be sourced. The Mayor could offer leaflets for advice and information.

Betsy agreed to become personnel manager, Candice was sending her on a special course regarding the latest legislation in recruitment. They would discuss the role in more detail after that. With years of experience in human resources, Betsy was keen to do things in a firm but approachable style. She was very enthusiastic.

Linda had limited time but agreed that Hal could have the opportunity to perform at the opening ceremony. He would put together a music group playing their own compositions. Linda would liaise with schools for competitions and work experience, etc. She would also investigate apprenticeship schemes. In school vacations Linda would source activities for kids so that parents could work. As an experienced hands-on teacher, Linda could help judge work.

Claire would not be leaving her full-time job but offered to help scientifically in any research. Her company may be interested in promoting science as a career and would be willing to install an information stand in the foyer.

In addition, Scarlett and Leo could test out sports gear, Ollie would continue to design store fittings; Sophie was tasked with trendsetting and advising on the social scene; Scarlett was invited to help organise fund raising events; Chloe was tasked with doing write-ups for youth 'What's hot in store' flyers; Jake was invited to test out the latest new technology and give reports to Chloe to write up and Zoe was unofficially apprenticed to Candice - her best assistant.

Mama was invited to run the 'What's On' store counter. She could give advice, tickets, place orders, offer assistance and generally oversee the needs of the customers. As a sociable and personable woman of experience, Mama would be an asset in the role.

Marie's mother was invited to share the role and offer French cooking demonstrations and lessons in the store. It would enable her to meet the community and make new friends.

There was the issue of supply and demand. With limited space Candice needed to efficiently resource supplies. An experienced manager would need to be found to source and maintain stock for the shop, the media and the LA office.

Henry would be supplying half the wares, he promised to deal with it and agreed to get backup. It was in Henry's interests to maintain production so he aimed for the best, however expensive. Candice agreed with Henry, she worried about how she could find time to cover everything, so she delegated and put her trust in people so sincerely, nobody wanted to let her down.

Ryan and Marie needed to discuss their future with their daughters. The job opportunities were exciting, Ryan wanted to stay and asked Marie to trial it for a year. The girls were ready to change schools to attend with their cousins. They loved being part of the family. Their home in Montreal was secure and the business was being run efficiently. Ryan felt it would be exciting to start over covering Allbrite and surrounding areas.

Marie needed time to think, she was afraid of abandoning her home in Montreal, of not being able to live up to the challenge of her assigned role which would be challenging but exciting. If Marie declined, she was afraid Ryan would stay without her so having missed him terribly when he went to Guatemala, she reluctantly agreed.

Marie's mother said this opportunity gave her a new lease of life. In Montreal she would be a sad lonely widow, here where nobody knew her, she could reinvent herself. Life needed to be lived she told Marie. Mama hugged Marie and sympathised with her dilemma. Marie confessed her anxieties and Mama promised to look out for her.

Meanwhile the foundations were laid for the store and the warehouse with the factory going up for the clothing. Wages were slightly above minimum, but the jobs were local, secure and with prospects, so people were happy. Demand exceeded supply. Lists were made of all the applicants which were put on a database for future reference.

Machinists, specialists in embroidery, trimmings, patterns and crafts were hired and began training as soon as the sewing room was set up, whilst building continued around them. Candice told the teachers to set up streams of classes so that all who wanted to learn could do so in sessions as there were not enough facilities for all in one go.

Marshall's take on the Wedding

Everything was progressing slowly to plan. On the wedding day, the whole programme came to a halt to cheer Candice on. Dr Wood looked radiant with joy. Candice looked like a film star. Ryan proudly gave her away. The family were groomed to perfection. The girls were bridesmaids, the boys were page boys accompanying the girls. A-listers and famous celebrities attended, and the media was in a frenzy trying to capture every moment and offering exclusive deals. Candice was famous in Hollywood and everybody loved true romance.

Everything ran smoothly, Candice was calm and posed willingly for everybody. The speeches were amusing, the meal was tasty, the happy couple moved around the room visiting the tables and didn't eat much. For the first dance the lighting flickered, sparklers were lit, and the atmosphere was magical.

When the new Dr and Mrs Wood slipped away to change to depart for their one-week honeymoon somewhere secret, everybody lined up to wish them well and cover them in confetti and good wishes. Allegedly, one of Candice's A-lister stars had given them an exclusive designer home on the coast to use for their honeymoon. Candice barely agreed to stay away for a week, although they had permission to stay longer. Zoe stayed with Mama for the duration and loved it.

While Candice was on honeymoon everybody worked hard through the list of instructions she had handed out. There was so much to do and most of it was intricate and time consuming. We could not understand how Candice could afford to launch such a big operation, but she told us she intended to make it pay by charging for everything it used. For instance, hiring space to display wares, charging for advertisements to appear in her catalogue or on her bulletins, parking, packaging, hiring out the facilities, offering events and demonstrations, anything she could think of.

Candice told Marie to advise potential suppliers and contractors that we preferred to use locals when possible. If locals were prepared to offer competitive quotations, they would be chosen over the big national suppliers who undercut them. There was no limitless budget however, so we were looking for value for money and continuity of supply. Contracts would be short term initially until suppliers established themselves. A quick turnover was forecast, and traders needed to constantly update their offers. The store would not continuously offer the same stock, its unique selling point would be regular changes and updates. Anything not selling would be moved on.

It occurred to Candice that there would be a high demand initially and with limited space, she came up with a novel solution. A week before opening Candice would invite viewings in sessions, furnishing attendees with an order form booklet and a pen. They would check out the store contents, note down the goods they wished to order including size, reference number, tag number, name and contact telephone number then collect and pay for the goods when the store opened. This would avoid disappointment and enable the store to get provisions ready. It would be bad news if they sold out due to a local stampede. Candice felt the ordering pads would be available all the time to avoid disappointment.

Staff training sessions would take place prior to opening, focusing on layout, facilities, advice regarding ordering, packaging, returns, customer service, queries, awkward customers, faulty merchandise etc. Dialogue with customers would also be discussed to ensure the right approach was taken. Preparations were being made to put together training manuals for all categories, plus employment contracts, supplier tenders. Endless paperwork had to be prepared and delivered.

Candice told everybody the success or failure of the venture depended upon everybody, not just her. She could not do this without each and every one of them, they were all in it together. This ensured that everybody felt committed and determined to do their utmost to make it work. It was 'our' store and future.

Whilst Candice was on honeymoon, Eric moved into his new house. He had proposed to Betsy, but she said she was not interested in marriage at present. He invited her to move in with him. Betsy asked him why he wanted her to. At a loss Eric replied lamely that he thought they would be good together. After checking out the new home and making suggestions regarding its furnishing and colour scheme, Betsy said she would think about it. Eric settled in roughly not bothering to unpack or decorate and took himself off taking pictures. He left Betsy to think about it and resigned himself to being single.

One afternoon he came back to find Betsy in the house, decorating. Surprised he welcomed her and asked how she had got in. She told him Mama had given her the key. Betsy decided that it would be convenient for work in the new store from his place. Eric asked about her present place, Betsy said she would rent it out for now. It seemed a good idea to try out how Betsy and Eric would manage together. Secretly Betsy was thrilled but maintaining her cool, she suggested that Eric should have a trial relationship with her. When they finally went to bed Betsy astonished Eric with her hot passionate love and he was captivated by her. He let Betsy do all the home refurbishment and was grateful to find her there when he returned each day.

The O'Brien kids and Matilda's became cool dudes at school. Everyone knew about the store and wanted to take part. They were invited to all the parties, sleepovers, everybody had opinions about what was cool and what was not. It made their efforts easier when they reported to Candice. Zoe wanted to follow Candice in her career. The others were pleased to be earning their own money and were cautious about spending it. The kids still had to do their homework and chores but found time to carry out their tasks for Candice.

Marie's mum practised recipes and techniques which she tried out on Mama and the family. They also went to various groups socialising and discussing the new store. The idea was to spread the word to encourage participation in its contents and activities. Everybody had ideas, Mama would jot down all the comments in a notebook. Marie's mother discussed food and recipes and was invited to try traditional family dishes in the community. Allbrite townsfolk were caught up in the excitement and were ready with advice and suggestions whenever they met any family members.

After the honeymoon, Martin came back alone looking tanned and relaxed. Candice had gone directly to LA where she and Henry shut themselves away to design for the next two seasons for all their endeavours. A 'Back to the Future' look was the idea behind the new look for the store opening and coming season. Samples were made up and sent to the factory to replicate in all sizes. Originals were kept for the store opening. Various ranges would be offered, featured in the catalogue and for collected shopping. There was enough work to keep a whole team occupied. Candice kept in regular contact with Martin but could not give him a date for her return.

Candice summoned Eric to LA to meet her professional photographer whom she used for photo shoots. Although this was not a field Eric had been interested in previously, Candice felt that with his gallery to run, his new home and love life to maintain, if Eric was planning to cut down on his assignments, he could get involved in store photography shoots. She offered Eric the chance to put his own slant on the shoots provided he made the goods look appealing. Eric and the professional took some shots and compared the results. No decision was taken, Eric needed to think about it.

To maintain supplies of clothing, Candice felt that samples in each available size should be displayed in store to try on with the offer ready packaged in transparent bags with clear sign indicators. Labels should contain size and length when appropriate. When customers wanted to buy, they could order their size if it was not available. Only the high-end special occasions sections would have fitting rooms. The youth and classical sections would be available to examine and try on in samples. A policy of return would be available if not suitable.

Ryan and Dan supervised the building process and helped with the planning and schedules. They oversaw the warehouse, the factory and the store between them. In addition, Ryan called Celia over to interview skilled workers to form a team for his new business. A series of questions had been devised by Ryan to check the professionalism of the applicants. Celia would carry out the initial interviews then Ryan would see the approved candidates. The weather was perfect when Celia arrived, so she was tempted to extend her stay declaring Allbrite a lovely old-fashioned, sleepy town just like in the movies.

Mama

With the store plans occupying all the family, it occurred to me that Theresa my sister could benefit. She would be ideal for a role as my stand in or even training up to help Ryan as Celia's substitute. I rang Theresa one evening and offered her the opportunity to stay with me and check out possibilities. Theresa did not like her current work, her kids had flown the nest. I felt that she may welcome a change and to be her own boss. It took some persuading and I had to let her think about it before she took time off to visit for a week. I met her on arrival, we hugged, and it was exciting to introduce her to the family and to Allbrite.

Theresa was very impressed with all the family achievements. Everybody made her welcome. I spoke to Ryan and Candice confidentially, to see if they thought she may be suitable. Ryan liked Theresa, he felt that if she could spend time with Celia to be trained up, he would hire her to become his right hand. Candice said she would be delighted to find a role for her if she rejected Ryan's offer. They took Theresa around the building sites, explained the set-up in detail and how they needed somebody reliable and trustworthy. Theresa was interested but was worried about her apartment and belongings.

Ryan said he had the same situation in Montreal. He was planning to return with Marie to sort things out. He wanted to rent the family home and check on his mother-in-law's place. Theresa said she lived in rented accommodation. Ryan said that made it easier, she could give notice, store or ship over her furniture and move in with Mama or one of the family. If the situation didn't work out, Theresa could move back and rent somewhere else. Theresa argued that she paid a fixed rent and it would be virtually impossible to get the same rate today. Ryan offered her a trial period whereby he would pay her rent until she decided. Hesitating, Theresa ran out of arguments and said she would think about it.

I enjoyed having my sister around, it made me feel young again. We used to share a room and catch up on all the gossip and wishful thinking young girls do. Now older and greyer, we were still the same young girls inside. Theresa was interested in all the details of the planned developments. She visited all the family, the school where the grandchildren attended, the parks, the malls and gave Allbrite a good rating. It was different to the lifestyle she was used to, but it seemed more laid back which Theresa found relaxing. She usually rushed around, suffered traffic jams and had been a bit lonely. Suddenly she was surrounded by enthusiastic family and it felt good, if a little overwhelming.

Theresa accompanied me to all the social events and centres I frequented. We discussed promotion ideas and how to circulate by networking. The more we planned together, the more I saw Theresa's interest kindle. When it was time for her to go back home, Ryan invited her to accompany Marie and himself to Montreal to meet Celia. If they got along, they could devise a suitable training plan. Ryan would meet all Theresa's expenses. Theresa nervously agreed saying she would have to arrange leave from work, but her eyes were sparkling. Ryan said it would give Theresa a chance to discover what would be involved, and how to sort out her domestic arrangements.

Ryan was an expert in home security and was busy developing systems for the store as well as enhancing the industrial units. My house was secure and I welcomed the prospect of Theresa sharing it with me, there was plenty of room with all the children gone. Even Eric had his own place now, he seemed happier with Betsy and was the most content I have ever seen him. Candice challenged Eric to take photoshoots of her fashions for the catalogue and shopping site. Eric was experimenting with angles, lighting and locations. He did not want to do standard poses and found the process intriguing.

It seemed the store would be like a catalogue shop with samples to feel and try before buying, apart from high-end. I was not sure how this would fare compared to traditional shopping. These days many people shopped buying from advertisement images, so perhaps I was old-fashioned. At least customers could check out the materials, the style and the fittings. I liked the idea of the quick turnarounds.

On the last evening of every month the windows would be blanked out, the floors would close and during the night everything would be changed over. On the first day of each month there would be a dramatic reopening. Candice had space in many leading outlets throughout the country, so she would have no problem shifting stock. I expected her to do well and hoped she could succeed well enough to meet all her expenses.

I think we must have worked some magic in Theresa's life because she met Ryan and Marie and got on well with Celia who showed her round Montreal. Theresa said she had more excitement since I had visited her than in all her life. It seemed Ryan helped her give notice at work, he paid her rent for three months and organised storage for her belongings. She had a number to call when she was ready. Later when she was settled and happy, Theresa said she hoped to stay permanently. Ryan arranged for Theresa to work with Celia for a month to get the hang of everything. Celia arranged accommodation for her.

The mayor rang to ask if he could visit me to discuss Candice. He said he was commissioning a sculpture of Candice designing, with a plaque to go in the foyer of the store for its opening. We should keep it secret. I found photos of Candice for him to choose from. I thought it was a lovely idea and swore secrecy.

Ryan

I told Marie we should invest in a home of our own if we were staying in Allbrite. Our landlord said he did not want to sell, he enjoyed the rental income. We went to look at houses and took Marie's mother along when she wanted. Marie's mother found herself a small house near to Mama which she bought and enjoyed furnishing with Dan's help. Marie's mum was enjoying Allbrite and seemed more vibrant and livelier than I had ever seen her. Our girls had made lots of friends and were enjoying school.

Whilst my family were looking for suitable properties, Marie came across an older house in town that needed renovating. It needed a complete make-over and everyone was busy working on the store. Nevertheless, if it made Marie happy, I said we could buy it and negotiated a decent price. This curtailed my activities because it needed a lot of work before it was fit to move into. It gave me the opportunity to try out some of the local builders and contractors. Some of my new crew were hired during this period. The old place had charm and scrubbed up well, we liked the spacious rooms with high ceilings.

I figured Marie and I needed to go back to Montreal to sort ourselves out. We left the girls with Mama and flew back one Friday night. It seemed very strange to return. Although the city was busy, our patch seemed very tame and quiet without all the family around. My mother-in-law's house was being maintained and secured, all was well. Marie sorted some things she wanted. I left Marie to sort both houses out while I went to see Brian who was running our business there. He was pleased to see me, I took him out for a meal and made him an offer of partnership for the Montreal end.

Business was good, demand was constant. Brian had used his initiative to make a few changes where necessary. He was happy to become a full partner of the firm with minimal investment on his part. My aim was to keep the company flourishing. I gave him full authority to run it in his style, he could hire and fire, I just needed to be informed. We then discussed my home in Montreal. I told Brian we were back to remove personal items before renting the home, furnished for the time being.

Brian told me his son Kevin was living with him with his wife and new baby, until they could save up for a deposit to buy. If I could agree a suitable rental rate, Brian offered to move into my house with his wife, leaving the young family in Brian's place. I had known Brian and his wife for years, they were like family, so this seemed an ideal solution. I knew they would look after our place. At the same time, I needed to cover running costs, so we haggled over a suitable amount and both agreed to consult our spouses.

This was a weight off my mind. Marie liked the arrangement. She asked what would happen if we decided to return. I said we would give Brian ample notice, he still had his own place, and the young family may be more settled by then. My dear little wife had changed almost beyond recognition with her new role in Allbrite. Dainty and feminine looking, Marie turned out to be a tough negotiator. Marie saw each contract as a challenge and used a French accent, feminine charms and determination to succeed. Marie sparkled with energy and was very hard to resist. I was incredibly proud of her. She told me she kept surprising herself and how alive she felt.

All weekend we cleared out clothing and personal possessions, took piles to the charity shop, threw some away, gave stuff to the shelters. Marie's mum did not want much from her house but did not need to let it out. She paid someone to take care of it. We left our house with relief, handed the keys to Brian leaving flowers and wine on the table and were glad to head back to Allbrite. I never imagined Allbrite would be more appealing to me than Montreal. Marie beamed when we got home, the girls had such a busy social life, they hardly missed us. Mama hugged Marie first then me, we were back to stay.

Sophie was always popular and the move made no difference. She was given the lead role in the upbeat school production of Snow White with a very modern interpretation. As a good singer and dancer, Sophie was very flexible and clearly spoken. There was no jealousy because she was a newcomer. Already a keen swimmer, Sophie earned her place on the girls' basketball team. In class she retained knowledge like a sponge and always volunteered. When Candice asked her to check out trends and happenings, Sophie was an instigator with new ideas.

Chloe maintained her media column but had renamed it 'Manoeuvres' as it sounded more upbeat. Her circulation rose slightly and gained new support in Allbrite. Always interested in current events, Chloe cast a discerning eye over her new town and her behind-the-scenes observations earned her a regular piece in the school magazine. The editor of the *Allbrite Times* offered her a weekly column hoping to attract younger readers. Candice had already designated the youth slot on 'What's hot' to Chloe for when the store began. In school, Chloe was among the top in English and an above average student. She had a dry, cryptic approach to life and made people laugh.

Marshall

I had never been busier and I loved it all even though it was exhausting. Apart from my own business, I needed to research pricing, wages, training costs, space hire costs, rentals, storage costs, transport, warehousing, factory costs, it was never-ending. I appreciated modern technology which enabled me to research anything and everything. My staff did most of the regular work freeing me up to consider store business. I had to recruit some young technological experts to help me along. It was truly enlightening to discover modern enterprise.

Linda was also busy looking into schools and education outlets in the area, planning competitions, prizes, courses, training, work experience, volunteers and qualifications on offer. She felt there was a unique opportunity for the young people to have a promising future in the town. Linda spared no effort in getting people on board with research, marketing and seeking new opportunities. If our kids had not been equally busy and involved with their school work, chores and Candice's instructions, they may have felt neglected.

I loved working with numbers and even with the overload it was stimulating. I passed on the paperwork and red tape to an associate who had patience for it. I needed to budget, estimate, forecast, make predictions for the future, all involving numbers. It felt good to be alive. Nothing was easy or automatic, everything had to be calculated carefully if there were to be no repercussions. Candice had no interest in the functions of the business, she delegated with strict instructions and expected it to work. It was flattering and terrifying in equal proportions.

Hal was making a name for himself in the music world. He could compose and play with ease even the most difficult pieces. Offers to perform were coming from many quarters. We knew he would leave us to go to a music conservatory to develop his potential and felt both proud and sad about it. Linda and I realised we had a specially gifted child and we would not stand in his way. A scholarship was awarded to the best gifted pupils, we knew Hal could be worthy. It seemed just a short time ago we held our firstborn baby boy.

The music for the store opening was written and Hal kept developing it and adding to his performance. A group of his friends performed together and wanted to make the opening a grand occasion where they would be noticed by celebrities and the media. Hal came home to sleep and eat, school, music and activities kept him occupied. His homework was delivered on time, his school reports were consistently good, so we could not complain. There was always a remote sense of detachment about Hal, as if his mind was elsewhere. He said he focused on the music only he could hear.

Jake was managing well at school with some extra tuition. He had an analytical mind with a flair for technology, particularly computer programmes. Although Jake was average at schoolwork in general, he had an inbuilt understanding of how technology worked and could apply it in multiple ways. We hoped this would provide him with a lucrative career one day. Jake's friends seemed to be nerdy types but were pleasant enough in company. They were not interested in fashion or cliques, they just got on with life and made their own fun. Often, they spoke in their own language using terms and initials only they understood.

In addition to all the work pressure, we also had to make time for school activities like fundraising, extra-curricular projects, fancy dress, social events, birthdays, civic events and appointments. It was a merry-go-round, a hive of activity, we were wired and like the rest of the family, in the public eye. I felt sympathy for famous celebrities who always had to appear at their best. Our kids were celebrities at school, Linda had respect and enthusiasm from the pupils who all wanted to contribute to the store. My business increased, and people specifically requested appointments with me. It was hard finding time to fit everything and everybody into my schedule.

Matilda

I always liked to keep up to date with new food concepts and ideas. All my business was based on old favourites and sampling new wares. So, I asked Candice to get somebody to send me menus from leading healthy eating places in LA. They were always inventing new trends and would offer a diverse range. Candice delegated her PA to trawl around LA collecting menus, taking photos of enticing food and then send everything to me. I found this fascinating.

For the store café I had already planned one counter with deli-style containers where people could choose their fillings and have sandwiches or rolls made up, or toasties. This would offer healthy salads, dips and vegetables. It was proving successful in town in my other outlets. I thought we could offer tasty snacks like tortillas but made in Allbrite style. I was developing these ideas while awaiting the menus. We had too many cake options. Pies also came to mind with savoury filling options, English style. Drinks would be sugar-free.

Candice decided that she would use local people to model her clothes and designs for the store. She chose Phil to model and told Eric to photograph him playing pool, leaning forward. Phil had to wear one of Henry's shirts and jackets. Eric was then instructed to take Scarlett diving in sportswear and to hunt out situations and local activity events. It all seemed very appealing. For catalogue sales Candice planned to use professional models, but everything connected to the store had to be local. I invited her to take shots of some of our food displays to whet appetites.

As time moved on, I hired the community hall to hold a home baking session. Bakers were invited to bring samples of their best endeavours to be considered for sale in our new cafe. This was so successful, we had to have sessions with people queuing to try everything. I picked out the best and listed everything submitted, telling people we would be changing the offer frequently so we would give everyone a chance to sell their wares. This seemed to be an excellent way to get people on board. Some of the home baking was delicious, I knew most of the recipes but there were some lovely surprises.

Scarlett tested all the sportswear. She was very opinionated and occupied with projects on comparative religions, new age therapies, women's rights and anything else she had time for. The more she read the more questions she had. I left Phil to cope with most of the answers pleading I had to check the oven which seemed to work even when I was not using it.

Phil thought it was good Scarlett was so inquisitive. I felt sorry for her teachers but expected they were used to coping. When I was her age, I had no interest in the big issues of life. I wondered whether her escape from her attacker had brought all this on.

Eithan shadowed Dan when he was not involved in his other activities. Every chance he got Eithan went over to Dan's or asked for a ride to the factory. Like his grandfather before him, Eithan enjoyed crafting handmade furniture and objects albeit with a modern approach. They both got pleasure at aiming for perfection. Their work shone and looked solid. Modern flat packs did not interest Eithan.

Eithan played on a school baseball team, had homework to do and reports to submit for Candy. As his mother I was very proud of his ability and noticed he was becoming a very attractive young man. I expected we would have girls sniffing around before long. Eithan seemed to be too preoccupied to be interested in chasing girls, but I expected that to pass.

I had to work with Ryan regarding the store coffee shop and cake shop layout. We discussed where the appliances would be situated, the seating arrangements, the counters and display areas. To avoid queues I decided on separate areas featuring various offers. Somebody wanting coffee and cake would go to one section, tasty snacks in another and so on. Seating would be along the windows and around the sections. Displays would be featured in window bays to tempt people in. It was a novel approach, but I figured it would save queues.

Eric and Betsy

We were like chalk and cheese so it shouldn't have worked. Both of us liked our own space and independence. I let Betsy do as she pleased most of the time because I was indifferent to routine and chores. My life had been simplistic and opportunistic. Betsy turned out to be liberal-minded so long as she knew where I was and if I would be returning. If I forgot to keep in contact, she would get mad. I got mad if she interfered with my work stuff which I kept in the spare room. It looked a mess, but I knew where to find everything, so I forbade her entry for cleaning.

 After both living alone for many years, it was surprisingly easy to adjust to having company. In the evenings over a glass of wine we would catch up on our day or put the world to rights. At night to snuggle and make love was divine. Early morning, Betsy set off to work. She was looking forward to her new role with Candice and kept a notebook jotting down ideas and strategies. I noticed her reading some personnel book, she was really keen.

 For my part I was finding the flexibility Candice offered me was quite stimulating. She didn't want contrived shots but wanted her clothing offset to look appealing. We had to dress the models and capture them going about their business wearing them. They had to be various sizes and ethnic backgrounds. Candice did not want to focus on skinny model types.

 When it came to Allbrite and surrounding countryside I was to capture it at different times of the day and night in all weather. Until Candice instructed me, I had barely noticed Allbrite. It was just a place I came from. Now I realised its light and shadows, the hills, the corn rippling, the seasonal changes, the workers. There was ample material to capture. Some of it came out so well, it challenged my best endeavours. When it was printed into commercial calendars, notebooks, cards, serviettes etc, I felt amused then slightly awed.

It got me so engrossed in planning my gallery and my schedule that I found assignments to be an interference in my new life plans. I turned down a couple because they were inconvenient. When I left to go to New Orleans after a hurricane, I missed Betsy so much I could not believe it. When I returned home, I proposed again and even offered to make babies. Betsy cried and said we would have a small quiet wedding somewhere and then tell the family.

I loved her because she was different. Most girls wanted a fuss and white weddings. We flew to Vegas for a long weekend, got married there quietly, Betsy wore a smart dress and put flowers in her hair. I smartened up the best I could, and we framed the photo. After seeing the sights, the light shows and the strip, we stayed in bed having fun. It was the best wedding I have been to. Of course, the family were disappointed to have missed out. Mama was sad to have missed it but congratulated Betsy on making a man out of me. We accumulated belated wedding gifts which came in useful in our new home.

Neither of us was ready to reproduce, Betsy wanted to establish her new role and I felt able to accept some assignments knowing she would be waiting for me at home. Whilst neither of us was particularly romantic or demonstrative, in private we created steamy passion. I hoped it would continue. When I did go away, I brought back stupid souvenirs to amuse Betsy. I never wanted to stay away long or travel too far unless Betsy came along. It was amazing how untrapped I felt.

"See, I told you I was right for you," Betsy said.

"Oh, my darling, you are always right," I said smiling.

"Smart aleck, what took you so long?"

"Sweet pea I was enjoying playing the field," I said innocently. "Field my ass, you just couldn't make a commitment," my wife told me.

We got along great like best friends. My family had already accepted Betsy into the fold mainly due to the long time she spent around us all in the past when I was too dim to notice her. The kids also enjoyed consulting her with their young angst. They did not confide in Uncle Eric, I was good for taking shots or giving them rides. My brothers teased me for getting caught but it was good natured, so I let it pass. Ryan was the worst telling me I'd be sprouting offspring next. I ignored him too.

Our house was fitted out basically. Dan was very generous with the furniture and Candice helped with the décor. Betsy kept it clean, I helped when I was home. Neither of us was really into home furnishing so we let them take over. We just wanted to flop in comfort when we got home and sleep in a comfortable bed. Tilly sometimes brought us leftovers or cookies. I know she took some to Mama and gave unsold goodies to the food bank and care homes. I reckon we got what Mama refused.

In the past I had always felt Allbrite was too small and confining for me. Suddenly, I became aware of undercurrents, intrigues and daily minor happenings that had passed me by. I enjoyed strolling through the parks capturing the light through the branches. Little things like a cat stretching out in the sunshine, or an older resident taking his dog for a walk, became appealing and eye catching. There seemed to be beauty in ordinary simple life. My work took on a new dimension.

Betsy had few girlfriends but knew many people. When we went shopping, she had to acknowledge people constantly. I asked her how she knew so many people when she was not very sociable. Instead of answering Betsy tapped her nose. Just because we were married did not mean she lost the art of being annoying. I had not met Betsy's family yet and she did not talk about them ever, so I respected her privacy and did not ask about them.

Of all the kids I became closest to Chloe. Perhaps it was her writing blogs or my familiarity with journalists. Chloe loved to listen to my stories about my assignments, the journalists I had worked with, the styles of writing. We discussed our visions, our creative urges, the finer details that were often overlooked. Chloe was a pretty girl, people sometimes thought I was her father although we did not look alike. When she had time, Chloe came with me to take photos and appeared in some scenes. I made her focus vary so that she transcended the shots.

It was lovely being an uncle in the heart of a big diverse family. We argued at times, disagreed regularly, yet supported each other throughout in sickness and health. Mama kept herself fit and active, always busy and hospitable. When Aunt Theresa came to stay Mama was made up. They giggled and gossiped like young girls. We enjoyed watching them both so happy. My aunt liked me, she always encouraged me and told me stories about when Mama and she grew up. I offered to take her back to their roots, but she was not interested and had been glad to get away.

Whilst in Allbrite I had been developing a series of books featuring aspects of my work. The project was going well, and my agent was doing some marketing hype to publicise them. She felt they should be released in time for Christmas presents. They would look good on coffee tables she said. Betsy helped me to choose prints for the store for display, developing into prints and for home features. With a good eye for details, Betsy made excellent choices.

We didn't get around to putting up any of my pictures at home until Candice told us off. She said our walls were potential marketing opportunities and expected to see them dressed next visit. Candice had a way of giving orders and expecting them to be carried out. Obediently, we did as we were told, most people did. I think we all fell under the spell of her angelic beauty.

Martin was the least likely husband I would have expected Candice to marry. He was calm, kind, patient and not connected to A-listers in any way. Yet without raising his voice or issuing orders, Martin ruled at home. Candice was a changed woman when he was around. Zoe followed Candice around like a lap dog. It was clear to see Zoe wanted to be like her step-mum. Candice had unlimited time and patience for Zoe. I wondered if Candice would have children, but I recognised she was too busy at present. I wondered if I wanted to become a father, it alarmed me but not as much as before. To be truthful, I was impartial so either way I would let Betsy decide.

Dan and Claire

My boat building progressed slowly due to time constraints and my need to escape. I was in no hurry, it was not going anywhere. Claire called it my man shed. I also undertook commissions for bespoke items of furniture which I really enjoyed. Most of the ready-made furniture could be done more or less automatically. I delegated that side to my staff. Over the years I had recruited fine staff with a constant intake of trainees. It remained popular and we tweaked designs occasionally to breathe new life.

Modern houses seemed to lack storage space, so units were always popular. Small rooms led to extensions, patios, decking, summer houses, always something. For a time, the DIY market proved popular and we opened shops supplying handymen with popular tool requirements. Once Ryan came fully on board, we would have in-house builders and electricians, plumbers and craftsman to outfit all opportunities. Everything wore out or needed replacing eventually, so it seemed a wise move. I realised Ryan was successful in Montreal, but in Allbrite we were all together.

I never asked Ryan why he did not join up, I heard him tell someone years ago that he lacked the urge to kill unknown civilians in a foreign country. Ryan was brave and bold, I reckon he was telling the truth, he was not shy of anybody or anything, putting himself forward to help others. He was still my big brother and I had always looked up to him. His wife Marie was turning out to be a real firecracker at drumming up business. There was nothing to her, but she had a first-class mind. Their girls were adorable. With two boys I was not used to girls so I tried to be gentle with them.

Claire enjoyed her work, she said Betsy had been replaced by a man who was an ex-New Yorker. The jury was out as to whether he would stay the course. We shared our chores and ferried the boys around. My wife looked out for Mama, checked on Marie's mother and remembered all the birthdays and anniversaries. Her charity group elected Claire to chair it for the forthcoming year, so we had regular meetings at our place. I headed for my boatshed. Our boys loved the leftover goodies because most of the ladies were on permanent diets.

Leo was actively pursuing his sporting interests and trying out new sportswear for Candice. He was a bit of a ladies-man, at his age the girls seemed to love him. An all-round good student, Leo was steady rather than brilliant but shone at sport. His only dilemma was what to major in. Leo had a good group of buddies who played music in Ted's garage drinking beer on the sly thinking we didn't know. Kids didn't realise we had been young before them.

Ollie was more serious and was always drawing or studying architecture. He had come up with some radical ideas for the new store that Candice loved. Candice took Ollie to meet her architect who was taking a keen interest in his progress. It seemed Ollie had years of study ahead of him, but he said it was worth it. Ollie's buddies included a girl called Lizzy who lived down the street. They seemed a chilled-out bunch and had grown up together. We knew all the parents so perhaps that's why they were always polite to me.

Rose, Claire's mother became good friends with Corinne, Marie's mother. They went out together and attracted a few admirers. When eyebrows were raised challengingly, they both told us they did not want to look after old men, they had done enough of that. They just wanted to go out, enjoy themselves and remain independent women. Sometimes Mama would accompany them, but she had her own circle. All these ladies were ageing well and seemed to have more energy than the rest of us.

Candice

Henry and I locked ourselves away for weeks designing for high-end specialist individuals, fashion shows and selected stores, our catalogue, the new store with its three ranges, seasonal trends, the 'What's hot' layout for the store and the new home furnishing ranges. We had to call in extra help and brief them. It was simply too much to cope with. Fortunately, we had trained up amazing staff who took direction well and could be trusted to deliver.

Although we were partners in all our endeavours, Henry preferred his name on the labels but not on site. He was well known and admired for his style, but only my name featured. We both had our wealth invested in the store and figured it could succeed if we kept turnover fresh, distribution nationwide. We engaged with media people and called in all favours owed. By hook, crook and bribery we managed to get co-operation.

We were both earnestly in love but could only go home to our partners at weekends. By then we were exhausted and never wanted to return on Mondays. The work seemed endless, the photoshoots, accessories, samples, were all delegated. I believed if people were entrusted with tasks they enjoyed, they would pull out all the stops. I did not want to be informed of detailed minutiae or need to supervise. It was enough to be told the mission was accomplished.

Eric was doing sensational work for me in Allbrite. The photographer in LA was accustomed to trendy poses which worked for the site. Each week I had a conference call with all my nephews and nieces to catch up with trends. They were proving useful and were quite inventive about what they thought they could wear and wouldn't be seen dead in. Zoe started designing and customising some of her clothes.

We had a big A-lister fashion show to present at a charity function with top names. Once that was sorted, we felt able to turn our attention to the store. Henry came with me to view the premises which were starting to take shape. We talked to the distributor, the textile merchant, the storage people and checked on supplies with Marie. It all seemed to be going to plan. There was not much to see yet, but nearer the time Linda was launching competitions at the schools.

Tilly did a home baking taster session which went down well, I was sorry to have missed that. Henry and I tended to send out for food which we ate carefully while we worked. I enjoyed food and probably would be fat if I lived a conventional life. When I was engrossed in my work, I often forgot to eat. Martin was the most understanding man, he knew the pressure I was under to get sorted and always encouraged me to do my best. I loved that man more each day.

As the building completion drew nearer, we began a campaign of publicity and enticement to build interest and excitement. Research was carried out inviting people to make requests, guess various statistics and any other ways we could come up with for participation. We kept our textile supplier happy, the machinists worked happily. They were not high earners but worked in good conditions, listened to music while they worked and built up skills and camaraderie.

Occasionally I would have nightmares of things going wrong. Everything depended on me. Was I too arrogant? Did I know what I was doing? What if the money ran out? All sorts of anxieties crept in until Martin held me in his arms and soothed me like a baby. I wanted to succeed, my whole career and security were at stake. Henry felt the same. We comforted and encouraged each other. Most of the time we were too busy trying to get everything designed and made up to suit us.

Eric was summoned to go out and take shots of locals wearing our designs. They were to go about their usual business suitably attired. When Henry saw the shots Eric took, he was amazed at how natural they looked. He reckoned Eric was setting a new trend. We introduced some seasonal beach wear and holiday clothing in cool fabrics. They photographed well. I just hoped we could be ready on time.

Aunty Theresa discovered a lump on her breast. Mama accompanied her for a surgical procedure and nursed her until she recovered. With modern technology Theresa did not have to have her breast removed, but she was sore and delicate for a long time afterwards. As her birthday was approaching, Mama told the whole family we should club together and treat Theresa to a special vacation. Theresa had struggled in life and deserved something she would always remember.

We found out that Theresa had always wanted to go to Asia, so we researched and found a ten-day trip to classic Malaysia and Singapore. Flights went from Los Angeles to Singapore on a spectacular Malaysian trip. Their itinerary included two nights in Singapore, one night in Melaka, two nights in Kuala Lumpur, one night in the Cameron Highlands and two nights in Penang.

They would have an English-speaking tour guide and most meals were included. Travel would be in a modern air-conditioned coach. A holiday brochure offered the ladies a chance to discover Singapore's Chinatown and Little India with its quaint shops, tour historic Melaka on the Malay Peninsula's southwest coast, view Kuala Lumpur's Petronas Twin Towers made of glass and steel, tour a working tea plantation in the hills of the Cameron Highlands, visit an Orang Asli village to see the unique traditions and lifestyles, visit the Ubudiah Mosque with gold domes in the royal capital of Kuala Kangsar and explore George Town, the capital of the island of Penang.

There was an option of travelling from Malaysia to China at the end of the trip for more sightseeing. On the trip they would encounter some uneven surfaces, stairs, steps and significant slopes. Some tours required walking about without shade. We discussed the trip and decided to include the China option at the end. Mama would accompany Theresa. We all gave them unwarranted advice such as: "Don't go off with strangers," or "Hide your valuables," etc. Candice organised their wardrobes. The grandchildren posed for a group photo to take with them. Eric took them to the airport to catch a flight to LA.

They had two weeks to go on vacation and would be ready to start training for the grand store opening. All the preparation they could make had been done. To watch them giggle and nudge each other was very amusing. As soon as they arrived, we expected to hear from them. Linda told them to keep a diary of each day. We hugged and teased them. Tilly got a text to say they had landed, it was very hot and sultry. During the week we got occasional brief updates. It seemed they were having fun. They were scheduled to fly to China for their last fling.

Their scheduled flight from took off but disappeared and we never knew what happened to Mama and Aunty Theresa. Anxiously we have waited for news ever since together with the other families who had passengers on the plane. Our prayers remain with them.

End

*If you have enjoyed meeting the O'Brien family and would like to know what happened to them, look out for "**Consequences**" which follows on from this story. It should be out soon on Amazon and will be on offer with sales of Allbrite.*